The Provocateur's Payback

Paco Muñoz-Botas

The Provocateur's Payback© 2015 by Francisco Muñoz Botas translated by Matthew Hovious

All Rights Reserved. No part of this book may be reproduced or transmitted in any form or by any means, electronic or mechanical, including photocopying, without permission in writing from the publisher.

For more information contact:
Riverdale Avenue Books
5676 Riverdale Avenue
Riverdale, NY 10471.

www.riverdaleavebooks.com

Design by www.formatting4U.com
Cover by Scott Carpenter

Digital ISBN 9781626011649
Print ISBN 9781626011632

First Edition March 2015 (English Translation of Qué Trastos! Copyright 2012)

To my parents

To my very best support, my sister Maru

And… to my unforgettable friend, Trasto

CHAPTER I

"Shit!" His heart skipped a beat as he stopped the car. He'd almost run over a stray dog. Back to square one. Time and again he just couldn't shake the lingering presence of his own dear departed dog. Curro knew he'd done the right thing, of course, putting Trasto's best interests first, wishing him a decent end, without him having to suffer endlessly. Wanting his death to be like his life, dignified, like a champ.

Where was the dog he'd slammed on the brakes for? Was it just his imagination – had it actually looked like Trasto? He thought he'd seen a flash of tawny coat, a certain distinction, like his dog. A proud, elegant vagabond that had come into Curro's life. No, not like Trasto, of course not.

Curro was driving back home after a weekend at a country house in Toledo, a guest of his friends the Aguirres. He and Pepe and Matilde Aguirre had been pals forever. Once a classmate, Pepe now ran the bank his grandfather had founded decades earlier. Life had sent Pepe and Curro down different paths. One spent his days focused on business, traveling the world, lecturing on the management of financial institutions like his own. Curro, on the other hand, traveled whereever fashion led him, partied non-stop, lost himself again and again in backrooms and underground clubs. Matilde had been Curro's first crush, a teenage passion on the Marbella coast, back when their families used to vacation together every Easter. She'd been a beautiful sapphire-eyed blonde, unusually demure for her generation. God, what he'd gone through just to steal that first kiss on the beach outside the hotel Marbella Splendor.

Once he'd reached their place the day before, he'd pretty much kept to himself. That Friday night, feeling unsociable, he'd gone straight to bed: they were all good enough friends, his hosts understood him.

Saturday dawned brightly enough to prove that spring had arrived for real. He was still in too much of a withdrawn mood to believably appear to enjoy himself, but he made an effort and stayed for lunch. Pepe and Matilde deserved that much. They tried to draw him out, recalling pleasant memories from their pasts together, anything to take his mind off of his troubles, but it had done no good. Despite the good intentions of hosts and guests, Curro's apathy was plain to one and all. The whole scene bored him, his mind wandered. In the months since Trasto's passing, his friends had grown increasingly worried about him. He wasn't himself. Once the life of the party, the most gregarious of them all, he'd become snappish, easily irritated. They'd tried to be understanding but were losing patience. Actually, they were getting fed up. What a drag he had become! He wasn't the only one who'd ever had a pet that died. Why didn't he just buy another one?

Pet! The very word, or what some people took it

to mean, outraged Curro. What exactly did they mean by *pet*? A toy? A passing fancy, a pastime? A dumb animal? Not for him. Trasto had been, was, part of the family, and one of its most beloved members, in fact, if not the most; his best and most loyal companion. Unique and irreplaceable. How was it that no one could understand this?

Seated at the right of the lady of the house, he tuned out the table talk. What a load of bull, he thought – society life sucks the big one. Aloof from the banter, Curro sullenly proffered monosyllables until one of the guests, a not particularly clever upstart, shared his thoughts about the finance minister in the Spanish president's cabinet.

Curro snapped, spurred by other frustrations.

"What nonsense! How can you possibly think he's the right man for the job? He doesn't have a fucking clue, he's just gonna sink our economy even faster than we are going down already. You ought to get out more, pal, try reading a paper sometime."

Curro's aggressive retort surprised the rest of the guests, but they were inclined to overlook it – except for the man Curro'd spoken to, a heavyset developer who'd made a fortune building cheap housing. The man stood up, gesturing towards Curro with his cigar.

"I don't know who you are, but nobody talks to me like that."

Curro stood up too. People who were that full of themselves really rubbed him the wrong way.

"I'll talk to you however," he glanced at his hostess and checked himself, "the heck I want. And put that cigar out when you're at the table, you hick. Hasn't anyone ever taught you any manners?"

The table erupted in alarmed chatter: the women were gobsmacked, the men were each weighing whether or not to hold Curro and the developer back. The developer came around the table towards Curro, who stepped out to face him – *lard-ass,* he thought – while Pepe stood up and came between them, raising conciliatory hands.

"Curro, please," he chided, "get a grip. Don't put me in a bind."

The offended party didn't seem inclined to bury the hatchet; he shoved Pepe roughly to one side and stood directly in front of Curro.

"I didn't know queers liked to fight. Come on, what else did you wanna say to me? Say it to my face."

"Oh, I didn't realize we'd met before. Haven't I seen you around the gay bars in Chueca?" he lied. "How about if we step outside?" Curro was in such a foul mood that he was prepared for anything.

Before he could say another word, the furious builder took a swing at him but was so off-course the punch landed square in the shoulder of an elderly Marquise – Aunt Isabelita, always a brave soul – who'd stepped in to see if she could get them to calm down. Howling, she crumpled to the floor, and that was the last straw for the gathering's increasingly distraught host. He made a gesture at the help, and two of Pepe's men stepped forward, waiting for instructions.

"Don Crescencio is leaving. Please go help him pack," Pepe told his driver, a sturdy kid from a town up the road.

The accidental boxer tried to keep arguing his

case, but no one really listened as he was hustled out of the dining room.

"Bye, Crescencio. See you around Chueca," Curro called after him, grinning slightly. He turned to his hosts. "Well, I'd best be off too," he said quietly. "Sorry, you two."

***

At least the drive back was pleasant. He'd lowered the top of his Jaguar XK8 convertible and had been enjoying the warm May breeze on his face, till he'd suddenly skidded to a halt at the sight of the dog. He took one more deep breath as he reached for the clutch, ready to keep driving.

Then from out of nowhere came a desperate plea from a man out of breath.

"Hurry, please! Quickly!"

Curro gaped at the rugged young man who'd just jumped into the passenger seat.

"What the hell is this!" Curro was more shocked than he was intimidated by the stranger. "Are you out of your mind?"

"Get going, please, they're gonna kill me!"

The young man pointed across the road. Curro looked up just as two thugs elbowed their way through the bushes: they looked vaguely Slavic. Then he saw their knives, and without a second thought he floored it.

Curro had never been more appreciative of the Jaguar's torque. He kept the pedal down till he was sure they'd left the goons safely behind. But who was this guy in the car with him? Before going any further it was time for some answers. He looked at his uninvited passenger. The guy was huge, looked vaguely Slavic, and was wearing jeans and a badly torn T-shirt. He was dripping wet.

"Get that shirt off, you're drenched!"

"It's OK, I'll be fine, just keep heading towards Madrid."

Curro was having none of it. He braked hard and pulled over to get a good look at the guy. Now that the shock had passed he saw his passenger in a new light. God, he was hot! Was it even possible to be that ripped *and* that good-looking?

"You don't understand," Curro said, returning to the matter at hand. "You're ruining my car." The man looked confused. "You're soaking wet," Curro intoned very slowly, "you're gonna ruin my upholstery. Look!" he said, pointing at the seat.

"I understand you, I speak Spanish," the man said, looking back towards the highway.

"Don't worry, they're not gonna catch up with us," Curro said as he opened the door. He went to the trunk and pulled out a hooded sweatshirt, someone's unfortunate idea of a Christmas gift that had been several sizes too large for him. "Here, put this on."

When his surprised passenger stepped out of the Jag, Curro finally got a good look at all of him – 6'2" and profusely tattooed beneath the shredded T-shirt he'd stripped off. He had the body of a 200-meter sprinter, though if anything more muscular. Curro thought it had to be partly inherited – you couldn't get that ripped just from lifting weights. The man's paleness contrasted sharply with his dark hair. His intense blue-eyed gaze and firm jaw were the strongest features in an even, symmetrical face. Curro noticed that the man's jeans were torn too, so he reached back into the weekend bag he kept in his trunk and handed the newcomer a towel and a pair of Jockey shorts sure to be way too small. There was something suddenly comical about the entire situation.

"Dry off the seat and put these on," he said, suppressing a grin.

"Are you kidding? Man, I'm not wearing these!"

"Well, I don't have anything else, so it's these or nothing. And ditch the jeans."

"I don't have any other pants!"

"You can't go anywhere in those anyway. I mean, look at them. When we reach Madrid I'll buy you something to wear" —Curro guessed the man had no money— "and then I'll drop you off downtown."

"But..." the Slav said, hesitatating, confused.

"No buts. Now come on, it's getting late."

Curro's passenger gave in and he swapped his torn-up apparel for the stuff Curro held out to him. He went through his pants pockets carefully, found nothing to keep, then wadded them up and went over to a drainage ditch and threw the pants in so no one would find them. Then he got back into Curro's car and they took off towards Madrid.

For the next several minutes they drove in silence. It occurred to Curro that he might be getting into trouble, and he wondered if it wouldn't be best just to give the young man some cash and drop him off at the next gas station. Weren't men picking up strange guys in need of a ride all the time, and didn't these encounters usually end badly, for the driver? As if he'd read Curro's mind, his mysterious passenger suddenly spoke up.

"Don't worry, I'm not going to hurt you or anything."

"Of course not!" Curro answered with conviction. "Why would I even think that?" And he wasn't afraid, perhaps more through gullibility than courage. *Besides*, he thought, *a guy this hot is worth taking a few risks for.*

"By the way," he held out a hand sideways, "my name's Curro."

The man gave him a firm handshake. "I'm Dima."

"Dima?"

"Short for Dmitri. And Curro's another nickname for Francisco, right? Like Paco?"

"Right. So you're Russian?"

"Partly."

"Hmm. I didn't know it was possible to be just partly Russian."

"I'm Russian and Spanish."

"I guessed you were from somewhere over there. You speak really good Spanish, though."

"It's not easy right now. Those guys back there." He nodded over his shoulder. "They drugged me."

Curro decided to change the subject. The less he knew, the better.

"Who do you live with in Spain? Family, friends? And whereabouts?"

"Man, I'm on my own. And now I'm out on the street." Dima closed his eyes and leaned back in the passenger seat.

"Well, get some rest. I'll let you know when we reach Madrid."

By way of acknowledgment Dima burrowed into

the headrest. Curro switched on the Jag's sound system and a Jamie Cullen tune filled the air between them. *Not a bad way to relax*, he thought, as he glanced at the resting Russian. *Not bad at all.*

***

Barely a half hour later they were in the heart of the city. Dima had finally dozed off and seemed to be sound asleep, though he twitched nervously a few times. Poor guy, thought Curro—he must really have been through the wringer before things even got to the point of being chased through a field at knife point. Curro briefly thought about taking Dima to a police station, but felt it would probably just aggravate whatever problems the Russian already had. No, he'd buy him some clothes as promised and drop him off wherever he wanted.

Curro drove straight to the El Corte Inglés department store midway up Paseo de la Castellana, which he was annoyed to find packed with shoppers. He felt very lucky to even get a parking space in front of the building.

"Dima!" Curro nudged the Russian with his elbow. Nothing happened. He grabbed the sleeping giant's arm— "Dima!"—and just had time to feel the rippling bicep flex beneath his fingers when Dima sprang to life. Before he knew it his face was jammed into the dashboard left of the steering wheel, an elbow in his back.

"Dima! Leggo, you animal! It's me, remember? The dumbass who's helping you?"

"Sorry, man, I'm sorry." Dima blinked,

sheepishly trying to help Curro back into a seated position.

"Never mind, I'll straighten myself out," he said, brushing away Dima's hand and trying to appear dignified, which might have been easier if he hadn't just been manhandled like a puppet. "You could have broken my back. Are you nuts?"

"I'm sorry, Curro. I'm feeling jumpy from..." He shrugged, then corrected himself. "I *am* jumpy. You don't know what I've been through."

"I can imagine. But you've gotta control that brutal, savage strength." He pronounced the last phrase with quasi-erotic verve. "Now stay here, I'm gonna go buy you some jeans and a few shirts and shorts. Underwear, boxers," he clarified, just in case. "All size XXL I suppose."

"That's right. Big, extra-long pants. XXL T-shirts."

"What size shoe do you wear?"

Dima stretched his leg, revealing an extremely worn, though not disproportionately large, sneaker. About 10½, thought Curro.

After a while he came back carrying a duffel bag containing everything he'd mentioned and more. He knew Dima had nothing. As he approached his car he caught sight of some commotion. Hurrying, he saw Dima sitting on the hood, the sweatshirt knotted around his waist like a kilt. Naked from the waist up, he was quite a sight.

A group of kids were goading him. "Show us your muscles," said one. "Come on, dude, flex those biceps." Dima didn't move. Curro thought he still looked sluggish.

"Come on, Dima," said Curro, tossing the duffel bag onto the passenger seat. Dima sat down, putting the bag on his lap, and finally flexed the tattooed arm he'd slung casually out the window. The kids standing around the car made a collective sound of amazement; one of them took a photo of Dima's bicep with his cell phone.

"Why were you standing around like that?" Curro asked. "What a show."

"It's really hot today."

"Ah," answered Curro drily. It would never have occurred to him that to a young Russian 60 degrees in the sun might feel like a scorcher.

Dima rummaged through the bag of new clothing and then said hesitantly, "Man, thanks for everything. I'll never forget what you've done for me. I can make it on my own from here. Can you drop me off on Gran Via?"

"No," said Curro, looking him right in the eye. "You're coming home with me."

***

Curro had made up his mind to bring Dima home to his place while doing the shopping. Dima seemed like a nice guy. Rough, no doubt, but a nice guy For all Curro knew, Dima might have grown up on the streets. Like Trasto, his beloved Trasto.

In a way, Dima reminded Curro of Trasto. He too had just walked into Curro's life without notice. He'd been at his mother's house in Torrelodones, like every summer, and the yearly town fair was getting ready to kick off. The carnies used to park their caravans just outside the edge of his family's estate and always seemed to have an endless number of dogs straggling along with them, and that year, one of them had been Trasto. He couldn't have been more than a few months old and he'd probably been abused, judging from his wary nature as well as his looks. Sick and underfed, he seemed to be all bones and legs. And ugly. Every day he squeezed through the wrought-iron gate to the family home, and every day he was thrown out of Eden. Till one day. The groundskeeper's daughter, an occasional visitor and an animal lover, felt sorry for him and took him in. After a trip to the vet (shots and de-worming) and after suffering through a bath, he became part of the family. Fearful at first, he didn't want to be around anyone, preferring solitude. The rough life he'd no doubt led before deciding to let himself be adopted had made him suspicious, even aggressive at times. Only after days of affection turned into weeks in his new home had the pup's self-esteem flourished enough to let him settle in.

Actually, no one in the house wanted a dog; no one less than Curro. His mother, Concha, definitely didn't; her parents had always had a dog, and one of her sisters had caught a life-threatening tapeworm infection from one of them. Gradually, though, the bond that formed between Curro and the stray convinced him to take the next step.

"Mom, I'm keeping Trasto," he announced. The name they had given him was an affectionate Spanish term for "naughty."

"Absolutely not. You weren't seriously thinking of taking him back to Madrid, were you? You know full well I don't want dogs in the house."

"Mom, he won't bother you. You won't even see him. I'll take care of everything, I promise."

"Sure, and I believe you. I said, no dogs."

"No dogs. Just... *ne* dog."

"No!" said his mother firmly.

"But it's my home. I have the right to have a dog if I want."

"It is *not* your house. It's my house, and I don't want any dogs in it."

"It's your house but it's also my home. I live here."

"No dogs, and that's that. This is giving me a headache."

"Mom..."

"No!"

And there would really have been no dog if it hadn't been for aunt Adelaida's timely intervention. Curro called his aunt, who was a nun, and she did the rest. Aunt Adelaida—Sister Adelaida—was Concha Solloso's favorite sister. Stirred by vocation, Adelaida had one day suddenly decided to embrace the contemplative life, knowing full well that none of those closest to her would really understand her choice. She'd been the most charming and fun-loving among her sisters. She smoked—they all did, but she'd done it provocatively, as if to draw attention to herself as a woman. At the time she'd decided to take her vows she had been in a formal relationship with a young man from a good family who ended up feeling all but jilted. No one around her had been particularly sympathetic except Concha, her eldest sister, who gave Adelaida her unconditional support. Having already been to college before she swore her vows, she became a worldly nun; she spoke foreign languages and was not at all prudish. She was the headmistress of a school operated by her order in Madrid and subsequently became her community's Mother Superior.

Aunt Adelaida's intervention was as decisive as it was divine. Concha never could refuse her sister anything, and so the next day she told Curro that Trasto could stay with them.

***

Like most of her family, Concha Solloso had been born in Madrid, but in spite of this she felt 100% Galician. She wasn't like her sister Adelaida, would never be quite as sophisticated as she was, even if she did speak French just as well as she did and could keep up an entertaining and varied conversation. On the other hand, she shared Adelaida's indifference to the frivolous lifestyle of their slice of society. Her extended family and close friends, along with her husband and son, would be the focus of her existence, along with selfless charitable work. In her younger years she'd been very animated when she did tag along to the trendy spots; but those days were long past. In what she humorously called "robustly poor health," she arranged her daily routine around Mass, Communion, and visits from family and friends.

While her husband was still alive, things had been different. When Paco Morante was in Madrid, for his sake she'd organized card games at their house every Sunday, and they went out more: concerts, the theater, dinners with friends, travel abroad. But after he died she disengaged from pretty much everything and focused on what really fulfilled her: spiritual life and her relationship with God. Of unshakeable faith, she loved high-minded chats with erudite souls such as Father Federico, her confessor, with whom she engaged in many a theological polemic over a comforting cup of hot chocolate with *churros*. She sought to apply the gospel to her daily doings, and it wouldn't be too much to say that she lived a saintly life. When Trasto entered her life she was already a widow, and after her initial reluctance she came to see the lively pup as a loyal friend and companion.

***

Once they reached Curro's spacious penthouse, Dima inspected the whole place carefully: how odd that the muscle-bound Dmitri Denissov should feel wary and rattled about his safety, while his host evinced supreme self-confidence. Curro showed him to the guest room and gently suggested a shower, which, frankly, Dima knew he needed. Curro grew tense and fidgety while waiting for the Apollonian youth to reappear. Was he all right? He was sure taking long enough. Curro couldn't take the wait any longer. Breaking all the rules of hospitality, especially as concerned a person like Dima—a foreigner with an unknown past—he opened the guest room door and found the getup Dima had worn that afternoon tossed carelessly onto the bed, the sweatshirt stained with blood.

"Dima!" he yelled.

No sign of the young Russian, and not a sound.

He peeked in the bathroom—empty too. Where was he? Curro crossed the room and looked out the door to the terrace that stretched all the way around his penthouse. There he was, stretched out on a chaise longue Curro liked to use on sunny days for reading and tanning. *Sweet Jesus*! With just the towel wrapped around Dima's waist, Curro could appreciate him in his full splendor. Once he'd gotten his breath back he spotted a trail of blood leading along the patio. He stepped outside, moved towards Dima, and lifted the towel, exposing knife wounds. Two of them were just surface wounds but the third, right above the groin, looked bad and was slowly oozing blood.

Shit, Curro thought, *what have I gotten myself into this time?* He tried to appear outwardly calm. Decisions had to be made, fast.

"Dima, why didn't you tell me? You can't just sit here like that. C'mon, lemme have a look," he said, reaching for the gauze and scissors Dima must have found in the bathroom. "I'll wrap it up and we'll get you to an emergency room."

"No way, no hospitals. I don't want any trouble with the police."

Curro shook his head. "Look, you've gotta let a doctor take a look at that or you could bleed to death, and then we'll both be in deep shit"

"I am *not* going to a hospital. If you're scared, I'll take off. Don't worry. Also, I am *not* bleeding to death," said Dima in a way that implied Curro had no idea what he was talking about.

"I'm sorry, but you just can't do this. We should see a doctor. And the police."

Dima got up and strode unsteadily towards the

shopping bag full of clothes Curro had bought that sat at the foot of the chaise lounge.

"Can I still have some of this?" he asked, and just then his left leg buckled beneath him, sending him to the floor.

"Will you give it up?" said Curro, exasperation mounting.

"No, no. I'm out of here. I am grateful, you're a great guy, but I want nothing to do with the cops."

Dima's face scrunched up in pain as he tried to get back up, only to lose his balance again. It hurt to see someone as strong as he was in such bad shape. Curro gave up and decided to jump in with both feet.

"All right, let's drop it for now. I'll treat you myself. Lemme have a look."

He eased Dima back onto the chaise lounge and moved closer to the wound. The day was starting to cool down, probably a good thing, he thought, if it made him more alert. Suddenly he remembered that for Trasto's sores the vet had prescribed some healing gauze he'd felt sure would help. In the end it hadn't done the dog any good and most of the box had not been used. He went and got it, fleetingly thankful that he'd kept it, though it had just been him keeping something that served to remind him of his dog. Along the way he scooped up some rubbing alcohol and Mercurochrome

He returned to the terrace and sat down next to Dima on the chaise lounge. "This is gonna hurt," he said.

"Never mind," said Dima, firmly.

Curro set about cleaning and disinfecting the cuts. Dima never flinched, his gaze steady on the amateur paramedic. As he neared the groin wound, Curro couldn't help absentmindedly caressing the rippling thigh. He rubbed in some medicated cream and began wrapping it in gauze.

"Hold it, man. Bring me some thread and a needle."

"Are you kidding? You don't really think you can just stitch yourself up."

"Sure, I do. Now come on, bring me the stuff."

Curro shrugged and went back inside. *You're the expert,* he thought. He rummaged through half the apartment looking for a needle and thread. *Dammit, why'd I have to let Jesús take his vacation early He knows where everything is kept.* He finally found some sewing items, in a drawer near the ironing board. Back on the terrace Dima looked eagerly at the makeshift surgical kit in Curro's hand. He unwrapped the gauze Curro had just applied and tested the needle, gently pricking the skin near one of the lesser wounds.

"OK, help me out." He looked up at Curro.

Now *that* was a whole other story. Dima needed him to help close the deepest wound, the one still oozing blood. Curro would have preferred to duck reality by looking away. But it suited both of them to make sure everything would be done right.

He murmured apprehensively, "What should I do?"

"Push the edges of the cut together, hard."

He pressed as hard as he could, trying to join the rent flesh, till all that showed was a vertical slash. Then Dima began stitching as if it were no big deal, applying considerable force in order to pierce the flesh six times. It became clear to Curro that somewhere along the line Dima had some form of medical training.

"Got it!" he said happily.

Curro exhaled a sigh of relief. "This calls for a celebration. Are you hungry?" He already knew the answer. "I'll rustle up something in the kitchen. You come lie down."

He helped Dima off of the terrace and onto the guest bed, propping him up on some cushions. Along with the tattoo on his right bicep, Dima had two more that wound symmetrically over his shoulder blades, two coiled snakes. Later Curro would learn that they were badges of rank in the mob to which Dima had belonged and ultimately deserted.

Curro returned shortly with two champagne flutes and a chilled bottle of Moët Chandon, which he raised aloft as he asked, "You like?"

"Of course, who doesn't?"

Then he went back to the fridge and came back with a tray of patés, cheese, and smoked meats. One look at Dima's face told him that this wasn't exactly what the Russian had in mind when it came to a celebratory feast; chastened, he returned to the kitchen where he grilled a couple of juicy steaks, which he served with toasted bread.

"Don't you want any?" asked Dima as he finished off the first steak. "Here, have some of this," he said, offering Curro a choice cut from the next one on the plate.

"No, thanks. I'm enjoying the champagne, it's great."

Dima polished off the whole thing in no time, while Curro quietly sipped his bubbly and watched. It occurred to him for the first time that the malaise that had been haunting his life for months, since he had been devastated for having to put down Trasto, had suddenly faded. For the first time since he could remember he was enjoying the company of another, enormously so in fact. Perhaps it was the absence of introductions between two complete strangers who could not have been more unlike one another—Curro a forty-four year old former playboy at loose ends, Dima no more than thirty, built like an ox and on the run from trouble. Curro sat there savoring the moment.

When Dima was done, he rose to take his leave. Explanations could wait. They'd talk the next day.

"Get some rest. Sleep well, you're overdue. And if you need anything, you know where I am. That room over there," he said, gesturing to the the left side of the terrace.

"Thanks. I won't forget what you've done for me."

Curro sat there alone with his champagne, the events of the day running through his mind. He would never forget that day. Whether Dima stayed or picked up and left in the morning, it was as if a page in his life had been turned by this stranger. He felt invigorated. Could this be the start of something interesting, new hope?

Of course not, he thought as he stood. *There will never be new hopes.*

CHAPTER II

Dima laid low for two whole days, barely getting out of bed except to eat and check on his wounds. They seemed to be healing well, with Curro focused entirely on his new role as nursemaid to the mysterious guest. For those two days he felt more tense than he could ever remember. They still hadn't sat down and spoken about who Dima really was and what had led to the goons chasing after him. Was Dima on the run from the law, a dangerous fugitive? Or was the mob out to get him? These thoughts and more turned over and over in his head during those two days that he too was out of circulation, keeping an eye on his patient's recovery.

On the third day as Curro was reading the paper over breakfast on the terrace, he was surprised by Dima's sudden appearance in the doorway. Till then he'd ventured no further than the bathroom down the hall.

"Morning, Curro."

"Well, good morning, Sleeping Beauty! How're you feeling?"

"Fine, just fine." Dima stretched out his arms like a cat after a long nap, then smiled. "Sleeping Beauty. Nobody's ever called me that before."

"Probably because nobody's ever seen you wake up after two days sleeping like a baby."

Dima's face broke into a puzzled smile. "But babies are awake half the night?"

Curro laughed. "It's just a figure of speech." Though each had reason enough to be wary of the other, especially Curro, their banter was relaxed, as if they were old friends.

"Help yourself to some breakfast. I've got just about anything in the kitchen—toast, jam, juice, sliced turkey breast..."

Dima returned with a well-laden tray bearing everything Curro had suggested, and more.

"You really gonna eat all that?" Curro asked wryly.

"I eat a lot. I need to bulk back up."

"Of course, a growing boy needs to eat if he wants to be big and strong," said Curro, grinning.

Dima didn't fully understand but sensed the irony and laughed, flexing a bicep. "Whoa!" said Curro, both amused and impressed. "You've gotta share some workout tips with me. You look ready to rumble!"

Dima laughed. "For a guy your age, you're holding yourself together pretty well. It's obvious you've put in some time at the gym and take care of yourself." He seemed to have recovered completely.

A guy my age? Curro thought. *I may not be running around like I once did, but there's no shortage of attention from anyone, let me tell you.*

Curro smiled, enjoying the playfulness. "C'mon, flex those guns!" he said, as awed as any of the kids who'd been staring at Dima in the parking lot. The Russian proudly lifted a huge bicep that Curro couldn't resist squeezing. "You can't get a body like this just by working out. You look more like a gladiator. Martial arts?"

"I was the Russian Army's champion," Dima said with a nod. "And European K-1—kickboxing—champion. I guess I've been practicing for one form of combat or the other my whole life. How could you tell?

"All it takes is one look." Curro paused, deciding how to broach the next topic. "Dima, we have to talk. All this, the last few days. Those guys chasing you, the knife wounds, how we met. It's a little unusual, don't you think?"

"That it is." Dima smiled. "I trust you. You know that? I've known you just a few days but I feel like you can be trusted. Ask me whatever you want."

"Where would you like to start?"

"Let's see. My name's Dmitri Denissov. I'm twenty-nine. I'm Russian—well, Russian and Spanish." He smiled. "My father rose to the top of the KGB during the Brezhnev years and was stationed in St. Petersburg in 1980. That's where he met my mother. I loved my mom and her family, too. Her father was a Spanish communist who went into exile in the USSR after the Spanish Civil War. He was no kid by the time he got married; my grandmother was a Spanish/Russian interpreter. This is why we all speak Spanish. I'm bilingual," he said, smiling again. "The other day I was in really bad shape, still half dopey from whatever those guys shot me up with. Thank goodness I snapped out of it enough to escape."

"Escape from whom?"

He paused before answering, self-conscious about broaching a subject he'd normally have been reluctant to discuss with anyone. Finally he said "Gagarin's thugs. One of the baddest apples in the New Russia. Drugs, money laundering, loan sharking. But before we get to that, let me finish clearing up how I got here. In 1991, when Yeltsin rose to power, everything changed. My father was seen as too close to Gorbachev, so he was relieved of his command. My family sent me away to a military boarding school when I was just nine. That's not really done much here, is it?"

Curro shook his head. "God, no. I mean, a couple hundred years ago there were military academies here where kids almost that young went to school, eventually graduating with a commission in the Royal Marines, but that was a long time ago."

"Well, it was no fun being separated from my family just like that, being put into a hostile environment, with a bunch of older boys bullying me. Besides which, my background was very different from most of them. I mean, my mother studied music in a conservatory, my father had been a high-ranking KGB officer; this flagged me as privileged."

My, my, thought Curro, *Who'd have thought....*

"They made life hell for me. Which is why I started boxing. I spent as much time as I could in the gym, till I could make everyone else steer clear of me. When I graduated from the Academy I was selected for a Special Ops unit, where my training continued in much the same vein. The different types of hand-to-hand combat fascinated me and still do: I've mastered them all. And when I left the army, I turned pro."

"Impressive. Your parents must be proud."

Dima swallowed hard, his whole expression becoming grim at the mention of their name, and

Curro wondered what Dima was about to say. "They moved back to St. Petersburg and my mother set up a music and dance school with a friend of hers who'd danced with the Mariinsky—have you heard of it?"

"Of course," said Curro, "I've been a couple of times."

"Things went well for many years. The school was a beacon for young students driven to learn but who couldn't get into the State academies. They even began putting on their own shows, and they kept tuition low. But a couple of years ago things went into a rough patch with the global economic downturn. You know how it is. And my dad tried every way to get a loan but nothing worked out, so he had no choice but to turn to Gagarin. He gave them a loan, all right, but the interest rapidly ballooned beyond anything they could pay. They started getting death threats so I confronted Gagarin. He knew me well enough to back off. My dad was really proud of me for doing that; though he was embarrassed that I'd had to ride to his rescue. He chewed me out, warned me to stay away from Gagarin because he'd gotten word that Gagarin had just signed up with the Kasparov brothers, the most powerful—and most bloodthirsty— mob in all Russia. Apparently Gagarin's first assignment was to launder fifty million Euros. But the cash disappeared."

"Dima, I still can't believe how well you speak my language," Curro interrupted, rather rudely. The Russian's family saga, interesting though it was, seemed to have made less of an impression on Curro than the fluency of Dima's speech. So fluid, so well-versed in popular slang, yet so academically correct.

"Look, Curro, if you're not interested let's talk

about something else. This was the first time I've ever tried to tell anyone..."

"Of course I'm interested, it's just that…"

"I told you, my grandmother taught Spanish. She studied Spanish Literature in Salamanca and after returning to Russia she was, for a time, the official interpreter for the top Comrades, even Brezhnev himself the year of the wheat crop failure and the aid from Argentina," he said, expecting Curro would know about that. "And yes, she probably did speak it more correctly than most Spanish academics. The language was her passion, a passion she spread to the whole family. At home we used to speak Spanish so often that even my dad ended up understanding it. I was a little overwhelmed when I first got here because I'm not used to hearing it outside the house, and all of a sudden it was everywhere. Now I'm just about used to it, even if my nerves sometimes get the better of me. Occasionally, there will be a phrase right there but I can't quite get it out. But that happens to me sometimes even in Russian."

"Well, you seem like a pretty laid-back guy."

"Most of the time I am laid-back, but not with the mess I'm in now."

"I understand. Go on."

"Fine, but please don't interrupt. As I was saying, my dad was able to keep tabs on what Gagarin's mob was up to through his KGB contacts; and that was his undoing. They found out he'd been keeping an eye on them, so they decided to pin the blame for the missing money on him. It was completely ridiculous—he'd never have gotten involved in a heist like that, and anyway he didn't have the means or manpower to carry it out. But the Kasparovs threatened to terminate Gagarin and his entire family if he didn't return every last penny. Unfortunately," Dima's eyes welled up, "I had to go to Amsterdam for a K-1 Tournament, and while I was there I saw something in the news about two bodies recovered from the Neva River, bound and gagged inside a car. My parents."

Dima broke down, sobbing bitterly and uncontrollably. Curro was shocked, both by the tragic story and his friend's sudden emotional outburst, but rose to the occasion, standing and giving the +-Russian a hug. It seemed the only acceptable response at such a moment, when no words are truly fit. Before retreating to his room, Dima pulled himself together for just long enough to finish his story.

"All this happened four months ago."

Just when Trasto died, thought Curro, beginning to feel some degree of emotional bond born of shared recent grief.

***

That afternoon Curro was dealing with some paperwork in his study when Dima walked up, already dressed.

"I'm going for a stroll. I need to unwind, clear my head."

"Fine, take your time, enjoy the fresh air." He pulled some cash off of his desk and stuffed it into one of Dima's pockets.

***

Curro's conversation with Dima had been one-sided, and understandably so under the circumstances. However, Curro wasn't sure he would have had the strength to open up the way Dima had even if Dima had asked. Curro had never been good talking about his feelings, something passed down from his parents. It wasn't that he didn't feel deeply—his devastation over Trasto's death was ample proof to the contrary. Rather he wasn't the type to share these emotions; in fact he wasn't equipped to even speak about them in the first place. The result was an emotionally stunted man who was ill-prepared for anything resembling a longterm romantic relationship. He was different and he knew it. Only Trasto seemed to accept him unconditionally just as he was, and for this he felt a lasting bond with the dog.

Curro Morante was shattered. The way things had ended up for his prized Trasto had made him bitter, depressed, inconsolable. Certainty, that was the issue that tormented him. He did not have complete and absolute certainty that he'd made the right decision when choosing to help his dog find peace. Yes, everyone told him he'd shown courage and love, thinking only of Trasto, wanting to spare the dog any more pain, wanting him to be able to die with dignity. Honestly, he hadn't seen any other way out. With a degenerative disease, barely able to walk, hobbling along, the sores spreading as his immune system shut down, life had little left to offer him. None of this now seemed to matter to Curro. Yet, anguish at having perhaps made the wrong decision still gnawed at him day and night. He had loved his dog, he still missed him every day, and the despondence that held him in its grip kept him from looking ahead with any hope.

Dima's sudden appearance couldn't have come at a better time for him. He could be a catalyst, or at the very least a distraction. And as for certainty that he'd made the right decision with Trasto, Curro would have to accept not having it—he would never know for certain that his decision about Trasto had been right. He'd get over that... ouldn't he?

To most women, and some men, Francisco Morante Solloso, aka Curro, was a real catch. He stood exactly six feet tall with a manly, athletic build . Tanned and green-eyed, he seemed quite youthful in his forty-fourth year. Nothing in his carriage, the way he walked or addressed others would have made anyone think that youth was behind him. He still dressed like a younger guy: jeans, banded collar shirts, loafers or sneakers. Always very casual. Except on formal occasions. At those times he gave free rein to his elegant side, showcasing his firm physique in tailored suits made to order at Calvo de Torra, just tight enough to make the most of his frame. Dress shoes from John Lobb, and always a pocket square in his blazer. Without ever nearing the sort of Italian extravagance he'd always found a bit tacky, his choices were sometimes daring, highly individual with regard to the colors and fabrics he expertly combined. He felt he had style. Even class.

Curro's had been a happy childhood, growing up in a loving environment, spending summers at his grandparents' homes in La Coruña or La Toja, until his dad's arthritis had made them try Marbella further south. Happy days, until *that* incident with his father; and then it had all changed. For better or worse? Who could say? From the time he'd hit eighteen he'd done his own thing, trading the repetitious trips to Marbella for the much more sensual charms of Ibiza, which he'd make the site of an annual pilgrimage to meet up with uninhibited friends from the four corners of the globe. *If it's September, it's Ibiza.*

He'd always been a bad student and all too easily distracted. At least his imagination had delighted his friends at school; he could spin the most trivial incident into an entertaining yarn. Subjects that appealed to his artistic side were the only ones in which he'd ever gotten straight As, apart from History and English—the latter achievement proving that his British nanny had done her job well. And then on to college to major in journalism, a degree that he would never finish. A shame, really; it could have been the ideal career outlet for the acute perceptiveness he'd been born with.

After that he'd spent some time working in his dad's office, watching his old man at the helm of a variety of ventures, managing the family assets; but the boredom nearly killed him. He could easily have been mistaken for the office gofer, since he jumped at any chore that would give him an excuse to head outdoors.

And even when he'd still been in high school, he'd snuck out every night to join in the ceaseless revelry that was Madrid after dark in the '80s and '90s. Just after he'd turned twenty-seven his father died, and the inheritance was comfortable enough to let him hang it up at the office and spend his time traveling and living it up.

His mother, whom he'd loved so much, had lived

for ten more years till succumbing to severe respiratory failure. She'd been so heavily sedated at the end that Curro would always feel the hospital had accelerated her demise. She went in for a nagging cold that wouldn't go away and died when her heart gave out. Damn hospitals, Curro wouldn't go near one. That had been seven years earlier, and it had really changed everything. The estate was sold for a small fortune and Curro, along with his faithful companion Trasto, had settled in a spacious penthouse on Salustiano Olozaga Street, a stone's throw from Madrid's sprawling Retiro Park.

***

When Dima failed to return that night, Curro figured he might have met some people at one of the local bars. The city was full of them, and most bars full of beautiful women sure to draw Dima's attention. But when he didn't return the following day, Curro grew concerned that he may have fallen into some trouble. Not that there was anything he could do about it. There was no way of reaching Dima, which made the wait that much more trying, and it wasn't as if Curro could go to the police. Truth be told it was more than just missing Dima; Curro missed the high spirits Dima had brought into his life. Was it possible he was gone for good, never to return? He didn't want to consider that option. So instead he busied himself, hoping to keep his mind off of his missing friend.

Finally Dima resurfaced on the third day, just as Curro was getting ready to go out for supper with a friend passing through Madrid. He looked neat and clean, as if he'd just had a shower.

"Where have you *been?* I was worried," Curro chided him. "I just about called the police."

"Are you out of your mind?" Dima said with an incredulous laugh. "The last thing I want is any attention from the Spanish police. Their noses get seriously out of joint at the faintest whiff of the Russian mafia."

"But you don't have a damn thing to do with the Russian mafia!"

"C'mon, think. Have you forgotten everything I told you the other day?"

"No, of course not." Curro wanted to steer clear of that topic, the less involved, the better. "So, how are you feeling? Are you doing better?"

"Fine, he said, taking a seat. "I was feeling really bummed out by my situation and didn't want to drag you along. I'm doing better now, but still not exactly carefree. Who did you think those guys were who were chasing me when we met? Gagarin's muscle. They've followed me all the way here, so they must think I know what happened to the missing fifty million euros."

"But you *don't,"* said Curro, sitting down opposite him.

"Not at all. I mean, I wish I did. Fifty million! I don't get it. They've already killed my parents, so why come after me?"

"They must have *some* reason. Either that, or they're totally dense. Here in Spain they might actually end up in jail. As you say, the Russian mafia is very high on the police shit list at the moment. Are you tied up with them in some other way?" he asked hesitantly.

"Well, I told you that when I left the Army I went on the European K-1 circuit. And I can't complain, things went well. But the big money's in the off-circuit fights. Gagarin controls that particular racket, and he has his own, let's say, 'stable.'"

Curro pictured a stable of young male fighters that looked like Dima. "Nice. And he signed you up to fight for him."

"More or less. He saw me winning a match in Paris by TKO and hired me for his team. I worked as one of his bodyguards for a short time, and did some things I now regret."

"What's a soldier like you doing with a thug like him?"

"Man, you don't know Russia. Mob families run the place and if you want to survive, especially in any field where betting is involved, you need the protection of one group or another. That's why I signed up with Gagarin, though I never felt like I was one of his guns. Even so," he took off his shirt, the same one he'd been wearing when he'd left three days before, and showed Curro the tattoos on his back. "These tattoos mean I hold the highest rank in Gagarin's mob."

The news that Dima was tied up with the highest ranks of the Russian mob and the blatant eroticism of the display of tattoos was for a second overwhelming. "What an honor!" said Curro sarcastically, wondering once again what he may have gotten himself into.

"Well, yes, frankly it is. Anyone who has these tattoos is untouchable. You have to pass some very harsh tests before you earn these."

"Like murdering someone, I suppose."

"Drop it, Curro," Dima said evenly.

"*Have* you killed anyone?" he asked, leaning in and looking Dima squarely in the eye.

"Yes," he said defensively, clearly annoyed with Curro for having forced it out of him. "And I'm not proud of it. But the people I killed were scum, they didn't deserve to live."

"No, no, of course not. Who better to know that than Gagarin?"

Dima shrugged impatiently. "You know what? I'm outta here. You seem like a decent guy, thanks for everything. I understand why all this would frighten you."

"Not in the least. I don't judge people. Your behavior towards me's been faultless, except for the lies."

"I haven't lied to you."

"Well, then except for the half-truths, or not coming clean at the beginning."

"I really haven't had time. We just met."

"It doesn't matter. You're staying," Curro said. He stood, moved closer, and clasping Dima on each shoulder, planted a kiss on his lips.

Dima was confused. In Russia men sometimes showed affection that way, but he knew it wasn't the custom in Spain. He thought perhaps Curro was trying to put him at ease by honoring his country's traditions. *Surely not*, he thought, but decided to pass it over.

Curro smiled inwardly at his advance. "Three o'clock already!" he said innocently. He was now very late for his lunch with Jorge, an old Peruvian friend, a surgeon, stopping off in Madrid on the way to a convention on face transplants in Vienna. He'd call him and make up an excuse for canceling so last minute, Jorge would understand. Many were the wild nights they'd spent together in some of the most dangerous nightspots on the outskirts of Madrid. When he'd visited Peru, Jorge had pulled out all the stops to make him feel at home, lending him a house with a pool and even a valet. Standing him up like this was unforgivable. He phoned, made his excuses, and promised to be there the next day.

"You hungry?" he asked Dima. "I'm starving. Jesús, my houseboy, is on vacation, and I don't feel the least bit like cooking. Let's go get something al fresco on Alcala near the park."

***

Once they'd been shown to their table—on the sidewalk, beneath an umbrella—Curro steered the conversation towards a different subject.

"So, what have you been up to while you were MIA the last three days?"

"First I went to the park, that one over there."

"The Retiro," said Curro.

"That's right. I spent a long time there, walking around, thinking, just soaking up the ambiance —so many people enjoying themselves. It's a beautiful park, I loved that glass house."

"The Crystal Palace."

"Is it a palace?"

"No," Curro said with a smile, "but they call it that all the same."

"Well, I spent a long time sitting on the grass in front of it. I lost track of the time. Some guys started a football game and talked me into playing along. It's not really my sport, but they needed a goalkeeper. Once they saw how big and strong I was they asked me to switch places with their defense. That was a mistake. I wasn't paying attention and went in too hard a few times, so I decided to call it quits and take off before I hurt somebody. Believe me, it was none too soon."

Curro was surprised by Dima's endurance; he could play football just a few days after receiving a large knife wound in the leg. But Curro said nothing.
"And then?"
"I went to Gran Via to get something to eat; I hadn't touched a bite since breakfast, so I was starved. And you're not gonna believe this, but I ran into a couple of pals from Moscow. One of them, named Vasili—we've worked together and saved each other's ass more than once. We went to a disco not too far from here, near Atocha Station—an old theater with a bunch of different levels. I had a fantastic time and was finally able to unwind. Then I went along with Vasili, who works as a bouncer by the way, to another disco on the La Coruña Highway. It was packed— I think some of the players from *Real Madrid* were there."
"I know the one you mean, it is pretty cool. There are a few more I want to show you too."
"Anyway, we stayed till closing time and then tagged along with some people who invited us to their after-party. It felt good just to speak Russian with a buddy again—I mean, the last few Russians I saw weren't too sociable."
"You can say that again. Where'd you sleep?"

"The house we went to, the one where the after-party was. There were a lot of people there, all seemed pretty nice. But by then I was pretty wasted. I ended up on a sofa at one end of the living room, and the next thing I knew I was—what would you say? 'Sleeping like a baby'."

"Well, I'm glad you were able to relax among your fellow countrymen," said Curro. "How about yesterday?"

"Once we were up, we spent the day at he gym, we even ate there. It's a huge gym, not just weight training, it even has a boxing ring. I sparred for a while with the owner—cool guy, used to be a champ a few years ago."

"Sparred? In other words, you mopped up the floor with him."

"No way, he's the instructor and the other guys really respect him, I didn't want to show him up. I pulled my punches. And after we ate I did something very Spanish." Curro looked blankly at Dima, who said proudly, "I took a *siesta!*"

"Heh, heh. Yes, Spain's greatest contribution to the world. Where at your friend Vasili's house?"

"No, right there in the gym, in the spa. Vasili was filling me in on his life here in Madrid. I was surprised to see him working as a club bouncer. In Moscow he was very well connected and used to handle a lot of cash."

"Life has its ups and downs," mused Curro.

"Tell me about it," Dima said with a nod. "Listen, I'm sorry I worried you, I didn't know where to call you and I just needed to clear my head, work out, and try to shake off the funk I'd been in."

"Say no more. Water under the bridge."

"I thought about coming back last night, once I'd rested I felt like talking with you. You're the only person here I can really open up to. Vasili's a great guy but it's not the same."

"I understand," said Curro, touched by this expression of trust. "Why didn't you come, then?"

"The owner of the discos Vasili works for called and told him to get over to a private party and take another strong guy with him. Some rock star was throwing a bash and they wanted us in there posing as guests just in case someone got out of hand. But in the end nothing happened, and I went over pretty well." Dima was beaming. "Lots of people flirted with me, and not just women, either. In fact, I think more men did than women. Man, there sure are a lot of queers in Madrid."

"You have no idea."

"Anyway I started talking with this stunning babe who waited till we were off duty and invited me to come back to her place. Vasili told me she's really famous, an international top model. I'll bet you'd recognize her if you saw her, her name's Eugenia."

Curro's eyes widened. "Eugenia?" Curro asked testily. "Eugenia what? Did you get her last name?"

"Osorio, Eugenia Osorio."

Shit, thought Curro. *Eugenia!* She'd be one hell of a rival.

***

After Curro got the check they stood up, having decided to stretch their legs before returning to Curro's penthouse. Dima drew his friend's attention to the cash Curro was leaving on the table as a generous tip; Dima thought he'd forgotten his change and started to reach over to hand it to him.

"No, no, leave it," Curro said. "They treat me very well here. I always have a table any time of the day or night, even if the place is full—and it's right next door, really convenient. So, Don Juan—you don't waste any time! What's your supermodel like?" Curro goaded Dima. "I've heard she's amazing in bed."

Leaving the restaurant, Dima said, "I thought she was really nice, I liked her. Actually she reminded me a little of you. She's, what would you say? A woman who knows what she wants."

"But in bed, is what they say true?"

"Man, you wanna know everything." Dima grinned at him. "Between us, it wasn't that big a deal. I'm pretty sure she was satisfied, though. At least, I haven't had any complaints!" Dima laughed.

Curro laughed too. "Eugenia! God, what a coincidence."

"You know her?" Dima seemed surprised at how amused Curro was.

"Of course, we go way back. She's like my..." he chose his words carefully, "my best friend, sort of a girlfriend."

"Your girlfriend?" Dima looked shocked, as if he'd overstepped boundaries.

"Well, not steady. A great friend, the best. But don't worry. You like her, right? Then go get her. Not a problem."

"Dude, if she's your girlfriend I'll pass. You're my friend and I owe you big time."

"No, seriously, we're not a couple. Anyway, tell me more. What did you two talk about?"

"Drop the act," said Dima. "Seriously, man, I'd never try to pull a fast one with your girlfriend. You're my friend, my brother."

From the looks of it, a very *big* brother, mused Curro. But he was pleased by his new sidekick's warmth.

"What did we talk about?" continued Dima "Just stuff, really. She tried to ask about my life. Hey, don't tell her anything. I didn't say a word about, you know."

"My lips are sealed."

"She asked if I was just passing through, had I been working as a bouncer for very long. We talked about Saint Petersburg, which she said she loves. You know, date chat. When I woke up this morning she was gone but she'd left me breakfast on a domed serving tray—toast, juice, bacon, and a card with her phone number on it. Said to call her next week."

That's very strange, thought Curro. Eugenia making breakfast! Usually she made it a point to avoid doing anything that compromised her image as an independent working woman. *Christ, she's really into him, all right. And I can't blame her, who wouldn't be? I sure as hell am. Taking off without saying goodbye—that's more like her, and so is taking home the first hot guy she bumps into, just like I would. Eugenia's like that. But her instincts are good, Dima's a good guy. Now the whole breakfast thing.* He smiled wryly to himself. *What a challenge. Which of us is going to end up with Dima? Eugenia's beautiful, smart, outgoing, bubbly—and super-famous. Not to mention the fact that Dima appears to be straight. Then again, nowadays, you never know.* Curro was a born seducer and provocateur. Taller walls had fallen.

"She's like that," Curro said to Dima, "charming and unpredictable. I think she told me she was going to Milan this week, some shoot for Italian *Vogue*. When she gets back, let's do dinner. We can make it a threesome."

CHAPTER III

"Taassiss, tassiss!" Eugenia shouted wildly, wildly mispronouncing the universal word for *taxi* as she tried to hail one.

She'd just stepped out of a restaurant opposite the Retiro Park, a Madrid eatery famous for serving wild game. Another dull business dinner, a prominent British editor trying to talk her into a lingerie spread. No lingerie! She never did those campaigns except for her yearly appearance with Victoria's Secret in the States. That was on a whole other level, and besides, they were friends. This night had been a waste of time for them both—Ian knew perfectly well that she didn't pose for lingerie spreads in magazines. He was just trying to score with her, and since he'd been in Madrid anyway invited her out to give it a try. *Another* try. When would he figure out that she was into jocks with attitude, not buttoned-down British gents? She didn't feel like beating around the bush, so as soon as she'd finished her Seared Venison and some of the exquisite San Vicente red that had arrived with it, she happily took advantage of a call from a telemarketer with a thick accent trying to explain the virtues of a cell phone plan. Unexpected, but timely.

"I'm so sorry, Ian, it's Mama. Another one of those migraines she's been having lately. She's whimpering in the dark in her bedroom, having an anxiety attack." She stood up, triggering a wave of attention among the other diners, as she usually did in most places. A kiss on each of Ian's cheeks and she was prancing towards the exit.

"Eugenia, darling," Ian called after her, his accent nearly as thick in its own way as the telemarketer's. "May I phone you later?"

"Better yet, I'll call you."

"Tassiss!" she shouted again, within earshot of the strolling neighbors and an elegant clique she'd jostled past exiting the same restaurant. "Taassiss!" As the cab pulled up she whispered to herself "Take me to Bilbado, passssing through Mesicosss along the way."

Sitting in the back of the cab she started giggling hysterically. She loved her little affectation, the release it brought. So much elegance, so much style, always having to be perfect. Sometimes it suffocated her, so she greatly enjoyed a display—a modest display, of course, being who she was—of a certain coarseness completely unbecoming to her, especially at times like that, stepping out of a venerable restaurant amid her peers.

Where to go, she thought, while the cabbie waited for instructions.

Curro's? His place was nearby, she'd surprise him. On second thought, better not. The fact they'd been such close friends for so long and despite the twelve-year age difference was due to certain basic, sacred ground rules, and one of those was: no surprises. Thoughtfully phoning ahead was the best way to avoid embarrassing situations, or just being untimely present when either of them happened to be enjoying some intimate solitude.

"Home. Corner of Hermanos Becquer and General Oraa."

***

Eugenia Osorio was on top of the world. In the relatively few years since she'd outshone all newcomers in Paris's most renowned new model search, she'd risen to the pinnacle of her profession. Possessed of radiant personality and flair, she not only shared a name with her fellow Spanish catwalk queen Eugenia Silva but enjoyed similar looks as well—both were tall brunettes with deep green eyes. Some years ago they'd walked a runway together, opening a highly anticipated show in New York. It had been put on by a Silicon Valley philanthropist to benefit victims of a Mexican earthquake, and society figures from across the globe had paid obscene prices for a seat, not necessarily front row but indeed anywhere they could get. The front row had been taken up entirely by princesses from royal houses, ruling and exiled, sprinkled with an Oscar-winning actress here or there. Billionaires and other A-listers got the next best seats. Spain's Infanta Elena, eldest daughter of King Juan Carlos, had been seated at the place of honor, next to the host; elegant as ever in a dress as sophisticated as daring, a dress difficult to wear without unshakeable confidence in oneself, confidence of the sort Infanta Elena possessed. The room's roar had tapered to a hush when the two Eugenias strutted onto the catwalk: serene, stylish, they looked as comfortable on the runway as they might in their own living rooms. After them had come the rest, stunning young girls of the most varied origins, radiant one and all. Feline Brazilians, frosty Eastern Europeans—the cream of every crop, but the Eugenias were something else. Their moves, their smiles, their air of distinction; something about posh Spanish girls set them apart. After the last walk, the models assembled one after the other to acknowledge the onlookers' cheering, and when the two Eugenias finally appeared the applause became an ovation, and Infanta Elena, ever so Spanish, had stood and shouted, "*Bravo!*" Ever since, Eugenia had reckoned that day as her enthronement in the modeling world.

Not that the Osorios had ever been that far from a throne. They were a lineage with generations of aristocrats and Spanish Grandees; but, like some of their relatives, they hadn't managed to hold on to their family fortune. Only Sonsoles, Eugenia's mother, had brought in the funds needed to reverse neglect and repel ruin at the Osorios' ancient palaces. Among a cultured and refined clan, Eugenia could be considered the most polished family jewel.

Millionaires, artists, sportsmen, Spaniards and foreigners, high fliers of every stripe had tried to win Eugenia's hand, and failed. She was in love with Curro, and the very knowledge that he wouldn't be an easy catch only made him more appealing. She knew how stubborn she could be and was convinced that she could make Curro love her, only her, and forget his fixation with muscled guys. She was convinced that Curro was straight, that he just, well, how did he always put it?:

"I have a thing for totally ripped guys."

***

The next few days at Curro's place were very busy. If Dima was going to stay there for a while—unless Eugenia had other plans!—then he'd need a complete wardrobe. Tailor, shirt-maker, shoe stores, the two men bought everything he'd need for a fresh start, a new life. And Curro did indeed see this as Dima's new beginning. It was clear that he could no longer go back to the Mob; in fact just the opposite. Curro would see to it that Dima started life anew on more even footing. In a few weeks the Queen would be the guest of honor at the Royal Opera House's charity gala do, and as both Curro and Eugenia were season ticket holders, it would be Dima's debutant event.

Spring was already showing signs of yielding to summer. The sultry season would soon have Madrid in its searing grip, so Dima needed linen shirts and pants, loafers, comfy Tod's moccasins, and some bathing suits. All first-class and what Dima deserved. To top it off, Curro gave him a Breitling chronograph he never wore and had forgotten in a drawer.

During those pleasantly hectic days a rapport grew between them, and Curro, departing from habit, was unassertive, even demure. No coming on strong, not this time. He'd hold back, it was an unusual situation with an exceptional prey. He would be patient. The comings and goings also allowed Curro to shake off, albeit temporarily, his lingering feelings of guilt over Trasto.

They talked about everything, opened up to one another. Like Curro, Dima felt guilt too, guilty for not having been there when his parents were murdered, for not having gone back to Russia at once. That had been his first reaction, thankfully quickly checked. It would have been madness, rushing right into the grip of Gagarin's mob, who'd have been only too eager to squeeze him about the missing money. Curro convinced him that delaying had not been cowardice but rather cleverness, reminding him of the old saying, "Revenge is a dish best served cold." Dima felt better and better, opening up to Curro in ways he never had to anyone. Some of the stories he shared made Curro blanch. And this was when Curro finally found out what had happened just before they'd met.

***

After learning his parents had been drowned in the Neva River, Dima decided it would be wise to lay low for a while. He couldn't prove that Gagarin was behind it, but his dad's warning and the information passed on by some old KGB contacts left him in little doubt. He couldn't go back to Moscow. He took the prize money from the K-1 tournament, left without saying a word to anyone, and bought a plane ticket to Saint Petersburg. Once there he planned to visit some relatives, pick up some personal belongings, and sneak off to spend some time abroad. But at the Amsterdam airport he'd realized he was being watched. If he boarded a plane for anywhere in Russia there would be a welcoming committee when he landed.

Fortunately, he had a friend nearby—a Dutch woman with sort of a crush on him, the widow of a well-regarded boxing judge. She took Dima in at her home in a suburb of The Hague, set well back from the nearest highway and train tracks. He spent his days training, putting out feelers to Moscow, and satisfying his benefactor. After a couple of months of this it was still not safe to return to Russia and he was ready to move on. The lady was starting to get on his nerves, and Dima had decided to check out the south. He'd always gotten along well with some of his Spanish cousins who lived near Cadiz, and he was back in touch with them. Since he was short on cash and wanted to avoid airports, he decided to hitchhike. He crossed Belgium and France this way, staying off of the main roads. Some nights he slept out in the open, gazing at the stars as he dozed off. It was slow going.

His first stop after entering Spain was Barcelona, where he made his first mistake. Tired of making such slow progress, he spent some of his last cash on a ticket for the high-speed train to Madrid, the AVE. He wanted to surprise an army buddy now stationed there as an attaché, someone who he was sure would help him out. Unfortunately, his friend was traveling with the Ambassador. This was a setback he hadn't planned on, and after breaking cover to ask about his pal he realized he was being watched again. Time to move on. Reluctantly he decided he'd have to hotwire a car—if possible he'd try to make it easy for its owner to recover after he reached his next stop, but for now he just needed to get away and get back under the radar as quickly as possible. That evening he ambled along Madrid's leafy Paseo de la Castellana, site of some of the sidewalk terraces so popular in the city's nightlife during the warmer months. Some of them offered valet parking. Dima hung back and watched till he saw one of the valets get out of a car in a hurry while leaving the keys in the ignition, and so he quietly snuck away in a nondescript Seat Ibiza hatchback.

His sense of direction was good and he'd quickly made it through Madrid's labyrinth of bypasses. But once he'd been beyond the city he'd mistaken the highway to Toledo for the one leading south to Cordoba and Seville. He retraced his steps back to Highway A-4 and stopped at Consuegra for gas. By then it was 5 AM and he'd stopped in the rest area just past the service station, meaning to catch a quick nap before he got back on his way. He fell into a deep sleep.

A blow to the head woke him abruptly. Shards of the car window cascaded down his chest as three goons placed him firmly in their grip. Within seconds he felt drowsy, disjointed, clumsy, as the drugs his attackers shot him up with took effect. What came next he remembered like fragments from a half-forgotten nightmare. He was tied to a chair, some guys were shouting at him. He looked around, it seemed like he was inside an abandoned cottage. He couldn't speak, he wanted to shout, "Leave me alone!" but his mouth formed no sounds. After a while he gradually became more alert and realized what might be going on. He tried to recognize any of his captors, but they were hired guns he'd never seen before. How the hell had they found him? He'd only been in Madrid for a day, and no one knew where he was planning to go next. The one who shouted the loudest and seemed to be in charge of the others waved a wicked-looking knife in his face. He kept asking Dima about the "fucking money from Moscow"—*How the hell should I know?* The other two stood near the door, smoking, bored into overconfidence.

Dima tried to pull his mind together and size up his surroundings. His senses were still sluggish, but he managed to get the lay of the land at a glance. The room was small. One exit, two barred windows. Essentially, a cell. Eventually, "Knife" took a breather, and Dima made an effort to shake off the grogginess and build up a rush of strength. If he was going to have any chance at all, he'd have to act now. When Knife came back toward him, Dima sprang forward and head-butted him right in the chest, as hard as he could. The thug fell sideways, dropping his knife with a gasp, and Dima made for the door, still wearing the chair. No good. The other two were coming right at him. The first one got a kick square on the jaw for his trouble; that put him out of action, but his pal pulled a gun. Things were getting ugly. Dima was so muscular that just by flexing he'd been able to create some wriggle room within his bondage and now he rammed his full bulk, including the chair, into the second guard, knocking him off his feet and then coming out of the melee with the gun in one of his hands.

Now he seemed to have things under control. Before leaving the makeshift cell, he wriggled free from the wreckage of the chair, still bound to his torso. But whatever they'd used to knock him out was still in his system, dulling his instincts. He felt the cold steel of the knife pierce his thigh a heartbeat before his erstwhile interrogator's hand was on the gun. He lunged to grab it but only managed to knock his assailant back: in a split second he had to choose between following through and fighting for the gun, or cutting his losses and taking the exit. He chose the latter and was out the door, sprinting away, the knife in his hand. Behind him he heard the wounded thugs starting after him. They must surely have been aware that they'd get a lot more than a simple scolding if they blew this assignment.

A BMW 850 parked nearby as he raced away from the isolated cottage so not scare drivers. A narrow dirt track led off towards a row of trees; beyond it he saw a stream and, maybe, the highway. Outnumbered and wounded, he nevertheless felt deliverance was within reach. But when he got to the trees, the thugs were on his heels and his bleeding leg gave out, sending him skidding down into the shallow stream. They caught up with him, and now he had no choice but to stand his ground. The one cocking the gun at him was closest; with his first thrust, Dima opened his face in to a bloody gash running from ear to chin. But the other two circled him, each gripping a glinting blade. He kept them both at bay, taking a few defensive wounds but giving as good as he got, stepping a few yards closer to the roadbed; and that was when he saw the car.

A convertible had braked on the road shoulder. It would surely take off again, any second. Dima had no time for second thoughts. He threw his knife away from his attackers and sprinted towards the road, through some bushes, leaping over the drainage ditch and hopping into the passenger seat.

"Hurry, please! Quickly!"

CHAPTER IV

That morning Dima had woken up earlier than usual and had gone out to get some *churros* with which to surprise Curro for breakfast. They were sharing them in the sun when the phone rang. Neither of them felt particularly like picking it up and it droned on until voicemail kicked in. *What a pain in the neck*, thought Curro. *Who would call this early on a weekend?*

The night before they'd gone to a play and then dined at the capital's latest fashionable eatery, a restaurant located in the gardens of a venerable palace in the Chamberi neighborhood. Dima had attracted his fair share of attention from the other diners: the linen slacks, Tod's loafers, and the tapered shirt, sleeves rolled up to his elbows—it all looked good on him. They'd gone home early, but stayed up late talking.

Dima had been completely won over by Curro's overwhelming personality. Despite his depression, Curro was so likeable, so natural, treated him so well, like an equal. Since the night with Eugenia, Curro had put Dima up in the guest bedroom adjoining his own. Until the nightmare. Curro heard Dima shouting in a language he didn't understand and leapt from his bed, concerned. He sat down on the bed next to Dima and shook the Russian gently to wake him. Dima trembled, wide-eyed and drenched in sweat.

"Dima, it's all right. It was just a dream."

"It was horrible, I dreamed of my mother. In it she was screaming for help from inside the car as it sank into the river. As she drowned, I was watching from a bridge over the river, just standing there, not even trying to help."

"It was just a nightmare. And that's the stuff dreams are made of: complete nonsense. You know you would have jumped in to try and pull her out. Don't torture yourself."

"I know you're right, but I still feel awful. It was so real. I could see her face, she couldn't breathe, she was begging for help." Dima began sobbing. "God, I still keep feeling I failed them. I should have been there, with them."

"Let it go, you had no way of knowing what was going to happen. How could you ever have known they'd pin the blame for the stolen money on your dad?"

Curro looked at him, so big yet so helpless, and the tenderness missing since Trasto's death came flooding back. Now he knew he would shower all of his affection on Dima and protect him. He wasn't sure what exactly that entailed considering the circumstances, but he felt like a man who had nothing to lose at this point. In many ways he felt half dead already. What was left of himself he would offer to Dima, no matter what came, he vowed inside.

Curro climbed into the bed next to his new friend and embraced him. Having him so close made Curro feel a curious sort of strength, as if he were receiving a transfusion of Dima's raw vitality. He tightened his embrace, feeling the colossus in his arms relax in acceptance and soon yield to deep, peaceful sleep.

The next few days passed in much the same vein. After supper Dima would chat online for a while with friends who kept him up to date with the latest from Moscow, and then get in bed; a while later, after the TV news, Curro would climb in next to him and cling tightly to him. The last time, it was Curro who awoke in a comfortably firm embrace. Curro couldn't believe his luck; he could only attribute Dima's acceptance to gratitude for his newfound safety and comfort. They never talked about any of it.

And there they were, having a laugh over breakfast about the gay couple who, the night before, had walked up to their table at the restaurant offering Dima the chance to appear on the cover of a men's underwear catalog. Were they for real, or just looking for an excuse to strike up a conversation? They couldn't be sure, and Dima said no thanks.

As they ate the phone rang, and once again they ignored it.

It was about half past one when they were surprised by the intercom's staccato tone. Curro rose and pressed a button.

"Yes?"

"Curro? Are you there? Can I come up?"

"Eugenia! What a surprise. I didn't know you were in Madrid."

"Well, you never answer your phone, and I was shopping on Serrano, so here I am," she said casually. "Besides, I need to talk with you. I've met this guy, you're gonna love him, you can't imagine what he's like. Think Tarzan, only more buff."

"In that case, come on up, Cheetah."

When she walked into the terrace, Eugenia's expression said it all: she'd broken the golden rule of never dropping by unannounced—and now she was paying the price. Lounging next to the man she loved was the man she desired, the one who'd made her feel amazing things she'd never felt before.

"Oh, so you know each other. I had no idea..." she said, trying to maintain her poise, while inside she felt more than a little out of place, ridiculous, even. She wasn't a fool, and the sight of Curro in his pajamas next to Dima in a bathing suit suggested intimacy beyond the casual.

"Yes, he thumbed a ride from me a few days ago. Charming, isn't he? I know he's been to your place—he told me the whole thing."

That was enough to finally get a rise out of Dima. "Eugenia! It's so good to see you," he said, standing and landing a kiss on her lips. "Let me just get a quick shower and I'll be right back."

Once they were alone Eugenia stopped trying to conceal her surprise. "How did you two meet?"

"Like I told you, I picked him up hitchhiking. He can tell you the rest. By the way," said Curro, "he *is* the Tarzan you were referring to, right?"

"The one and only," she said taking a seat. Eugenia sounded both bewildered and upset at this surprising turn of events. "So, was he a good lay for you too?"

"You're way off base. He's not the least bit gay."

"I know that; but I know you too."

"Well, nothing's happened *yet*," said Curro provocatively. "Do you really like him that much? Just say the word and I'll leave the field clear for you. He's crazy about you. Then again," he said, smiling wryly, "here I thought you were hung up on *me*."

"Oh, come on, you've never given me the time of day. You know damn well I've been in love with you for years. If you didn't have this unhealthy fixation on gym rats, we might just stand a chance."

After a while Dima returned, freshly showered and shaved, dressed to the nines and his long dark hair still glistening with moisture. He looked so stunning that Eugenia did a double take.

"Uncle Curro here," joked Dima, gesturing towards his host, "took me shopping and bought the whole shop. Do you like it? I've never dressed like this."

Eugenia smirked knowingly. She knew Curro all too well. "It suits you. All of it. You look like a prince."

"And you can be his princess," interjected Curro, eager to get back into the conversation. "Shall we have a bite to eat? How about if we go to Currito's?"

"Currito's?" Dima said with a laugh at the play on Curro's name.

"Yes, inside the Casa de Campo, a huge park on the west of the city. The food is to die for."

***

Casa de Campo was a bad idea. Curro hadn't stopped to think how he'd feel about going back for the first time to the place that had once meant so much to him. And to Trasto, especially Trasto. Over the course of years, every weekend, rain or shine, it had become a tradition. At first Curro had found it a complete pain in the ass: walking for exercise was anathema to him, even more so in such a crowded place where it was almost impossible to find spaces devoid of boisterous families or training athletes. In time he'd grow used to it.

He loved sports; he could point with pride to his years of judo, to the tennis matches—later replaced by racquetball—swimming, riding. And there'd been all that time working out at the gym. That he actually hated, but kept it up anyway in the name of looking good, of being desirable Apart from the fact that they were good places to score, of course. Gyms had developed into a swingers' scene all their own, places to hook up for later or even have quickie sex on the spot.

But just going for a walk—that was something he'd only done with his parents, when they were getting on in years and had been under doctor's orders to get some exercise. Even then it wasn't something he'd needed to do all that often, since they'd both had caregivers looking after them.

Curro was a man of his word, and he rose to the challenge. He hadn't wanted a dog, but the dog had wanted him. Having accepted the responsibility, he'd have to accept its consequences. Trasto was a German Shepherd and Podenco mix; quick, strong, energetic. He wasn't a lap dog, he needed to run. His owner understood this and took him places where he'd be free to run and roam. In Madrid, Casa de Campo was where Trasto could feel free, chase rabbits—which he occasionally caught and made a meal out of—and have the run of the place. As they got to know the park better they discovered areas away from the beaten path, all but empty, where Trasto could vanish into the brush while Curro relaxed on the grass with the papers or a book. He grew to enjoy silence in the company of his dog; and he learned to go for a walk. Trasto taught him.

***

Eugenia decided this was going to be an all-out war, one she intended to win. Over lunch at Casa de Campo, she realized that there could be no holds barred. For all the attention either man paid her, she might as well have been invisible, or homely. She could understand why Curro might be withdrawn—the park, Trasto, the memories—but what really threw her was the evident complicity linking the two men. Eugenia Osorio, international supermodel, was learning how it felt to be ignored.

She wasn't going to take this sitting down. She liked Dima, he was an amazing lover, his innocent sense of humor had made her laugh, but that was it. A committed relationship was out of the question—not in a million years, with some Russian who'd just blown in off the steppes! She was in love with Curro, her confidant, the man she wanted to raise a family with, to live in the country surrounded by dogs and horses— and kids. No Dmitri Whatshisname was going to derail the dream she'd been nurturing for so long.

She had an idea. She would reel Dima in just to make Curro jealous, and once she had him wrapped around her little finger, Curro would realize exactly how the handsome foreigner saw him—as a giant-sized Visa Gold card, like so many boys had before him. Dima was straight, no doubt about that after the night she'd taken him home. It had been clear that he was enjoying himself, and he in turn had made sure he satisfied her. She was mystified by how buddy-buddy Dima was with Curro, who was old enough to be his father and who anyone could tell had a crush on him. She wondered if the secret might be in how they'd met—she was sure she still hadn't heard the whole story on that.

She'd have to handle Curro with care—any inkling of what she was up to and she might lose him forever. Curro acted as if Dima were his possession, proudly displaying him at every trendy spot in Madrid, showing him off without the slightest compunction. That didn't surprise her; Curro always did whatever he damn well felt like—as did she. *Focus, baby. Roll up your sleeves and get to work.*

Eugenia knew that Dima had settled into a comfortable routine—jogging, gym, martial arts. She made a few discreet inquiries as to which Madrid gyms focused on training for boxing and other combative sports. She knew that as far as Curro was concerned, only the best would do for his new young friend. The one that seemed to be on the tip of everyone's tongue was a new facility that offered training in traditional disciplines as well as the highest echelons of hand-to-hand combat and self-defense. It was run by Ignacio Manjón, a noted Taekwondo Olympic medalist, and was located in the posh neighborhood of La Moraleja. Dima attended every day, arriving at the wheel of Curro's Jaguar, while Curro drove around Madrid in a

Mini Cooper that was easier to park. It was a fashionable place attracting a varied clientele: there were long-time residents of the neighborhood, successful pro athletes, staples of the showbiz gossip mags, also martial arts professionals seeking to hone their skills under the master's guidance.

Dima had become popular at the gym in record time. People used the flimsiest excuses to strike up a conversation with him. Where are you from, what diet do you follow, can you help me get going with this machine? He received invitations galore, all of which he politely declined. A few times he tried to convince Curro to come along with him, but Curro no longer worried that much about staying in top shape.

Dima training was a sight to behold: Shirtless, sweaty, sparring in the ring, holding court amid a throng of admirers of both genders. Oddly enough, whenever he went for a shower the men's locker room suddenly got crowded. Whispers here and there, heads turning in his wake; his magnetism left no one indifferent and more than one of his sparring partners felt inadequate in the face of such raw virility.

When Eugenia walked into the weight room a buzz of expectation crackled through the place. Eugenia Osorio, the supermodel! Stolen glances tracked her progress across the floor. All very discreet; so much the better. Members of this gym were people of the well-mannered variety, not the kind who would smother a celebrity by begging for autographs or a picture and spoil his or her time off. Was Spain changing? No, thought Eugenia, this gym just happened to be an oasis of urbane, worldly people.

She spent some time stretching her legs and

toning her arms, then set off to reconnoiter the terrain. She made small talk with a few acquaintances but all the while kept an eye out for her prey. Where could Dima be hiding? He was nowhere to be seen. The Jaguar was still parked outside so he had to be there somewhere. At last she caught sight of him just as he was heading for the exit.

"Dima! Long time, no see. You've been neglecting me," she pouted.

"Oh come on, you're the one who's always flitting off somewhere. You know Curro adores you. And so do I." Dima flashed an irresistible smile.

"Curro, Curro, Curro. I've seen enough of him to tide me over for quite a while. Wouldn't you like a wild night out, like the night we met? If Curro wants to tag along, that's fine. If not, then it'll just be the two of us. He hardly goes out on the town anymore anyway, he's been in such a deep blue funk."

"I know, I know, since his dog Trasto died." Dima was fully up to speed on Curro's frequent mood swings. "But he can be a really fun guy. I have a great time with him, although it'd do him good to get out more. He's spent the last few days all cooped up alone in his apartment."

"He's like that, he always needs his space. Actually, I never thought you'd last this long at his place. Curro's fiercely independent. He's breaking his own rules for you. If Trasto were still alive you'd already have been shown the door." Seeing the mystified look on Dima's face, she explained: "Trasto was an amazingly jealous animal. He wanted Curro all to himself, and as far as Curro was concerned, Trasto always came first."

"Ahead of you?" Dima was getting more confused by the minute.

"Ahead of anyone. Curro and Trasto, now there was a real bond. True love for sure," she said, matter of factly. "Or the closest I've seen Curro get to true love at least. Anyway," Eugenia changed the subject, she was more than fed up with that one, "Tonight. You. Me. What do you say?"

"I dunno. Curro may already have made plans..."

Eugenia was losing her patience. *What a dork,* she thought. But she was a great actress; after all, she spent her workdays trying on different poses, different personalities.

"Come on, I just got back from Milan and I need a night on the town. I was so bored. The Italians seem to have all lost their charm, they don't know how to flirt. Give me a Russian savage any day." She realized she'd stepped in it and without missing a beat tried to recover. "Or better yet, a Russian-Spaniard, they're my very favorite—refined, lively, but with an animal side. Like you, my Russian-Spanish giant."

Eugenia heard herself and inwardly cringed. She never babbled like this, never said this kind of bullshit; but then she'd never had to work this hard for what she wanted, either. Usually it was men who made fools of themselves to win her affections, not the other way around. But as the saying goes, *All's fair in love and war.* So, "my giant," then, if that's what it took.

Before Dima could answer, Eugenia was distracted by a woman approaching them at a firm clip. Aunt Matilde, Pepe Aguirre's resolute wife. Matilde was not only Eugenia's aunt—her father's sister—she was also Eugenia's godmother; and for some time, the loudest cheerleader if not the actual matchmaker for a Morante-Osorio wedding. As she saw it, what more could one want? Curro and Eugenia had known each other for a lifetime, and this was the essential element for a successful marriage among their social class. A quick glance at her contemporaries confirmed Matilde's impression: the relationships that had lasted were those in which both partners came from the same background, shared the same views, the couples in which one spouse was unlikely to surprise the other through some unwelcome unorthodoxy. Besides, they were both gorgeous, and Curro was well-off enough that no one could accuse him of being a fortune hunter. As for Eugenia, allure was hardly the only asset of Matilde's darling niece; one day she would split a sizable inheritance with her younger sister Fabiola—currently studying at the Sorbonne—but as the eldest daughter, Eugenia would inherit her father's title and so in due course become the 21st Duchess of Luaces. In Matilde's eyes the match was beyond perfect.

"Eugenia, darling, fancy meeting you here!"

"Aunt Matilde!" Cheeks were kissed.

"I didn't know you came to this gym too. Isn't it awfully out of your way? And as long as you're in the area, why haven't you called?" Matilde gently chided her niece.

"I would have, only since it's Friday I thought you'd be on the way to Toledo already. I'm meeting Maru Vallejo for lunch, she's around here somewhere trying to burn off an extra pound," lied Eugenia serenely.

"Well, we're not leaving till after lunch—your Uncle Pepe has a meeting with some Belgians, or

Frenchmen. Somebody foreign, anyway," said Matilde while eyeing Dima, a mute spectator to this unplanned family reunion.

"Auntie, let me introduce Dima. I'm sorry," she said to him. "I've forgotten your surname."

"Denissov, Dmitri Denissov."

"Of course, Denissov. Dima, this is my Aunt Matilde."

"Delighted to meet you," said Dima, clasping and formally kissing the offered hand.

Matilde acted as if Dima were transparent and launched into a lengthy conversation with Eugenia, one in which Dima was clearly not expected to participate. Dima took the slight as an opportunity to bid both ladies farewell.

"I'm sorry to run off, but I have to go. Curro's arranged for paella at this legendary seafood joint."

"The Saint James?" asked Eugenia

"The one and only," he said and nodded. "And you know he is about being on time—if I'm late he'll hit me," Dima quipped. "Nice to meet you, ma'am."

"But are we on or not?" As he turned to leave, Eugenia called out after him.

"I'll call you later," said Dima as he strode towards the parking lot.

"Who was *that*?" Asked Matilde, her curiosity piqued.

"Just a Russian friend, he's really charming. What a hunk, don't you think?"

"Sure, but where did you two meet? He's not really your type."

"Anyone can be my type, Auntie. Just like any other woman with good taste." The undertone of classism in Matilde's remark irked her. "Anyway, he's Curro's new best buddy."

"Oh, of course, I should have known at once. That must be Curro's Greek god, the one everybody's been talking about. Curro never changes—he must be out of his mind, inviting someone like that to move in with him. Half of Madrid's talking about it, he takes that kid everywhere with him —I think he does it just to defy convention. Your father's going to be furious, it might be seen as a slight to you. I've half a mind to start believing those rumors that Curro's turned gay."

"Nonsense!" Eugenia snapped. "And I'll thank you not to repeat trash like that about my fiancé."

"I just hope he makes up his mind sooner rather than later."

"What's gotten into you, Aunt Matilde? You've always been for Curro—in fact, you were the first person to encourage me as far as he and I being a couple. And Uncle Pepe loves him."

"And so do I," she said soothingly, "you know that. But I think he's going too far this time. Mark my words, it will end in tears."

Eugenia looked at her watch, eager to end this conversation. "I'm awfully sorry, Auntie, but I have to run. I shouldn't keep Maru waiting."

They exchanged pecks on the cheek, Matilde squeezed Eugenia's forearm, and they were off in separate directions. After a few paces Eugenia turned and waved energetically as she walked away. "Bye, Auntie! Auntiiee! Byeee!" shouted Eugenia, giving vent to one of her episodes of exorcism.

That girl, thought Matilde, shaking her head. *I've half a mind to believe her father.*

CHAPTER V

Something wasn't right, Dima was sure of that. His instincts were sharp enough to sound the alarm at the faintest hint of danger—a sure sense that things that were out of place. Like now at the gym. Something didn't fit. He'd also felt it the moment he'd stepped off the train in Madrid, which was why he'd lost no time in trying to get away from the city that fateful night. They'd been waiting for him. They must have followed him since the moment he'd set foot in Spain. How else to explain Gagarin's thugs appearing right on cue? Dima hadn't told anyone he was coming, not even his cousins in Cadiz. He'd meant to surprise them, confident of being well received.

He smiled briefly as he remembered those summer vacations with his Spanish cousins; the fistfights they'd gotten into with the kids from the next town over, nearly every weekend. His cousins had been pushovers till Dima had taught them how to defend themselves.

Dima's thoughts were darting between past and present as he reached for his car keys. Just then two of the bigger guys he'd seen around the gym, fellow K-1 practitioners, sauntered up.

"Dima, my man, we're gonna hit the town tonight with our squad—you in? Wait till you see the babes."

"Not in the same league as Eugenia Osorio, of course," said the blonder of the two, grinning. Dima thought they had to be brothers—both big, blond, same swagger.

"Sorry, guys. Love to, but I already have plans."

"Oh, I'll bet you do—with Eugenia Osorio! Son of a bitch." The other one shook his head jealously.

"No, just some friends." Dima didn't feel like getting into specifics. "I gotta go, I'm expected for lunch downtown. See you Monday. And thanks." He'd started walking again when one of the two caught up with him.

"Fine, dude, no biggie. But if you change your mind we'll be at the Ganvino Club on Orense. We run security there. It draws a good crowd—probably some people Eugenia knows, no gangbangers. I'm Tony Martinez Porras and this is my brother, Andy." They shook hands and Dima got into the Jag.

Andy Martinez Porras—that name rang a bell. Dima realized that was the Spanish K-1 champion. Dima had seen him fight, one tough customer. His big brother, the one who'd done most of the talking, didn't seem the shy and retiring type either. What a pair.

Dima put the convertible's top down and as he drove along he began turning the issue of his arrival in Madrid—who'd found out about it, and how—over and over in his mind. It was no use; he just couldn't figure it out, maybe it would come to him when he least expected it. As he drove along, the sun's benign warmth on his skin made it easier to put the whole thing out of his mind for the time being; the gradually spreading ebullience tipped the scales. He'd call

Eugenia and take her up on that night out—with or without Curro. He needed to unwind, needed to let his hair down. He needed a wild night out.

Indeed, later that evening Dima fleetingly reflected that Madrid by night was indeed all that it was cracked up to be. He hadn't enjoyed himself so much in a very long time.

As he'd expected, Curro had politely declined his suggestion that the three of them have dinner together, offering the clumsy excuse of not wanting to miss a TV show. Heaven knows he hardly ever switched the damn thing on. So, with Curro's approval, Dima took the keys to the Jaguar and left for Eugenia's.

He was impressed by Eugenia's apartment. Like Curro, she too lived in a penthouse, but her interior decor was much more daring and avant-guard than his. Dima loved Curro's penthouse; very comfy, masculine yet welcoming, its design scheme built upon wall-to-wall carpeting linking walls covered in designer wallpaper or fabrics, rooms that house sofas and easy chairs, and scattered modern artworks coexisting with a few antique heirlooms; all very well arranged, elegant. Eugenia's home exuded a completely different charm: slate flooring, travertine walls, a minimalist, functional *leitmotiv* with a decidedly New York touch. Which did he prefer? He wasn't sure. Both were special, but for now Curro's place felt like home. It *was* home.

As soon as he arrived Eugenia offered him a cocktail; instead, he asked for freshly squeezed orange juice. *A bold, assertive woman's place is in the kitchen squeezing oranges,* thought Eugenia ruefully as she helped herself to a glass of chilled white wine, keeping the bottle in the fridge for later.

There wasn't much in the way of preliminaries, not that there was really any need; they liked each other, they were attracted to each other, and almost from the moment drinks were served they began to kiss, to caress. Like an old movie, the leading man scooped the lovely heroine up in his powerful arms and carried her effortlessly to bed—or in this case, the larger of the sofas in the living room; the first step on the players' road to ecstasy.

Eugenia enjoyed it even more than she had the first time. She explored every inch of her lover's body, more minutely than she had before. She let her senses lead her, she stroked, licked, sucked every bulge and jut of Dima's rugged, rippling form. No taboos, no restraint. She'd shared her bed with handsome, worldly men, with elite sportsmen too, but Dima was a different experience altogether. His every pore exuded a sexuality that pushed her time and again beyond her previous limits. She was used to calling the shots, to demanding the treatment due a goddess from those fortunate enough to have possessed her; Dima left her reeling. He took her in positions she'd never known existed, leading her to the entirely new sensation of savoring submission to a dominant man. The call of the wild changed her forever; she found herself accepting her new role with pleasure. At last she fully, profoundly understood that reverently mentioned yet always elusive concept, multiorgasm.

At the end she lit up a smoke—how long had it been since she'd done that? —and snuggled up in Dima's arms. She thought about the times she'd been with Curro: what a difference!

Dima would become the object of her desire, her

yearning, the man to whom she would give herself up completely. From that night on, in his presence she would always feel expectant, nervous, excited, and his love would be the goal she sought.

"You're looking really elegant tonight," she said approvingly, as they began putting themselves back together to go out. At first she'd been surprised to see him so nicely done up: beige chinos, a pale pink shirt, brown Sebago moccasins, and a navy blue blazer. She'd been expecting jeans and a tight T, which she knew looked so good on him. But Curro, knowing her, knew she might take her date somewhere classy for dinner, so before Dima left he'd recommended to the Russian that he dress up a little more. Dima felt invigorated after standing under the largest showerhead he'd ever seen, and with the strongest water pressure too. "I'll be ready in no time," she told him, "and we can take off."

Eugenia emerged from her wardrobe looking very casual. Working in the fashion world had made her weary of trying to keep up with each season's ins and outs, so she'd developed her own elegant yet daring freelance style. She hated black, except for at the very formal occasions that required it, and in spring and summer she always went with as much color as possible. Now she topped gray slacks with an Ibiza-style printed blouse, and wore comfy flat sandals; they'd be the best choice if they went dancing later, and standing six feet in her stocking feet she didn't need any extra lift. She'd always secretly found ridiculous those of her fellow models who insisted on tottering around at all hours on six-inch heels that made most of them at least two heads taller than any of their beaux. Not to mention the fact that she'd seen more than one of them stumble over and end up in an unbecoming heap on the floor, sometimes bleeding.

"Let's go try our luck at getting a table in El Paraguas," she said to Dima as they walked towards the elevator. "It's not just fashionable, the food is exquisite."

Dima guided the Jag down Serrano to Jorge Juan Street. Outside the restaurant the two guys handling its valet parking service were having a hell of a time trying to managing the Friday night mayhem. A murmur went up among the crowd waiting for a table around the door. Eugenia was used to that low rumble, she heard it wherever she went and was recognized.

"Wait here," she said to Dima, nimbly exiting the car. "I'm going to find out if we've any hope of a table. There's no point in parking if we're just going to have to leave again."

She greeted some acquaintances then strode resolutely through the door, sure of achieving her goal. A short time later she reappeared, arm-in-arm with a gentleman whose deportment suggested he might well be the owner of the place.

"Dima!" she shouted. "Leave the keys, we've got a table!"

Dima sprang from the convertible in a gymnastic bound and in a blink was standing before Eugenia and her companion.

"Dima, this is Agustin, he's in charge. He's been charming enough to have a table prepared for us at once."

They went in and were seated in a small, intimate dining room just off the passageway that led to the rest of the restaurant. Some friends of Eugenia's had already finished their meal and she stood for a moment to say goodbye, ordering a chilled bottle of Moët Chandon as she passed a waiter.

Dima had been taking in his surroundings. Their cozy little dining room branched off of the hallway through which all of the other diners came and went, so it was a privileged location at which to see and be seen. Just as the waiter approached the table with the champagne, Eugenia was back like a whirlwind.

"No, wait. Excuse me, we're moving to a different table, in the other dining room—the one at the end, next to the window." She sidled up to Dima. "This room's fine during the week when the place is full of stuffy suits, but the other one's much more enjoyable tonight. It's bigger and you can see everyone. Follow me!" she said, tugging at his hand.

She felt ecstatic. How long had it been since she'd felt such excitement, such a thrill, and such contentment? For all the glamour the fashion world had to offer she'd grown bored with its predictability. Always the same faces saying seemingly the same things from one season to the next. Only the colors changed. Dima was surprising to her. Without knowing quite why, she felt more alive than she had only a few weeks before, and lucky to be at his side. Sex can create a bond, making lovers accomplices in something shared, intimate, sublime... And if it's something with multiple orgasms, so much the better.

Heads turned as they approached their new table. *What a couple!* The stunning model was only too happy to acknowledge those who greeted her, proud of the hunk by her side. As soon as they were seated she started in on the champagne, convincing Dima that it was a special enough day for him to bend his own rule against alcohol. After all, didn't Dima drink red wine with Curro every day? The only difference between his tipple and the one she was offering was that her drink was as bubbly as she was.

Eugenia was positively gabby, making plans, planning trips, laying out a new life for them both. She, who had never been in love except with Curro—and how silly and hopeless that now seemed—with suitors spread halfway around the globe, many quite obscenely rich, was now completely hung up on an enigmatic young foreigner. She, Eugenia Osorio, who as the future 21st Duchess of Luaces possessed the ancient right to address the King as "Cousin," had gone nuts over a simple Russian named Dmitri.

Dmitri whatshisname. Dmitri, *Her* Dmitri! Not for a second did she doubt he'd feel the same way about her, feel in fact as if he'd hit the jackpot. She probed him with question after question, trying unsuccessfully to form a clear picture of her beau but hearing only vague, opaque answers in return. *"So what brought you to Spain?" "Do you see your Spanish relatives often?" "How about your Russian relatives?" "So what line of work are you in exactly?" "Fighting? You mean, you make a living out of that?"*

"So, tell me, Dima," she said, once she'd had enough champagne to stop beating around the bush, "how did you really meet Curro? You're not one of those guys who gets by through sponging off, um, homosexuals, are you?"

"Whaaat?" Dima said, repulsed and defensive of his friend. "Curro's not gay—"

"Heh, heh. Of course not, he just, um, *has a thing for totally ripped guys.*" She snorted. "Guys like you."

"Drop it, Eugenia. You're drunk." Dima didn't like where this conversation was heading.

She raised her hand and called out to a passing waiter.. "Another Moët Chandon! Iced, please!"

"Wasn't the last one to your liking?" asked the maître d', solicitously.

"Yes, it was fine, but I want the next one seriously cold. Bring an ice bucket or something. And for dinner we'd like, umm, something we can share for an appetizer. And the calamari."

"Pan-fried Calamari it is. And for the gentleman?"

"The gentleman will have the same thing."

"Excuse me," Dima broke in, "what else do you have that can be shared?"

"To share? Here," and he handed Dima a menu, pointing at the house specials, then looked back to Eugenia. "And would you prefer a meat or seafood entree?"

"Meat," said Dima, before Eugenia had a chance to open her mouth; his eyes skimmed the menu as he talked. "As appetizers we'll have the *fabada* croquettes and the Cantabrian anchovies with avocado. And some clams."

"Very good, sir. And the entree?"

"Oxtail meatballs," said Dima. He smiled at Eugenia. "The other day we had oxtail at home," (*at home?* thought Eugenia, miffed) "and it was fantastic. I'd never tried it before."

"Thank you, sir. Well chosen." The maître d' nodded towards Dima and headed for the kitchen, leaving Eugenia bemused. *I should have expected as much; Curro, teacher of the year.*

"So, someone's got the munchies?" she asked ironically, cocking her head to one side.

"After a workout like that," Dima said with a smile, remembering their time in bed.

"Come on, have some more bubbly, don't be a stick in the mud."

"We've already had enough, Eugenia. Let's give the champagne a rest."

"Are you kidding? It's perfect now, just the way I like it. Freezing!"

Dima had been having a great time: at Eugenia's place, in the car, even enjoying the interest they'd elicited as they walked into the restaurant. Until he realized Eugenia had morphed into a spoiled little girl demanding to be the center of attention and determined to be obeyed. She refused to accept his circumspect answers about his past or respect his privacy: she'd been all but interrogating him, pushing him, clearly irked by his close friendship with Curro, to the point of badmouthing him with those remarks about his orientation. It was as if she felt left out the Boys' Secret Club and couldn't handle it. All of a sudden the mask had slipped and she seemed a far cry from the cosmopolitan, outgoing, cheerful girl who'd begun to fascinate him.

And, to top it off, she wouldn't let up on the booze. With each passing minute she became more and more of a loose cannon. It was all getting to be too much for Dima, who had made discretion his watchword. True, Curro could be reckless, but he was very good at judging the time and place for everything, and when he thumbed his nose at convention he usually did so in ways that amused Dima, without making him uncomfortable. Didn't Eugenia realize that everyone was looking at her? If she wanted to be the center of attention, she certainly was now. She shouldn't lose sight of the fact that she was famous and should tone things down a bit; her behavior was becoming downright vulgar, nuzzling him while she stuck her hand inside his shirt in full view of the other diners.

"Eugenia, we're leaving," he said firmly, giving her no chance to argue. This time he was the one raising his hand to call the waiter over, but only to ask for the check.

Once a date starts going badly, it usually gets worse; and that was just what happened. A famous French rugby player, in Madrid to lead the national team, had recognized her. The previous summer in Monte Carlo he'd been turned down none too graciously by Eugenia, in a way that had embarrassed him in front of his teammates. Now the rugby player stood up and lurched towards Eugenia, stumbling over most of what he found in his path. A few diners muttered under their breath at him, and one of his tablemates, big and tough-looking, tried to coax him back to his chair but was roughly pushed away for his trouble.

The massive jock walked right up to the table and stood right in front of Eugenia. After a second she recognized him, then grimaced and stared coldly in the opposite direction. Her rejected suitor began gesticulating while bawling her out in his native tongue, which—thankfully—most of the diners didn't understand. Dima didn't understand it either, but his date's face told him all he needed to know about the general tenor of the Frenchman's remarks. Dima stood up to defend Eugenia just as the other man's gesticulations were becoming aggressive. The convenience of having a table near the window became more apparent as the Frenchman careened through it headfirst, dragging tablecloth and cutlery along with him, once Dima's punch had landed squarely on his face.

The restaurant broke into spontaneous applause at Dima's gallantry, while the Frenchman's companions apologized for his behavior as they went outside to offer first aid.

Dima calmly repeated his request for the check and insisted the restaurant also bill him for the damage, which the management dismissed at once. He paid with the credit card Curro had lent him, along with its pin number. As the couple left the restaurant, Eugenia whispered into Dima's ear, "Sorry about the show."

"Which one?" he answered drily. Dima had things firmly under control.

While they were waiting outside for their car, Dima approached the French huddle to ask how bigmouth was doing. He'd come around by now—he was a rugby player, after all—gotten to his feet and, like a gentleman, offered Dima his hand, which Dima accepted.

"Auntiee, Aunntieeeee!" Eugenia suddenly shouted as if possessed.

"Eugenia, darling, are you all right?" asked Aunt Matilde, timely as ever. "I heard from Agustin that you were behind this ruckus."

"It wasn't my fault, Auntie. There was this crazy Frenchman."

"Of course there was, dear." Matilde looked at Dima. "Thanks. You behaved like a real gentleman. Thanks for standing up for this crazy niece of mine."

"Auntiiee, enough already. Anyway, what are you doing here? Weren't you going to Toledo?"

"Your uncle ended up having to stay in Madrid, to entertain his French clients—I hope they have better manners than that bunch," she said, cocking her head towards the athletes sauntering away down the sidewalk with their bruised leader.

"So you're hanging out with your peeps!" giggled Eugenia.

"I was, until I had to take you home. Come on, I won't have you out in public like this."

"Like what? What do you mean?"

"Drunk as a skunk, that's what. And please, please stop calling me Auunnntiee."

"It's nothing to do with you, I'm just like that. And no way am I going home. Don Juan here was just taking me out on the town," she said, gazing devotedly if unsteadily at Dima.

"No, I'm gonna call it an early night," said Dima, "I'm beat. Besides, Curro said something about going somewhere called San Juan tomorrow to ski.

Matilde smiled. "You must mean water skiing at San Juan Reservoir."

"Whatever. Shall we go?" he said, politely but with firmness enough to indicate that it wasn't really a question. The valet stood next to the car waiting for his tip. "Get in."

Technically, having more than two people in the

front of the car was a moving violation, but it was late and Eugenia's place was only a few blocks away, so the women squeezed into the two-seater.

As he pulled out into traffic he realized they were being followed. It was a Porsche, keeping a prudent distance. His mind raced with worry as he tried to project an outward coolness. Taking Eugenia back to her place could be dangerous; they'd know where she lived and might use her to get to him. Curro's place was out of the question. Not only did he not want to put his friend in harm's way, that would blow his cover too, revealing his secret hideaway. Now, Eugenia's aunt—no one would associate her with him and if they'd been following him they wouldn't take her for part of his inner circle, but rather just someone he'd met by chance and given a ride.

"Matilde, where do you live?"

"A little further up the street from the French Embassy on Serrano—do you know where that is?"

"I'm afraid not."

"All right, keep going straight up Velázquez and I'll tell you when to turn left."

When they pulled up outside Matilde's place, Dima did a double-take. He'd been expecting a nice condo, but instead found himself parked outside a free-standing, multi-story home-cum-palace. *Well, well, Auntieeee,* he thought.

Dima sprang out of the driver's side and around the car to help them out of the passenger seat. He saw them as far as Matilde's gate, which she unlocked; he was invited in for a cup of tea, which he politely declined. The night had been exciting enough and he wanted to rest. Eugenia began whimpering in protest and, when she saw that wasn't getting anywhere, tried grabbing hold of Dima and refusing to let him go.

"My love! My beau! My knight in shining armor—"

"Try not to be so corny, dear," Matilde interjected as she took Eugenia by the arm.

"He saved my life!" babbled Eugenia, still several sheets to the wind.

"It wasn't that big a deal, honestly," said Dima.

"No big deal! Why if you hadn't stepped in, I might have been publicly embarrassed—"

"I'm off." He gave Eugenia a peck on each cheek, waved at her aunt and was in the car and away from the curb in a flash. His stomach was turning and it wasn't because of the food.

CHAPTER VI

Dima was in serious need of a breather. Since he'd gotten to Spain it had been one hair-raising experience after another. Of course, apart from the knowledge he was still being followed and spied on for thugs working for Gagarin—who else? —he had to admit that his life had taken a 180 degree turn. Curro and Eugenia had shown him a new world that fascinated him, but it was only a distraction from his status as an exile. He wanted revenge for his parents, he needed to clear their names. Gagarin's muscle boys had put the screws to him over the missing cash, but they hadn't killed him when they'd had the chance. Why? Was his hard-won freedom part of their plan—were they following him to see if he'd lead them to the loot they thought he had? Or had they simply bungled the job, intending the knife wounds—one of which, at least, had been deep—to finish him off?

He was still mulling all of this over when his thoughts returned to that Porsche, which had disappeared once he'd dropped off the ladies. Who was it? The same crew who'd kidnapped him, or a fresh team sent to tail him? He doubted it was the kidnappers. Russian hired guns didn't usually get around in a Porsche; their bosses did, but they were usually more discreet. He'd spotted this car as soon as they'd left the restaurant.

He decided to shelve the issue till the next morning. It was still early and he had plenty of time to enjoy himself. He thought of that disco the guys from the gym had mentioned—Ganvino, on Orense. He thought he could find it.

When he pulled up outside the nightspot he couldn't believe his eyes:what appeared to be the same silver Porsche that had been tailing him was parked near the door amid other high-end cars. Andy, the younger of the two Martinez brothers, was working the door and as soon as he saw Dima he strolled over, all smiles and good cheer.

"Dima, my man! Glad you decided to give this place a shot. Nice wheels, by the way. José there will take the keys for you." He gestured towards a young man already approaching the driver's side, and bumped knuckles with Dima as he stepped away from the car, leading him through the clutch of people on the sidewalk near the door. As Dima stepped over the threshold he felt a hand clamp down firmly on his shoulder.

It was Vasili, his Russian friend. They chatted briefly and promised to catch up later.

"Eugenia didn't feel like tagging along?" Vasili asked.

"Nah, she went to bed. She was tired." *How did he know I was out with her?* wondered Dima.

The place was full but not uncomfortably so. He'd never seen a disco quite like this one—the place was full of plants, making him feel as if he'd stepped into some tropical locale. Pretty, stylish people, mostly young, around his age. They walked through the table area, past the bars and dance floors, to the VIP zone, where the cream of Madrid's social scene were enjoying themselves. At the very last table sat Tony, who managed the place, surrounded by spectacular babes and his eclectic retinue: B-list celebrities, a couple of toughs, and some preppy kids. Tony stood up and greeted him with an enthusiastic hug.

"Hey hey, my man Dima, what a surprise. This morning you didn't seem too warm for the program. C'mon, grab a seat and a drink." Tony, who clearly ruled this particular roost, gestured impatiently for one of his hangers-on to give Dima his seat, then nodded towards the nearest waiter. "Bring us some bubbly—the *good* stuff." Tony beamed at his table. "This calls for a celebration—we have among us a genuine machine, the European K-1 champ. Man, I've watched you fight so many times on Eurosport. That match with the Dutch guy was insane, you almost killed him," Tony said with a laugh, as if he found the idea quite amusing. "Players and pimps, I give you—as seen on TV—Dimas Denissov, the fucking master."

The new guy's achievements didn't seem to impress—or interest—Tony's retinue all that much. The tougher ones sized up Dima's strength—he'd taken of his blazer and rolled up his sleeves—and decided Tony was probably too easily impressed; they were tough guys too. The girls, on the other hand, were more intrigued. They liked buffed guys, and Dima had the novelty factor going for him as well, so one after another tried to attract his notice.

"So, Dawg, whatcha doing in Spain? When my

little bro and I saw you workin' out at the gym we flipped. We've followed all your fights. I train Andy—he's good, you'll see—and I always use you as an example. You're rapid, you're rough, you're raw. I've seen this guy bench-press 530 fucking pounds!" he told his crew, before snapping at the waiter, "Is that goddamn champagne here yet?" The waiter weaved towards the table at last. Tony reached for the bottle, poured a glass for himself and Dima, and not bothering to wait for the rest, raised his glass: "To Dima!"

Dima was already feeling a little wobbly from the last bottle of champagne at the restaurant, but he could hardly snub his host after such a generous, eloquent introduction. Tony seemed like a nice enough guy, although he probably hit the bottle—and, maybe, other things—a little too often, and he was a little too wired for Dima's liking. Dima was by nature more low-key; he didn't like being so loud or attracting so much attention. But as long as he was up for a night on the town, it looked like he'd come to the right place. The Spanish girls in the place were neither shy nor flat-chested, especially not the brunette he danced with a few times before checking out some of the other talent in the room. He thoroughly enjoyed the way each rubbed him, rubbed herself against him, making no secret of what was on their minds. After a while he decided to look for Vasili and see if he had any fresh news from Moscow about the missing money. Vasili had been—and, Dima assumed, still was—very well-connected in the Moscow underground. Dima was still puzzled by what Vasili was doing in Madrid. When they'd first bumped into each other, and again the day after, he'd tried to get a straight answer out of him, but no dice. They'd been pretty good buddies, so Dima didn't really think Vasili had been sent to Madrid to find him.

Dima completed a tour of the whole disco with the voluptuous brunette clinging to him, but made it to the front door without seeing any sign of Vasili; he peeked outside and saw that the Porsche was gone too. Dima turned to steer his curvy companion back towards the VIP room at the end of the club, where Andy and Tony were holding court with their increasingly raucous friends, looking as if they had had something else besides alcohol, but just then a burly guy with a shaved head stepped out in front of them, blocking their path.

"You the famous Dima from Moscow, invincible fighter, eh?" The guy brayed like a hyena.

"Yeah, my name's Dima, and I'm from Moscow. Can I help you?" Even with the Porsche now gone, Dima kept up his guard.

"We see how strong you are, yes?" laughed Shaved Head, who pitched his jacket towards a bystander then pulled off his tie and unbuttoned his shirt. Although Dima didn't know it, his unexpected opponent was a Turkish ex-mercenary who'd been working lately as a bouncer and wanted to earn points with the Martinez brothers by showing them what he could really do.

"Tarek!" shouted Tony. "Stop fucking around and get back to work on the door. This guy's my guest. Beat it." Andy was alongside him, arms crossed over his chest, his pose clearly underscoring who was in charge.

"Fine, boss, no worries, I stronger than this Russian."

"What's his problem?" Dima asked. "He wants a fight? Here?"

"Naw, he can't be that stupid," said Andy. "He's won a bunch of arm-wrestling contests and it's gone to his head. Just ignore him." Andy looked at the Turk and sneered, "Idiot."

Dima didn't take a challenge lightly. "OK, so you're a strong guy, huh? Let's find out together."

Dima had started unbuttoning his shirt, slowly at first, as the disco patrons around them became more and more excited. Then he pulled it off all at once, revealing such a rugged physique that the crowd broke into applause, cheers, and wolf whistles. The Martinez brothers bumped fists, both smiling like the cat that ate the canary; they began steering the gladiators towards the dance floor nearby, now empty, as one of the waiters placed a table in the center for the contest. The contenders played to the tightly-packed crowd, each showing off what they brought to the table. Dima, a little tipsy by now, was enjoying the moment and approached his position, flexing his muscles to the delight of those present. His opponent, unbowed, broke in to the crab pose, his arms tautly displayed before him, lumbering towards the table with the unhurried might of a grizzly bear.

Tony took the stage as referee, and the contest began. Both men leaned into the table that supported their elbows, and the Turk, a veteran of many such moments, channeled as much of his upper body strength as he could focus into a fierce opening push. But Dima met the onslaught with the stoicism of a confident god, Dmitri the omnipotent. Staying firmly put, making no irregular movements, Dima yielded some ground to the Turk's strength and weight. Tarek, the mercenary hardened by war, took his apparent advantage at face value and put all his chips on the table, throwing the rest of his strength into the match. Dima, the fighter educated by experience, now had the measure of his opponent and started the pushback, unbowed. Gradually, but continuously, he won back the lost ground and when they were back to where they'd begun, he pushed on, tenaciously, aiming to utterly smash his opponent's resistance. He took the lead with a brusque movement, a surge built from every fiber and tendon of his biceps and triceps, that destabilized the Turk. It was the beginning of the end. With a final exertion of his forearm and wrist, Dima brought the Turk's knuckles down solidly on the tabletop. The crowd erupted in cheering. Tony lifted Dima's arm, and the Turk accepted his defeat in a surprisingly sportsmanlike fashion and discreetly withdrew toward the bar, in search of a well-earned pick-me-up. Dima, on the other hand, was touched, squeezed, groped by women and men whom the anonymity of the crowd spurred into indulging their secret fantasy of enjoying such a champion.

After things had settled down and they were back in the VIP area, Dima sat talking to Andy— whom he liked better than his older brother—and saw the chance to steer the conversation in a direction of interest to him.

"That's some amazing luxury horsepower you've got parked out front," said Dima. "Your disco has a seriously well-to-do clientele."

"Thanks, but it's not *our* disco, man. People think we're the owners," he said with a laugh, "but we just run the place and restrict entry to the seriously wealthy. We do have our own place, but it's just a little hole in the wall joint—we'll take you to it, too."

"All the same, looks like a sweet deal. That was some Porsche I saw outside."

"Ain't complaining, but it could always be better. Now, the guy who's absolutely swimming in cash is the guy who actually owns this place. He's got discos all over Madrid, and his fingers in a lot of other pies as well."

"So do you guys, from the looks of it."

"You don't miss a thing, dude. We're into this and that. Use your imagination. You're a cool guy, maybe we can do some business together if you stick around. How long you gonna be in Madrid?"

"Awhile. I have relatives I'm going to visit."

"You got Spanish relatives? No shit. Where at?"

"Down South." Dima didn't want to be any more specific.

"Right, so that's how come you can speak Spanish." Andy laughed again. "Hell, you speak it better than me." He wasn't just trying to make Dima feel good.

"So is that silver Porsche yours? It's totally cool."

"Yes it is; and it sure as hell cost us enough too, I can tell you. Nobody gives us shit for free." With that he cocked his head towards the dance floor, then got up. "Sounds like a scuffle out front—I gotta get back to work. I better give the whole place the once-over, we operate a strict no-lowlifes policy here."

Dima stayed where he was for a while, not sure

what he wanted to do next. He was tired and he'd had enough to drink; besides, he didn't like staying out till the break of dawn, and he couldn't believe how quickly time had flown. He was just about to step out of the place when he bumped into Tony, who was coming back in alongside a blond kid with long sideburns. They gestured for Dima to follow them and the three of them went into the men's room, where— once they were locked in—the blond kid pulled out a folded piece of paper with what turned out to be cocaine inside. They offered Dima the first line, which he politely refused; he'd never liked drugs, despite the circles he'd moved in in Moscow, among drug traffickers and other outlaws. He'd just unlatched the door to take off, when in walked the brunette who'd been coming on to him all night, who obviously knew what was going down. Tony and Sideburns did another line each and this time shared their stash with Big Titty Brunette who happily joined in. Dima was starting to feel like the third wheel, so he turned around and headed for the exit again; but Brunette caught up with him and tugged him towards the next stall, pushing him inside then unbuckling his belt. Dima decided to just relax and enjoy himself.

When he got back to his table, everyone who'd been there before was gone, replaced by a different group, sitting around Sideburns: thoroughly stoked young guys with their dates, the black sheep of several prominent Madrid families, all drunk and high.

Near the exit he started to feel like he was going to throw up and had trouble staying on his feet. They'd played him. Idiot. The way he felt didn't just come from too much champagne. It must have been some kind of narcotic, his legs were giving way and he felt incredibly drowsy. Things started to spin around him, he stumbled trying to get a grip. Who had done this and why? Now where were all those people who spoke so admiringly to him, the Martinez brothers, Big-Titty Brunette, his pal Vasili? He blacked out.

***

When Dima awoke, hours later, his head throbbed. He rolled over, leaning on one elbow as he rubbed his temples and forehead, before his eyes slowly came into focus on the grubby mattress. As he lifted his gaze, he caught a glimpse of Madrid's skyscrapers far off in the distance, through a small, dirty window; but the light hurt his eyes and his head, and he quickly turned away. On the opposite wall, empty hangers dangled from a bent pole spanning the open closet. His eyes widened as he took in the rest of the closet's contents: automatic weapons leaning against one corner, crates of ammo stacked beside them. After a glance at the door, he crept quietly toward the closet, eyeing the other firearms perched carelessly on top of the ammo. Dima's face showed his puzzlement. Clearly whoever had brought him here didn't mind him knowing about this weapons locker; they trusted him, even. A friend, then? Suddenly he heard approaching voices, and before he had time to finish weighing up whether or not to arm himself, the room's door flew open.

"Vasili!" he shouted in spite of himself, his own voice resonating through his hangover as painfully if someone were holding his head t o a hi-fi speaker. A familiar-looking brunette stood next to his friend.

"Dmitri!" said the other man, good-naturedly firing off a series of remarks he didn't understand at first. With his ear having lately grown more accustomed to Spanish, it took him a moment to realize he was being addressed in his native tongue. At the same time, a thought occurred to him. Dmitri was the name he'd been called by his classmates at the military academy and, later, by his those he dealt with in the underworld after he began moving in Gagarin's sphere. Only his family and closest friends called him Dima, except for the time he'd used it as a *nom-de-guerre* when fighting outside Russia: "Dima, the Polar Bear" or some similar nonsense. So why had he introduced himself to Curro as Dima? An interesting question that Dima pondered as he continued to emerge from his drugged stupor.

CHAPTER VII

The absence of the beloved means the desolation of the soul.

Desolation, absence; empty words. It's the feelings they evoke that have true meaning; the words themselves mean nothing. How then to explain the feeling of loss, of the absence of the being that made you happy, that gave meaning to your life, that helped you pass the day with optimism and vigor, with happiness and even joy, through this isolating, barren existence? For that was what Curro felt his life was: isolated and barren. Whereas he once lived in a playboy's world and would have had the option of returning to it following Trasto's death, that ended years ago. Trasto had in fact replaced that world and now he was gone, so what was left? That was the truly difficult quandary. An impossible one to answer.

Like so many other nights, Curro couldn't get to sleep. Fits, starts, anguish, the unending presence of Trasto's absence was Curro's penance. Penance for what? Why? It didn't matter. He was an orphan now, and he would be till the end of his days.

Orphaned in a way he had not been by the death of his father, or even of his beloved mother. In spite of how many times he'd been around the block by then, one or two of Curro's closest friends had been afraid he wouldn't be able to go on without her; they'd been worried about what he might do, so close had been his bond with his mother, so many secrets had they shared. Yet in the end none of this had been comparable to the listlessness, the tedium, the enduring malaise suffered by his spirit and the impossibility of his recovering enjoyment of life that had all been brought on by Trasto's death. He, the most hedonistic among all his wide circle of acquaintances, the one who'd been burning the candle at both ends, could find no consolation or joy. Living without his dog felt like dying. He had not given any serious thought to joining him; suicide would be a sin. Not against God, against himself, against the singularity of his chancing to exist. Anything so implausible as life itself must not be disdained so casually, it had to be accepted as something sacred, something out of the ordinary; it would be an insult to raise one's hand against something so anomalous.

He was sick of thinking, sick of reasoning, of looking for answers. There were no answers for him, he'd accepted that now. Time to face reality. His feelings of guilt at having to choose to have Trasto put down were consuming him. He'd given up trying to explain this to anyone. Which only fueled his feelings of isolation from the world.

Dima! The earthquake that had rocked his world for the better. What a guy. If only their paths had crossed years earlier, when Curro had Trasto in his corner, he wouldn't have gotten away. A thousand Eugenias couldn't have kept them apart. Dima, the perfect man, brutal yet educated, with a physique that was beyond Olympian. Gods and heroes—how they would have envied such perfection and strength! *Dima, I love you*, thought Curro. *Like a Modigliani drawing, like Callas, like Don Pablo Picasso, like José Tomás the bullfighter. I love you as much as all of them, and more; and as little as any of them. Not at all. I don't love you at all. That's a lie, I love you, I love you so much, I love you like I never loved any man...or woman; but I have nothing to give you. Nothing from inside. I love you without being in love with you. I have no love left to give.*

It was another bad night—maybe he should have gone out with his friends. Then again, what good would that have done? Nightlife and partying; all that was over for him, it bored him now; and they'd be better off without him looking over their shoulders, they'd be having fun. Eugenia didn't know it yet, but she was crazy about Dima, Curro could tell. And he accepted that. He loved her, she was his friend, his twin soul, and he knew Dima could give her what he couldn't, hadn't, and didn't want to. *But don't be greedy, Eugenia dear*, he thought. *You'll have more than enough time. Let me have one last, mind-blowing whim.*

He'd never had a stable relationship, nor felt unfulfilled by the lack of one. His emotional needs were more than met by his family and friends. He'd had his "seasonal" flings, as he thought of them, but nothing serious, just fun times with people his own age. Every summer he'd find someone entertaining to pass the time with, and things would last as long as the vacation or voyage in the course of which he'd met the lucky one. He was always very clear: no strings, just good times to be enjoyed for as long as the fates decreed—which usually wasn't very long at all. After that, to each his own. He'd been with countless lovers, hundreds, couldn't even remember all of their names but how much fun it had been.

From the end of the '80s all the way through the '90s he'd never slowed down. With a few close friends and a horde of casual acquaintances he'd toured the globe like a runaway stud. It was a miracle he'd managed to side-step both AIDS and drugs: with the latter of the two he'd had a passing acquaintance—more of an extended flirtation really. Several of his friends—some of the closest ones—had fallen through the cracks, gone headfirst into the opportunities for pleasurable self-destruction that were all around them at the time. Curro had drawn a line under all that, never to revisit it.

Ten years earlier, everything had changed. A routine check-up revealed a liver deficiency that was to be his salvation. It had been his safe-conduct out of the breakneck race on which unbridled pleasure had been leading him towards an uncertain and probably inglorious end. After a delicate liver operation and the requisite time in recovery, he decided to begin waking early and getting more out of his mornings by rediscovering exercise and sports he'd all but forgotten. He began limiting nights out to dinner with friends, private parties, or inescapable commitments. Without, of course, giving up altogether those sporadic instances of complete abandon occasionally warranted by special circumstances—such as when someone new and interesting drifted onto his radar screen.

This new routine would have been change enough, but the advent of Trasto would be what really turned his world upside down. Less traveling, less partying, less dull schmoozing; in their place, more long walks in the country, healthier living, more get-up-and-go, more optimism. A new way of looking at life. He'd come out ahead on the trade.

That long night of contemplation left him with many conclusions. Dima would not be his salvation; no one could. The way they'd met, the man's own personality, the empathy that emerged, had made him think he just might have had a chance. But no. He wasn't really bothered by Eugenia as a rival, Dima's problems with the mob and all the rest of it There was no cure for his existential emptiness. Still he promised himself to try, and try he would, in spite of that conviction about his true self and his all-embracing indifference.

He got in and out of bed, lying down time and again without achieving quietude. He went in the kitchen and poured himself a Scotch—twelve-year-old Chivas, his favorite, the only one he'd drink—then went out onto the terrace to gaze at the starry sky, which that night seemed dark and threatening, more immense even than at other times he'd looked at it, and he started trying to find the different constellations. This kept him busy for quite a while, over two more glasses of Scotch in fact. But since nervousness had him in its grip, anything seemed preferable to thinking. He just wanted to rest and let his mind go blank.

He went back in the kitchen for the last glass and, on his way back to his bedroom through the study, spotted on a shelf something that had been his best ally over the last several months. He popped two sleeping pills that would tip the scales in his favor in his running battle against insomnia.

***

"Curro!" Dima was shaking his friend briskly. "Wake up, I need to talk to you."

"What's the matter? What time is it?" he asked, groggy from mixing booze and downers. God, what nausea he felt!

"Curro, wake up!" Dima repeated. "Grab a shower, I'll make some coffee."

Curro slowly got to his feet and went out on the terrace, where he found springtime in glorious possession of Madrid. What time was it? He craned his head towards his study, where he could see the clock on the highboy—*Half past three already*, he thought. He was starved. Coffee wasn't going to be enough.

"Dima," he called out, "forget the coffee, let me shower and we'll go to Manolo's, they put on a splendid brunch. Just you wait and see."

Dima came out onto the terrace. "Brunch? What's that?"

"It's like breakfast, only way bigger," he said, not wanting to get bogged down in details. Some places offer it every Sunday."

"But today's Saturday."

"Is it? Well, whatever. They'll serve us something, I'm sure. Let me get dressed." As he went toward the bedroom he asked, "Anyway, how was last night? I'll bet you two had a hell of a good time."

Dima followed him inside. "That's what I need to talk to you about. I am so pissed off at some of the shit that's happened "

"What, you mean you and Eugenia didn't get along?" Curro interrupted.

"No, that's not it. I'll tell you about Eugenia later. But when I dropped her off last night—"

Curro stopped and turned. "You mean you didn't go home with her?"

"If you'll just listen, I'll explain.

Curro gave in, and sat down. "I'm all ears."

Dima took a seat opposite him. "After I dropped Eugenia off I went out with these guys from the gym who'd already invited me out yesterday morning. Two brothers, they do K-1, too. Anyway, they introduced me to some girls, you know how it goes; next thing I know they're stuffing me full of champagne, only it really did not agree with me. I think one of the girls spiked my drink, you can't imagine how queasy I felt. I was out on my feet. I remember staggering towards the exit... hen it's all a blank. So I wake up today and I'm at Vasili's place—the Russian I ran into last week, the guy who works at the disco—"

"You think someone spiked your drink?"

"Yeah. At any rate, I woke up in Vasili's and I have no idea how I got there."

"What's so weird about that? This Vasili fellow must have noticed you were a little worse for wear and taken you back to his place. He had no way of knowing you live here."

"No, and I'm not going to tell him, either. The whole thing smells fishy to me. Like the fact that he's working at one disco one day and a different one the next, or the fact that I even ran into him at all in a place as big as Madrid on my third day here. Don't you find all this a little bit strange?"

"I don't know," said Curro. "The mafia here divvy up the nightspots among themselves, so it doesn't really make any difference to them if they send one of their muscle boys to a different disco every night of the week. Like the night you met Eugenia, Vasili had been 'assigned' to that private party, remember? I don't know too much about how these things work, but I imagine they're much the same in Russia."

"No, it's not the same," Dima said shaking his head slowly. "I'm telling you, something's fishy about all this. Vasili's not a bouncer, he's going freelance to the highest bidder. Besides, this morning he kept trying to steer our conversation towards my dad and the missing money—very odd. He wanted to drive me back here but I made up an excuse to get rid of him so I could find my way back alone. I don't trust him any more."

"Weren't you two pals back in Russia? You kept telling me you'd saved each other's asses more than once."

"When it comes to our line of work, there are no friends. I just meant that before we'd worked together and helped each other out. No more or less than expected. I mean, if your group's in a fight with somebody else's, you wanna know your guy's got your back, right? It's the same here, isn't it?"

"Yes, I suppose so."

"But friends, real friends—no way. People there don't have the same notion of friendship that people here do. I mean, what you've done for me... obody there would ever believe it. Nah, he and I aren't friends the way you and I are; I don't trust him that much. Besides, I thought I saw the girl from the disco at his place."

"What girl from the disco?"

"The one who was on my heels the whole damn night. She's the only one who could have spiked my drink—she was on me like a bad suit. Very forward, she followed me everywhere. She even pushed me into a stall in the men's room so we could make out—"

"See? Your night wasn't *all* bad."

Dima shrugged. "It was just a blow job. Pretty good one, though," he said, savoring the memory. "Anyway, like I said, I think she was the woman I saw when I woke up at Vasili's place—which looked like an army guard hut, by the way. Everything was dirty, a complete mess."

"No kidding," said Curro, suddenly more curious.

"Man, you wouldn't believe the firepower he has in there, the place looks like an arsenal. I was surprised that he had a Makarov—they're so old, no one even carries them anymore. I felt like he was trying to intimidate me—as if he didn't know me better than that. I mean, like I'd give a shit!" Curro had never heard Dima use this sort of language before. He seemed to be going street quite quickly. "I dunno, Curro—I think something's gone wrong. He didn't seem like the Vasili I used to know. Hell, he even seemed different from the other day, the day I met Eugenia. I forgot to tell you that when I dropped her off at her Aunt's—"

"Her Aunt? You mean, Matilde? How'd you end up with her?"

"We ran into her on our way out of El Paraguas."

"That's my Eugenia," Curro said, beaming. "Wasn't the food fabulous?"

"Forget the food, Curro. Eugenia was completely wasted, and she was being a total pain in the ass, but please don't interrupt me—I'll get to that. From the restaurant back to Matilde's house we were being followed by this Porsche—Dude, don't look at me like that. You don't seem to have grasped what deep shit I'm in. They're after me, I've already told you that."

"I'm sorry, Dima. It's just that all this is new to me, and..."

"Curro," Dima cut him off. "I'm prepared for this kind of thing, OK? I know when I'm being followed, and I was being followed. Once we reached Matilde's, the car disappeared. Guess where I saw it next? Outside the Martíneze's disco."

"The Martínezes? Who are they?"

"Those guys from the gym I told you about before!" Dima was losing his patience. "Vasili was roaming around the place like it was his his living room—"

"Well, he *does* work there."

"I know what I'm talking about," he said impatiently, standing up. "The car was parked right in front of the door, like it had just got there. But Andy was working the door and Tony was inside drinking, surrounded by babes. He sure as hell hadn't been out tailing anyone."

"You mean, Vasili took those Martinez guys' car and then followed you all over Madrid with it? With their permission? Or because he just felt like it, or someone told him to? Or maybe those Martínezes are the ones who are supposed to be keeping an eye on you? I don't know, Dima, it sounds like something right out of a movie."

"Curro, I just can't get through to you. You're a posh guy and you're loaded, and you don't seem to understand. This is what my life is like. No movies."

"I'm sorry," said Curro. "We've had so much fun the last few days I keep forgetting about the trouble you're in. I've been a jerk. Forgive me. Anyway, please go on."

"Apology accepted. Basically that's it: they're still after me, which isn't too surprising if they think I know where the fifty million Euros are stashed. They're very rough customers, and I don't want either of us to get hurt, especially not you."

"Nothing's going to happen to us," Curro said firmly. "We're in Spain, this is a civilized country, not the jungle. Justice works here, we have an effective police force. Granted, though, it wouldn't hurt to watch our step."

"I still think it's really weird that Vasili's already so settled in as a bouncer at Madrid's discos. His line used to be protection rackets, same as mine," he said with a shrug, in a way that suggested it had not been his vocation of choice. "Maybe he's sold out to Gagarin now and that's why he always seems to be underfoot. His real job is keeping an eye on me."

"On the other hand, if he's already at a certain level in the organization, like you say, maybe he's supposed be learning the ropes here: finding out how to move dope, looking into distribution channels. Not a day goes by that I don't see something on TV about some Russian crook having been arrested here—you'd think Spain was heaven for them. So maybe he's just here trying to establish a beachhead."

"But not alone. Or at any rate, not for himself. You think I should drop the gym I've been going to? Am I attracting too much attention?"

"No way. La Moraleja doesn't exactly seem like the thug's hangout of choice. Just watch your back. I'm going to do a little digging on those Martínez brothers and see if I can get the lowdown on Vasili too."

"Don't tell me you have contacts in those sorts of circles here? Come on!"

"I know more mafiosi than you do," Curro said with a laugh.

"Yeah, right." Dima raised his eyebrows. "Take a look at this." He lifted a gun with a handle so big only someone with a huge hand could safely operate it. "While Vasili was trying to impress me with his firepower, I spotted this Viking 446 stashed under some magazines. It's an updated and improved version of Russian army standard issue. It's pretty damn good. I stole it." He grinned. "Fuck him, and fuck Gagarin too!"

"Well, well," said Curro, taking it from Dima and giving it the once-over. "This is perfect for guys with oversized paws like yours. I like it, you could even use it in competitions."

"How'd you know? You're right. And here I thought you'd be mad."

"Ha! No way, I love guns. When I was growing up we used to go hunting and I've also gone in for skeet shooting and event shooting. I'm very familiar with firearms. You look surprised. Did you think I was just another idle rich guy who never gets his hands dirty? I like this one, it's very well balanced," he said, weighing it in his hand. "Since I have a license, if push comes to shove we can always say it's mine. Now—let's lunch, brunch or something! It's getting late."

Dima was pleasantly surprised by Curro's reaction. He would never have thought that his refined friend would be conversant with firearms.

They went to the Mallorca pastry shop near Puerta de Alcala and over their snack Dima finished telling Curro all about his adventure with Eugenia the night before; Curro just about split his sides laughing.

CHAPTER VIII

The Royal Theater was packed, and those attending were dressed with an opulence not seen since the first shows after the remodeling was completed fifteen years earlier. A lot of the regulars who'd been skipping recent events, like Eugenia and Curro, didn't want to miss this evening, a charity fundraiser for multiple sclerosis research presided over by the Queen and sponsored by some of the country's top corporate names, among them the Aguirre Bank. Tonight's musical program was back to basics: Verdi, Puccini, Rossini, Mozart, Bizet, the composers Madrid's opera enthusiasts most wanted to hear.

It had been almost impossible to get a ticket for Dima. Fortunately the Aguirres had their own box, the one that belonged to their bank, and were happy to offer seats to their friends, who in turn gave their tickets—Mezzanine, Row 6, near the aisle—to some Japanese guests their hosts had invited. They got Dima into the theater with a nosebleed seat ticket they'd obtained from a scalper at a slightly higher price than Beluga caviar.

The gents in tuxedos and the ladies in formal gowns vied with each other for who could be most elegant. Amid this dazzling crowd, the handsome and dapper Curro still commanded attention, as ever; but this time he had a formidable rival in the room: one Mr. Dmitri Denissov. Dima was overwhelming, his handsomeness well adorned by the formal wear they'd bought for him and which he wore with confidence and ease, as if he'd always moved in such circles. With the sapphire cufflinks and his pocket square he looked every inch a prince of the Russian steppes. They could even have introduced him as one; he wouldn't have been the first phony prince in circulation around Madrid.

And Eugenia? How to describe style and elegance incarnate? Even though this spring was shaping up to be a warm one, many of the ladies had gone for basic black, always a safe bet. But in this as in most things, Eugenia delighted in going against the grain. She showed up in a Valentino evening gown upon which gray, burgundy, red, and silver mingled smoothly, and as her only ornament, golden earrings, delicate loops set with eight carat diamonds; a lot of carats for such a narrow space, yet a design so simple as to preclude any suggestion of ostentatiousness.

The ticket holders stood around in the main hall, awaiting the beginning of what promised to be the gala of the year. The Aguirres were among those charged with welcoming the most distinguished guests, while Curro and Eugenia introduced Dima to no small number of curious acquaintances who were by now well aware of the Russian's privileged position alongside the "perfect couple"—a phrase that Aunt Matilde had just happened to blab to about half of Madrid.

Dima was behaving like the perfect gentleman he bore within himself, but part of him was on constant alert, checking the lay of the land. Curro spotted the enormous bulge in his pants. Was that…? No, Curro had seen him stepping out of the shower more than once. Then what...

The oversized pistol! Curro took Dima aside and quietly read him the riot act.

"Are you out of your mind? What the hell made you bring a gun here? Don't you know the Queen is coming? This place is crawling with cops—uniform and undercover. If anything goes wrong, Pepe Aguirre will really be in the soup. Christ, the embarrassment!"

"I know what I'm doing," Dima said confidently. "Trust me."

"Trust you! What does that have to do with you sneaking a gun into the Royal Theater?"

"Curro, listen to me. It's for safety's sake. I don't for a second think I'm safe anywhere, not even here with all this security. You don't know Gagarin and his men like I do."

Just then the loudspeakers sounded the final call for all ticket holders to take their seats. Everyone who'd been standing around chatting hurriedly made their way inside.

The Queen's entrance hushed the low roar in the room. Absolute silence gripped the hall as the Royal Theater's orchestra in residence struck up the long version of Spain's National Anthem. After the final note, the entire assemblage turned towards the Royal Box and broke into spontaneous applause, which gratified Her Majesty. At her side were the King's sister, the Infanta Margarita, and her husband, the

Duke of Soria. Behind them, members of the Royal Household.

The concert began. They'd all come: Placido Domingo, Carreras; even the legendary divas Caballé and Berganza, their voices still excellent. Joining them were promising up-and-comers for whom the evening provided a priceless opportunity to make a name for themselves.

Curro, though always an opera lover, found himself unable to enjoy the event despite the caliber of the voices filling the auditorium. He sat lost in thought, trying to figure out Dima's absurd actions. Dima stood at one end of the box, having refused the seat Pepe offered him; he could hardly have asked for more, his host having kindly offered to give the handsome foreigner his own seat when he learned Dima had a seat high up in the theater. Curro found himself able to concentrate only upon hearing the opening notes of the aria "Casta Diva," which Caballé sang as beautifully as she had at her peak.

Soon it was intermission, and the audience filed out to meet and greet as the last shouts of "Bravo!" for the stars died down. At the start of the ovation Pepe looked at Curro and then nodded approvingly towards Dima.

"He is one hot son-of-a-gun," said the banker.

You have no idea, thought Curro.

***

During intermission the cream of Spanish society descended on the bar for a glass of Spanish bubbly, Cava. Nothing else would do. On nights like this, champagne would have been an unwelcome interloper.

The Queen, discreet as ever, sipped a soda in the Royal Box. She was always "on duty," with none of the outgoing, crowd-pleasing stuff the King was so good at.

The Aguirre's box had emptied out along with all the others. It was one of the better ones on the Dress Circle, just two spots away from the Royal Box. Matilde, Eugenia, Dima, Pepe, and Curro were sharing it with two young couples, Central European princes, who wouldn't have missed this event for the world. The four ladies had had the choicest seats, the front row, with the gentlemen seated behind, Curro at the end next to the door. To German eyes, accustomed to inflexible observance of rules, the idea of someone sneaking into an opera box, especially one so close to the Royal one, was worthy of at least a raised eyebrow or two; but Their Serene Highnesses had graciously overlooked this indiscretion: in truth they too were captivated by the magnetism of the "Spanish Giant," as they later called this Mr. Denissov. They spoke Spanish just well enough to take Dima's superior command of the language for that of a native, and so remained ignorant of Dima's origins; he was still fidgety, remaining on the lookout. Their group stayed on the mezzanine level because Matilde had arranged for some light catering, a snack prepared by the theater's restaurant.

People came and went, exchanging brief greetings. Eugenia chattered away with the two princesses; they had crossed paths countless times before, at events and parties in this country and on other continents.

Pepe and Matilde left their group for just one moment, to go and pay their respects to the Queen. Her Majesty shared her refreshments with the heavyweights of Spanish song. They talked of Carreras' well-nigh miraculous recovery from leukemia and the endurance of the great Placido Domingo's tenor voice. Of course there were also words of praise for the divas, especially that last aria, which left Queen Sofía especially moved. Berganza, asked what she would be doing next, smiled and replied "It's a surprise, Your Majesty—I hope you'll like it."

The Infanta Margarita and her acquaintances agreed that so far the evening had been every bit the success they'd all hoped for. People had come from far and wide for this glittering evening; around the Infanta alone the group was varied enough to allow her to practice six of the twelve languages she commanded.

Curro, meanwhile, knocked back the Cava and was bemused by the effect Dima was having on their Royal Highnesses and the two German couples. One of the Germans seemed to be sizing up the enormous bulge the gun made along the inside of Dima's pants. He stepped backwards, slightly off-balance, and steadied himself by reaching for Curro, to whom he said, in shaky English, "May I have some more champagne, please?" All bubbles appear equal, though they're not.

"Yes, Hans, of course," said Curro, raising his arm to signal a waiter, who approached immediately bearing a full tray.

"Thank you," the Germans said in unison, though after a single sip Curro called the boy back over—the bubbly clearly was not chilled to the right temperature.

The waiter was back in a flash with an ice bucket, which he offered to the gentlemen; the Spaniard in turn offered the foreigner first pick, which he summarily declined, faintly shocked by this "Spanish custom." Curro, not the slightest bit offended, was grateful for the ice now cooling his drink. He was a consummate gourmet, who found there was nothing worse than a glass of insufficiently chilled bubbly. Not in Curro's book.

Then it happened. Matilde returned from Her Majesty's box to rejoin her own group when a woman's voice boomed, "Matilde, how delightful! How long has it been—?"

The speaker was Grand Duchess Anastasia, a member of the Romanov clan and longtime resident of Madrid. She and Matilde had been classmates at school and close friends.

"Anastasia, darling, where have you been hiding?"

"Well, part of the time in Saint Petersburg, now that I'm allowed to go as often as I like. Let me introduce you to someone. This is Alexei Gagarin, Russian oligarch," she said, in a tone that hovered between playfulness and sarcasm.

At the sound of this name, Curro glanced anxiously at his friend. The look in Dima's eyes reminded him at once of a Chinese folk tale that centers on the power acquired by an orphaned young boy abandoned in the woods, to whom the forest gods granted such strength in his gaze that a look from him was enough to wipe out entire cities.

That sort of gaze was precisely what Curro perceived —what he felt almost physically—when he heard the name "Gagarin." He saw that his friend's eyes were boring into those of his parents' killer, whose extended hand he plainly ignored. Curro, seeking to defuse the situation, nudged him to one side. But Gagarin stepped closer, almost in pursuit, smiling, and said something in Russian to which Dima did not reply. The Grand Duchess mouth was agape, not sure if she could believe what she was hearing.

A disembodied voice sounded throughout the theater: "Seats please, the concert resumes in one minute!"

The members of both groups strolled back towards their places. After a few paces, Dima turned and looked at the crime lord, who'd struck a defiant pose, standing firm amid a group of his toughs. While he knew all too well that he was being chased by Gagarin's men, Dima hadn't considered that the boss himself might also show up in Madrid. Being seen out in public like this, at a royal reception no less, was not Gagarin's style. No, he moved behind the scenes, careful never to be linked directly with anything he chose not to be. Seeing him now so suddenly, Dima wasn't about to back down. Dmitri Denissov, no shrinking violet himself, took a firm step forward. The challenge had been met.

Mercifully, the goddess Fortune chose to intervene, sending Eugenia as a guardian angel. Having been held up by the long line outside the ladies' room she was now rushing back to her seat and firmly tugging her beau by the forearm, leading him reluctantly through the door to their box. The second act began.

Inside the box, and seeing as how Pepe had not

returned—they would find out later that he'd gotten tied up greeting the president of a small dictatorship seated in a nearby box—Curro was at last able to sit next to Dima. Both men shifted their seats slightly further back into the box, the better not to be overheard.

"So that fat ass is the infamous Gagarin. How very dashing," deadpanned Curro, before adding "Grand Duchess Anastasia has absolutely no idea who she's invited into her box."

"I'm gonna kill that piece of shit," said Dima as if he hadn't heard Curro at all. Dima shifted his weight, about to get up.

"Are you nuts? Sit down," Curro whispered, tugging on his friend's sleeve as hard as he could. "Sit down... it down! Cool it, will you? Now is not the time! What are you trying to do?"

"Curro, you just don't get it. Gagarin wants me out of the picture. He knows I'm the only one who can prove my father's innocence. First chance he gets, I'm toast. Here or wherever. He doesn't give a shit about the police or the royal protection squad. You don't know what he's capable of doing."

"But didn't you say the guys who kidnapped you kept trying to get you to tell them what happened to the money? If they really think you're still holding back 50 million Euros, they won't kill you just like that."

"I know. Honestly, it's hard to figure out exactly what they want with me. If they meant to keep me alive all along then they kind of got carried away. I mean, you saw the knife wounds: but you're right, that bunch just saw me as a means to an end, it was the money they were really after. Now things have changed. Gagarin wants to kill me, I could see it all over his face. I'm an inconvenient witness. I think he stole the missing money from his partners."

Curro tried to stop his friend from fidgeting, but he wouldn't keep still. Every few minutes he leaned over the edge of the box to look into the seating area below, where one of his enemy's thugs was standing guard near the exit. Dima's restlessness was beginning to annoy the other guests in the box, especially the two princely gentlemen who each directed a withering stare at him. The situation was becoming critical; even Matilde and Eugenia had turned around more than once, sensing the constant movement at their backs. Finally, Curro decided to act.

"Dima, what exactly do you want? A shootout with Gagarin? Here, in the Royal Theater, in front of the Queen and half the Madrid police? You're out of your mind, we'll all end up in jail with you. Trust me, man, please. I'm sure there's something we can do, but now is not the time. You need to keep a cool head, pick your own time and place for payback, and then blow the bastard's head off if that's what it takes." Curro was surprised to hear himself talking like this; but since Dima had come into his life he wasn't quite the same person. "Leave this to me. I know the theater's head of security, I'm going to go see what he knows about the Russians. It doesn't make any sense, the way Gagarin's boys are prancing around in here like they own the place, in the presence of the Queen no less. How did they all get in? I'll be right back—stay here!"

"I'm coming with you!" said Dima, getting halfway out of his seat yet again.

"Absolutely not. If they see you it'll just make things worse," said Curro as he placed a hand on his friend's shoulder to gently, but firmly, guide him back into his seat.

"Please! Enough is enough!" growled the Prince who had been shaky on his feet during the intermission.

CHAPTER IX

Curro expected the hallway outside the box seats to be completely deserted but no sooner had he stepped through the door when he was blindsided by someone plowing into him at full speed. Fortunately it was just Begoña Perez, rushing back to her seat after a hasty pee break. *The untold advantages of box seats*, Curro thought.

Stealthily he descended the stairs towards the main entrance where, apart from the royal security detail chatting with some of the theater staff, all was quiet. They gave him a bored look without interrupting their conversation. Curro kept going and crossed to the side on which they'd spotted one of Gagarin's thugs guarding the door, but as he tried to open one of the lateral doors he was intercepted by an overzealous usher.

"I'm sorry, sir, you can't come back in till there's a break."

"But there are no entr'actes today, just a brief interval between one song and the next."

"That's right, sir."

"Anyway, I'm in a box upstairs. It's just that I looked down here and thought I saw a man leaning against this door in the inside, and he's not a theater employee. He looked very suspicious and I'm concerned for the Queen's safety."

"That's impossible, sir," the usher replied politely. "No one but the security detail is allowed inside like that."

"I'm telling you, I saw it. How can you allow such a suspicious looking stranger inside so close to the Royal Family?"

"Absolutely impossible, sir. It's not allowed."

"Well, how about if we check to make sure?"

"That's not allowed," he said for the third time. "Sir, why don't you return to your seat? You're missing the show."

"Look," Curro said, beginning to get hot under the collar, "I'm telling you I saw something suspicious. Now, let's check to make sure," he said, his hand already on the door handle.

Tempers were still rising when several members of the Queen's guard detail came along to find out what was causing the commotion. All of them were tall, handsome, and buffed fellows—*whoever does her recruiting has good taste,* Curro thought. He explained again what he thought he'd seen from his perch in the Aguirre Bank's box, and that as one of the sponsors—a white lie—he was concerned about the Queen's safety.

Suddenly they heard a loud thump on the other side of the door and the guards sprang into action. One of them gently opened the nearest door, through which floated the celestial voice of Placido Domingo as he sang "Addio alla Vita" from *Tosca*. *God, please don't let them close it again,* thought Curro. The guards carefully checked all entrances to the orchestra seats, finding neither a Russian nor anything else that resembled an imminent threat to Her Majesty's well-being. False alarm. The Russian that Curro had seen had vanished.

"Would you mind just letting me stay here till the aria's finished, please?" Curro asked the guard who seemed to be in charge.

The Chief Colonel of the Royal Guards was happy to oblige. After so many years by Queen Sofia's side, some of her love for timeless classics had rubbed off on him. He understood. Curro lingered by the door transfixed, oblivious to everything, and didn't notice that Dima had watched it all from up above. When Placido Domingo finished, shouts of "Bravo!" went up all around the room, and Curro turned around to seek the closest route back to his box. Unfortunately, as he passed the restrooms the Cava he'd consumed was too much for him. He bolted through the door and hurried to the stall at the end. As he entered it, he heard footsteps rush up from behind as rough hands shoved him forward.

.There was no time for anything else. The stranger slammed him up against the wall, holding his forearm to Curro's throat. He tried to call for help, to scream, to wriggle out of the lethal embrace, but it was no good, the attacker was far stronger. Light-headedness and nausea were overcoming with a blackout imminent.

In the final seconds a disjointed flurry of thoughts went through his mind, unanswered questions: *Who the hell is this guy? What does he want from me? To kill me, just like that? Has he got me mixed up with someone else?*

***

Curro's senses had all but collapsed when, suddenly, a sharp jolt revived him. For a moment he felt flattened, with the mystery man on top of him and the stall door from behind, both suffocating him. Air flowed slowly back into his lungs, consciousness came streaming back. *What happened? Where am I?* Dima helped him towards the sink, gently holding his head underneath the faucet to invigorate him and then splashing water on his face as well. He was coming back to life. And then he saw the body of the guy who'd tried to kill him, lying on the floor with a broken neck, like a marionette on severed strings. Dima picked up the inert body and hauled it into one of the stalls. Then he approached Curro, who was still a bit groggy, and slowly explained:

"I saw the whole thing from the box. This bastard went out one of the other doors just before the security detail checked the one he'd been leaning against. I feared the worst, and I was right. It's a damn good thing I heard the noise he made in here before it was too late. Quick, let's get back to our box. No one will know we were ever here."

"The Germans…" Curro wheezed, still not fully himself. "And the security guys? Although from the lower level I don't think they would have seen you coming…"

"The Germans are wasted, they didn't even notice me leaving. There's nothing to worry about. Now come on."

"Like this?" said Curro, looking in the mirror. "Go get me Eugenia's shawl, so I can at least dry my head."

"Forget about that, let's get out of here!"

"Dima, listen to me! I can't go outside looking like this. Besides, I really need the toilet. My stomach," he excused himself, seeing the look on Dima's face. "Lock the stiff in the stall, try to do something so it can't be opened. Now come on, just this once, follow my lead."

"I always do," Dima protested.

A couple of minutes later Dima reappeared, and Curro could at least dry himself off enough to not attract undue attention. With his hands he smoothed his hair back.

They returned to the box as all voices joined in Agustin Lara's "Granada." The show must be nearly over; Curro knew that "Granada" was one of the stock encore pieces at events like this. The curtain swung down, the bravos resumed and as the standing ovation went on the minutes ticked by, with nothing else happening.

The Queen, not to be put off, kept applauding while remaining seated—a sure sign that the show was not over. The clock kept ticking, the frenzied audience stood its ground; it would be considered rude to the Queen to exit the hall before she did. Fifteen minutes, then twenty.... Twenty-five! Palms were growing red, and then something unexpected occurred, something extraordinary: the Queen herself stood, flanked by the Infanta and her husband, and approached the edge of the Royal Box saying, "Bravo!" No one in the audience had ever seen anything like this. With the Queen still standing, the shouts and applause from underneath built to a new pitch. One cannot, one must not, keep Her Majesty standing any longer than absolutely necessary. And then, Berganza appeared on stage, most elegant and every inch a *madrileña,* and launched into Mozart's "Non sò piu". Her clear voice reverberated through the room, lending its owner a touch of agelessness. As she finished, the ovation resumed, only this time much more briefly, as the evening's entire star-studded cast now took to the stage to wind things up with the brindisi from *La Traviata*, another classic. More applause, more raising and lowering of the curtain, till the opening bars of the national anthem—its official name, the "Royal March"—silenced the room. With a sweeping wave, a delighted Queen took her leave of all others in attendance. How she'd enjoyed the night's raptures!

After Queen Sofia's departure and the courtesy farewells, some—the lucky ones—dined in the Royal Theater's restaurant; among them the Aguirres and their guests, and Grand Duchess Anastasia with hers, Gagarin included. He seemed not to have noticed that he was down one flunky, or at least his mien betrayed no concern. His other two thugs were nowhere to be seen; Curro assumed they'd be wearing a hole in the carpet outside the dining room.

At length the four *divos* appeared, their entrance eliciting a standing ovation. They were getting ready to dig into a very well-deserved dinner when Eugenia, exhibiting the eccentricity and candidness that were her stock in trade, approached Placido Domingo and sweetly asked if he would sing her a *Ranchera.* "I just adore *Messicoss,"* she said firmly.

"Young lady, I've just spent two and a half hours singing, don't you think that's enough? Did you enjoy our little recital?"

"Oh, of course! I loved it! You're the best. Listening to all of you together. Why, it was ecstasy."

"Well then, go savor your ecstasy," the tenor said with a twinkle in his eye, turning back to his meal.

Eugenia looked crushed as she returned to her table, where Aunt Matilde was waiting to chew her out.

"Darling, how could you be so stupid?" asked Matilde, as if the remaining guests were not even there. "Who in their right mind would pester Placido Domingo just as he's sitting down to dinner after a concert like that? Did you happen to notice it was almost three hours long?"

"Well, would it have killed him to do a few verses of "Yo Soy el Rey"? You know I'm crazy about it. And he didn't even recognize me! After all the times we've bumped into each other at the same events in New York. Just this year at the Hispanic Society..."

"Eugenia, listen to yourself!" Now it was Curro. "He's Placido Domingo, international superstar! Supermodels are nothing special to him. He probably knows thousands."

"Am I not the *top* top model?" Eugenia pulled a childish pouty face.

"Eugenia, let it go," said Curro wearily. "Things will look different in the morning. You've had too much Cava."

"Well then I'll balance it out with champagne. I prefer sssssmall bubblesss anyway."

"I ask only that in my presence you will never again," Uncle Pepe said solemnly, "address Placido Domingo as if he were one of your young friends. Or anyone else of his caliber, for that matter, and especially not after they've addressed you formally. It was embarrassing to watch. "

"Sssssorry, Unkie—really, I am."

"And drop the damn clown act! I don't want to hear more *Unkie* this or *Auntieee* that."

***

Curro was beginning to suspect that there might really be something wrong with Eugenia, or at least her judgment. Of course she was eccentric, with that whole act about *taassiss* and so on, and he'd understood when she'd tried to explain to him the need she felt to expiate some of her exquisite perfection through studied coarseness. But lately it seemed to be getting out of hand and it was starting to worry him—she spent all day in that mode.

He knew she was of more than average intelligence; she spoke perfect English and French in addition to her native tongue, and she'd studied literature at the Sorbonne. It was safe to say that Eugenia Osorio belonged to that select group of people who were as refined on the inside as on the surface, who could carry on a conversation about any aspect of current events and clearly express well-informed opinions. So what was it, then? Could the so-called "Luaces Gene" be coming to the fore? Curro didn't know precisely what this hereditary condition entailed, what the telltale warning signs were, so he couldn't really hazard a guess. But something was wrong. Speaking to Placido Domingo with such familiarity! That should have been impossible if Eugenia were fully in control of her senses. Curro cast a sidelong glance at Pepe, who seemed to have a concerned look on his face as he looked at his wife, a carrier—like Eugenia—of the Luaces' genetic heritage.

By the time dinner was over, both Curro and Dima's nerves were on end. During the meal they kept their eyes on Gagarin's table, where he and some of the other diners seemed to be enjoying a good laugh, while the Grand Duchess' smile had begun to look a bit forced. When she and her guests stood to leave, the Aguirres went over to say goodbye, accompanied by the Germans. They walked down the stairs with her as far as the exit, with Gagarin hanging back. When they returned, Pepe and Matilde looked concerned.

"Anastasia was in a strange mood. She told us…" Matilde paused and looked over her shoulder. "…that the Russian fellow she introduced us to had threatened Dima in the theater. She heard him say something—in very gutter terms she could barely understand—to the effect that Dima would end up just like his parents."

Dima had heard Gagarin's threat loud and clear too, but just at that moment Curro had steered him away and then Eugenia's unexpected appearance had at least temporarily defused the situation. Now being reminded in front of others of his parents' murder was simply overwhelming for him. He wasn't going to let Gagarin get away with it. He sprang to his feet and made for the exit, with Curro on his heels. Dima had made it through two of the theater's large formal rooms and was just steps away from Gagarin and his remaining bodyguards before Curro caught up with him. The tension was thick with the hatred between the two antagonists, so palpable it could have been worthy of the operatic stage a few feet away from where they stood.

The Russian thugs pulled out their guns and pointed towards the nearby restrooms. For Curro and Dima the immediate future began to once again cloud over with uncertainty. But then along came the Germans, who'd dawdled behind their hosts when taking their leave of the Grand Duchess; and with them, three members of the German embassy's security detail, a small courtesy shown by today's Federal Republic towards these scions of two families whose princely houses had been especially prominent in the German Empire of times past. The three military attachés escorting the princes this night were a token of that esteem. Curro fell effusively in step with Hans, bringing Dima in tow. The situation was, at least for the time being, defused again.

Just then the Aguirres came down the hallway towards them, Eugenia at their side. All three were quiet, pensive as a result of the disturbing end to the evening's festivities. The Germans, on the other hand, oblivious to the threats to Dima, were in high spirits and ready to continue the evening elsewhere. The Aguirres begged off.

"Another time I'm afraid, Hans. Thanks, but we're ready to call it a night. Eugenia, you're coming with your aunt and me. You look worn out, let us take you home."

"Thank you, Uncle," Eugenia said confidently, "but I'm going with them for a nightcap. Curro and Dima can see me home later."

***

They walked back down into the main hall, where there was no sign anything out of the ordinary had taken place. The theater's staff were as attentive as ever, and the drivers and bodyguards of a few Madrid A-listers were still pacing around waiting for their charges. Gagarin was only a few feet away with his pair of guards. What would happen next was anyone's guess. Curro knew he had to avoid them and decided to play the card offered by the princes' security escort.

"Come back to our place. It's a beautiful night and we can sit outside on my terrace." He shot Dima a look of complicity.

"Excellent idea," said Dima encouragingly. "Better at home than out on the town. It's Saturday, everywhere'll be crammed."

"Ah, you live together?" asked Hans.

"That's right. So what do you say? Are you in?"

"All right, let's go," said Hans. "Our car's over there."

"We're heading back to our hotel," said Ernest, the older of the two princes. He and his wife Olympia were more quiet and understated than Hans and Charlotte. "We're staying at the Villa Magna. Can you drop us off?" he asked Pepe. "I think it's right along your route,".

"We'd be happy to," the banker answered, signaling his chauffeur, who soon pulled up outside at the wheel of a late model Bentley.

The two groups took their leave of each other.

"Which car is yours?" asked Hans.

"We came in a cab," lied Curro; he noticed the look of surprise on Eugenia's face, but at least she said nothing. "Do you think we can all fit into yours?"

"Of course. Here it is." The Germans had been using a minivan to see Madrid. It was more than big enough for the group of them now. They each took their seats, Curro and Dima keeping an eye on Gagarin and his hired hands, who had boarded a top-of-the-line Mercedes. By now he would surely have noticed that one of his boys was missing.

Curro suggested a route back to his place, which took his guests along some of Madrid's most scenic and brightly lit streets. Once they reached his block they stepped out of the minivan and Curro's guests admired the neighboring area. Several old mansions dotted the streets, including that built by the Marquis of Salamanca, the illustrious financier who'd designed and had built the graceful neighborhood that today bears his name; now the headquarters of an important bank, Salamanca's palace still spoke eloquently of the refined tastes enjoyed by Madrid aristocrats in the nineteenth century. As the small group strolled around, followed at a discreet distance by the Prince of Anhalt-Reuss-Holms' security detail, Curro saw Gagarin's car drive by. No doubt Gagarin was making his point: *You can't hide from me*. But Curro wasn't really concerned. Apart from the protection by proxy he'd acquired with the Germans' presence, his street was one of the safest in Madrid: his penthouse shared its sidewalks with embassies, government buildings, and the bank itself, so everything that happened on his street did so under the watchful eye of several dozen CCTV cameras, apart from which police cars drove up the street every so often. Nothing unwelcome would happen here.

They went upstairs to Curro's, where Eugenia sportingly played the hostess, and they settled in on Curro's spacious terrace. Eugenia stuck with champagne, while Curro and Hans went for Chivas on the rocks. Charlotte asked for Vodka with beer, no less—*Hell of a ride,* thought Curro. Dima wouldn't touch anything alcoholic.

Charlotte was a lovely young woman whose olive skin and hawklike nose were proudly-borne tokens of her mother's Sephardic heritage. The Tolosanos still possessed the ancient key that supposedly came from the front door of their ancestral home in Toledo. After the first drink, and egged on by her husband, she began singing charming, romantic songs in *ladino,* which delighted the small gathering of music lovers. Although her father had been a German count, her mother's Jewish roots had been no small obstacle to overcome – the rules by which the German upper nobility lived were very strict indeed. Hans' father – in view of the fact that Hans was his eldest and the heir to the title – had needed to put up quite a struggle against his own clan to ensure they would not try to strip his son of his hereditary rights. In the end, the changing times – and especially the considerable assets Charlotte's parents were willing to settle on her – smoothed over the objections from some quarters of the House of Anhalt-Reuss-Holms, whose members needed cash to refurbish the confiscated property they'd recovered in the aftermath of the German Democratic Republic's dissolution. Charlotte was more of an extrovert than her husband and after her third Vodka with beer, she sat down very close to Dima and began openly flirting with him. Evidently such behavior was par for the course with the couple because Hans didn't even blink, preferring instead to keep on pontificating to Curro about what he saw as a worrying decline in European values.

Hans, a very cultured individual, now managed his family's international business interests, which included the newspaper that had published the notorious Mohammed cartoons and in so doing had made him a target for certain radical Islamic groups. This had meant a few changes in the couple's routine but in no way put a crimp on their ebullient social life, which led them hither and yon in search of pleasures high and low up to and including the extreme. They had come to Madrid purely for the pleasure of hearing the celestial sounds of what would be remembered as the recital of the decade. Hans' sexual appetites were well known and had landed him in hot water more than once, like the time he'd been arrested for propositioning an undercover cop in the public restroom of a New York park. That had cost him a night in jail, since his New York lawyer couldn't post bail before the next morning. Hans had sworn then that he'd never again set foot in a country so invasive of consenting adults' right to do whatever they wanted in private. Naturally, it was a promise he hadn't kept. Life without a couple of trips to New York each year? Unthinkable.

Charlotte, ever more frisky, wasn't letting up on Dima. A hand on his thigh, whispers in his ear. All of this had Eugenia livid, and if she was trying to hide her jealousy and irritation at the moves Charlotte was putting on *her* beau, she wasn't doing a very good job of it. Dima meanwhile couldn't have cared less about any of it, he had other things on his mind. Eugenia on the other hand was just about to blow her top—*Slut! How dare she!* —and with all the champagne she'd had it was only matter of time before she did so, in spectacular fashion.

Charlotte stood up and asked Dima to see her to the kitchen to make a snack—"Anything'll do, even a sandwich," she said. Once there she seemed to lose her appetite—for food, at any rate— wrapping her arms around Dima instead. She whispered to Dima, trying to coax him away to spend the night, a threesome with her and Hans at their hotel. She even mentioned money. Her husband had trained her well: after all, they'd been enjoying this sort of pastime together ever since they got married. Dima politely declined and gently brushed off her advances, but if he thought he'd get away that easily then he hadn't reckoned with all the booze Charlotte had already drank, or indeed with her insistent personality. She was resolute as she was uninhibited and in response to Dima's rebuff she simply thrust a fine, delicate hand down his waistband into his pants.

Dima disentangled himself and backed out of the kitchen towards the terrace, with Charlotte in hot pursuit. Dima doubled back around the outside of the penthouse, intending to seek safety alongside Curro and Hans. But when he rounded the corner he saw that the mix of sultry spring temperatures and Scotch had led Curro to take off his tuxedo jacket and then unbutton his shirt. Curro was no Dima but was still quite fit and attractive for his forty-four years; at least, Hans certainly seemed to think so, judging from the way he was cornering Curro at one end of the sofa, trying to slip his hand inside Curro's shirt to feel up his well-defined pecs.

"Hans, for God's sake!" Curro said with a laugh. "Come on, give it a rest."

"Curro, just let me touch you, only a little. Let me

stroke that firm chest of yours," begged Hans in a way most undignified for the head of a princely house.

Just then Curro and Dima's eyes met and they both burst out laughing. This brought Eugenia out of her hiding place, from which she had watched—with increasing envy—Charlotte's attempt to sexually harass Dima in the kitchen.

Champagne vs. a vodka-beer cocktail. Who'd come out on top? Who'd be the first to blow? Should be the vodka, but no, it was the champagne.

"Will you keep your hands OFF my boyfriend!?" shouted Eugenia.

"Your boyfriend?" Charlotte answered sarcastically.

"Yes, my boyfriend. Keep your hands out of his pants. You've got a lot of nerve. Some princess," snorted Eugenia.

"Don't you mean *Curro's* boyfriend? Or his, let me see—protegé? Gigolo? His, you know what I mean, his butt boy!"

That was the last straw. Eugenia had had enough. *Bitch!* she thought. Without a second thought she stepped up to Charlotte and slapped her so hard that the tipsy princess lost her balance and tumbled to the floor.

"What the —! Get your hands off my wife!" Hans lunged at Eugenia, but was stopped midway by one of Dima's arms. "Savages, that's what you people are. Every time I come to Spain some shit like this happens. This is what I get for treating people like you as my equals. Fucking Spaniards!"

Curro sat back to enjoy the show, amused. He knew that Eugenia could take care of herself perfectly well.

"Savages? You're not even a savage, you're just a hick," Eugenia said with a sneer. "A bunch of jumped-up operetta princes who talked your way to a station you didn't even deserve, a mere two centuries ago. *My* family descend from the kings of Asturias and before that from the Visigoths. In Spain there are two hundred families older than yours. Fucking yokel!"

With this exchange, Hispano-German relations plummeted to a new low. The Prince and Princess of Anhalt-Reuss-Holms, heads held high, stalked out of Curro, Eugenia and Dima's lives for ever. They swore then and there never again to set foot in Spain. Naturally, it was a promise they would fail to keep.

***

"C'mon, let's all get some sleep, it must be way past our bedtimes," said Curro, whose face was finally showing the strain of the evening.

"Five-thirty. Yep, that's late all right," said Dima. He too was ready for some shut-eye.

They both looked at Eugenia. She couldn't go home now, the Russians would be circling outside. It would be better if she stayed with them. She'd be safer that way.

"Eugenia, sleep here if you'd like," Curro offered.

"Of course! No way am I going back out now, I'm beat. Where should I bed down?" she asked hesitantly.

"Wherever you like," answered Curro.

"In that case I'll stay with Dima, if you don't mind," she said, grabbing hold of his arm possessively. Dima looked at Curro quizzically. This wasn't in the script. Curro nodded his assent.

Eugenia, after all that she'd had to drink, was now feeling wired and not at all in the mood for sleep. She was more inclined to make the most of the experienced lover she now had at her disposal. She craved another helping of what she'd tasted the other evening, another night of total abandon: besides, it would help her come down from the rush left by the altercation she'd just been involved in. As soon as they were in the bedroom she began stroking Dima and trying to incite his lust in a way more overt than she'd ever done. She stretched out on the mattress, on her back at first and then face down, with moans and lascivious glances, like a slut. It took some effort just for Dima to get her off of him, but after all that had happened that night he really was not in the mood. He got up and left the room. He went to Curro's study and returned with a glass of water and two sleeping pills that upon returning to the bedroom he all but forced Eugenia to swallow. They took effect almost at once, and she dozed off in the fetal position, clasping a pillow tightly.

Dima actually had no intention of dropping off peacefully—at least not just yet. Truth was, he really couldn't. A long time after having put his past life behind him, he'd had no choice but to rediscover his deadly combat techniques: as soon as he'd arrived in Madrid, and now again this past evening. He kept trying to get away from the old days, but they kept catching up with him. Against the old rule from his fighting days, he poured himself a Scotch on the rocks, in a balloon glass like Curro always did, and plopped down on one of the sofas on the terrace. It was some time before he noticed at the other end of the terrace, leaning against the railing, his friend – and now, accomplice – who was drinking too, his gaze lost in the night sky. He walked over to join him, without saying a word, and it was Curro who leaned over to clink glasses with him.

"Thanks, Dima. A toast—to you."

"Curro," Dima began, "I'm sorry... I didn't mean to..."

"Dima," Curro cut him off, firmly, "cut the crap. And don't apologize. You saved my life: that guy in the bathroom would've killed me. They were trying to send you a message, through me. Like a Christmas card," he said ironically. "I'm glad you came along when you did and broke that son of a bitch's neck. He asked for it. Now we're both going to have to watch out for Gagarin, he won't take this lying down. You know that better than I do. But there'll be time to talk about all this tomorrow. I'm going to turn in now, I'm dead tired. But I'll never forget this day. Because of your friendship and because I saw death up close, beckoning me forward. And you know what? I wasn't the slightest bit afraid to take that trip. I was ready to go quietly. Now, give me a hug, champ. And don't ever apologize for saving my life. All right?"

Their long, tight hug filled Curro with a wave of sensations: affection, love, maybe? It wasn't anything sexual, just a profound, closely-felt sensation. He went to his bedroom, stopping along the way for a couple of sleeping pills. A short time later Dima too came indoors, and after walking right past the bedroom in which Eugenia was sleeping like a schoolgirl, he got into bed with Curro, one arm firmly around him.

CHAPTER X

"Fucking faggots!" Eugenia bawled after receiving the shock of her life. Still drowsy and a little worse for wear after the previous evening, she'd reached out across the mattress expecting to find the object of her affections reposing beside her. There was no one there. *Maybe he's in the shower, or getting some breakfast,* she thought. She glanced at the clock: 3 PM! At least she felt well-rested. She slipped into the en suite bathroom—*No Dima here*—for a quick shower and then pulled on some comfy togs: Curro's place had long been like a second home to her, and she kept a well-stocked closet there. *OK , time to find the boys.*

When Eugenia walked into Curro's bedroom, she was stunned. She found him spooning with Dima, whose face suggested he was in the grip of a pleasant dream. The sight of those two together in bed, in that position, turned her stomach. She couldn't handle it. The fact that they were the only men who had ever really mattered romantically in her life just made it that much worse. Curro, who she'd had a crush on for so many years, the one she considered her twin soul, snuggled up next to the man who might become the all-around mate she'd so yearned for. And in *that* position!

"Faggots!" she said again, hoping it would wake them from what looked to be a very satisfying rest.

They were slow to react, which just stoked Eugenia's anger even more. She let out a torrent of invective, sparing them nothing. At first Curro and Dima just lay there, registering her fury. Dima was nonplussed to hear himself the subject of one epithet nobody had ever called him. And Curro, who wasn't in the mood for drama, just got out of bed and went into the bathroom, leaving a puzzled Dima to face Eugenia's wrath alone.

"You're really something, Dima! Here I thought there might be a chance for us. Boy, was I wrong. I don't know what it is about Curro, it seems like he has you hypnotized."

"You've got it all wrong. Curro is not gay, please get that through your skull. He's my friend and I love him as a friend. He's been really good to me and he has a big heart."

"Yeah, right, a huge one! Curro has never loved anyone in his whole life except his mother, and Trasto," she said scornfully, just as Curro walked back in, dressed in a fuzzy bathrobe. "And I'm not even sure about them. I have never seen Curro shed a tear for anyone. Not once. Not even for his precious dog." She turned and faced him accusingly. "Isn't that right, Curro?" She went on, not waiting for an answer. "You tell me, Dima—have you ever known anyone that you've never seen cry? Not me. Curro's a selfish loner and everything else means dick to him. And that's what you are to him, Dima, dick!

Curro had reached his limit. "That's enough, Eugenia, must you be so common? It doesn't suit you."

"Common? I'll give you common. You're nothing but a common thief," she sobbed, her self-control slipping. "One time that I find a guy I really like, did you have to steal him from me?"

"Eugenia, if you'll just shut up before you blow it with hysterics, I think you'll find that Dima was, and will be, yours. But did you ever stop to think that maybe I liked him too?"

"You like everybody. Anyone who's ripped. But you don't love any of them, you just use them. You've never loved anyone in your whole life, except Trasto, I'll grant you that. You've only ever loved a dog! And even that was a very odd kind of love. Very selfish, very typical of you! I don't buy this show of mourning you've been putting on. He did love you, he adored you, he'd have given his life for you."

"Out of my house, Eugenia," Curro said, crossing the room to take Eugenia by the arm and lead her out. She'd touched a nerve and he'd had enough. How the hell would she know how he'd felt about Trasto? "I said get out! Let's go!"

"What's the matter with you two?" asked Dima, baffled by everything that was unfolding in front of him.

"Fine, I'm leaving all right," Eugenia said to Curro. "And I don't think we'll be seeing each other for a good, long while."

***

As soon as Eugenia was gone Curro realized the mistake he'd made by snapping. With the Russians sure to still be keeping an eye on the place, Eugenia was in certain danger. He and Dima looked at each other, both thinking the same thing, and they immediately bolted down the four flights of stairs to street level. As soon as they were outside they looked towards the corner of Paseo de Recoletos and spotted Eugenia's svelte figure, one arm aloft as she called out, "Tassiss! Tassiss, taassiiiss!"

They dashed back upstairs to get dressed. Curro was the quicker of the two, pulling on some jeans and a T-shirt, and slipping on a pair of deck shoes, the first footwear he laid his hands on.

"Meet you downstairs. Hurry up!"

By the time Curro reached the street, Eugenia was gone. Dima burst out onto the sidewalk looking for his friend moments later. Curro rode up on a Vespa that had been gathering dust at a nearby parking garage.

"You know how to ride one of these?" he asked Dima.

"Sure. I used to have one in Moscow."

"All right, hop on," said Curro, passing Dima a military-style helmet. "You beat it over to Eugenia's place. I'm going to call her neighbors to tell them to keep an eye out. And the police. Then I'll follow. Here," he said, handing over the Viking 446.

***

A few minutes later Curro pulled up outside the front door of Eugenia's apartment building. He spotted the Vespa, badly parked in the middle of the sidewalk, just before the building superintendent walked up to him.

"Don Francisco," he addressed Curro, "is something wrong? Miss Eugenia's foreign friend just got here and went up to her place. He convinced me it was urgent, that she was in some kind of trouble, and I gave him the spare keys. I hope that's all right."

"Yes, José. You did the right thing."

"Nothing's happened to Miss Eugenia, has it?" José had been linked to the Osorio family for many years—they owned the building—and he'd known Eugenia since she was a little girl: his face now evidenced both affection and concern.

"No, I'm sure she's fine," said Curro soothingly. "We just need to get hold of her, something urgent's come up."

"Can I help, Don Francisco? Is there anything you want me to do?"

"No, but thanks anyway. What you could do is keep your eye out for someone named Inspector Jiménez. As soon as he's here, bring him up. Then get back to what you were doing. Enjoy your Sunday."

"I'll stay around here. I'm not moving till Miss Eugenia is back."

"Thanks," Curro repeated, "but there's no need, really. I'm sure she'll be along any moment now."

Curro went up to Eugenia's penthouse, where he found Dima and Eugenia's downstairs neighbors, the Abrisquetas—the husband was a well-respected retired judge, a relative of the Osorios. A judge's retirement pay didn't stretch very far, and he and his wife had for years been paying merely symbolic rent, thanks to the generosity of the Duke of Luaces. All the ruckus Dima had made, racing up the stairs three steps at a time and then charging through Eugenia's front door like a commando had left them just a tad concerned, especially when they saw the door had been left open.

"What's going on here?" the judge asked Curro warily. "Who is this wild young man?"

"He's a friend of ours—of Eugenia and I. Nothing's happened, we just need to get hold of Eugenia. But don't worry, it's nothing serious."

"Really? The way he was carrying on, it sure looked like it was," said the judge's wife. "Well, we'll leave you to it then. If you need anything, we're right downstairs."

"Thanks," said Curro

Once they were finally alone, Dima brought Curro up to speed. No sign of Eugenia, nor any indication that she'd already been there and left. Besides, she wouldn't really have had time, since Dima and Curro both had arrived in record time, and the building super said he hadn't seen Eugenia since the day before. Curro reached for his cell and called Matilde, who had nothing to contribute except hysteria, the grip of which made her insist on phoning Eugenia's parents in Paris, where they spent a lot of time with their younger daughter Fabiola.

Curro tried convincing Matilde to hold off phoning, saying there was no reason to jump to conclusions. Eugenia, being who she was, could have flounced off somewhere, or she might simply have gone away with one of her girlfriends. Curro pleaded with Matilde not to alarm Eugenia's parents before they'd checked for her with all of the friends she might have gone to. He finally got Matilde calmed down and they divvied up a list of the friends and acquaintances Eugenia spent the most time with. They agreed to touch base later on.

The door phone buzzed. It was José announcing the arrival of Inspector Jiménez, who was on his way up in the elevator. Curro had just enough time to issue a warning to Dima: "Not a word, all right? Leave this to me."

Inspector Jiménez walked through the open front door, a hint of a smile on his face. "Curro!" he said, extending his hand, "God, it's been a long time."

Curro took his hand and embraced him. "It sure has. What—ten years or so since we last saw each other?"

"Since you disappeared off the face of the earth, and the brass stuck me behind a desk."

"Yeah, well. Liver problems, among other things. I finally ended up having to pay the piper. Too much of a good thing and all that. Don't know if you heard."

"There *was* some talk. They way you were headed, it's probably a good thing you took early retirement." Jiménez smiled again, fondly remembering the bad old days.

Carlos Jiménez Moreno had been—years ago—the police's undercover man in Madrid's elite circles, put there to keep tabs on who was moving what in the city's burgeoning cocaine trade. Madrid's coke traffickers were usually Spaniards from Galicia, or Colombians, and in Madrid's frenzied night scene they regularly rubbed elbows with the city's upper crust. Carlos had been young, handsome, well-mannered, and blended in well; he'd been invited to all the right parties and had fit seamlessly into the coked-up debauchery, so well in fact that more than one society girl would have married him; but in real life he actually had a steady girlfriend. With his cover he could have married any of his playmates and spent the rest of his life living like a millionaire; but he hadn't really been interested.

Carlos came from a rough background on Madrid's meaner streets. You had to watch your back around him. He was a tough guy even before taking up martial arts in a serious way. When he'd joined the force, as the reigning Spanish champion in Full Contact Fighting, it hadn't taken the higher-ups long to work out how much mileage they could get out of him. Night after night, Curro and Carlos had run into each other so many times in so many of the same places that they'd struck up something approaching friendship. Carlos had gotten him out of a bind more than once. Eventually, life had led them in opposite directions and they'd lost touch. Until today. Curro had called Carlos because he was sure of Carlos' discretion. He knew he could count on him.

Carlos eyed Dima curiously. *Some guy*, he thought. Time was, Carlos would have been quite an opponent, even for Dima. Now he was forty-four, the same age as Curro, and Dima could surely take him. Even so, Carlos still sparred at the gym every day; he was the best boxer on the force and the younger cops couldn't handle him.

"Carlos, meet Dima, a Russian friend of mine. A good *friend*," Curro emphasized. "Dima, this is Carlos. He's a policeman—an inspector—and we go way back. Also a friend."

Having sized each other up, the two men held one another's gaze. They shook hands firmly.

Curro gestured to them to take seats in the living room.

"So, Curro, tell me, what's all this about? You said something about a friend in danger?"

"That's right. It's about Eugenia Osorio, the model. She and I are close. I can't be positive, but I think something's happened to her."

"What makes you think that?"

"Dima here is Russian, as I said, and since he's been in Madrid someone's been following him. Don't ask me who or why, because we don't know, but we're sure they're tailing him. Last night we went to the Royal Theater and on our way home I'm positive they followed us back to my place. Eugenia spent the night at my place, and hasn't been seen since she left this afternoon. We're still calling friends of hers; I mean, she could just turn up out of the blue, but I've got a bad feeling the guys who were following us have kidnapped her."

Jiménez sat there impassively for a moment, impossible for Curro to read. Finally he said, "So, you're Russian, eh?"

"Carlos, I've already told you that. Dima's a trusted—"

"Yes, I know, you told me. But in case you haven't heard, in the wee hours of the morning we found a Russian stiff at the Royal Theater." Carlos looked at Dima. "It was a hit, no doubt about it. Done by a real pro." By now Carlos was staring at Dima intently.

Curro knew he had to work fast. "We had no idea. I mean, we haven't watched any news today."

"This won't be on the news. It was a charity do, the Queen was there. It would look bad for this to get out."

"I understand," said Curro.

"Anyway, the guy who was offed was just a peon. Hired gun for a Moscow mob boss by the name of Gagarin, who it's our good fortune to have here fronting Russia's leading crime family. Gagarin's a slippery little bastard and we haven't managed to nail him yet on drug running, money laundering, or any of the other sleazy sidelines we're sure he's into. At least, not yet. But we will. You know him?"

"No," said Dima.

"Yes," Curro said firmly. "He knows him. Gagarin killed his parents in Saint Petersburg. We know he's a crook. Apparently, Gagarin kept a consignment of dirty money he was supposed to be laundering for his bosses, and pinned the blame on Dima's father. He and his wife then turned up drowned in the Neva River. Gagarin wanted to make it look like he was settling accounts. Son of a bitch."

"You're in one hell of a mess," Carlos said to Dima. "I'm afraid you're going to have to come to the station with me."

Curro shook his head emphatically. "No. No way."

"He just lied to me."

"Carlitos," Curro calculatedly blurted out the nickname from times past, "don't do this to me. I'm telling you, he's not mixed up with this bastard Gagarin. Didn't you hear any of what I just told you? Gagarin killed his parents!"

"Exactly. So he has a motive for offing that guy at the Royal Theater. Now come clean. What do you two know about the stiff?"

"Carlitos, are we friends, or not? I'll vouch for Dima. I assure you, he had nothing to do with this murder you're talking about. We spent the whole evening with Eugenia Osorio, the Aguirres, and the Prince and Princess of Anhalt-Reuss-Holms. Ask any of them, they'll back me up. Anyway, you owe me one, man."

Back in the day, Carlos had been harassed by a superior jealous of the lifestyle he enjoyed as part of his cover. Carlos was handsome, he had socialites knocking down his door, and although he stayed with the same girlfriend throughout, he could hardly have passed up so many opportunities for a little fun on the side. Internal affairs had tried to link him to the very same drugs ring that he was spying on. Things got ugly, and Curro had hired Madrid's top lawyer for Carlos, picking up the tab himself. Carlos wouldn't forget that.

"All right," he shrugged. "Let's leave it there for now. But I want you to keep me in the loop on all aspects of this mess, including Eugenia Osorio's angle. I'll put out some feelers to try to trace her movements. If she turns up, you let me know."

"I will—promise," said Curro, with a sigh of relief. "But I'm sure she's been taken."

As soon as the Inspector had gone on his way, Dima angrily confronted Curro.

"What's the bright idea?" he said, leaping up. "Why the hell did you tell him all that? Now he wants to lock me up!"

Curro held up a hand reassuringly and said, "Like I told you, he's a friend. We can trust him. Let me handle this."

Dima had no idea what Curro had in mind, but he decided to drop it. He trusted Curro. Never more so than in that moment.

***

The next few hours brought no relief from uncertainty. Matilde and Curro worked their way through the list they'd made of Eugenia's acquaintances; zero results. Some of them had been at the same event at the Royal Theater the night before, but none had seen her since.

That afternoon at the Aguirre's—where they'd established their command center—stretched into the evening, and then into the early hours of the following day. Matilde, always right on top of things, discreetly set up drinks and cold cuts. No one ate a bite, but she found the drinks needing replacement more than once. Even Dima poured himself a stiff Scotch, which—to his dismay—he was starting to grow fond of.

Curro and Dima suspected the wait was in vain. During the first few hours, her disappearance could simply have been put down to her tantrum. But as the day gave way to nighttime and mention of Eugenia's disappearance on the nine o'clock news—Inspector Jiménez in the headlines once again, leading the investigation—Curro and Dima really had no doubt Eugenia had been kidnapped. And they knew Gagarin was behind it. But how to explain that it was all part of an attempt by a Russian crime lord to intimidate a blameless, handsome young man? No, it was vital to keep the backstory under wraps for now.

The situation put Pepe Aguirre between a rock and a hard place. He couldn't let his brother-in-law, Eugenia's father, learn about her disappearance from the TV news. Around sundown he'd gone into his study, with Matilde trailing dejectedly behind, to make the call. Once shock had given way to anger, the frantic father had vented his emotions on them: understandable, perhaps, but unfair, since they'd always kept an eye on their niece when she was in town, while her parents spent most of their time in Paris. Besides, Eugenia was all grown up and supposed to be able to take care of herself.

But Ignacio Osorio, perhaps out of guilt at having failed – or not really tried – to keep his oldest daughter on a tighter leash, was looking for someone to blame. Anyone beside himself would do. He'd been one of the best-connected men in Spain since the early seventies, when he'd been a regular on the cover of society mags on two continents. His affairs with some of the biggest names in Hollywood had made him a household name. It had the been the daughter of a Spanish insurance mogul who'd finally gotten him to the altar, a beauty named Sonsoles Pérez de Torres.

Or was she? It wasn't so cut and dried. Sonsoles' surname had changed over time. Spaniards customarily used two surnames, their father's followed by their mother's maiden name. Sonsoles' father was surnamed Pérez Muñoz; her mother, Torres Quintana. But Sonsoles introduced herself as Pérez *de* Torres, and that had eventually mutated to Pérez-Benzo de Torres, all together. Curro was very fond of Eugenia's mother but had no idea exactly what name was on her driver's license. At any rate, this was the kind of thing that just happened, when the prosaically named Mr. Pérez Muñoz married off his only child and heir to the 20th Duke of Luaces.

Among those friends who dropped by to offer the Aguirres their moral support was the majestic and rotund Grand Duchess Anastasia, this time with her very own coterie of elegant ladies-in-waiting, all friends of Matilde's. Curro saw the chance to strike up a conversation and make some headway.

"Ma'am," he approached respectfully, "please allow me to introduce one of your fellow countrymen, Dmitri Denissov. He yearns for Russia's monarchy to be restored," lied Curro charmingly.

"You don't say," came the blasé reply.

"That concert last night. What a splendid success! And your guests—so charming." Curro had decided to get right to the point.

"You're Morante, aren't you? Concha Solloso's son?"

"Yes, that's right. My mother held you in the highest esteem."

"As I did her, she was a delightful person. You needn't be so formal towards me, I've known you since you were in knee-pants.... Anyway, I've no idea who you're talking about."

Curro pressed the issue. "The foreign gentleman with you—I believe he was Russian as well?"

The Grand Duchess wrinkled her nose. Now she knew exactly who Curro was talking about and recognized the handsome young man by his side. In her mind's eye she saw the scene last night when that lowlife Gagarin had threatened him right in front of her. She could kick herself for having included that little creep among her guests. Who was it that had recommended him? Ah, yes, her Spanish lawyer, who knew Gagarin from Marbella where they both had homes and—she suspected—were probably partners in something shady. Her pride was slightly wounded by the fact that one of her friends had warned her not to let Gagarin within a mile of her, but she'd trusted her lawyer. That was a mistake she wouldn't repeat.

She looked up at Curro. "Don't even mention that rascal and his entourage to me." She lowered her voice. "This morning the police were at my house. It seems they found one of his bodyguards who'd been beaten to death—right there in the Royal Theater! With all of us in the same building, including the Queen! Can you believe it? Shocking, truly shocking. I don't even want to know what he does to attract that kind of attention. As far as I'm concerned there is no such person." She made to leave, as if to show that the very mention of Gagarin was odious to her. But Curro hadn't finished.

"Well, that puts me in a spot," Curro said, taking her arm in a manner most contemptuous of protocol before she could get away. "It's just—he asked me if I'd arrange a fitting for him with my tailor, and now I don't know how to get in touch with him."

"Marbella," she answered, jerking her arm out of Curro's grasp. "He told me last night he was flying back to his place in Marbella."

***

In the hours before dawn the hosts retired, the sympathetic visitors took their leave, and Curro eventually decided it was time for him to go home, too. The gathering had dwindled down to just Curro, Dima, and a couple of Pérez cousins of Eugenia, who followed Curro's lead and went home as well. It was almost 5 A.M. That evening Pepe had told those gathered that Ignacio and Sonsoles would land in Madrid the next day. For a moment, faced with so much worried frenzy, Curro wondered if perhaps he'd overreacted in assuming foul play was behind Eugenia's disappearance. She was so unpredictable, but in his gut he was grimly convinced he was right. He felt awful, guilty even; he had told her to get out of his house after he himself had brought her there for protection. But regrets were pointless. What's done was done. Now the focus needed to be on finding Eugenia.

Curro lowered the convertible's top and as they drove away from the house dawn's cool breeze caressed their faces. As they drew nearer to his penthouse, Curro changed his mind.

"Hey, where's that disco you were at the other night?"

"Disco? You're thinking of going out at a time like this?"

"No," he said impatiently, "where's it located?"

"Over on Orense. It's called Ganvino. Ever been there?"

"It rings a bell. I don't know, I may have been there sometime, but discos bore me—I got fed up years ago. Anyway, let's go over and see if we can catch up with the Martinez brothers or this Vasili guy. Maybe they can help us with a lead on Eugenia."

"What, now? They'll be locking up."

"Good. If they're locking up, that means they'll still be there."

CHAPTER XI

As they arrived it was plain that the party wasn't over. Huddles of stragglers stretched up and down the sidewalk outside the nightspot. They pulled over to the curb and Curro killed the engine; Dima scanned the area for any sign of Vasili or the Martinezes, but didn't even see a lone bouncer or valet attendant. The place's unguarded entrance was as good as an engraved invitation. Downstairs the atmosphere wasn't at all what they expected. Laughter and noise surrounded them. That night's entertainers, an American group called the All Jazz Band, were relaxing between sets with their devoted fans (plus groupies and spongers), the staff, and the venue regulars. Out of the darkness came Tarek, the overconfident Turk whose challenge to Dima hadn't worked out so well for him. But he was gracious and invited them to stay even though they'd be crashing a private party.

Curro and Dima found a seat at one side of the dance floor, where those still on their feet were dancing any which way and some were singing along to the music. Then the musicians took to the stage and struck up an improv jam session, to the delight of their audience. For Curro, fond of jazz in general and this band in particular, it was like a front-row seat at his own private concert. Dima caught his eye and pointed out two shirtless guys who were dancing without a break—the Martinez brothers. After a while they sidled up to the bar but the only person behind it turned out to be the sideburned pusher Dima'd seen the other night, who was pouring himself a drink. He nodded at Dima, and at Curro too—whom he'd seen before—and then excused himself and returned to the floor, where a hot brown girl was waiting for him. In a flash Dima was over the counter and ready to tend bar.

"Evening, sir, what can I get you?" he asked Curro with mock formality.

"Chivas on the rocks, please, bartender," Curro said with a grin.

Dima checked the shelves, then the cabinets, with increasing dismay—no Chivas. But he was determined not to come up empty-handed and he spotted something that would be just the ticket.

"I'm so sorry, sir, we're fresh out of Chivas. As a token of our apology, may I offer you this champagne instead?" He raised a bottle of Moët Chandon he'd found in the freezer. "It's been chilled just to your taste, sir."

"Champagne it is then."

Dima had begun developing a taste for alcohol since he'd been in Madrid; he sipped a beer as Curro enjoyed the champagne, but all the while he felt more than a little guilty. It was as if drinking and joking with Curro was a betrayal to Eugenia. They were supposed to be there to chase down any leads, not to drink and listen to music. He was sure she'd be having a very hard time of it if she had been kidnapped, and meanwhile here were he and Curro drinking in a noisy disco and looking for all the world like they'd forgotten about her.

"Dima! Dawg, where've you been at? Some disappearing act you pulled the other day, man." It was Andy, the younger Martinez brother who danced up to them in the grip of a foreign babe who held tightly onto Andy's sweating pecs as if they were a trophy she was proudly parading before her friends. She did a double-take when she saw Dima, as if she were briefly contemplating a swap.

"Curro, meet Andy, from the gym—"

"Your homie Andy, you mean. I mean, we're good, right?"

"Absolutely. Andy, this is Curro, my best friend here in Spain." Andy looked Curro over and his first thought was, *What the fuck is Dima doin' with such an old dude?* On second glance, he thought Curro looked familiar, but he couldn't say where from.

"Hi," Curro said shaking Andy's hand. "Curro Morante. This is one hell of a party you've got going here."

"Yeah, the band totally kicks ass. We rolled up the welcome mat once the concert itself was over, but as you can see, the party just keeps on rockin'."

"Hey, the door was open!" Curro threw up his hands in mock apology.

"Don't sweat it, dude. Dima is on the home team, but I'm gonna tell Tarek to stop slackin' off. These guys," said as he jerked a thumb at the band, "invited some of their peeps to come hang with us and someone better be workin' the door."

In the end Andy needn't have worried about

gatecrashers so much as guests. The band's friends turned out to be most of a British soccer team who'd lost that night's match to Madrid's less-prominent team, the Atlético. They were still smarting and looking to blow off steam. Having already drunk half the booze in Madrid, when the last bar they'd been at closed its doors they'd moved on to the private after-party being held by their American friends.

Unfortunately, they lived up to the stereotype British "yobs" had for mindless intoxicated violence beyond their shores. It seemed like they'd barely gotten there before the first chairs flew, followed by tables, bottles, and clothes belonging not only to the team and their handlers but the bimbos they'd brought with them as well. The carnage was a highly entertaining spectacle, unless you were the management contemplating the bill and how when you were going to present it to the owners. That was the position Tony and Andy were now in—it looked like what had been a great night was going to end with the club they ran completely trashed.

Eventually it became apparent that nothing short of general mobilization would be enough to stop the drunken mob that randomly yet effectively was smashing everything in its path. At first the Martinez brothers tried to go easy on them but, not for the first time, found that there was no reining in a booze-fueled yob mob. They had no luck getting through to them and things quickly degenerated to the point where only the use of force could save the premises. Except for Tarek and two other bouncers, all the rest of the club staff had left hours ago. The Martinez boys were badly outnumbered and even underpowered. They started to lose their cool and really rip into the drunken revelers, but these in turn just laughed the blows off, and responded with even harder punches of their own. In the end it was Tony who caught Dima's eye and signaled for help; Dima in turn looked to Curro for his go-ahead, and Curro shrugged in a way that said, *Up to you.*

When all was said and done, the tide was turned by the intervention of just one man—a particularly nononsense man, to be sure. Andy, Tony, Tarek, and the rest were still trying to play it by the book; but Dima wasn't on the club payroll and besides, he needed to blow off steam. The shit he'd had to put up with the past two days had him so wound up that some extra exercise could only do him good. He hammered all comers, left, right, and center, till he had the rats on the run. Sooner than any of them thought possible, the disco was empty, and the two brothers had the Russian to thank for saving their livelihoods.

"Aw, fuck, would you look at this. Can you believe this?" Tony swore his way through the disco, shaking his head. "Man, the cleaners are gonna have their hands full here, I'm tellin' ya." At length he looked at Curro and Dima. "Hey, you two, wait a second. Don't go anywhere, the next drink's on us."

When the four of them stepped onto the sidewalk the sun seemed blinding. It was just past 8 A.M., but by then Orense Street was in the grip of Monday rush hour. Cars hurrying to and fro, pedestrians charging down the sidewalk, horns bellowing over the growl of engines. Curro and Dima would've been happy to get some sleep, but the chance to pick the Martinez brothers' brains was too good to pass up. Curro and

Dima followed their car (that notorious Porsche) to some neighborhood neither one of them recognized on the outskirts of Madrid. Eventually they pulled up outside a seedy-looking joint called the Scorpion's Tail, where Tarek was already on duty working the door. He herded the people standing around towards either side of the door, where they stood, a warped echo of an honor guard, as Curro and Dima strode through the entrance.

They went down a dark, narrow staircase and found themselves in a stale basement where people of every description were polishing off the dregs of a night that had already ended, still searching for God knows what. By that stage of the game, with so much liquor and other substances coursing through their systems, it was anyone's guess what sort of personal nirvana any of those present were after. As they made their way in, the customers began greeting the two brothers, warmly yet respectfully—it was obvious they knew who was boss. Among those drifting through the semidarkness, Curro wasn't too surprised to see a controversial politician who was cuddling up to a huge, tattoo-covered Afro-Caribbean guy while in turn a small, pale Asian boy sucked his ear. In the penumbra he also caught sight of, and attempted not to be noticed by, two young girls whose parents he knew; they were performing a striptease while being groped by leering stoners. *Just when you think you've seen it all,* thought Curro. Things rapidly started to get out of hand and the girls suddenly found themselves cornered by the guys they'd led on, looking for all the world as if they were about to start gang-banging them. The girls tried to cool things down—*A joke's a joke, this is going too far*—but no one really seemed to be listening.

Curro leaned towards their hosts, "Listen, those two airheads are the daughters of some good friends of mine. Could you guys do something?" he said, pointing at the two brats in the corner, who would never forget how close they came to being gang-raped.

"Sure, hold on," said Andy, moving towards the group around the girls. He dispersed the troublemakers in no time flat. The leader of the pack, a tall, skinny kid, made like he was going after the girls again; Andy dealt him an open-handed slap so hard his friends had to pick him up off the ground. After that, without saying another word, Andy pointed towards the stairs leading to the exit, and the would-be rapists filed obediently up the stairs and out of his bar.

"Now *that* guy knows how to get results," Curro said to Dima "Listen—would you mind seeing those two young ladies to a cab?"

"No problem," said Dima, gesturing—*after you*—to the two frightened girls. They would never walk this far on the wild side again. As the three of them started up the stairs, Curro called out after them, "Wait till they're safely in the taxi!" then ran to catch up with the Martinez boys.

"You guys are fucking ace!" said Curro, figuring it best to address the brothers in their own lingo.

"Ahh," Tony said as he waved dismissively "this place is full of dipshits. I'd happily rip the heads off most of them." Curro thought Tony seemed more reserved than his younger brother, at least towards him.

"Do I know you from somewhere?" said Andy.

"I don't know, I used to go out a lot at night, but not for the last few years. These days it's mostly just dinners with friends, that sort of thing. Speaking of friends," he said, changing the subject, "is Dima's Russian pal around? He wanted to catch up with him."

"Joker's disappeared," snorted Andy. "He hasn't showed up for work since the first night Dima was at Ganvino. Neither has Sonia. You know, his girlfriend? If he ever *does* come back, his ass is history, I tell you that. No way we're keepin' someone that unreliable on the door—"

"We'll see about that," snapped Tony. "Remember—he came highly recommended. We don't wanna step on our dicks."

This exchange intrigued Curro. Who were they talking about? Whose good graces was Tony worried about staying in?

Dima burst in looking rattled. "The street's full of cops, I think it's a raid!"

Tarek bolted back downstairs. "The pigs!" Hot on his heels, a sergeant in a flak jacket. "Police! Hands on your head!" He gestured at Curro. "You fucking deaf? Hands on your head!"

Outside, chaos reigned. Several paddy wagons were parked in front of the place, a couple dozen uniformed officers at the ready. The joint's best customers—the ones who were still inside, midmorning—lined up with their faces to the wall, like punished schoolkids. The left-wing politician was having his *don't-you-know-who-I-am* moment, trying to talk his way out of the scandal his arrest in circumstances like these would mean with his friends and family (but not his party, which was very liberal on morality). His fame, such as it was, didn't seem to cut any ice with the cops either, unless one counts the dubious distinction of being the first guy cuffed and loaded into a paddy wagon. One of his paramours, the Geisha-faced Asian kid, was screaming about police brutality; the other one, the tall Afro-Caribbean who knew the drill—went quietly, despite the two grams of coke in his pocket that he hadn't managed to ditch. He was sure that Spanish justice would, obligingly as ever, excrete him back out onto the streets before too long.

Out of the corner of his eye, Curro caught a glimpse of Inspector Jiménez, who was questioning the two girls he'd helped; just as their taxi had been about to pull away, the police had stopped it and forced them to get out, and now they stood answering questions monosyllabically, shaking and pale beneath the morning sun. Curro, ignoring the cop who told him to stand still, pulled away from the wall and walked towards Jiménez; Dima too broke ranks and followed his friends. Two of the cops pointed their weapons at the rebellious pair.

"Carlitos!" shouted Curro.

The Inspector turned his head, more than a little surprised that anyone would call him that at a time and place like this. He saw Curro on the ground, one cop's knee on his back, and the Russian he'd met the day before, surrounded by officers with their guns drawn.

"Stand down! Put your guns down, now!" Jiménez shouted.

"But Inspector—"

"Antúnez, I said put your gun away, NOW. You, Almodóvar—get that guy off the ground and bring him over here. And his pal, too."

The Vice Squad officers were surprised, but did as they were told. Inspector Jiménez was respected—and feared—down at the station. Word was, you did not want to get on his bad side.

"So, what brings you to this distinguished establishment?" Jiménez said with a smirk at Curro. "Missing the club scene that much, are we? I don't suppose you'd care to explain how you know the Martinez brothers."

"I only just met them, they work out at the same gym as Dima. They seem like nice guys."

"Yeah right. Two-bit pushers, that's what they are. And—"

"Carlitos, please." Curro nodded at the girls. "Let these two go. They're in over their heads, they had no idea what kind of place they'd walked into."

"Sure, they just stumbled through the door on the way to choir practice, right?"

"Take a good look at them, Carlos. They're just overgrown kids looking for a rush in the wrong place. I know their parents—hell, so do you. Remember Ana Pidal? The blonde's her daughter. C'mon, let them go home. They're so scared they're pissing themselves."

Carlos looked at the girls' IDs; Curro was telling the truth.

"Almodóvar, get these two the hell out of here. Put 'em in a squad car and take them home."

"Yes sir, Inspector."

"Everyone else, down to the station." The other officers had just about finished loading the rest of the people from the club. "Antúnez, get the keys off of Tony Martinez, lock the place up, and tape the door. You two, follow me," he said to Curro and Dima.

Once they were in his squad car, Carlitos let rip. "Mind telling me what the *fuck* you were doing in this shithole, hanging out with two lowlifes like the Martinez brothers?"

"I told you, they work out at Dima's gym. They're all into K-1. We dropped by the disco they manage, Ganvino, and when they locked up over there they invited us to come here for one more drink. Very nice guys."

"Yeah, a couple of real saints. Regular Mother Teresa material. Look, Curro," Jiménez was about to lose his cool, "your two Boy Scouts there are pushing coke. Not a lot, true, but they're in with this Gagarin we were talking about yesterday. I was gonna lean on them anyway to see if they knew anything about the stiff in the Royal Theater, but then an informant told us they're keeping a pound of Colombian marching powder in their stinky little club."

"A whole pound, huh? Wow, the Godfathers of Madrid," said Curro laconically.

"In case you didn't know, there are people doing time for a lot less than that, my friend. My men are gonna pull that place apart and if we find anything at all, those two are going down. Welcome to the real world."

"This informant—did he have an accent?" Curro was starting to suspect he knew why Vasili had made himself scarce. Dima looked at Curro, not knowing where he was headed with this.

"Yeah, he had an accent. Russian one, in case you're wondering. What, now you think Gagarin's behind the tip-off? Why the hell would he do that? These guys are part of his network, they help move the merchandise and launder the cash."

"I don't know," Curro said hesitating, and wondering if he should share his thoughts aloud with Jiménez. What the hell, they were friends. "You ever heard of a guy named Vasili? Works as a bouncer?"

"Sure, one of Gagarin's lieutenants. He's been here for a few months now, he oversees his boss's distribution network through the discos. Gagarin has nearly a dozen in Madrid, fronts for dealing. That Vasili's a nasty piece of work. He's a suspect in at least five murders throughout Europe, but no one's ever managed to make anything stick. Why, you suspect him? What of?"

"I'm not sure, but something smells. I've never met him, I just know what Dima's told me about him—dangerous guy, looks out for number one."

Carlos parked in the lot next to the station. As they walked from his car into the building, Curro got a look at the circus shaping up outside. The station was downtown, just off of Gran Via, and a crowd of gawkers had assembled on the sidewalk opposite, attracted by the sirens, paddy wagons, and squad cars. Their curiosity was rewarded by the freak show as the cops began herding the suspects out of the vans and into the station: pimps, stoners, pushers, transvestites, prostitutes. In other words, best in show.

Unfortunately for the politician, a famous actor was already inside the station on a domestic violence charge, so TV cameras and reporters were circling outside when he was pulled from the police van. He tried not to attract any attention and raised his cuffed wrists in front of his face to cover it. But his geisha, proud to have such a prominent john, had other ideas and tried to link arms with him as they ran the media gauntlet. He roughly elbowed the Asian away, causing them both to lose their balance and triggering a barrage of insults. The geisha's falsetto morphed into a deep bellow worthy of a truck driver, with which the scorned hustler worked his way through the colorful repertoire of Spanish insults he'd learned while working in Madrid. Cameras flashed, lenses zoomed... liver Regás would not be returning to Barcelona nor would his very conventional family ever forgive him. But he would still hold onto his seat.

***

They went up to Jiménez's office, where he left Curro and Dima for a moment with his secretary. She seemed to be checking police reports against a printout of sets of fingerprints. Someone somewhere had just been identified. Curro and Dima stayed quiet. With a witness like her, it wasn't the time or place to discuss the day's events so far. Curro's eyes strayed around the room: he gave the decor high marks. Sober, understated, appropriate to a dedicated servant of the law, yet indicative of good taste. Nice desk, comfortable chairs for visitors, table lamps, carpeting in warm colors. As a whole they spoke of an occupant who attached a certain degree of importance to his workspace beyond the merely functional. At the far end, on a table near the window, Curro spotted a photo of Carlos horsing around in a pool with two kids. He hadn't known his friend was now a family man; he hadn't asked. Next to it, a black-and-white studio shot of Carlos' wedding day: Carlos with Mamen, whom Curro had met a few times. They'd made a good couple, as was still evident from the photo: young, both attractive, both with the same dreamy gaze that seemed to denote true love.

Nearly an hour went by before Carlos came back, and when he did he did not look like a happy camper. He politely told his secretary it was time for her break and waited till she'd left for the coffee shop across the street before turning his gaze on Curro.

"The Martinez boys have clammed up. They say they've never heard of Gagarin. Lying bastards. Before I'm done with them they're gonna hand me their boss on a silver platter. He's slipped away too damn many times already. They're staying put till they decide to play ball. We were lucky enough to catch Tony holding fifty one gram folds of cocaine, their Turkish pal had about the same and I can hold Andy as an accomplice. They're gonna do time. And then there's the theater murder—"

"Carlos," Curro interrupted his friend, "I assure you, believe me, the Martinez brothers have nothing to do with the body at the theater. Don't ask me how I know, I just do. And don't look at me like that. We talked with some of the Russians at the Budax Club in case they might have heard something about Eugenia," Curro lied, "and Dima and I got the impression the Russians here are involved in some sort of turf war. It wouldn't surprise me if there's a struggle on to control drug sales through Madrid discos."

"Stop bullshitting me. I know the guy who owns the Budax. He's not mixed up in any of this shit."

"I know that, he's a friend of mine too. I meant the people around the disco ownership, the gofers." Curro was making it up as he went along and was unsurprisingly quite adept at it. "They're the ones trying to cut each other out of the picture."

"No shit. You've just reinvented the wheel. Drug gangs want to crowd each other out of the market. You don't know what you're talking about. Sorry, man, but that's the truth."

"Excuse me," said Dima, who'd been silent until now. "Inspector, I'm just as interested in seeing Gagarin go down as you are. I don't know how important he is in the drugs scene here, but in Moscow he was a major player and from what I gather he probably is here too. I've known Vasili for a long time. He's usually a lone wolf, although he seems to be in Madrid to do Gagarin's bidding. Vasili and I hung out last month at the Budax and from what I've heard from other bouncers—also Russians—I think he was sounding them out to set up a drug pushing operation on the side. Look, give me some breathing space and I promise to help you lock up Gagarin for good. And let the Martinez boys go. I agree, they know more than they're letting on, but they're comfortable around me. They'll let their guard down, I'll get something out of them. They look up to me from having seen my K-1 matches on TV."

Curro and Carlos glanced at each other. "Well well, this kid's got balls," said Carlos. "I'll give you that. You may even be right. But no way am I turning those two loose."

"Carlos, I think Dima's onto something. Give us a chance. Think of Eugenia, too. It may be the only way we can get a lead on her whereabouts. I mean, no one really has any clues at this point, we just have good reason to believe Gagarin's got her."

"You're outta your minds, both of you. You're gonna get me in deep shit. My team's supposed to turn the Scorpion's Tail inside out tomorrow and if we find the stash after I've already let those two go, how'm I gonna look?"

"I've got a feeling you won't find anything."

"Hell, I hope not!"

For the sake of appearances, Curro called in his lawyer to demand that, in view of the fact that no charges had been filed (the coke Andy and Tarek had been carrying having mysteriously disappeared from the evidence room), his new clients, the Martinezes, be released immediately. The Inspector had no choice but oblige, and after they'd all thanked the lawyer for his diligence, Curro told the Martinez brothers to come back to his place for a chat. At first they weren't having it: they were tired, they hadn't gotten any sleep, and they were worried about the shape their bar might be in. Dima knew he was better at handling these kind of people than Curro was and decided it was time for him to step in.

"You're coming with us, and that's that. We need to talk, and you wouldn't be out at all if it weren't for Curro. Tarek can drive you over. The Inspector was gonna keep you two under lock and key until you gave him enough to nail Gagarin. Well, the two of us have our own beef with him."

"So? None of our business," snapped Tony.

"Maybe not, but that hundred grams of blow that magically disappeared is definitely your business. Voilà," said Curro, tossing to Tony the two baggies he'd had in his pocket. "And that other pound of coke you've hidden somewhere in the Scorpion's Tail is your business. Add all this up, I think it's enough to send you two to prison for quite a while. Now, is *that* any of *my* business?"

"Dude, you a cop or what? You sure don't look like one," said Andy.

"No, I'm not a cop. But the Inspector and I go way back. He's after Gagarin – and so are we, for different reasons. I convinced—*we* convinced—him to turn you loose and look the other way because you were going to help us help him put Gagarin away. I hope we did the right thing; otherwise, you may walk away from this one but Inspector Jiménez is going to be so pissed off that the sooner or later—my money would be on sooner – he'll find a way to lock you two up and throw away the key."

"All right, all right," said Tony. "What do you want us to do?"

"First of all, tell me something," Dima broke in. "The other night, before I went to Ganvino, your Porsche followed me through half of Madrid. Why?"

"Dude, it wasn't us!" said Andy defensively. "You trippin' or what? You saw me as soon as you got there, workin' the door. And Tony was totally wasted, he wouldn't even have been able to find the fuckin' car keys, let alone follow anyone anywhere. So, like, no way was it us. Anyway, why would we follow you at all?"

"That's what I'd like to know. Because it was definitely your car."

A shout went out for Tarek, who had been chilling in another room, uncharacteristically quiet and retiring since Curro and Dima had begun calling the shots. "Hey, Tarek, you know anything about this? You were on the door too. You see anything?"

"I, yes," the ex-mercenary began, speaking sheepishly to his bosses. "I see Vasili come back with your car. He say he make delivery you sent him on."

"What? Bullshit," said Andy. "We do make, uh, home deliveries for some of our best customers," he said with a shrug, "but it's always Tony or me, or lately Tarek—we trust him enough for that—but no way were we gonna send Vasili out on a delivery round. We don't know him that well. Now as for the car keys, we leave 'em behind the bar, anyone could've borrowed 'em."

"So you didn't notice that Vasili and the car weren't around?"

"No, I mean, the car's always parked out front when we're not using it, and if one our guys wants to borrow it, he can, if he asks first. But Vasili'd never driven it, much less without asking. Vasili's not part of our crew, man. And he never spends the whole night around the disco. He works directly for Gagarin, who not only owns the disco, he also supplies our product line—"

"Dammit, Andy, enough already with the details," snapped Tony.

"Don't you see they got it all figured out anyway? Besides, I tell you what—I damn sure trust Dima and his pal here, who's already done us one helluva big favor, more than that two-faced playa Vasili."

"What do you mean, 'two-faced'?" asked Curro.

"Something about him's just not right. Always on his own, never chillin' with anyone. Lotta smiles, lotta back-slappin', but he's not foolin' me. He's a fake. He's just hangin' around to look over our shoulders. Besides, he's been askin' a lot of questions. Don't forget, we've been in this biz for a long time, a lotta people know us.

Tarek's heard that Vasili was goin' around checkin' up on us: do we handle a lotta merchandise, do we front for other wholesalers? Stuff like that."

"Gee, sounds as if someone doesn't trust you."

"It happens," Andy said with another shrug. "We're not afraid. Never mind all that talk about the Russians, we're on our home turf."

"One question," said Curro, hesitantly. "Did you two by any chance 'lose' some of Gagarin's goods, or maybe some of his money?"

"Whoa, whoa, whoa," Tony stood up, followed by his brother and Dima. "What the fuck, man? Who you think you are?"

"Cool it, Tony." Curro remained seated and unperturbed. "We're here to talk about solutions. You two are in trouble with the cops and, worst-case scenario, also with the Russians," he said, stressing the latter as the more dangerous of the two. "We're worried about a friend of ours, Eugenia Osorio, the model. She's disappeared. We think Gagarin's got her."

"What makes you think that?"

"We crossed swords in Moscow and he's a complete son of a bitch," said Dima. "He's after me, I'm after him. But that's my problem. What really worries us is, we think he took Eugenia to send me a message. Whoever has her, they still haven't gotten in touch with her family, the police, or with us."

"To me Eugenia's like my little sister," said Curro. "I've known her since she was a baby. But right now we don't even know where to start looking. Have you heard anything? Do you know anything else about Gagarin?"

"Naw, man, just word of mouth," said Andy.

"Vasili's been our go-between lately—he delivers the goods, he sends word back up the line. Before him, it was somebody else. Gagarin doesn't get involved personally at our level."

"Well, if you don't deal with him directly and the one running things for him is Vasili, that solves the mystery of the tip-off. Where'd you get that pound of blow? Who else knew you were keeping it at the Scorpion's Tail?"

The two brothers huddled together briefly, and Tony finally decided to trust the odd couple.

"Vasili gave it to us. He said we had Gagarin's go-ahead to 'grow emerging markets,' as he put it."

"Christ, you guys really aren't too bright, are you?" Curro blurted out. "I'm sorry, but it's obvious that you two have been played. Vasili wants exclusive control over Gagarin's distribution for the entire city and he wanted you two out of the way. He starts by telling Gagarin you two have kept merchandise that belongs to him without paying for it; then, just to finish things off, tips the police off to make sure you guys are out of circulation for a long time. Leaves both of you in the pen with your former employer only too happy to be rid of you. Don't you see? I mean, if the only people who were in on all aspects of this were you and Vasili, well..."

"Okay, I get you. Vasili was tryin' to fuck us over big time," said Andy quietly. He was nervous, fidgety. "Son of a bitch! If I ever get my hands on him..."

"You ought to try to get to Gagarin first. Tell him the truth, make him see that Vasili was trying to play him too. I don't think he'll be too amused, and Vasili's reputation isn't exactly spotless to begin with—right,

Dima?" He nodded. "You can outflank Vasili if you move quickly enough."

"And just where are we supposed to find Mr. Fucking Gagarin?" asked Tony.

"Marbella. I hear he has this huge house—no, a mansion, really," Curro said with a sneer. "And a yacht in the port. Puerto Banús."

"And how do we recognize him? What's he look like?"

"He's one fat bastard, I can tell you that," said Curro.

"Great, you just described half the people in Russia," Andy snickered. "Well, with exceptions. Like Dima here, the lean mean killin' machine."

Before going their separate ways they shook hands, promising to keep in touch as each group approached its goals from different angles. Considering the topics they'd been discussing and the way it had started out, all of them ended up feeling a surprising degree of camaraderie.

In the hallway outside Curro's, as Dima stood next to Tony and Tarek while they waited for the elevator, Andy turned to Curro and said "Dude, I *know* you. I can't remember where from, but I know we've met before. You remember? Don't I ring a bell?"

"Sorry, Andy, I'm afraid not. If I'd met you, I'd remember. I mean, who could forget a pair of guns like these?" he said, squeezing one of the young fighter's biceps with mischievous twinkle in his eye.

After the elevator doors closed, it suddenly dawned on Andy and he burst out laughing. "I´ll be dammed if it isn´t... Now I remember," he said. "Fucking A!"

CHAPTER XII

Darkness on all sides. And a terrifying sensation of narrowness. Fortunately, Eugenia's perception was still quite significantly dulled, which at first allowed her to take stock of her surroundings with a drowsy detachment. When she was a teenager the onset of claustrophobia had become serious enough to require psychiatric treatment. She'd long since thought she had it licked; these days she could step into an elevator and ride up forty floors in any building in New York without a second thought.

But now, as she tried to stretch her arms and they butted up against the cramped reality of her tiny enclosure, panic gripped her all over again, a panic greater than any she ever remembered. Trapped! She couldn't breathe, she started to pant, it was as if there were no air around her. She felt like she was drowning. Self-control abandoned, she started pounding on the surfaces that trapped her. The blows sounded metallic, like some sort of percussion. She gathered she was in the trunk of a car. Her mind spun madly out of control, she couldn't form a single rational thought or begin to calm down. *I want to die,* she screamed in her head.

All at once a glaring light blinded her, from a flashlight it seemed, and she heard as if from far away a sound, the tone of reproach. The light filled her eyes: she was trying, clumsily, to cover them when she felt something cold that dissipated any will to resist.

Some time later she awoke again, lurching upright from the mattress she'd been lying on, gasping for breath. The feeling of having been trapped in a tiny space still had her in its grip and her senses were slow to assimilate the change in her surroundings. Gradually, as the mist lifted from her thoughts, she understood what had happened She didn't know where she'd been taken since being kidnapped in Madrid. At a glance she realized the nature of her prison: a cabin on a yacht. She sprang towards the door and tried the knob: no luck. She was locked in. Why? What was she doing there? It had to be a mistake. It certainly couldn't be any of her friends' idea of a joke, any of them would know that this was way, *way* over the top. She wanted to scream for help, but something told her that wasn't the best idea. Instead she moved over to the porthole and looked out.

Marbella! Specifically, its marina, Puerto Banús. After so many summers at her parents' place in Guadalmina, she knew the whole area like the back of her hand. She tried to pry the window open but there was no handle or lever. She tried hitting it but soon realized it was reinforced glass, unusually thick. Although the cabin was wide enough to feel comfortable, mercifully with a window and daylight, her panic at being locked in started to return. She could feel the self-control over her phobia that had taken her years to develop crumbling. At last she began pounding on the door, screaming, crying, rage mixing with tears of fear.

Eventually she caught sight of herself in the mirror of the cabin's bathroom. A thread of blood ran down her face from a cut along her cheek. Nothing serious. She washed her face, moistening her hair too., but not daring to drink from the tap. Then she went to the minibar in the room, downing a bottle of water all at once. In an instant her nervousness returned, she began pacing back and forth, and then she exploded again. More shouts, more banging on the door and window, eventually she even began throwing things... Her rage went unanswered. She seemed to have been left alone on the yacht, which, judging from the size of the one next and the space between the slips, must be a pretty large one.

Exhausted, and on some level finally convinced of the uselessness of her fury, she sank to the bed, tired enough to calm down and assess her situation. She looked at her watch: 4:30 PM, Monday the 13th. May 13! She'd been out for a whole day.

In her mind she tried to review everything that had happened, if only to make some sense of her situation. After that unpleasant exchange with Curro, during which she'd received no support at all from Dima—*jerk!* —she'd boarded the first cab she found, intending to cool off at her penthouse. She was convinced that sooner or later Curro would come to her and apologize. Although, maybe not. Deep down she knew she'd gone too far when it came to Curro and his devotion to Trasto. It was the one, the only, subject that was off-limits with her friend and she should have chosen her words carefully. Trasto. What was she thinking? Besides, she'd lied out of spite. She knew, they all did, that Curro had truly felt—still did—deep, irrational love for his dog. But neither of them were much given to holding grudges. They'd make up, somehow, and everything would go back to the way it had been, with Dima at their side.

"Stop here, please," she'd told the cabbie upon spotting the frankly provocative window display at the Mallorca deli on Velázquez. She got out of the cab at the nearest corner, walking back to the shop; on the sidewalk she'd bumped into her friend Piluca Silva on her way back home loaded with treats for whiling away a Sunday afternoon. She'd stopped just long enough to be congratulated on that hunky new boyfriend everyone was talking about—she smiled as she walked away; *News always travels fast in Madrid,* she thought. In Mallorca, Eugenia took on sumptuous provisions for an evening on the couch in front of the TV: Nadal was into the final of the Monte Carlo Masters and she didn't want to miss a minute. Eugenia found him charming. They'd met years ago in Miami just before he'd served notice of his awesome talent to the world, nearly beating Roger Federer who at that time had been cloaked in an aura of invincibility. She'd gotten along well with the athlete; they'd even done an ad campaign together for a Spanish fashion label now wildly popular in America. Who was Nadal playing? She couldn't remember and didn't really care. Nadal was a safe bet.

She decided to walk the rest of the way home, the fresh air would do her good. She stopped at a newsstand for the Sunday papers: she scooped up the *ABC*, the *El Mundo* and *El País*; she loved the weekend sections. She had a sudden, fleeting urge to call Curro but she dismissed it. Let him call; after all he was the one who had told her to get lost, while Dima stood by and said nothing.

"Eugenia! Hi, you remember me?" A tall, heavyset guy stood before her, a young woman at his side. He vaguely registered as Eastern European, and for a moment she thought he might have had her mixed up with someone else.

"Actually, no, sorry," she said, continuing on her way. She wasn't in the mood for any nonsense. She was looking forward to getting home and relaxing on the couch, watching Nadal trounce whoever he was playing and waiting for an apologetic phone call from Curro. Then she stopped and turned. "Do I know you?"

"Yes, man! I pals with Dima. I Vasili." *And I'm Cheetah,* she thought sarcastically, looking at this orangutan of a man. But upon hearing Dima's name she stopped for a moment and got a better look at the Russian and his sidekick. Suddenly her supermodel side took over as she critically evaluated the couple standing before her. *What a pair,* she thought. The guy was as tall as Dima but any resemblance ended there. He wasn't nearly as handsome nor as graceful as Dima. His clothes—*Kitsch Sunday Best*, Eugenia decided. White pants too tight for his bulging legs, a white shirt struggling to contain his beefy trunk, white patent leather loafers that looked at least a size too small for his huge feet. The brunette was no less of a sight; curvy and six-feet tall but towering on huge white heels, dressed to match her guy except for her nails and lips, both a garish shade of red.

"Oh, *right*," she half remembered. "Basilio, Dima's friend from Moscow."

"Vasili, I Vasili. And this Sonia, my girlfriend." Sonia leaned forward as if to kiss Eugenia's cheek, a move Eugenia aborted with an outstretched hand.

"Pleased to meet you, Basilio and Sonia," she said, then kept walking. So far it hadn't exactly been a great day and she didn't feel the least bit like socializing. "Bye, Basilio, bye Sonia. Enjoy your Sunday."

The big Russian sprinted up beside her, cutting her off. "I tell you, I Vasili!"

"Basilio, Vasili, whatever. Do I look like I care? Look, I'm in a hurry. Excuse me!" she said, stepping to one side so she could keep going.

"Who you think you are, rich bitch?" said Sonia, who had grabbed Eugenia's forearm. "You think you better than us, you fucking whore?"

Eugenia dealt the foul-mouthed Russian a loud slap. Sonia screamed and Eugenia, sure that retribution would follow in short order, began sprinting down the sidewalk towards her apartment. *God, I wish Dima were around now!* she thought.

Eugenia's long agile legs carried her away quickly. Just her luck—no one on the streets. Sunday afternoons were quiet in the Salamanca district and there were few passersby. After helping his girlfriend up, Vasili began charging after Eugenia. She turned off Velázquez onto Diego de León, her building almost within sight. For his bulk the Russian was surprisingly fast, though, and it wasn't the first time he'd chased someone. Eugenia realized she wasn't going to make it to her front door and desperately changed course for Serrano, where there was always a sizable Spanish police presence standing guard on the sidewalk in front of the U.S. Embassy. She picked up speed, firmly convinced she would reach her new goal, and then she slipped in dogshit.

Filthy fucking hicks! Eugenia thought. She didn't fall, but the effort to steady herself cost her vital seconds and before she knew it, Vasili had roughly grabbed hold of her. Eugenia tried to shout for help, but Vasili had one hairy paw firmly over her mouth.

A car screeched to a halt on the sidewalk next to the Russian. Sonia leaned away from the steering wheel and threw open the rear door: Vasili shoved Eugenia into the back seat like a sack of potatoes and then piled in on top of her. Without a single witness, the car had sped off.

***

That was the last thing Eugenia could remember clearly. The Russians must have had something in the car to knock her out with. She could vaguely remember having been semi-conscious for a few minutes, the claustrophobia that had gripped her—she shivered as the memory came back—and then they must have given her drugs again. They'd moved her at night, she was sure of that—she remembered a blinding light in her eyes when she'd briefly woken up.

And that was it. *Now what do Basilio and that slut want me for? I met him the same night I met Dima. What could Dima have to do with this?*

She got off the bed and went back to the porthole,

where she could see the early evening crowd building up along the marina's fashionable waterfront. Puerto Banús—so many people strolling along without a care in the world, so close to her. She tried to attract someone's attention, waving frantically behind the porthole; maybe the glass was tinted. At any rate, no one seemed to notice her. Unfortunately her cabin was on the side of the yacht furthest from the gangway to the jetty. It was no use. She slumped back down on the bed.

She was stunned to spot, in one corner of the room, the Loewe handbag she'd been carrying, which someone had carelessly tossed down on the floor. She grabbed it and shook its contents onto the bedspread. Coins, keys, pens, makeup, all the useless junk she couldn't get by without, and her cell phone! She couldn't believe her luck. The battery was almost gone, but she got a signal. At once she dialed 091 for the police: a recording. Shit! What was that other number? She'd never been in a situation like this before, her nerves were getting the better of her. 012? 111? No, 112! That's it! She was trembling, panicked by the idea that salvation might be so close but slip out of her reach. She dialed. A robot voice again reminding her that this number was only for emergencies and to hang up if she was calling for any other reason. She was shaking like a leaf by the time an actual person spoke to her.

"112, what's your emergency?"

"Someone'sss taken me hossstage; I need the policccce pleasssse." Lately, the affectation Eugenia had begun employing as a token of her freedom to be as inelegant as she wished had become the tail that wagged the dog; with increasing frequency it appeared unbidden. The operator had been in dispatch long enough to have heard pretty much everything from the life-threatening to the mundane.

"You want the police? Where are you?"

"Yess, I need the policcce pleasssse. Someone help me, I'm so scared!"

The operator's patience was wearing thin. She'd already had one crank caller that afternoon. "Miss, tell me exactly what's wrong."

"Passssss me the policccce pleasssse!" Eugenia trembled, unable to bring herself under control.

"Look, this is an emergency line. You should be ashamed of yourself." And with that, the operator hung up.

"Idiot!" Eugenia shouted. She steadied herself, biting her tongue, and when she was sure she had recovered control of her speech, she dialed 112 again.

"Operator, what's your emergency?" This time it was a man, with a South American accent.

"I've been kidnapped in Puerto Banús, I'm on a yacht, please give me the police." She gritted her teeth, determined not to lose control again.

"Patching you through, please hold."

"Miss? Police dispatch desk. I understand you're calling from Puerto Banús and you've been kidnapped?"

"Officer, I'm Eugenia—"

The door burst open. For a split second Eugenia thought of trying to hide the phone in her clothes, but it was no use, they'd seen it. Sonia, two burly thugs in tow, grabbed the phone out of her hand and smashed it on the floor. "You really believe we are so stupid? See those things in the corner near ceiling? Cameras and microphones. For fun we let you get just close enough to think you'll actually get away with it, we watch and hear everything. 'Policcccce Pleasssse'. Miss Model is a fucking wack job, heheheh—"

Sonia couldn't finish snickering because of how quickly Eugenia, surprising even herself, lunged forward, reached around and pulled Sonia's head backwards by her hair, felling her with a deft karate chop from her other hand. As Sonia went down Eugenia leapt astride her and began bating her with the kind of passion only pure hate could fuel. The two thugs looked at each other, disinclined to intervene for now; they didn't like the boss's girlfriend and the didn't mind seeing her taken down a notch or two. If and when they were really needed, they would act; otherwise, they could always say they hadn't stepped in sooner because Sonia knew how to take care of herself and they'd thought she'd prefer to. Sonia was nearly as tall as Eugenia, but with a huskier build. She was determined to have the upper hand, Eugenia was determined not to give in. Eugenia had Sonia right where she wanted her—pinned to the ground while Eugenia beat her remorselessly.

She knew the fun was over as soon as she saw Vasili in the door way. He shoved the two thugs aside roughly, muttering something in Russian, and with a single move picked Eugenia up and threw her backwards against the wall, which she hit with such force that she nearly passed out. The wind knocked out of her, she lingered on the floor for an instant, all the time Sonia needed to spring to her feet and kick her in the face. Sonia punched, kicked, and scratched until

Vasili judged that the real winner of that particular hand-to-hand combat was in as bad a shape as the woman she'd bested.

The remains of the phone cluttered the floor, having been crushed underfoot during the struggle. The officer had heard just enough to make him send a patrol car to Puerto Banús so local cops could take look around.

CHAPTER XIII

Curro and Dima spent several days trying to develop leads from friends and contacts in Spain and Russia, days when there was no news on Eugenia and during which Inspector Jiménez wasn't returning their phone calls. They came up empty. Dima's Moscow contacts said that Gagarin was watching his step: he hadn't shown his face around there and probably wouldn't as long as the Kasparov brothers were still pissed off at him. Gagarin was believed to be holed up at his Marbella mansion. Curro and Dima had also paid a courtesy visit to Eugenia's parents, who didn't really want any visitors and were still coming to terms with the shock of her disappearance. Curro's relationship with the couple was merely formal, nothing like the connection he'd always shared with Aunt Matilde, who was nearly the same age as he was. Ignacio Osorio was the eldest son of the previous Duke's first marriage, and Curro had never gotten along particularly well with him. Curro thought Ignacio was awfully arrogant for such a pinhead, and found Sonsoles' *nouveau riche* ostentatiousness tacky and tasteless. But good manners required that the courtesy call be paid, and so it was. Curro was sorry not to see the younger Osorio daughter,

Fabiola; she had decided to stay on in Paris owing to academic commitments. She always treated Curro like a brother, but he was sure she'd made the right decision by staying at school.

Since Eugenia had been kidnapped, Curro was sleeping even worse than usual. He'd spent part of those long insomnia-ridden nights secretly exploring his comrade's curvy form, inch by inch, with Dima's rather loud snores providing welcome confirmation that he remained oblivious in deep slumber. These forays never failed to turn him on, and he always ended up rubbing one out. Then one morning, as dawn took possession of the room, he decided it was time to make his move. Enough with the waiting! It had gone on for far too long. He grabbed Dima from behind, rubbing himself against the Russian's back and buttocks. He was hard in no time, and clung more tightly to his buddy's ripped form. Curro boldly pressed on, exploring every hidden aspect of Dima's warm anatomy, till he came to an unexpected discovery: Dima had a hard-on too!

"What the—? Knock it off, you fag!" spat Dima before jumping out of the bed they'd shared so many times. Dima stood glaring at Curro, hands on his hips. "Eugenia was right, you *are* gay! If it wasn't for... don't know, I'd beat the shit of you. You took advantage of me!" he shouted, moving menacingly towards Curro.

"Well, go ahead then, beat me up if you want," said Curro, a response Dima hadn't expected and which momentarily left him even more off-balance.

"You're gay! And I've been sleeping next to you all this time!"

"Dima…" Curro knew he had to choose his words carefully, he didn't want to offend him. He knew how sharp Dima was with his hands and knew that he was on edge because of everything that had happened lately, as he himself was. "Dima, if I was cradling you while we slept it was because you were crying out for affection, albeit not in words. I can hear you having nightmares so often. That's why we started sleeping together, isn't it? You felt safer and even I got a better night's sleep."

"Some affection, you've been copping a feel every time I dozed off!"

"No, no, not at all. This was the first time," replied Curro, looking amused.

"Yeah, right. Sure, you fruit!" Dima took a step closer.

"Man, how can you say that? Look at yourself!" Curro said, pointing to Dima's underwear. "You've got a woody!"

"Son of a bitch! How dare you!" Before Curro knew it, Dima had taken a swing that knocked Curro clear out of bed.

The punch landed him on a settee next to the wall. "Animal," wailed Curro, hamming it up. "You nearly took my head off!"

Dima instantly regretted his temper. "Jeez, Curro. I'm sorry, but don't exaggerate, it's not that bad."

"Maybe not for you, dumbass,"

"Stop whining, I'm the one who got groped, remember?" Dima said irritably. "I ought to have you charged with sexual harassment," he added, with an odd and forced expression that may have been intended to look like a smile.

"And I oughta have you run in for domestic violence," Curro replied as he stood up. "Dima, I'm sorry. But please, get your head out of the clouds. Of course I'm gay! Why the hell else would I bring you home, get involved in all these headaches of yours, *and* run the risk of ending up six feet under?" He saw the disappointment on Dima's face and changed his tone. "Don't get me wrong, I don't regret a minute of it. I'm proud to have been able to help you. And you've brought new meaning to my life. When you came along, I was fed up with everything. That's changed, thanks to you. But I'm not going to lie to you. I like you a lot," he said openly to Dima's face. "Matter of fact, you know what? I think I love you," he lied, not knowing quite why.

"Oh, spare me the act," said Dima, rolling his eyes. "Like Eugenia said, you don't love anyone, you're incapable of that. And as for you being gay? Truth is, part of me suspected as much, but I didn't want to see it. I guess I thought if I admitted the truth our friendship would somehow have to end." He moved towards Curro and offered a conciliatory hug. "Hey, no groping, though," he warned Curro.

"Kiss me," said Curro, wanting to see just how far he could go. When he saw the surprise on Dima's face, he went on. "What do you care? You guys kiss each each other in Russia all the time. Pretend I'm your cousin," he said, tiptoeing to within an inch from Dima's lips while gently pressing the Russian's face towards him.

"On my face," Dima muttered, offering a cheek.

"On the lips, Russian style. Or even better yet, how about a French kiss?"

"French?"

"Yeah, you know. Tongue."

Dima's shove sent Curro several feet backwards, but at least he came over to help him back up. He put his hands beneath Curro's armpits, raised him up till Curro was eye-to-eye with him, and quickly gave him a kiss, "Russian style." Curro didn't want to push things with Dima any further, he'd already tested him more than enough, but he couldn't keep his hand from imperceptibly grazing his confused friend's crotch. He *still* had a hard-on!

***

Dmitri Denissov had a lot of questions. He'd had his doubts about Curro's sexual orientation, but had simply assumed his friend couldn't possibly be gay. In Russia he'd never seen a gay man like Curro, a regular guy he could walk down the street with without feeling embarassed. When he'd been with the Special Ops Unit, one of the other guys in the unit, a strong, handsome kid, had been discovered one night in a bar in drag as a cabaret *artiste*. He'd had a hard time coming to terms with seeing a guy he'd been out drinking with, a guy he'd *showered* with so many times in the barracks, dressed up like that. Once his secret was out the guys ganged up on him and beat him to a pulp and then the commanding officer expelled him from the unit; his military career was over. The past few years, more and more gays had been out campaigning for equal rights. Dima felt it sometimes degenerated into the grotesque—limp-wristed queers parading through the streets trying to attract attention. Here in Spain it was different; gays seemed to act naturally and were treated normally by most people, without resorting to public spectacles that damaged their own credibility—save for a few exceptions he'd seen, which confirmed the rule. From the beginning Curro had seemed to him like a regular guy, a mature friend he could confide in, a guy who even exuded a feeling of security: by his side, Dima felt protected. A man's man, from head to toe. All the more reason why Dima wanted Curro to explain how he'd become who he was. Curro seemed comfortable in his skin. Dima wanted to know how that had come about.

Curro had gone for a shower. He was singing Spanish songs Dima had never heard before. They must have been hits from those years when Curro had been out every night, the Madrid *movida* scene of his bygone youth. In his mind Dima went over the questions he wanted to ask Curro. He didn't want to sacrifice the friendship, but there were some things he needed cleared up, and he needed to satisfy his own morbid curiosity about Curro's initiation into the gay world.

"Curro!" he shouted, once the off-key singing and the monotonous sound of the water jet had stopped. "Come on out to the terrace. I've made toast and coffee."

"Thanks! I'll be right out," Curro answered. He appreciated the gesture. Jesús, his valet, was still on vacation and Curro decided to call and tell him to take some more time off. He trusted Jesús completely but he didn't really want an extra pair of eyes around the house now, things being what they were. More importantly, he didn't want Jesús drawn into the complex web that linked them, Eugenia, the Russian, and all the other extraordinary happenings.

They settled in on the terrace, and Curro made short work of his favorite breakfast: orange juice, toast with olive oil on it, and coffee. He hadn't slept well but that wasn't hurting his appetite. Dima watched him quietly, not eating a bite.

"Don't you want any?"

"I'm not hungry."

"It's not my fault, is it? I hope it wasn't my hugs. Come on over here, have a seat," said Curro, patting the empty chair at his side.

"Gimme a break, Curro, that's getting a little old."

"Oh no it's not. I'll be having *you* for breakfast, with a side order of fries—just you wait and see."

"Dude, give it a rest. Listen, tell me about your first time with a guy, how you got into... his. I mean, your *first* first time was with a girl, right?"

"Hmm," Curro looked down pensively. "You really want to hear this? It's no big deal. Okay, there was one strange thing..." he said, his voice trailing off, unsure whether or not he should continue. "I've never told anyone about this, not even Eugenia. I've always been embarrassed, it's so intimate."

"I've told you my entire life."

"Fair point. Okay, here goes. You were right about the first time I got laid, it was a girl. I was a punk kid, all of fifteen. And it was awful. A whore. My dad took me, if you can believe it."

"Your dad? At that age?"

"Yep." Curro fell silent for a few seconds. "My

dad. I still despise him. He was one handsome son of a bitch, though."

"What are you talking about? I don't get it."

"You will. Listen: My dad spent most of the year traveling around, one place after another. My mom's the one who really raised me. She was the constant in my life, the one who was always there for me. I hardly have any memories of my dad, much less any photos. Till I hit thirteen. He was on one of his trips abroad, with this lover we later found out about." Curro stopped, smiling suddenly. "This is good, lemme tell you this part. She'd been a German spy stationed in Madrid during World War II—I don't know if you know this, but Spain was officially neutral. She was supposed to collect information about Franco and his inclinations with regard to the war. Anyway, once it was all over and all of her people had been rounded up and jailed in Germany, she stayed in Madrid. She'd hooked up with a famous aristocrat who supported Franco. This guy, he was a second cousin of my grandmother's, someone she saw from time to time— he died years later, flat broke and a bachelor, because as long as his mother lived she wouldn't have him marrying the ex-spy. Well, once Uncle Ricardo died, his former lover shows up one day demanding the deed to a home she said she'd inherited. My dad was out of town and my mom wouldn't even speak to her. Years later, when my dad died, we found out she'd seduced him and he'd promised the house to her, but when the estate went into probate, Villa Amelia still showed as being in our name. Turns out, my dad had given her this big stack of phony papers he said was a deed to the property, so he could screw her too!" Curro broke out laughing. "Poor bitch, she was afraid she was going to get evicted. My mom let her stay in the house till she died. Even invited her to tea once or twice. By the time I met her she was old, but still had amazing looks and this... bearing, know what I mean? Anyway, that's what my dad was like."

Dima laughed. "What a bastard. Sorry, I didn't mean—"

"Don't apologize, he was a bastard with a capital B."

"Anyway, tell me about how you got into guys."

"Enquiring minds want to know, eh? Come over here," said Curro, "sit next to me." This time, Dima did.

"As I was saying, when I turned thirteen my dad stayed home for a longer stretch than he usually did. Maybe he thought his position as head of the family required him to take certain steps he couldn't delegate to my mom. I remember it all like it was yesterday. It was winter—the kind of winter we used to have in Madrid, when we got two or three big snows a year and they'd last for days. I'd been skiing in Navacerrada with my classmates, and when I got home I ran a hot bath and jumped in. My dad came into the bedroom, calling my name. He saw lights on in the bathroom; the door was open and he just came right on in. I felt violated, like he'd overstepped a line no one had given him permission to cross. Well, he wanted to know if my masculinity was developing normally, if my foreskin retracted as it should. Can you imagine? On reflex I immediately covered myself with my hands, feeling more than a little bashful. He insisted, so I gave in—I thought, *Hey, this must be something dads are supposed to check.* So I stood up in the tub and showed him everything was in order. 'All right, that's the way I like it!' he said—he was beaming. 'You're a real stud, just like your old man. Look how strong I am,' he said, and started to undress. 'Look at these big hairy muscles,' he said. I didn't know what to do or say next. I'd sat back down in the tub, while he was showing off. I have to say, my dad was always an athlete, it must have been partly genetic, his muscles were unusual for that day and age. He'd boxed and he was still ripped. He finished taking of his clothes, all the while going on about how fit he was.

"Finally, he got in the tub with me, and it was more of the same. 'Here, touch these pipes,' he said, flexing his huge, perfectly shaped biceps. They looked as if they were carved in marble, like a Greek statue. A *hairy* Greek statue, heh heh—he always bragged about that too. I was so intimidated I didn't know how to react. I was scared but I touched his biceps, I admired his hairy, ripped chest, and then... I don't really remember but I think I got a hard-on. That's when my dad must have noticed something—he was out of the tub and my room like a streak, and I'll never forget the look of distaste on his face. It was an absurd, ridiculous situation, it never happened again. When I look back, I think he must have been drunk. I still don't understand it."

Dima sat there with a look of disbelief. "Fuck! Dude, I'm speechless. But that's not why you turned queer, is it? Sorry, I mean, gay."

"Hah, hah. Queer, queer. That word's fine with me, as long as it's not used with the intent to offend."

"Of course I don't want to offend you. You're my buddy—"

"Yeah, right. C'mere, come to your gay buddy," said Curro, openly provocative.

"Jeez, Curro, will you give it a rest! I don't know what's gotten into you."

Curro laughed. "You remind me—your attitude, your security in yourself—of my father. Or rather, the vague memory I have of him. We didn't have much to do with one another. Fourteen years after that he died, when I was a wild kid drinking Madrid down by the gulp."

"What did he die of?"

"Relax, we'll get there. Back to the story. As I was saying, our relationship was never particularly smooth—I was rebellious, he traveled non-stop. After that night in my bathtub, something changed. Radically. He started avoiding me, he spent more and more time on the road. But while I was still little, right after the bath incident, I started asking him to show me his muscles. He'd try to give me the runaround, but as you know," he reached for Dima's crotch, "I can be very persistent. Exasperating, even."

"Knock it off, will you? I don't want to have to punch you again."

"Whoa! Look at you, just as much of a macho, hairy-chested dude as my father. Hah, hah."

"I'm *not* hairy..."

"Ha, ha. No, you're not. Not the least bit," Curro said with a laugh.

"Aw, fuck. Curro! Can we please get back to your story?"

"Not that much to tell, really. Buff guys like you started turning me on." Once again he leaned in close to his friend. "Actually, some of the stuff I did was downright scandalous."

"Like?"

"Well, with the chauffeurs in the building where we lived. Almost all of our neighbors had mechanics who doubled as bodyguards. You can imagine... I felt up just about every one of them. And some of them let me!" Curro smiled. "Ah, the memories. When my dad took me to the whorehouse, it was a disaster, although I managed to rise to the occasion. But over the next few years, when he realized I wasn't hooking up with any of the girls in our circle—daughters of friends of his—I think he started to feel guilty, like my preferences were his fault, and he started spending more and more time away from home. I hardly ever saw him, he was always out with his buddies, his cheap sluts... And his lovers. There was one period when everything got better, the summer that I hooked up with this little French beauty, Dominique, in Marbella. I still remember her fondly."

"Did you fuck her?"

"Yes! You don't *know* how much fun I had that summer."

"I'm listening."

"See, I also flirted with her brother Pierre. I found him much more attractive than Dominique. It was just some petting, nothing else. It was all new to him, and I think he liked it but that in itself made him uncomfortable. I didn't push things, I didn't want any trouble. Tell you who I did score with, though—one of the waiters at the hotel. God, he was hot. It was a real turn-on, having this guy wait on you in the dining room, sitting next to your parents, and then secretly meeting him after work. It was like a comedy skit: out one door with Dominique, in through the other with...

What was his name? Ahh, who cares. It was an intense summer, I enjoyed it as much as any kid my age."

"How old were you?"

"Seventeen, maybe eighteen—no more. That must have been the last summer I spent with my parents—the whole summer, I mean. We always used to go to Torrelodones when it started getting hot in Madrid, around mid-June, and we'd stay there on and off till September, when we went to Marbella. Up in Torrelodones the temperatures can be ten or fifteen degrees lower than downtown Madrid. Anyway, after that year I traded Marbella for Ibiza, I'd spend at least one wild month there every summer. I've never enjoyed anyplace more. I get nostalgic just mentioning it. Ah, the memories..."

"So what happened to your relationship with your dad? Did it get any better?"

"Not really. I mean, even though we technically lived in the same house, I was hardly ever home, nor was he. We'd see each other at the office, where he oversaw the management of the family businesses. My mom kept nagging me to spend more time with him at the office so I could learn how everything worked, and I had just caved in and started doing so when he had the accident that killed him."

"He died in an accident?"

"Yep. He'd gone to Estoril, with that German lover I told you about; they were at the casino on the outskirts of Lisbon. He'd had too much to drink and insisted on driving back to the city. They tried to talk him out of it, but he wouldn't listen. He ran smack into a tree. We never heard all the details, my mother preferred not to know. Despite everything, she was still madly in love with him, and I think he loved her too, even though you wouldn't have thought so from the way he was living his life. The German woman had stayed behind at the casino, she was fed up with his benders. Later on, the times she visited us, we didn't talk about that trip."

"Hell of a story, man. I'm sorry. Did you find out anything else about, you know, the end? I mean, knowing you."

"Not really. I heard from our chauffeur—apparently Dad used to open up to him, he said Dad never really got over how I'd turned out, realizing he couldn't expect any heirs to carry on his name and the family fortune. Honestly, I didn't want to dig any deeper. Better to leave it at that, I thought. It didn't feel right, snooping around my father's death."

"What a shame. He sounds like an interesting guy."

"You know, now I'm sorry I never got to know him better. Truth is, he avoided me. I think he felt guilty because of that scene in the tub. I don't know, man. Life's like that. I wish we could have talked more, I wish he'd told me more about his younger life. He was an adventurer—sort of a Spanish Indiana Jones." Curro smiled bitterly.

***

Francisco Morante García could be considered a self-made man. Born in the mountains of Santander, he came from a proud gentry family that by then had no assets beyond honesty and arrogance. The younger of two brothers, he'd been studying Agricultural

Engineering when a visitor from overseas changed his life, and that of his whole family. Fermín Usher Smith—a born and bred Uruguayan, in spite of his surnames—arrived in Madrid on the last stop of a European sales trip, in the course of which he'd made a fortune selling vast quantities of beef wholesale throughout the Old Continent. Europe was hungry, and the Ushers of Uruguay were livestock farmers on a grand scale, owning hundreds of thousands of cattle.

It was the early '50s and Uruguay was still seen as the Switzerland of South America, enjoying economic buoyancy that would soon disappear. In Madrid the Uruguayan ambassador hosted a reception for Usher which was well attended by Madrid's polite society, the daughters of marriageable age gazing dreamily at the wealthy and exotic guest of honor. Among those making eyes at him had been Marimén Morante, Francisco's vivacious sister, then studying in Madrid. To everyone's surprise, Usher fell head over heels in love with Marimén and, after a very brief courtship, they were married. Spain ended up being the least profitable stop on his European tour from a business standpoint, but the Uruguayan went home with an attractive, ingenious wife who—once they'd recovered from their initial, understandable qualms—charmed her in-laws completely. Father, mother, and sister Usher had been delighted with Fermín's bride.

Once Marimén was settled in, hot on her heels came Francisco, who left college without a degree. Francisco immediately perceived the opportunities presented by the country and his sister's new family. Fermín Usher was a pleasure-seeker who didn't really care about anything except bedding whoever was fashionable that week. He traveled all the time, neglecting the family business to the considerable annoyance of his aged father, a methodical Englishman born to parents from the Old Country, whose son perplexed him utterly. Marimén soon realized that Fermín would never make her happy but, rather than mope about, she seized the reins of the business with the blessing of her father-in-law, who saw in the pretty Spaniard the dedication and capability lacking in his son. Marimén had studied accounting in Madrid, and now she found herself managing the Usher's business empire. And who better than her brother Paco to oversee the livestock and the land. It was hard at first, the rough cowboys and tenant farmers on the Ushers' land were used to dealing with the easily deceived Fermín: but Francisco didn't intimidate easily. When the head herder tried to humiliate Francisco in front of the ranch hands, Francisco rose to the challenge: they agreed to a duel, cowboy-style: bare-knuckle boxing. The herder was tough as nails and well over six-feet tall, but he hadn't perceived Paco's inner savage and that would cost him dearly. Francisco Morante was tall and strong, and well more muscular than average; but beyond that, he had balls and a burning desire to make the most of the chances Uruguay and his sister were offering him. The fight ended in no time, and from that day on it was quietly accepted that the Morantes were now at the helm of the Usher estates.

A twist of fate then gave the Morantes the final push needed to reach the top. The whole Usher family, Fermin included, used to travel to Europe every spring, a tradition popular among the well-to-do families in the Southern hemisphere. That year, Marimén and Francisco Morante would stay in Uruguay to run the estate. But fortune's whim sent a Titanic-sized iceberg into the path of the steamer carrying the Ushers from Buenos Aires to Lisbon: there were few survivors, none of the Ushers among them. As sole heir of the entire Usher fortune, Marimén found herself unexpectedly propelled to a prominent place in the world of international trade and finance.

The Morantes were clever and enterprising enough to sense that their adopted country was approaching the down side of the curve, and so they began seeking opportunities elsewhere. In the US, department stores were fast becoming consumers' destination of choice for one-stop shopping; the Morantes simply applied this idea to their native Spain, with excellent results. In Uruguay they'd leave behind vast land tracts and livestock holdings: but the country's political drift and economic decline, coupled with homesickness, made up their minds. Marimén went back to Santander and eventually married a prominent notary, whom she promptly retired. They spent a quiet life together, focused on their collections and on charity: and she also went into cattle ranching locally. Francisco, on the other hand, claimed his place among Spain's financial elite, organizing and financing an array of entrepreneurial ventures that would one day put him at the forefront of Spain's blossoming industrial sector. Along the way he met the captivating and cosmopolitan Concha Solloso, and she stole his heart.

***

Curro had always been guarded and reserved about his feelings and how to express them. He'd opened up to Dima like he never had to anyone before, and regretted it at once. Why did he have to talk so much? Why open his heart to such a recent acquaintance? Now he would feel more vulnerable. After this unexpected confessional, he excused himself and went for a drive in his convertible, not having any particular destination in mind. He ended up spending the day touring places emotionally significant to him. He visited the family crypt in Torrelodones, and prayed a rosary for his parents. His mother would really have appreciated the gesture. Later on, not really remembering how he'd gotten there, he found himself wandering along the well-trodden paths of the Casa de Campo parkland. Under cover of night and with the stars as his witness, Curro began sobbing uncontrollably. He returned home, found Dima had gone out, and took two sleeping pills as the opening volley in his nightly battle against insomnia.

CHAPTER XIV

Trasto! He'd dreamed of Trasto. At last. Ever since he'd died Curro had been yearning to see him. Not as a ghost suddenly popping out of thin air, or as an obsessive, imaginary hallucination. He had just wished he could somehow be with him again so that he could tell him how sorry he was.

Curro had sworn to the dog that he'd see him through his health problems, a promise he'd made with true conviction. They'd make it through this. Of course they would! The two of them, a team, like so many times before. Didn't Curro always have his way in the end? Well, this time, the most important time, he would too, he had thought. Yes. Trasto would return to the fields to chase rabbits, they'd resume their long walks together. But it wasn't meant to be. The tears came quietly, yet unstoppably. "Oh Trasto, I'm so sorry," he sobbed.

They'd tried everything. Curro had brought in Madrid's best vets, who'd tried all the latest treatments for neurological recovery. He'd even imported a magnetotherapy machine from Italy after hearing it might help; no dice. Then there were those special mushrooms harvested in Galicia, supposedly the last hope for patients in critical condition. There hadn't been much research into their effect on dogs, but they tried it anyway to no avail. The degenerative disease that had his beloved dog in its grip advanced a little more each day. Trasto's abilities slowly declined, leaving him exposed to new ailments that found their opportunity in his weakened immune system. It was such a hard decision in the end. He was clearly suffering, there was no hope of recovery—what to do? As he weighed the options, Curro came down time and again on the side of whatever diminished Trasto's dignity the least. And that's what he'd chosen. To bring to an end the suffering, to fend off the final and complete paralysis that the future had held in store for Trasto.

It had been a stimulating dream, one that restored his faith that he had in fact made the right choice. And how he'd needed that. It had been a brief yet liberating moment, to feel himself once again strolling alongside his dog with the serenity that routine brings. Trasto darted back and forth, cheerfully, with as much vitality as ever. Far away, then nearby, but always aware of his master's location. Just like so many times before.

***

A muffled *thump* roused him out of his pleasant reverie, dragging him back to the real world. He turned and looked at the other side of the bed, which—for the first time in quite a while—was empty. He heard another *thump*, louder this time, on the other side of the penthouse. He almost called out Dima's name, but something made him hold back. He checked the clock—just past 4:30 AM. Dima had been sleeping much more soundly the past few weeks, so it seemed odd that he'd be awake so early. Not to mention making so much noise.

When he walked out of his bedroom he noticed that outside, at the other end of the terrace, the scaffolding around the penthouse next door—undergoing refurbishment—had come loose, part of it dangling onto his terrace. Something was wrong. He started in the direction the noise was coming from, then turned around and slipped into the kitchen for a knife. He grabbed the longest one, the one he used to thinly slice Spanish Serrano ham. Then he stepped out onto the terrace and soundlessly crept in the direction of the noise.

Through the dining room window, Curro caught sight of Dima struggling as three large figures held him against the wall. Curro felt a sudden rush as he tried to process the situation. What to do? Those guys looked like pros, he knew he wouldn't stand a chance with the ham knife. He thought of the Viking 446 Dima had lifted from Vasili. Could it still be in his bedroom, in the drawer they'd hidden it in when he'd first brought it home? Curro quietly raced back for it, but no luck—the gun wasn't there. Ever since what had happened to Eugenia, the gun had practically become an appendage of Dima, who took it with him everywhere. How about the guest room? Curro crept in, rifled through the drawers and the closet: nothing. He heard footsteps and ducked into the bathroom. The creaky parquet portended the approach of Russian voices, getting closer by the second. Just in the nick of time, through the crack between the door and its frame, Curro saw them coming. One of the Russians was coming right for his hiding place. Curro squeezed into the shower, which was separated from the adjoining tub by a pane of frosted glass from which hung a thick bath towel on a peg; this partly concealed Curro. He saw the thug's reflection in the mirror over the sink. *God, what do they* feed *these guys? They're* all *giants.* The newcomer washed his face and leaned in close to the mirror, checking the bruises left by Dima before he'd been overpowered. His nose was bleeding and he cursed in Russian before spitting out two yellow, blood-flecked teeth. When he looked back up, the mirror revealed Curro's presence. A chill ran through Curro as he saw the Russian's gaze meet his own in the mirror. The thug spun around and grabbed him by the throat, squeezing, breaking into a broad smile: *Sadistic bastard enjoys his job,* thought Curro, before his head started to spin and he moved towards unconsciousness. His arms were limp, the gap-toothed smile and stinking breath seemed certain to be the last sensory experience of his life. "You die now!" the killer growled. And then Curro, fading fast, discovered that the ham knife was still in his hand and somehow, as if guided from without, his arm sank the blade as deep into the Russian's neck as he could.

Blood spurted from the thug who kept his hold on Curro's neck even as the grin became a frozen grimace. "Let go of me, asshole!" Curro snarled, as he pulled the blade back out only to sink it into the Russian once again. He broke free and made for the bedroom door, but tripped and fell, knocking over the nightstand. As the contents of its upended drawer fell to the carpet, Curro spotted a shining barrel. The Viking! *Shit! Empty.*

The ruckus had alerted the other two assailants, who dragged Dima down the hallway, his hands tied behind his back. Curro went back into the bathroom, exiting onto the terrace through the back door. He would have to try to gain an advantage from his greater knowledge of the apartment's layout. It was a big place with a terrace that went all the way around it. For a moment he considered escape, going for help, but he'd be jeopardizing Dima's life even if he did manage to get away, and his own too if he didn't.

Given the crisis at hand and his chance to rescue his friend, Curro suddenly felt more alive than he had in memory. He'd just killed a man, and nothing in that moment, he felt, could stop him from killing two more if it meant saving Dima. He was prepared to do whatever was called for. What was there for him to lose at this point when already he had lost so much?

He went all the way around the penthouse on the terrace and in the living room next to his study he poured himself a Chivas on the rocks. Not even those two goons down the hall could rattle Curro. He savored the drink for a moment. Where did Dima keep ammo for the Viking? He had no idea and there was no time to look for it.

Before heading back in the direction of the Russians, Curro decided to put on a María Callas CD at full blast, which would boom through the whole apartment and mask any sounds he might make.

At the same time, it would attract the attention of police on duty guarding nearby embassies. The walls began vibrating to the sound of *Un bel dì vedremo*. Then, he reached into the little compartment that concealed the master switch for all of his lighting and plunged the penthouse into absolute darkness.

Curro felt enboldened like never before,

bordering on delirium as he braced for the fight to come. "Come and get it, punks!" he shouted. He stepped into his study where he remembered to pick up a walking stick that had once belonged to his dad; it concealed a razor-sharp blade long enough to have been used for fencing. Curro, of course, had other ideas. Serenely, arrogantly even, holding his saber the way he imagined a captain of the Spanish infantry of old would have, he headed off in search of his prey. And that's how he saw them; hitmen who had broken into his home, beaten his friend, and therefore deserved whatever was coming.

He felt more than found his way to the guest room, avoiding the terrace this time. Holding the sword-cane out before him, he entered the darkened room and promptly tripped over the inert body of his former attacker. He fell right onto the thug's chest and discovered that the unpleasant breath of a few minutes earlier had given way to a new, more rancid odor. Once he was back on his feet, he almost tripped again: the place was such a mess, it was hard to keep one's balance amid so much debris. Curro was grateful for the way the great diva muffled the racket he was making. But where was Dima?

He tried the kitchen next, its door out to the terrace opened onto the least well lit area of the entire apartment. Cautiously, he moved ahead, flattening himself to the wall, step by step, till he saw them at the end of the terrace where the scaffolding was, Dima being held with a knife to his throat as if his attackers were deliberating over how to escape with him alive. At least Curro didn't see any firearms. But what did they have in mind? Down the scaffolding to the street?

It was four stories. Why not the elevator, or the stairs inside the building? Just then the attackers reached the same conclusion, and as they started to move Curro could see why: they had to drag Dima along with them, he could barely stay upright. *Bastards, they've drugged him again*, thought Curro.

As soon as they were gone Curro leaned over the parapet and looked down towards the street, where a young couple were being questioned by two Civil Guardsmen; one of the patrolmen glanced up briefly. The music had achieved one of his objectives! Curro started waving his arms, trying to attract their attention, but the Guardsmen were still focused on the couple outside. He didn't dare shout, that would give away his position to the Russians. He had to try to get the Guardsmen up here to help him. The scaffolding? No, he didn't like his chances on that shaky metal frame, and he was a little old for that kind of acrobatics anyway. He'd have to try to get to the staircase ahead of the Russians. He backtracked through the kitchen but to his surprise the attackers had made it through the house to the front door already, and he just had time to duck into the guest bathroom to avoid being seen.

Dima was trying to shake off his stupor and was writhing furiously in his captors' grasp. One of his exertions was so violent that it knocked the larger of the two off balance, and he stumbled in the darkness, landing just inches away from where Curro was hiding. What to do? It was a chance: possibly, the last chance. Curro took the challenge. As the Russian got to his feet he met a vengeful stare. Without a second thought he charged the unexpected figure who received him in the same pose a bullfighter uses in the ring, firmly gripping the saber's handle. The charging beast skewered, he crashed lifelessly to the floor, the tip of the blade protruding out the other side. Dima realized what was happening and headbutted the last assailant so vigorously that it knocked him out. Unfortunately, the Russian tough fell with exceptionally bad luck for Dima, opening his old leg wound with his knife, digging right in to it as the man dropped to the floor. *Shit, of all the things...* thought Curro as he opened the front door to let in light from the landing.

The last assailant was trying to get back up: Curro, drawing on his long-ago Judo days, applied a strangulation lock to the Russian's neck. The more he moved, the more he choked himself; even so, the man was so big he almost freed himself. Then Dima limped over and simply flopped down on top of the man. With that much weight on top of him, the attacker stopped moving and Curro could now apply his deadly technique with unfettered precision: meeting his comrade's gaze, as if to say *This one's for you,* Curro squeezed the attacker's throat as hard as he could. Then he shifted his own position slightly, better to see the last breath the thug exhaled on his way to hell.

The landing lit up and they heard the elevator's whirr. Curro just had time to dash back to his study and switch off the stereo—Callas had moved on to *Turandot* by then—and run back to the landing, shutting his front door behind him.

The elevator opened and the couple from the second floor stepped out, pleasant young newlyweds who spent more time traveling the globe than in their recently inaugurated Madrid home. Behind them was an aloof Civil Guardsman who'd been stationed at one of the embassies nearby. He was the first to speak.

"What is this circus? Do you know what time it is? You've woken up half the neighborhood."

"I'm so sorry, officer. I'd just meant to turn the volume up slightly but the knob got stuck and I kept thinking I could fix it. I finally just pulled the plug, which I should have done in the first place. I'm really sorry."

"Are you all right? You're bleeding."

Curro had forgotten how he must look. In his disheveled pajamas, barefoot and stained with the blood of his attackers, his improbable reassurances didn't have a very soothing effect.

"It's nothing, I'm fine—I cut myself and then spilled the Mercurochrome trying to treat the wound." As lies go it wasn't a great one and he regretted it immediately. *God, was that really the best I could do?* he chided himself.

"You think you're funny? Open that door."

"It's nothing, officer. Honest, look," he said, unbuttoning his pajama top to show his unscathed torso. "See? I'm fine, nothing's wrong."

"Sir, open that door," insisted the Civil Guard.

"Officer, I'm a lawyer and I know my rights," lied Curro boldly. "Let me repeat, you needn't worry. Everything's fine, nothing to see here."

"You're coming with me," said the Guardsman, resting his palm on the handcuffs clipped to his belt. "And you two may go, I'm sorry about the inconvenience," the Guardsman said to the couple from the second floor.

"I'm sorry, officer, but I'm not going anywhere with you. Call Inspector Jiménez Moreno, at the

Central district station. He'll explain."

"I don't need any kind of explanation from any policeman. I take orders from my superiors in the Guard, not from some cop."

"Well then, let's wake up my uncle General Gómez-Ochoa," Curro lied again. He'd never met the General, wouldn't even have known who ran the Civil Guard if he hadn't read it in the paper. But he had no qualms about dropping his name. Some relative of his was sure to know the General.

"You're a nephew of General Gómez-Ochoa?" the Guardsman asked hesitantly, until then unflappable.

"Yes. My late father was his cousin." *This guy's a cool customer,* thought Curro, feeling in spite of himself a sort of pride in the man's dedication to his job. "May I have your badge number, please?"

"I'm Corporal Guerra Ordóñez. Jerónimo Guerra Ordóñez!"

"Sir, yes sir!" On reflex Curro was trying to be funny, but it wasn't really the time and as usual just made things worse.

"All right, have it your way," said the Guardsman, ignoring Curro's snide comment. "I'm going to go report on everything I've seen here tonight and your uncooperative attitude." He started down the steps. "I'm not leaving till my superiors arrive."

***

"How are you doing?" Curro asked, once he was back inside.

"Not good at all," said Dima from the floor. "I'm gonna bleed out if we can't find some way to stop this," he said, pointing at his leg.

Dima was right—the wound didn't look good at all. As the knife tore through his skin on the way down it must have sliced through something vital, maybe even nicking an artery. Blood was seeping rapidly out even though he'd tied his T-shirt around his calf. Curro grabbed a necktie and with that and a cane put together a makeshift tourniquet that would do better, at least for a little while. If he didn't get this taken care of quickly, his friend was in deep trouble. He already looked like he might be close to passing out. Curro had an idea. Actually, the same idea he always had: Carlitos.

He called the station but it wasn't Carlos' shift; he asked for Carlos' home number but the Desk Sergeant just hung up on him. Now what? He still had all of his appointment books from the good old days, in a drawer in his room. He dug through all those half-forgotten papers... and there it was. He quickly thumbed to C for Carlitos and pounded the number onto the keypad. After two rings he heard a well-rested, energetic voice, ready for the day ahead.

"Who is this?" Carlos was surprised to get a call on his cell that early in the day, it was a number only his closest friends and senior colleagues at the station had. Curro was fleetingly grateful that he'd caught him at the station the day Eugenia disappeared.

"Carlitos, it's me, Curro. Let me talk. I know it's too early, but I've got a real problem and I need your help."

"Oh great, Curro. Here we go again. You and your problems."

"Let me talk, it's important, there's no time to lose. I need an ambulance at my apartment with a police escort. It's for Dima, he's been injured." He had to get Dima out there, quick, before the Civil Guard returned.

"But—"

"No buts. I'll explain everything later. But send the ambulance, with a squad car escorting it. Don't ask me why, I promise I'll explain everything." He heard his friend pick up his land line and give someone some orders, then hang up; then he was back on the cell.

"All right, let's hear it, blow by blow, nice and slow. The Russians, right?"

"Russians, Russians. Forget about them. I got jealous, I lost it and I stabbed Dima," he improvised, unable to do better for the time being.

"Say what? Curro, stop, I'm pissing myself. You really expect me to believe you stabbed the Jolly Red Giant you've been playing house with? C'mon, April Fool's Day was last month."

"I know, it sounds crazy, but it's the truth. We started arguing about Eugenia and I lost it. Of course I couldn't lay a finger on him in a fair fight. But he threatened to hit me, and then didn't. You know I was always a vindictive bastard. I grabbed this old sword concealed in a walking stick... God, I feel awful now. It was cowardly, I waited till he'd let his guard down. But I hate him, he's been toying with me!" As he finished his lines, Curro could only feel that he was a loss to stage and screen.

"Aha! So you *did* hook up with him. I knew you hadn't changed," Carlos said with a laugh.

"As if."

"I knew it all along. How bad is it?"

"He's lost a lot of blood. I think I nicked an artery."

"What about the police escort? I mean, if it's not for the Russians—"

"Forget the fucking Russians, it's the Civil Guard! I made an awful racket with my stereo system and someone called them... Listen, I've gotta go, I hear the siren from the ambulance outside. Come by here. Please."

Curro hung up the phone and went over to Dima, where he knelt down next to his friend. "Dima," he began whispering in his ear, "it's going to be all right. The ambulance is here. You'll be fine. Good as new in a few days."

"Thanks, Curro," he answered, a wheezing voice so different from his usual tone. "You've got balls. I knew that already, but you really impressed me tonight. You're a champ." Dima tried to smile.

"Hey, don't wear yourself out. Be quiet, get some rest. As soon as I can, I'll see you at the hospital," he said, squeezing Dima's hand.

The next few minutes were the most stressful of Curro's life. With great difficulty he managed to get Dima out to the landing, only because Dima was still able to help, though only just. He was there waiting for the paramedics when they stepped out of the elevator, accompanied by the two cops from the squad car Carlos had sent. As soon as they were gone, he set to work frantically trying to find a way to hide the three dead Russians in the shed on his terrace. After considering, then rejecting, a dozen different ideas, it finally came to him: his Samsonite suitcase! The wheels would move the bodies, the suitcase itself was sturdy enough to take the weight. No sooner said than done; one after the other, all three corpses were wheeled away. He hosed the blood trail off of the terrace, then straightened up inside the house as best he could; he didn't need to worry about the rest of the mess too much, because Dima's injury could justify any lingering blood stains and the mess itself was consistent with his story about a jealous rage.

He was still out of breath and disheveled when the doorbell rang. No time to clean himself up now. He drew himself up to his full height, for want of a better way to appear dignified under the circumstances, and opened the door. It was a curious trio: Inspector Jimenez, Corporal Guerra, and a third gentleman who looked as if he'd been roused from his bed especially for the occasion. Curro, flouting any conventions of hospitality, kept them out on the landing without inviting them in.

"Commander," Jiménez began "allow me to introduce Francisco Morante Solloso. Mr. Morante, this is Commander Leiva. Commander, I've recently become acquainted with Mr. Morante as a result of my investigation into the murder at the Royal Theater and the Russian mafia —you're familiar with the case, correct? —and he's informed me of an unfortunate accident in which, while he was trying to show the injured man a family heirloom, an antique sword concealed in a walking stick, he tripped and was unlucky enough to stab his friend with the very artifact he'd been displaying." *Wow,* thought Curro, *Carlos can be a real silver-tongued devil when he wants to.*

"So, you're General Gómez-Ochoa's nephew?" This seemed to be the only relevant topic as far as the Civil Guard officer was concerned.

"That's right, Commander, we're related. Call

him if you like, he'll vouch for me. Francisco Morante Solloso."

"Oh, that won't be necessary, I know who you are. You're quite the celebrity." From his tone, Curro couldn't be sure if he was being sincere or ironic. "My wife buys the gossip mags each week and apparently you and this Miss Osorio feature often enough to be on the payroll." Ironic, then.

"Please, I'm cracking up, Commander. I'm so sorry I can't invite you in, but if you'll please excuse me, I need to get cleaned up and head for the hospital. You can imagine how I feel at being responsible for my friend's injury. If there's nothing else I can do for you." Curro turned around, indicating that the meeting was at an end. "Oh, Inspector, there is one more thing I'd like to discuss with you, if you can spare a minute."

Jiménez reacted before the Guard officer had a chance to. "Don't worry, sir, this matter falls under police jurisdiction. I can, however, send you the full police report if you like, when it's ready; but this is nothing more than an unfortunate accident."

"No, that won't be necessary. Thanks anyway," the officer replied, a bit confused.

"Commander, thanks for your interest," said Curro as he backed away. "And I must congratulate you on the dedication shown by the personnel under your command. Specifically, Corporal Guerra Ordóñez, who does his job with efficiency and bravery, as every soldier should. Well done. I'll mention you both to my uncle." He stepped forward, shook the officer's hand first, and then the corporal's, winking as he did. "It's been a pleasure, Corporal."

***

Once they were inside and the door was closed, Curro tried to distract his friend's attention from the evidence.

"You blew me away, Carlitos. I had no idea you could talk like that. Such decorum. You sounded like a nineteenth-century orator."

Jiménez smiled dismissively. "All these years rubbing elbows with classy guys like you, something was bound to rub off on me. So, jealous rage, eh?" His tone changed completely, making it clear he wasn't buying it. "Looks like the First Cav rode through here," he said sarcastically, glancing up and down, left and right, as he walked through the apartment. "Man, this must have been one hell of a battle. I'm not blind, you know. You don't trust me, fine, that's your problem. It's clear as hell something big's gone down here and your pal Dima was bang in the middle of it—you're not really gonna deny that, are you?" Carlos stepped over an overturned chair. "So, the Russians decided to drop by for tea and crumpets, then all hell broke loose. You're lucky to be alive. What, were you out on the town or something?"

"Give it a rest, Carlitos, will you? I've been here all night. *If* you were right, and those Russians had dropped by, I'd be waiting in line for my autopsy by now, don't you think? And yet, here I am, alive and kicking. Unless you think I sent them packing all by myself. Curro Morante, lean, mean ass-kicking machine!" he quipped.

"Very funny. I'm just saying—what I see here? No way this was a jealous spat. Besides, your pal

Dima would kick your ass from here to next Tuesday if you laid a finger on him. Unless he's one of those S&M guys who likes to stand around with his hands in his pockets while some other guy beats the crap out him. Sorry, Curro, I'm not buying it."

"Carlitos, let's talk about this later. I'm going to take a shower and see how Dima's doing. What hospital did they take him to, anyway? He's my top priority right now, and he was in bad shape, you know. And hey, thanks for everything. You're a pal."

"I'll wait, lemme drive you. I'm not in a hurry."

"No way! I mean, thanks, but I've put you out enough already."

Curro was trying to convince the inspector that his presence was no longer necessary, and put his hand on his back to gently guide him towards the door. But Jiménez really *was* in no hurry—he was still looking around in every direction, trying to find some additional clue to confirm his suspicions.

"Some host you are," he snorted as they reached the door. "You know what? I could really go for an ice cold beer. Bet you've got one in the fridge."

"Carlitos, this is no time to knock back a cold one together. Besides, you're on duty."

"Stop being such a pain. Go on, go take your shower, I'll help myself to a beer."

Curro gave up and went to the bathroom where he stood under the shower head for all of about thirty seconds, till he caught sight of his friend on the terrace, leaning over the parapet. Grabbing a towel to cover his modesty, he dashed out the side door onto the terrace.

"Carlitos, what gives?"

"Relax, man. What's with you? I'm just checking out the scene down below. You sure caused one hell of a mess."

"I didn't cause anything. And stay away from the scaffolding next door, one of these days the whole thing's going to fall over one someone out here."

"Hey, you got a bathroom in here? I gotta take a piss," said Carlos. , turning the knob on Curro's shed.

"Carlitos!" shouted Curro. He was relieved beyond words when the door didn't move. He couldn't remember having locked the shed after dumping the corpses inside, but apparently he had on reflex.

"Carlitos, Carlitos. You're gonna wear my name out if you keep on using it like that."

"Use my bathroom, it's just right through there. Your memory's not so good, man."

"How should I know where your pissoir is? I've never been here. Back in the day, you lived in this huge house with your mom... Oh, and at the place in Torrelodones. Now that I remember, and fondly, too. Swimming in the pool there, and the parties you threw when your mom was out of town. Ahh, good times."

"If you've never been here, then how did you know where I live?"

"Dude, I'm a cop. Besides, haven't you heard? You're famous! Gossip mag centerfold," Carlos snickered.

"Yeah, right, a regular A-Lister. Go on, take a leak and let's get going."

Truth be told, Curro welcomed the breather offered by Carlos' pit stop. He checked the lock on the shed then popped two anxiety pills. He had to decide what to do with the bodies. It was going to be a hot, sunny day and the stink of decomposition wasn't too far in the future. Before leaving he chained and bolted the door between the kitchen and the stairwell; while Jesús was away, the building super's wife had been coming in every afternoon to earn some extra money cleaning. As soon as Carlos reappeared, they took off.

When they stepped out onto the sidewalk, Curro was taken aback by the brouhaha on the street. The super, the Civil Guard, neighbors, onlookers, and the police, whose patrol cars were blocking the street—all together, it was like walking onto a movie set. Carlos reiterated his offer of a ride and they drove together to the Hospital de la Princesa on Diego de León Street. They parked outside the emergency room and went to Information to ask about Dima. He was in surgery, being operated on at that very moment—sectioned femoral artery, according to one of the cops who'd escorted the ambulance. Curro prepared to settle in and wait for an update from the surgeon.

The inspector had to get going, he was needed to wrap up a sordid case on the other side of the city. His men had located a Belgian pedophile on the run from Interpol, holed up in Madrid after being charged with the disappearance of several children in Portugal.

"... nyway, Curro, play it smart. Keep away from people who aren't your own class."

"My class? Hah, hah. Carlitos, you're killing me."

"I'm just saying, watch your back, those Russians are bad news. Anything comes up, you can count on me."

"I'll hold you to that."

"Shit, now I'm really scared."

CHAPTER XV

Curro had never yet come up against an injunction he didn't want to flout, so he soon went through one of the doors marked RESTRICTED ACCESS—MEDICAL PERSONNEL ONLY and idly snooped around some of the offices where patients were being seen, till someone spotted him and—as on other occasions, in other hospitals—he was ordered to leave. Curro ended up outside, milling around with other worriers who were trying to face up to whatever misfortune had befallen them. Someone offered him a smoke, which he politely but firmly rejected. He'd kicked smoking years ago and it was one vice he had no intention of revisiting. After an hour, during which he'd tried to take a break from reality with the aid of a newspaper and some coffee at a nearby kiosk, he returned to the hospital only to be told that the doctor who'd operated on his friend had been looking for him, had long since given up and was now in the operating room with another patient. But he'd left word that Curro could visit Dima in Intensive Care, where he should be waking up by now.

It was a brief encounter, one in which the patient could only manage weak gestures in response to Curro's questions: *Do you feel all right? Does it hurt a lot? Is there anything I can get you?* The usual questions at a time like this when the patient really just wants to be left alone. A short, tubby nurse came along: she fussed solicitously over Dima, then told Curro he needed to let the patient rest. At least he knew Dima would be in good hands. As he left, he leaned in close.

"Dima, the operation was a success. You'll be home in a few days, you'll see."

"Thanks, Curro," he whispered. "I owe you my life."

Curro left the room, lavishing his most endearing smile on the nurse as he did. The more the troops were on his side, the better they'd treat his friend—now his accomplice. Curro waited patiently for the surgeon to finish his next operation, then caught up with him in the hallway. The surgeon confirmed what Curro had dared to tell Dima before knowing for sure: the operation had gone well, no complications. In a couple of days the patient would be discharged, but he'd be looking at a lengthy convalescence at home before he could be up and about.

I owe you my life—God, that sounds grandiose, thought Curro, who'd decided to clear his head with a long walk home. *No, you don't owe me a thing. Nothing at all. It's been a pleasure to find within myself a sense of resolve I didn't know I had. I'd never thought taking a life would be that easy. In the end it was a purely mechanical action, one where there were only two possible choices: life or death. And I chose life, even though I no longer feel attached to it. And I don't regret what I did. I don't feel guilty about a damn thing.*

***

Back in his apartment, Curro spent the next several hours rearranging everything: straightening the furniture, his belongings, the clothes and other stuff that had fallen out of the overturned drawers; then a second round of cleaning, starting with the terrace then the rest of the house. He put all the blood-stained clothes and sheets in the washer, and also called a locksmith who changed the locks on the front door and the service entrance; he himself replaced the lock on the terrace shed, adding a sturdy padlock.

He needed to decide how to dispose of the bodies. It was a challenge. His building had been built in the 19th century and had no garage through which he could try to descend and leave with the bodies. Additionally, there was surveillance 24/7 on the adjacent buildings, so it wouldn't be easy to smuggle them out. For the time being, he opened the two small windows, one on either side of the shed, so it could air out. He bought a dozen buckets, and that night he drove to a gas station and bought every bag of ice they had. He'd keep the buckets full of ice, change it every day, and try to keep the temperature down inside the shed. As homemade solutions go it was creative enough, but it wouldn't do in the long term.

Over the next three days Curro visited the hospital, where Dima was getting better by the minute thanks to the diligence of successive shifts of besotted nurses. As soon as he felt fit enough to really talk, Dima told Curro that the attackers had been the same men who'd trapped him shortly after his arrival in Madrid.

"The funny thing is, though, I don't recognize any of them from Moscow, or from Gagarin's group. Remember I was sure that he was behind the kidnapping? Now I wonder. It's funny, these guys all had slight accents. Maybe Russians born somewhere else—Estonia, the Ukraine... Something like that.

"My my, you're a regular Henry Higgins."

"Who?"

"You know, the guy in *My Fair Lady* with Audrey Hepburn? The one who was obsessed with accents? Anyway..."

"Remember my Spanish grandmother!" Dima pointed out in jest. "I have a good ear for accents."

"Yeah, yeah. Russian, Spanish, German, and English. Not too bad for a musclebound jock," he teased Dima.

Curro devoted those lonely nights to reading, trying to finish books he'd earlier given up on. Like *Disgrace* by Coetzee from South Africa, which had been languishing on a shelf. A good friend had suggested he leave that particular pleasure for another time, upon hearing that Curro had started it. At that point, what had happened to Trasto was still too recent, and he thought the aspects of the novel that involved dogs might depress Curro. As it turned out his concern was well-meant but misplaced, as the story had nothing to do with his dog. Trasto had lived surrounded by love, right up to his inevitable end, at home, in Curro's arms, and that after having been given a sedative before the arrival of the friendly vet Curro had asked for the house call. No, they were completely different stories.

When he went to the hospital to bring Dima

home, the Russian was sent off like a celebrity. The surgeon who'd operated on him, the nurses, even the orderlies—all came by to say a few words of farewell. The surgeon took Curro aside and warned him:

"He's doing a lot better, but he needs rest. The guy's in amazing physical shape, but there's always the risk of the wound, which was deep and affected his femoral artery, opening back up. If he doesn't take it easy for at least a week, there could be dangerous consequences. You have to convince him to stay off his feet."

"Doctor, consider it done."

***

After leaving the hospital they heard from Inspector Jiménez, warning them of tensions gripping Madrid's underworld. They were now squarely in its sights. A low-level pusher they'd busted outside a disco told the police, after Carlos paid a personal visit to his cell, that there was talk about a Russian traitor and his Spanish partner who were going to pay dearly for dissing one of the Moscow godfathers. Word was, a famous model was being held in Marbella as bait to try to lure the unlucky twosome to their fate. At first Curro thought this was good news: surely now his friend could lead the cavalry to Gagarin's mansion to free Eugenia, search warrant in hand.

"It's not that simple, Curro," Jiménez said quietly over the phone.

"Why not? You're a cop, act like one."

"I repeat, it's not that simple. Gagarin has a healthy network of flunkies and fall guys looking out for him. He's greased half the palms within twenty miles of Marbella—he and his lawyer, greasy bastard named Basurto."

"Basurto? Fidel Basurto?"

"The one and only. You know him?"

"We went to school together."

"I thought you might. Posh guy, *almost* as much as you," Jiménez said with a grin.

"I remember him well. He wasn't much of a talker. Kind of dull, really, I think he had sort of a complex. The other kids were always bragging, you know, their parents' cars, their boats, that sort of thing. His family was well-educated but they didn't have the proverbial pot."

"Well, he's not so quiet now. Shows up at every party in Marbella with different eye candy, and he's loaded. More than you, even."

"Wow..."

"Okay, maybe not *more* than you, but he's definitely loaded. Riding shotgun with Gagarin, he's managed to build quite the real estate empire."

"A real estate empire!" Curro repeated sarcastically. "Then he probably *is* more loaded than I am. Times have changed, Carlos. You know I'm just living off of the income and haven't done an honest day's work in forever and a half. Sooner or later, it all runs out..."

"Boo, hoo. Poor Curro. That's why you're in the Spanish *Forbes* rich list, right? 'Cause things are going so badly?"

"Talk, just talk... Listen, I can't believe there's nothing we can do for Eugenia. I mean, I know people—who do I have to talk to?"

"No one. Marbella's a backed-up septic tank of vice and corruption. And those are just its good points. The powers that be all have their fingers in too many cookie jars—fraud, embezzlement, influence peddling. Too many of them watching each other's backs. Anyway, this isn't exactly top secret."

"I know. But you're telling me we've got this young lady, famous model, daughter of a duke who's schmoozed everyone on four continents, and of his wife, who *is* on the *Forbes* rich list, and the daughter is being held hostage by a second-rate Russian mobster and there's nothing anyone can do? I don't buy it."

"That's pretty much how it is, Curro. All we have is hearsay, and we can't act on that. And your so-called second-rate mobster is actually one very dangerous guy with a rap sheet in half the countries of Europe, and who has all the local powers that be firmly buttoned down in his pocket."

"So?"

"So we wait. Sooner or later, he'll slip up. Listen, the last thing we want to do is force his hand and lose him. I know she's your friend, I know you're worried, but there's more at stake here than a fashion model kidnapped. You and Dima should make yourselves scarce for a while. Get outta town, go somewhere quiet where Dima can rest and get his strength back. Got it?"

Not on your life, Curro thought. He knew exactly where he could take Dima to rest and recover,

But Curro wasn't going to be idle in the meantime. Eugenia's life was hanging by a thread.

CHAPTER XVI

It hadn't exactly been easy for Curro to convince Dima to take shelter where they were going. There were complaints, long faces, and the odd mention of hell freezing over, but all to no avail. Curro had made up his mind.

The sun set as they were driving across Guadarrama Ridge through a forest of elegant, distinctive Valsaín pines. Curro's car stereo played classic tunes by The Doors as they drove along in silence, their thoughts lost in the striking landscape and Jim Morrison's voice. They were both tired of arguing. Curro had been firm, inflexible. He had to be, for the good of all of them. After their last conversation with Carlos he'd realized that he would have to swing into action because Eugenia's life was hanging by a thread and when it came to saving her, Spain's justice system wasn't up to the task. Besides, he'd taken an unexpected and singular pleasure in his new incarnation as Hero to Order. He'd always dreamed of feeling useful to others, nurtured childhood fantasies of saving the planet since those long-ago afternoons reading fare that ran from *Capitán Trueno* to *Captain America*. Suddenly, *he* was the

Captain. He was heading down a path he'd never anticipated, but their current impasse called for a hero and he'd decided to answer that call. He'd make a merciless avenger.

At first Dima had insisted on coming with him; he'd more than earned his stripes and he wasn't one to shy away from a fight. His experience would have been a huge asset, but he wasn't even close to being fit for duty. His recovery, his health, depended on his taking it easy for a while. Curro would have to go it alone, or at least try to. He lied, promising Dima that he was just going to Marbella to check out the situation on the ground, to see if he could get wind of what Gagarin had in mind for Eugenia and for them. Curro insisted he'd be safe at the house in Guadalmina that he'd inherited from his parents. It was still registered in his mother's name, there was no way the mob could trace him to it.

Segovia loomed before them, the dying sunlight gilding its charms. The Alcázar castle, the city walls, the aqueduct, the spires that dotted its landscape... An unusually well-preserved gem of medieval Castille. Though it had been sunny that spring afternoon, as the sun sank behind the horizon they felt cool, chilly even. They bypassed the city, taking the crossing over the river; on one of its banks stood the Carmelite Convent that was to shelter Dima till his recovery was complete.

Curro had called his Aunt Adelaida to see if she could take Dima in for a few days at the school her order ran on the outskirts of Madrid. Adelaida was nobody's fool and quickly spotted the holes her nephew's sob story was full of.

"Tell me the truth, the whole truth and nothing but the truth," she said firmly.

Curro brought her up to speed, leaving out the sticky details. He mentioned a bar fight that got out of hand, the bad luck of having it involve people tied up with the local mob. Dima needed to lay low for a few days till he was well enough to go home to Russia. Aunt Adelaida was sympathetic, but resolute in her refusal: in a school building, with kids in and out all the time every day, an injured foreigner wasn't exactly going to blend into the scenery. She had recommended instead her Order's cloistered convent at Segovia, where a great-aunt of Curro's, now approaching her hundredth year, ruled as Mother Superior. She was known as Mother Amparo.

Stepping out of the car they admired the majestic edifice, which comprised several different wings arranged around linked courtyards. From the main façade rose a Gothic turret that served as a watchtower. The building evinced a succession of different styles that had at one time or another been architecture's dominant trends. Romanesque and Baroque features mingled with Gothic and Renaissance traits. The building had once been a Hieronymite monastery and sprawled out over an area much greater than that really required for its current purpose. Since the eighteenth century it had housed a community of Carmelite nuns devoted to prayer. The sisters didn't live on charity alone; the popular butter cookies they baked were now distributed throughout Spain.

Curro and Dima walked through the main door, which was open, and found themselves in an enclosure. On their right was a small revolving compartment through which the cookies routinely departed, and on their left, an ancient bell pull. Curro used it to rend the shrouding silence. They were expected: a short time later, they heard a voice.

"You're Francisco Morante, aren't you? This is Sister Maravillas."

"That's right, Sister. Pleased to meet you. Is Mother Amparo there?"

"Of course, she's been expecting you. We all have. It's so nice to have you here. Currito, Concha's son! Your mother was like a saint, the way she concerned herself with our wellbeing."

"Thanks, sister. We've brought a few things in case you might all enjoy a change of menu—shall I put them through the revolving door?"

"If you would, please."

Curro and Dima gingerly stacked up the provisions they were carrying on the tray in the revolving compartment. Curro had outdone himself; the nuns would feast for days.

Shortly thereafter the Mother Superior came to them. Adelaida had convinced her of the seriousness of Dima's plight and so she had agreed to break the rule of the cloister as a favor to the son of the convent's late benefactress. Curro didn't remember Great-aunt Amparo, though he'd been taken to visit her a few times—a grating always separating them, to maintain the nuns' professed isolation from the outer world— but remembered having been told that she was once a great beauty. Once the gate had been pushed to one side and they were face-to-face, he was impressed. Though nearly a hundred years old, she retained a commanding presence. She was more than tall, her taut, pale features dominated by intense aquamarine eyes. In spite of the simplicity of her tight headwear and the habit, belted at the waist with a knot, Curro thought her bearing more that of a princess than of a woman withdrawn from earthly affairs.

After the requisite greetings and introductions she asked them to follow her in absolute silence as they walked down hallways and through courtyards to the place where Dima would live incognito for a few days. Only the congregation and the gardener who helped the sisters with their fruit and vegetables would know of the exceptional favor granted to Dmitri Denissov.

The place chosen was on the other side of the convent, far from where the nuns went about their everyday chores. Immediately after passing through a Baroque courtyard they came to some disused cells that would serve as their rooms. A glance sufficed for Curro to be convinced of the austerity with which the community lived: a cot, a thin mattress, a sheet and a blanket. That was it.

"Here it is, make yourselves at home. The rest of the community's already had supper—we wake up and go to bed with the hens here—but I waited so we could eat together. You are staying the night, right? I have so much to ask you about. Your friend will be brought dinner on a tray which will be left there," she said, pointing at a stool outside the room's door. "He speaks some Spanish, right?"

"Yes, Aunt, fluently."

"Yes ma'am, I speak Spanish," Dima chimed in.

"Every day at 6 A.M., 12 noon and 7 P.M. he'll be brought a meal," she said to Curro. "A little bell will be rung when it's there. It would be better if Dima stay out of sight till the food's been left. We've already broken a few rules," she said, smiling.

"Six A.M.? But Aunt Amparo—"

"That's fine, Curro," Dima cut him off. "That's just about when I need to take some pills and check the wound. Anyway, waking up early'll be nothing new after the army."

"Ah. You're a soldier?" inquired Sister Amparo. "So was my father."

"Yes ma'am, I was an officer in the Russian army. But I'm a civilian again now."

"That's too bad. I always looked up to the army. In our family," she looked at Curro, "there have been many officers. Ah, such memories..."

"So, Aunt, when and where should we meet you for dinner?" *Or a snack, more likely,* thought Curro.

"Someone will come for you. They'll ring the little bell—follow the sound at a discreet distance."

"Fine."

"Don't be nervous," she said, looking at Dima, "tomorrow the gardener will brief you on our customs here. We've set up another cell over here—the only one in this wing that has electricity—with a small TV, and you'll be brought the morning papers. Arsenio, the gardener, will show you the way to an old orchard adjoining this wing; you can get some fresh air there, and use the hose for bathing. Of course, there's also the river—"

"That's fine, Aunt Amparo. There'll be plenty of time tomorrow for Arsenio to bring him up to speed."

***

Once they were alone, and seeing the look of utter dejection on Dima's face, Curro tried to cheer him up.

"C'mon, it's not that bad."

"No, it's great! I'm going to be locked up like a monk. I'm sure I'll have a helluva time!"

"Heh, I wish you could see your face," Curro said as he burst out laughing. "Look, you'll be able to rest, go for walks, even go for a swim in the river if you like. Just make sure your stitches don't get infected. Anyway, your wounds are doing better, right?"

"Yes, but..."

"And you've got the laptop, you'll be able to surf the net. Plus, they have a library. You can catch up on your reading."

"All the latest page-turners, I'm sure."

"Hah, hah."

Ting-a-ling-a-ling. The bell! By the time Curro had set off in its wake, the nun (a novice, he presumed, judging from her spry pace) had disappeared. He guided himself by the receding notes, never once catching sight of the bell's bearer. They retraced the route he'd taken on the way in; Curro marveled at the craftsmanship, the load-bearing arches and the ornamentation that made up the building. The erstwhile monastery was so sprawling that he could easily have gotten lost in its courtyards and corridors without a guide to lead him along. This sound had ceased once he'd reached the Romanesque courtyard, the oldest and the one closest to the main building. He was admiring the splendid capitals atop the columns, each one different from the next, when he heard a well-modulated, slightly high but firm voice. The Mother Superior.

"Currinchi!" she called out. "Currinchi!" It had been his mother's pet name for him, when he was a little boy. Her female family – sisters and aunts – had eventually picked it up too; even so, it had been so long since he'd heard that name that it felt strange, though not unpleasant. Once he'd followed the sound he found himself in a huge room with high ceilings adorned with mudejar decoration, all in perfect condition. From floor to ceiling the walls were covered with elegant tiles bearing a pattern he identified more with Portugal than Seville, and which made the chamber seem unexpectedly exotic. The room's scant light came from candles large and small, strategically placed on tall candelabras.

"What a place. It's beautiful, Aunt Amparo."

"Yes it is. One never stops marveling at it, even after a lifetime here."

"Those tiles seem very unusual."

"Aren't they? I'm glad you noticed. They're Portuguese. One of the Portuguese noblemen who stayed in Spain after Portugal became independent in the seventeenth-century gave a whole shipment of them to his Confessor, who was the prior here when this was a Hieronymite monastery. They are one-of-a-kind. Look very distinguished, don't you think?"

"It sure does. What is this room, anyway? It's huge."

"It was the Romanesque refectory. Once long ago this part of the building burned down and when it was rebuilt it was the dining hall until we Carmelites came. Now it's a waiting room; relatives who are coming to visit the sisters wait here for their turn to speak with them through that grille down there," she pointed off into the darkness. "Anyway, let's get on with it. You're in luck, you'll be dining from the stuff you brought, otherwise I'm afraid you'd have gone to bed hungry. We're very frugal here."

"Aunt Amparo, you look great," he said, changing the subject. "Still a beauty."

"Flatterer. You know that we here attach no importance to such earthly things."

"I know. But you really do look radiant. And you transmit such inner peace. Now I'm glad I came, even if it had to be because of this unpleasantness with Dima."

"Who is that boy?"

"A dear friend of mine who through no fault of his own got caught up in a stupid fight at a discotheque."

"Kids today. He's quite handsome, by the way."

"Yes he is. He has people falling all over him."

Over dinner they talked about family, the nun eager to hear more about the new generation she hadn't met. Times had changed and visitors, once frequent, were now few and far between. Except for the odd great-niece or -nephew like Curro—and very sporadically, too—no one visited her any more. The nieces and nephews she'd once been closest to, her siblings' children, were now old themselves, decrepit even, and had stopped visiting years before.

They enjoyed reminiscing, retold the stories of childhoods long past. Aunt Amparo, with a prodigious memory and still in full use of her senses, was a walking encyclopedia when it came to baptisms, first communions and weddings. She remembered everything, even admitted to Curro that she still kept a scrapbook with newspaper clippings about assorted family events. They also spoke of her life dedicated to prayer—she promised to pray for Dima's full recovery—and the sense of fulfillment it had given her. She urged Curro to open up more to God, to follow his mother's example of daily saintliness. Curro fidgeted, unsure what to say. "Oh dear, someone's wavering," she reproached him. After he'd promised to take part in some spiritual exercises and find a good confessor, she rose, bringing the evening to a close. It was ten P.M. on the dot. As they took their leave, both convinced that they wouldn't meet again—at least, in this world—and after a warm, heartfelt hug, Curro saw in Aunt Amparo's eyes the strength of her faith. Back in the cell with Dima, they went over the next steps one last time. Curro would be leaving the following morning for Marbella, where he'd join in the same social scene as Gagarin, and he'd be on the lookout for any means of finding Eugenia. Curro would stay in touch with Dima by phone and e-mail, keeping him up to date. Curro had promised Dima not to rush into anything alone, but to wait till Dima had recovered enough to join him, and to ask for Inspector Jiménez' cooperation too. With this understanding, and with both of them thoroughly worn out from their trip and the latent stress, they each withdrew to their respective cells hoping for sleep enough to restore their strength.

CHAPTER XVII

After the beating she'd endured on the yacht, Eugenia was sedated again and moved to a new location. As soon as she came to, she found herself inside a spacious home. Through a window she saw a garden and caught sight of the mountains and knew at once she that was on the ridge overlooking Marbella.

The first few days were both monotonous and nerve-wracking, with no sign of what anyone wanted or expected from her. Worse, there was in fact no sign of anyone at all except for a young redhead whom Eugenia took to be foreign; the girl acted both as her servant bringing her meals and her guard. Eugenia tried to talk with her but silence was her only response. By guiding her to the pool, the girl indicated that she was allowed to go outside for relief from the heat of that unusually warm spring. At first she balked at leaving her room, where there was a TV with lots of DVDs, but watching movies did nothing to relieve her own feeling of being watched, kept under lock and key with no chance of escaping. *Who was behind all of this*, she wondered, *and what do they want with me?* She couldn't begin to guess, and felt she was a victim of some horrible mistake. Surely they had intended on kidnapping someone else, not her. Only on the fourth day did her boredom and latent claustrophobia force her to accept the favor of time outdoors offered by her mysterious kidnapper.

The grounds were ample and well cared for. All manner of plants flourished in the benign microclimate. The villa, though sprawling, was all on a single story and not as garish as what Marbella's *nouveau riche* Eastern residents usually inflicted on the area. The pool was surrounded by a well-trimmed lawn; the water looked inviting, and having found in the closet of her room a brand new bikini her size, Eugenia tried it on and was ready to dive in when at the last fraction of a second she heard the sounds of two men and shivered. Turning around she and saw them at the end of the garden, snickering and mocking her. She felt like prey for vermin. Two burly guys she'd never seen before were standing there in trunks far too small and tight for their rugged bodies, both with a hand on their crotch. The tiny swimsuits made it amply apparent that both of them were getting turned on by the sight of her in her new bikini. The darker-skinned of the two broke into a wide grin, revealing two rows of perfect white teeth, and moved confidently across the grass towards her, a cocksure strut meant to say *Hey babe, real man approaching.*

"Well hello, baby. My name's Alex, and I'll be looking after you while you're here," he said in fluent Spanish, running one huge hand over his privates. "Wanna take a dip with me?"

Eugenia felt a tremor of fear pass through her. She turned to run back to her room, leaving Alex laughing in her wake. He cannonballed into the pool behind her, the wave he made soaking the grass with droplets that glistened in the sun.

The following day she was finally hauled before her captor, Gagarin, for the first time. When she was taken into his office he was on the phone, his back to the door, and when he put the phone in his pocket and turned around, she didn't recognize him. The loud, unbuttoned flower-print shirt, the several gold chains glinting on his chest, the gut spilling over his waistband, his greasy, unshaven face... It was a long way from the figure he'd cut in formal dress at the Royal Theater. At the sight of her he leered from ear to ear, then addressed her in lightly accented English:

"Well, look who we have here, the famous model men everywhere yearn for. Do you know who I am?"

Eugenia still hadn't recognized the man behind her nightmare, though he gave her the creeps in a way no one else had since she'd been taken.

"I'm afraid not. Should I?" she asked hesitantly.

"Allow me to refresh your memory. Dmitri, that concert the Queen was at."

That Russian hick at the Royal Theater, the one who Dima stared a hole through, she thought, dismayed. She remembered it all now; he'd said something that had shocked the Grand Duchess, the remark later relayed to them all by her aunt. At the time none of it had made any sense to her; now everything took on a new meaning. Now she realized just what deep trouble she was in.

She put on a brave face, even though Gagarin's appearance and self-confidence frankly scared the hell out of her. "Why have you kidnapped me?"

"Relax, nothing bad's going to happen to you.

Let's just say that you're going to be my *guest* till your friend Dmitri returns something that belongs to me. Come, let's sit together," he said, gesturing to the couch.

"What do I care if you've got some problem with Dmitri?" she shouted, standing her ground. "I demand to be released at once!"

Gagarin chortled. "Ah, I do love Spanish girls' fiery personalities. You're like Russian girls, you know that? All passion."

"Listen, pal, in case you haven't noticed, you're not in Russia anymore. You're holding me against my will! You'll go to jail for this! My family will see to that," Eugenia said furiously.

Gagarin's chortle broadened into a belly laugh. "This is *better* than Russia! Nothing ever happens to anyone here. I repeat, you're my guest, my very special guest. I hope we'll be friends. You have the run of the place, you can go for a swim, anything you like—except leaving."

"Here, and anywhere else, that's called kidnapping." Seeing her threats had no effect she changed her approach. "Look, please let me go. I won't tell anyone, I swear. I could say I left Madrid in a huff, wanted to be alone for a while, and now I've cooled down. I'll talk to Dima, convince him to make things right with you. Please."

Gagarin grinned sadistically in reply, underscoring the hopelessness of her predicament. Eugenia broke down. The open-ended nature of her captivity was more than she could take. She was a temperamental creature, used to doing whatever she pleased, and now she found herself in a situation where her free will was to be thwarted indefinitely. The sobbing model's captor approached her, gently moving her tangled hair out of her face but then extending the gesture down her cheeks to the corner of her mouth. In an instant Eugenia's hand slapped his away.

"Oh dear, we're off to a bad start. Beauty rejects Beast."

"No, it's not that, it's just... Put yourself in my shoes, sir, I feel like I'm under a lot of stress."

"*Sir*, is it now? Please don't go all formal on me. I mean, are we advancing backwards, like crabs?"

"What?" Eugenia failed to see where his remark was headed. "Look, just let me go, please. Knock me out again, leave me somewhere. I have no idea where I am, I could never find this place again."

Gagarin snorted. "Turn you loose? I think not. Well, I have someplace to be, so see you in a few days."

She blocked his path in desperation. "Give me a phone! I'll call Dima, you can work out whatever it is right now."

"You can phone him when I return—you'll be more convincing by then. So long, my dear! Do keep in touch."

Gagarin walked out leaving behind him an utterly despondent Eugenia. It had finally sunk in that things wouldn't be getting back to normal for her anytime soon. She tried to think of anything that could give her additional insight into her captor and the reasons for her kidnapping. She thought back to that night at the Royal Theater, just a few days ago. She couldn't remember anything particularly striking about it, except for the latent tension already palpable between Dima and the man she'd just seen. What was his name? Tavarin, she thought. She'd assumed he must be loaded, though his manners struck her as pretty gauche; that was all she could remember about him. On the other hand, between all that cava and champagne she hadn't really been at her sharpest. But there hadn't been anything particularly remarkable about that fat guy no one had even bothered to introduce her to.

She was still racking her brain, trying to figure out if there had been some warning sign she'd missed, when the door opened again and in walked the guy who'd hit on her the day before by the pool. He was wearing nothing but a pair of tennis shorts, a striking, brief contrast to his smooth olive skin. He fixed her in his gaze, his eyes as dark as the lustrous hair flowing away from his temples. He stood as if he were giving every muscle in his body time to introduce itself to her. Then he came closer, and she flinched at the thought of the submission that such an arrogant alpha male could—would—subject her to. She knew she should be frightened, but at the same time she couldn't control the sudden arousal that was coming on. She realized the battle was lost as soon as she felt herself moistening.

Alex approached her, flashing his pearly whites. As she accepted the inevitable she offered what might have resembled a lukewarm smile, which bought her a slap that landed her on the carpet.

"What'd you expect, bitch, hugs and cuddles?" He picked her up by her hair and shoved her towards the other end of the study. "You're gonna get just what you're asking for. I'm gonna treat you like the cheap slut you are." He punctuated this with a kick to her ribs.

Eugenia squealed in pain, disoriented by the unexpected blow and his inexplicable rage. She just sat where she'd landed, trying to guess what the next move would be. Alex had had women like this before and knew the game well. He motioned her towards him, and Eugenia, guardedly, crawled towards him on all fours.

"That's more like it. The way a bitch in heat should approach her master."

"Don't hurt me!" she begged, "I'll do whatever you want."

"No shit, and here I thought you were gonna play hard to get." He laughed. "Wanna see raw power, the power of a born winner, someone who takes what he wants, when he wants it? Well, take a good look, 'cause here it is." He stood over her, clearly savoring their respective roles.

The moment was interrupted by the sound of the doorknob. The other tough she'd seen in the garden the previous day walked in. Eugenia, on the floor in the fetal position, didn't dare look up as the two men began arguing in a language she didn't understand. The tone, though, more and more shrill, told her enough to know that it wasn't a friendly chat.

Eugenia turned just enough to catch sight of the newcomer. She could see from his angry gestures at her that he was complaining at not being invited to take part. Tempers finally reached the boiling point and Alex let out a bellow worthy of Tarzan; the other punk would have been well advised to let that be the last word, but through being foolish enough not to shut up, he earned an uppercut that landed him on the carpet next to Eugenia. Another howl from Alex filled her with fright, which turned to revulsion when she saw how Alex intended to make the other man acknowledge his submission: he stuck his bare foot out on the floor next to the fallen man's face, demanded, from what she could tell, that he kiss it, and then forced his foot partway into his victim's mouth. Alex's braying laugh provided additional evidence, were any needed, of his emotional imbalance. He then pulled his unwelcome companion to his feet, and made a pantomime gesture of pointing a finger at his head and pulling a trigger before shoving him back out the door, slapping his ass as he went.

They were alone again, and Eugenia's eyes were fleetingly drawn to the massive bulge that seemed about to rupture Alex's tennis shorts before his foot slammed down challengingly next to her face on the carpet. She knew what was expected of her, and meekly delivered; and once she had also seen to Alex's foot, without being told to she moved up his leg, where she knew her attention was urgently required. *Good God!* Some of her more risqué friends in New York had been heard to brag about the package on their latest catch, but Eugenia was willing to bet none of them had ever taken on that many inches.

Once she'd done everything asked of her, she left Alex, still panting, and stepped into the bathroom of Gagarin's study where she got into the shower and stood under the jet for the longest time, strangely content at being ordered and manhandled like no one had ever done. . When she turned the water off, Alex was waiting for her in the doorway—looking hot as hell, she hated to admit—wearing nothing but a beaming grin of contentment. He held his arms out in a welcoming gesture and she clung to him without saying a word. Equal parts ashamed and flustered, she feared a sudden change of mood from the man who had so easily made himself her master.

"See? We can get along after all," said Alex. "You'll be my slut, and I'll be your stud."

Eugenia couldn't think of a response under the circumstances so she answered, "Anything you say."

"No, no, no. It's not what I say, it's how things are gonna be. I'm your stud, you're my verrry fancy little slut. Now, who am I?"

"My stud, my powerful stud. And I'm your little slut." *Is this really happening?* she wondered. *Could this kind of role play actually turn me on?* Somehow she now felt less fearful but couldn't say why.

"You learn fast, I like that."

"Yess ssssir, you are my sssstud and massssssster."

"What?" said Alex, oblivious to Eugenia's quirks.

"Yes, I said yes. You're my all-powerful stud and master, and I'm your slut, your bitch. Bitch!"

Alex held her tighter. "You're one *crazy* bitch, I tell you that. But a beautiful one. You're a countess or something, right? I never have been able to figure out rich babes like you but I at least know what you like and need."

Alex led her out to the garden and urged her to cool off in the pool; a hot wind was blowing through the grounds. She wasn't really in the mood but didn't want to set him off, so she swam a few laps. Later, reclining on a deck chair, she watched the childish horseplay that the pool brought out in Gagarin's bodyguards. For a while they held an impromptu dive contest, each trying literally to outmaneuver the other; the kid Alex had humiliated such a short time before played along as though all was forgotten. It looked as though the mindless roughhousing would have been enough to keep Alex entertained for the rest of the day; and every time he'd shown his long-suffering colleague who was boss, he'd look over at Eugenia, dedicating to her each new display of his alpha male supremacy.

The redhead appeared mid-afternoon with snacks for them all: some sandwiches Eugenia wasn't in the mood for and beer, which she had to replenish several times. At least they were drinking Eugenia's favorite brand——Alhambra 1925——and they were ice cold. No one bothered to tell Eugenia the redhead's name but she spent the rest of the afternoon with the group, having been forced by Alex's second banana—Adrian was his name—to stay and be groped. It must not have been the first time, Eugenia thought; the redhead accepted her fate with indifference albeit not enthusiasm. The women's eyes met and from their shared isolation grew a sense of complicity.

That night Eugenia was to learn more. She'd sought refuge in her room, hoping not to receive any nocturnal visitors but listening intently to the sounds surrounding her. She'd heard the guys pass by her window, talking; as usual it sounded as though Alex was giving orders while Adrian muttered something that sounded vaguely submissive. For a while she heard laughter and clinking glasses in the garden, as though a celebration were underway. Then all was quiet.

In the wee hours, the doorknob's squeak sent a chill through her.

"Hello," she heard a voice say, the redhead's freckled features visible on the other side of the door.

"Hello," Eugenia said with a sigh of relief.

"Don't worry, they went out a while ago. We're alone here now, except for the two men out by the front gate. They stay there day and night with their dogs."

Eugenia sat up in bed. "Huh, so you *can* talk. I thought you were mute." Eugenia smiled. "You speak Spanish really well. Where are you from?"

"I'm Russian," she said, closing the door behind her, "but I was born in Estonia. My parents moved to Valencia when I was a little girl."

"Ah," said Eugenia. "How'd you get mixed up with this bunch?"

"Last year my whole family packed up and moved back to Tallinn, except me, I wanted to stay here. I got a job in Marbella as a sales clerk, but at the end of the summer I lost my job, couldn't pay the rent… Well, you can imagine the rest."

"No, I can't, actually."

"Prostitution."

"Oh," Eugenia answered, not expecting that explanation. "Right. It's just that you look almost kidnapped yourself—I mean, they won't let you talk to me."

"They told me not to, or else. You don't know how hard it was for me not to answer all those questions you asked me in the beginning. Yeah, I guess I am sort of kidnapped too now... They don't want me to leave, they think I know too much now."

"What exactly do they think you know?"

"When I first came here, some other girls came along with me—we were the party favors, the boss had guests, we were supposed to keep them happy. Unfortunately I saw something I wasn't supposed to."

"Well, come on…tell me more."

The redhead took a seat near the door. "So my john was this Italian guy, and the boss handed him a briefcase, and the guy opened it up and started going through it right in front of me. And it was completely full of cocaine."

"The boss is this Tavarin guy, right?"

"Gagarin."

"Whatever. The fat bastard who left this morning?"

"That's the one."

"Asshole. So what did he say?"

"He told me I'd just been hired as an interpreter—Gagarin doesn't speak Spanish—and that I'd be staying here at the house from then on." Her tone was resigned, as if her fate had been set in stone by Gagarin.

"Didn't you tell him, I don't know," she said, looking around, "someone was waiting for you to get back or something?"

"They know I'm alone here—no family, no boyfriend, no one to really notice that they'd stopped seeing me around. The only people I still know here in Spain are over in Valencia. So once the party was over they never let me leave, and that same night I had my first visit from Alex. Need I say more?" she asked disdainfully. "He's a fucking animal. Worse even. I still get the creeps when I think of what he made me do."

"Are you ever allowed off of the reservation, or are you locked up all the time like me? At first I thought you were one of them."

"No way. I'm just the help. I have the run of the place for as long as it takes me to cook and clean, and that's it. Plus they know where my family live in Tallinn, as they're only too happy to remind me... But I can't take it anymore, I've got to get out of here or I'll go nuts. I've been palmed off on Adrian now, and he's a sorry excuse for a man. At least Alex... Well, he has his good points, as you know."

"No, I don't... Oh, wait, you mean his huge cock. Yes, I noticed."

"He's brutal, and yet he can be strangely addictive. Watch out with him."

"Where's he from? His Spanish is good but not perfect, and he looks too dark to be Russian."

"He's Moldavian. He comes from a family of carnies. I heard his father, who he never talks about, was a lion tamer—Romanian gypsy, from Moldavia. His mom's a Spanish acrobat, retired now, she owns one of the big traveling circus companies. He speaks Russian, Romanian, and English, besides Spanish."

Imagine that, thought Eugenia, *a savage polyglot.* She didn't want to give too much thought to the effect Alex's possessive brutality had had on her self-esteem or how it made her feel deep down. But she wasn't going to delude herself. As soon as she'd gotten one look at him, she'd known that she'd end up fighting with herself.

Just then the sound of somebody moving outside made them both jump. They looked at each other in silence, neither wanting to be discovered in conversation with the other. Someone down the hall shouted "Ekaterina!" Eugenia looked at the girl, who nodded. Their time was up. A handshake then a hug sealed a deal of silent support. As Ekaterina crept out, Eugenia whispered, "We'll talk again tomorrow. I'm going to escape, and you're coming with me."

"Ekaterina!" the shout rang out again, only this time in a voice Eugenia hadn't heard before.

Only a few days later the mere thought of Ekaterina's warning made Eugenia burn with shame. She'd been warned, all right, but she hadn't been able to resist him, or indeed herself. When she thought about it, she despised him for the way he took her without a second thought, degraded her. Then she wished she'd never laid eyes on him. At the same time, part of her feared that his visits had unleashed new desires in her, desires more risky, more violent than those she'd been awakened to by Dima.

The day after their brutal introduction a timetable had been established, which had evolved into routine. After Eugenia had spent a boring afternoon lounging by the pool while Alex saw to some mysterious obligations of his, he'd show up every night around nine and take her as roughly as he wanted, with the same possessive ferocity as the first time. Their relationship had become so intense that both seemed to have forgotten their initial positions as captor and hostage, acting instead as though they were partners in perversion. Eugenia had never before experienced total submission, the suppression of the self in anticipation of a word, a gesture, from one's master. She'd enjoyed the novelty of being passive and obedient during her trysts with Dima, but it had felt like a game she could have called off whenever she pleased. This was different; the situation was out of her control, her only thought was for her master, for his pleasure. She felt overwhelmed, as if she were another person, and spent every afternoon yearning for the visit, and if he didn't come, or was late, she was overcome with rage.

One night, after he'd failed to turn up the evening before, Eugenia ripped into him as soon as he was through her door. "Son of a bitch! Bastard! Where the hell were you yesterday? Why didn't you come to me?"

"What did you just say, bitch?" He stormed over to her, hand ready to strike. "You better watch your fucking mouth. Don't forget your place!"

His words ignited her. "I'm your bitch, your slut, your slave. Come here, my darling."

This time, Alex really wasn't in the mood. He'd gone to collect a debt on Gagarin's behalf, only to find that the guy being extorted had skipped town. The boss would hit the roof and take it out on him, and Alex was fed up already. Gagarin treated him worse and worse, like some dumbass errand boy. He turned around and walked out. Behind him he could hear Eugenia's plaintive whine.

"Don't leave, Alex, please! Come back! Please, Master, please!" she sobbed, sounding lonely and forsaken, just as she felt.

CHAPTER XVIII

Home. Going back to the scene of so many long summer days, so many youthful memories, was comforting for Curro. Despite the time passed since he'd last been to Marbella, nothing seemed to have changed, it had just become easier to get to. Not only had the spindly coastal roads of his childhood long since mutated into to four-lane highway, he was now able to come down from Madrid on the high speed train that linked the capital and Málaga in just two and half hours

Curro enjoyed the train ride. Though the Sierra Morena range was still vividly green, the central plains were starting to yellow. He couldn't help being reminded of Trasto; it was familiar turf, after all. More than once he and Trasto had gone away to spend a few days on Aunt Marimén's sprawling estate. Whether on foot or horseback, the vast expanse of grassland where livestock marked with the Aguilar-Morante brand roamed had been an ideal place to get away from the excess of the big city.

When Curro's taxi pulled up outside the big house in Guadalmina he found Angelita waiting for him by the door. She was a daughter of Maruchi, who had been his parents' cook in Madrid for nearly thirty years, Maruchi, who had died only a couple of months earlier, struck down by a rapidly spreading cancer. Everything was just the way he remembered it. The house by the beach, its lush gardens, the tennis court, the pool. It brought back memories of his youngest escapades with his Marbella pals, Matilde Osorio and Pepe Aguirre among them. The groundskeeper's house was by the side of the driveway: Maruchi had spent her last few years there, retired, and it was now occupied by Angelita and her husband, the Guadalmina home's caretakers. They had three kids, all of whom looked disapprovingly at Curro as he got out of the car, knowing that his arrival meant no more swimming in the pool while the owner was home. Curro settled in on the top floor, in his parents' old room, which apart from its spacious bathroom and walk-in closet boasted its own living room: he planned to make it his base of operations for however long he was in the area.

After leaving Segovia Curro had spent two days in Madrid organizing everything. At least the most pressing claim on his attention had been taken care of. Once Dima'd gotten out of the hospital and seen Curro's makeshift morgue, he had stepped in. He did what only he could do for Curro: he called in a favor from his underworld connections to make the bodies of the dead hitmen disappear. Curro didn't know how they vanished or who was involved, they were simply gone when he came home from Segovia. But the less he knew the better, so he just let it go. Besides, he had enough on his mind without worrying over the fate of three hired killers.

The night before heading for Marbella, Curro surfed the net for a while. Nothing in his inbox looked particularly interesting so he dumped all of the new messages except two from Dima. That worried him; did two messages in so short a space of time mean his pal's little spiritual retreat was driving him up a wall? As it turned out he needn't have worried. Dima said he was working hard to recover, exercising near the river every day. Beyond that, he was bored, because the old TV set the nuns had hooked up for him didn't get the national channels, just some local Segovia TV and a few religious channels he'd never seen before. To make matters worse, his dial-up connection was shaky too and it took him forever to log into his e-mail account and read the messages. This was, in fact, the subject of the second message. Dima had received an e-mail from an anonymized account, no return address, and he couldn't open the attachment over his weak connection, so he was forwarding it to Curro. Could Curro take a look and tell him if it was anything important? Curro couldn't get it open either, and soon forgot about it.

***

The search for Eugenia couldn't be put off any longer. The night after his arrival, he borrowed Angelita's husband's car and headed for Puerto Banús, to scout the area. He chose a perch at one of the bars facing the marina. It was Thursday night and it wasn't even the high season yet, but he found the marina already quite animated. The crowds had changed a lot since way back when. Here were some loud young sailors who looked like they might be crew from one of the big yachts. There went a group of British tourists, looking like they just got off the bus from Manchester. Next were some Spanish tourists, well-dressed but inattentive, wondering what the hell they'd walked into. Marbella was another place now, and once he'd finished his business Curro had no desire to ever return. Nothing tied him to the place any longer: not old friends, his gang having long since dispersed; not the beaches, their former tranquility having long since vanished; and certainly not its present social scene. Marbella had sold itself, if not too cheaply then too indiscriminately. After all its years as a playground for the jet set, famous artists, refined aristocrats, and the recently enriched, the area was now heading downhill fast, just one more destination for the cheap package tours flooding the country.

These were his thoughts as he sat slowly sipping Chivas on the rocks, when some movement at the next table snapped him out of his reverie. The bubbly, gregarious troupe of youths at the next table had suddenly broken off conversations to greet the titan who'd just approached their table. Curro found the young man unsettling at first sight. He had a vaguely gypsy air, his tight T-shirt made the most of his rock-hard pecs and abs, and his raw magnetism was strikingly apparent. The whole group shot to their feet, the guys giving him the firmest handshakes they could muster, the girls leaning in close for kisses on cheeks. The newcomer stood alongside the group for just as long as it took to let them all admire him, then went on his way. As he walked off his gaze met Curro's, and for a second Curro thought the man had smirked at him, a tight-lipped, faintly obscene grin. Then he was gone and Curro blinked back to reality. *I must be overtired,* he thought, *I'm seeing things.*

"Cugggo!" When he heard that he was *sure* he must be delusional. No, no such luck—it was Pamela Sundheim, who in spite of all the time she'd been hung up on Curro, had never managed to master the Spanish rolled r's in his name. Pam's father, so he'd been told, headed up one of East End London's roughest blackmail and protection rackets. Curro hadn't ever bothered finding out if it was true.

"Pam what a surprise!" *You've put on a few more pounds*, he thought. Her short, freckly frame was—to Curro's eye—drifting towards Rubenesque.

"I should be the one saying that, we've not seen you around here for ages! It's as if you were avoiding us," she said with mock seriousness, completely unaware of the fact that she'd hit the nail on the head.

Pam was with an entourage that was now greeting people at the table next to Curro, the one the striking young man had just left. Pam reached over and grabbed one of her companions by the elbow, pulling him slightly off balance as he turned so she could introduce him to Curro.

"Cuggo, allow me to introduce my fiancé, Fidel Basurto—*Count* of Basurto," she stressed proudly. "Tonight's our engagement party, you mustn't miss it!"

Fidel turned and found himself face-to-face with his old classmate. If he was trying to hide his annoyance, he didn't do a very good job. In truth, a sizable proportion of the Costa del Sol's residents had made up their pasts. Some of them in time actually seemed to have forgotten the truth, to have assimilated a vanity commensurate with their bogus new status. Even so, *Count of Basurto!* It was all Curro could do to keep a straight face. *So, the Basurtos, that middle-class dynasty of more or less prominent judges, have traded in the bench for nobility. Well, whatever floats your boat.*

"Delighted, my lord," said Curro solemnly.

"Oh, come off it, Curro!" Basurto turned redder than a tomato, despite his deep tan. While Pam was distracted in conversation with someone else, Basurto leaned towards Curro. "You know what people are like around here. Pam's family got it into their heads that I was a count, because the Daoiz-Basurtos are distant cousins of ours, you know, and—"

"Say no more. And don't apologize, I mean, a trivial thing like this. If your being a Count turns them on, then be a Count. I won't be the one to tell them any different. Besides, who knows—maybe you were a Count all along, and we just never noticed."

He made his remark in a neutral tone, perhaps with just the faintest hint of mockery, though it was taken as a personal insult by the prospective consort to the heiress of the Sundheims' hard-earned (or not) millions. Basurto shot Curro a dirty look and walked off, joining a group that seemed to be hosting a local politician, the alderman with authority over zoning permits in a nearby town with a coastal wildlife reserve.

Still clutching his Scotch, Curro stood, suddenly alone and openly laughing. *The way things are going around here,* he thought, *I'm going to have to make up a title if I want to get a decent table in a restaurant. Or even be invited out for drinks.*

"Cugggo! We're leaving. The party starts at one. Do you remember the way?"

"To your place in Los Monteros? Sure. Or is it being held at the Counts of Basurto's mansion?" he asked pointedly, oblivious to the daggers his former classmate was staring at him.

"Now don't forget, Cugggo, I'm counting on you. We'll have a blast. The civil ceremony's being held in London, by the way. Daddy insisted. Oh, listen, when you're ready to come on up, would you mind bringing Alex there? He's a friend of Fidel's and he doesn't know the way."

Curro turned around and nearly walked straight into the dark stranger whose arrival had been so celebrated, whose good looks Curro had found so disquieting. Alex looked at him intently, as if he were under a microscope. Curro didn't mind this in the least, it gave him more time to bask in the sex appeal that positively emanated from this swaggering new acquaintance. Curro thought something had changed. Of course! His outfit, now it was much more brash. Alex had changed from the tight T-shirt into an unbuttoned vest which only drew more attention to his physique, a daring look he was nevertheless able to pull off with ease. Curro made no attempt to hide his interest and shot Alex a look loaded with innuendo, a look Alex acknowledged with a possessive smile after swelling up like a peacock.

"Of course, it would be my pleasure. In fact, I'll be happy to take your friend to dinner, and when we finish we can head on over to your place. See you at one sharp." He gave Pam a peck on the cheek and then nodded formally at the somber, bitter-faced Basurto.

"See you later, my lord." Curro sat back down. His erstwhile neighbors, Alex's friends, had already left for dinner. He gestured towards Alex. "Grab a seat. What're you drinking?"

"Nothing. Pay up and let's go."

"No way, man, I'm not going off and leaving this half-finished," he said, raising his Scotch. "In fact, I'd like another one before dinner. Waiter," he said with a gesture, "can I get another Chivas on the rocks please?" He turned back to Alex. "Hey, listen, go have dinner with your friends if you want, I can wait here. Or are any of them going to Pam's party? I'm sure there'd be room for one more. Have to be a *lot* of room to fit you in. But I'm sure any one of them would be delighted to give a guy like you a ride."

Alex chuckled. "You can say that again. Anyway, I wouldn't give a damn whether they were delighted or not. But I'm going with you."

"Have a seat then, chief," Curro repeated, tugging on Alex's arm.

When the waiter brought his drink, Curro, provocative as ever, spoke before Alex had a chance to.

"Please bring this gentleman brown rice and chicken. Better make it an extra large helping." Alex started laughing.

"I'm sorry, sir, we only serve drinks. And bar snacks."

"Well, if you don't have food, you'd better find some, don't you think? I mean, are you really going to say no to a guy who's this buff and starving? Flex those guns," he said and nodded at Alex. "Show yourself to the gallery, please! Astound us with your brutal strength! Show your superior dominance!"

Alex, who was laughing so hard his sides hurt, stood up and flexed his muscles for all to see, having flung off his vest. Curro's little charade had drawn a curious crowd of passersby and the bar's owner had come out to see what was going on. He knew Alex, knew what kind of set he ran with, and how suddenly—and violently—his mood could change. For the time being Alex seemed happy to keep performing, Curro keeping up his ringmaster's patter; no one at the bar dared check the behavior of someone who was living proof that the raw power of the jungle walks among us. They were taking things too far, sure, but it was all in good fun. Or would have been, if the guys sitting at a table in the next bar over hadn't gotten jealous of the way their dates were gaping admiringly at Alex. They were four Argentine polo players whose team was touring Europe for a competition. They were all tall, handsome, and seriously put out at the way their beautiful companions were getting worked up about Alex's show of strength.

"*Oshe, pibe,*" one of them called out, "enough of that shit, all right?"

"Dude, I'd button your lip if I were you," Curro said. "I don't think you really want to feel the uncontrolled rage of this portentous champion, half man, half god, whose gaze alone could cut you in two."

Curro liked to hear himself dramatizing out loud. Dramatics could invest any event with a grandeur it otherwise lacked. And multiply its intensity exponentially. It transformed any scene.

Aching to show the beauties at his table that no matter how impressed they were by perfectly shaped and proportioned muscles, he wasn't going be silenced by the mere sight of him, the man who'd called time on Alex's exhibition got to his feet. His pals followed suit.

With three glasses of Scotch under his belt and the onset of the loose, euphoric state they triggered, Curro was delighted by the effect his over-the-top act was having. *Let's see what Big Boy here can do,* he thought. Alex hadn't made a move yet, hadn't shown any reaction to the Argentine gauntlet. He stood his ground, self-possessed, supremely serene no matter how many guys were in the other group. He shot Curro a sidelong glance, looking faintly amused; he was egging Curro on. In fact, Alex himself was surprised to find himself letting someone else call the shots.

"Okay, guys, you might as well drop your panties," Curro called out, provocatively. "You're already beaten and you don't even know it yet. My friend here will now proceed to humiliate you all while your tramps watch."

"Wha—? *La concha de tu madre* —!"

My mother's conch shell? Curro thought. He wasn't entirely sure what the Argentine meant but vaguely remembered having heard that it wasn't a term of endearment in the southern hemisphere.

Every so often people face a choice between two opposing ways to save face: standing firm or standing down. This was one of those times when in the long run standing down would really have been the better choice, for the four Argentine guys. They mistook Alex's stillness for hesitation, even doubt. They rolled up their sleeves, handed their watches and rings to their dates, and stood together facing Alex and Curro.

At that point Curro metaphorically washed his hands of the matter; it was time for Alex to take the lead. Alex gently pushed Curro to one side, where he found a front-row seat convenient for the show. Curro had a feeling any participation by him wouldn't tip the scales either way; he took a small sip of his scotch and waited for the curtain to go up. Then, as if on cue, an Alex he had guessed at but not yet seen emerged to face the four.

"What?!" he said, taking one step forward, a new expression on his face. "What?!" he shouted again, leaving the lounge area and standing in the middle of the street that ran along the waterfront.

Now the Argentines hesitated, surprised at the aggressiveness shown by their lone opponent. That was when they realized they might have bitten off more than they could chew. Alex's body and the resolve that went with it spoke for themselves. It was too late for them back down now, in full view of their girlfriends and the rest of the onlookers. The leader of the group looked at his three pals and shrugged, expecting an answer.

"What, changed your mind now, ladies?" Alex sneered. "Think again." He looked at Curro. "You didn't really think interrupting us like that was gonna be free, did you? I sure hope not."

He grabbed the first one by his neck, easily lifting him several inches off of the ground. The others hesitated briefly before their pride spurred them forward in support of their buddy. Alex didn't even break a sweat. He repelled the lanky horsemen's crude onslaught with a few rapid moves that left two of them in the water and a third moaning on the sidewalk with a broken leg. Meanwhile, their leader, purple-faced from suffocation with his neck still firmly in Alex's grasp, looked as if he wished to just be put out of his misery.

Curro admired both Alex's technique and his boldness, but could see from the faces of the ladies and of the bar's owner that it was time to wrap up the show. Besides, the police could show up any minute. He got up and quickly grabbed hold of Alex's wrist.

"Okay, that's enough."

"Says who?"

"I do, man. Seriously, that's enough. You're the fucking master, no one can possibly doubt that. Now let's get out of here."

Alex relented, dropping the man he was still holding. Relaxed, cocky, he sauntered back to their table and dropped a couple of 50 euro notes, more than enough for the drinks they'd had. Curro and Alex made their way through the crowd, which parted respectfully to one side, and took off in search of new thrills. On their way back to the parking lot, where Curro had parked the car he'd borrowed—a *Seat Ibiza* that was ready for retirement—Alex stopped when they were even with a top-drawer motorcycle.

"Let's take my bike. Dinner's on *me*," he stressed.

"Whatever you say. I thought you didn't have any way to get to Los Monteros."

"Well, I've got this. Hop on."

"What, without a helmet? We could get one hell of a fine for that."

"Wear mine. Here."

"Okay, put this back on," Curro said, handing Alex the vest he'd picked up as they'd left the bar.

Curro straddled the motorcycle, holding Alex's waist firmly. The vest was open and a touch of his warm, smooth skin gave him an agreeable feeling of familiarity, of being at home. Curro's hands went up to Alex's pecs, which he grabbed firmly, while pulling the driver's torso back towards him. Alex turned just enough to shoot him a condescending smirk. Curro, oblivious to the surroundings, nibbled on Alex's neck. Alex stopped the motorcycle and got off, laughing, looking at Curro incredulously.

"Dude, are you outta your mind? You know who I am?"

"Of course. You're the fucking master. Hunk among hunks. The one who could kill with a single look. The one everyone fears, no one dares challenge. And a helpless creature in need of protection, which I'm going to give you."

Alex kept on laughing. "Dude, you're a complete nutjob, you know that?" He got back on the bike and kicked off again. "Yes!" said Curro. "I'm passionately crazy about your power, your awe-inspiring strength. I'm crazy about the most lethally powerful man ever seen."

With Curro in full verse, ad-libbing a speech that surprised and amused even himself, they pulled up outside the restaurant Alex had chosen, near the Don Pepe Hotel. The staff greeted them very coolly, suspicious of such an odd looking pair, and a young waiter warned them that a table outside, on the terrace, was out of the question; they were all reserved already. Curro and Alex were discussing whether to hope for better luck somewhere else when a tanned, attractive gentleman with piercing eyes and whose age was hard to guess strode confidently up and interrupted them:

"Why, Curro! It's been a while."

"Manolo?" said Curro distractedly. "I didn't know you were around. Still in the saddle, I see. Nice place you have here. Did you ditch the Beach Bar?"

"Hell yeah, long time ago. This place is much more profitable. It became fashionable a few years back. Still doing pretty damn well," he said, looking at Alex disdainfully. "You here for dinner?" Curro nodded. "In that case, hang on for just a minute while I set it up."

Manolo went off into the far end of his restaurant and emerged onto the terrace carrying a table himself, followed by waiters carrying chairs and a table service for two. It was set up in no time and Manolo discreetly withdrew, though not before he'd cast another disapproving glance at Curro's company.

"Asshole. He knows me perfectly well but didn't even bother to say hello," Alex muttered furiously as he took a seat. "He does one more thing to piss me off, I'll rip his fucking head off."

"Relax, I've known Manolo for years. He's not a bad guy."

"Well, I'm gonna rip his fucking head off. Son of a bitch! I've been here like a million times, with *really* important people."

"Ahh, let it go," Curro said, unfolding a napkin on his lap. "Let's not let it spoil our dinner."

They ordered only sardines roasted on a spit over an open flame—afterwards, they asked for seconds—and Sangría—there'd be seconds of that, too.

"Dude, you oughtta keep your hands to yourself, you know that? No one feels me up like that. I mean, not a guy. I let girls do it—I let some of them, anyway," he said with a smile, starting to relax. "You were groping me like some kinda queer. Do I look queer to you?"

"No way, man. You know damn well you don't. I couldn't help it, sorry."

"Forget about it. So, I take it you're loaded? Basurto, Pamela, the kinda service you get here... and that whole posh schmuck look you got going on."

"No need to exaggerate, but what I do have will be yours. I want you to ruin me, take all my money, beat it out of me. I come before you on bended knee, oh King of the Jungle," said Curro theatrically.

"Stop acting like a faggot."

"It's true, chief. When I saw you I felt something I can't explain, I've felt really strange ever since. It's like I've turned into someone else. You've turned me gay."

"Give it a rest."

"I'm confused, almighty Thor. Seriously, man, I'm straight, I like girls with huge tits," he lied brazenly, performing a role that had suddenly occurred to him unbidden. "But your strength, your power, it's thrown me for a loop. It's like a teenage crush."

"Fine, whatever. What do you do? You some kind of millionaire?"

"Money, money, money—what a drag. 'Money makes the world go round'," said Curro as he began humming the song from *Cabaret*. "Of course I have money, man. I wouldn't even dare to look at you if I didn't. I want to take care of you, treat you like you deserve to be treated. Let me be Uncle Curro, or the daddy you always needed. What, you think I couldn't tell? Your eyes, man, they're screaming for someone to treat you like a human being, not just like an omnipotent giant."

Curro was a big fan of the need-for-love gambit, it had always worked really well for him. Was there anyone who didn't need it? Except him. But he knew he was exceptional, a singular case of independence and fulfillment in solitude. He'd never needed anyone except Trasto.

"How could you tell?" asked Alex. "It's true, dude. Except for my mother, everybody's afraid of me. Even my family, even friends I've known my whole life. And girls, they're terrified of me. Oh, they like it when I'm doing them, but that's all they see in me. I mean, they don't even try to see what's inside, get to know me. Friends are pretty much the same. They just want me along when we go out at night in case a fight breaks out or so I can introduce them to chicks. That's all."

"Everything's changed, little tyke. *My* little tyke," he said with a knowing smile. "Daddy's going to take good care of the most fearsome man who ever saw the light of day, the terrible warrior who kills for fun and looks into his victims' eyes while he gulps down their souls. I love you, Alex, you are power itself. From this day forth, your name will be power. Tell me, mass murderer, how many men have you killed with your bare hands? How many have shit themselves at the mere sight of you?"

"So many questions! You can't expect me to tell you everything the first day."

For a moment Curro paused his fevered monologue. *What an answer,* he thought. *So it's true. Not only is this guy capable of killing, he's already done it.* It didn't really surprise him that much. With the kind of power he'd displayed and the kind of personality Curro suspected, he thought Alex seemed perfectly capable of killing with his bare hands, of slowly choking the life out of any opponent and holding tight till the last gasp. The conversation picked back up, though in a different tone. Then Alex surprised him.

"Dude, I dunno, I feel confused too. I could tell from the minute we met that you're an ok guy. More than that..." he said, trailing off. "You'll think this sounds stupid, but I," his voice rose, his ego still showing through the words, "a big, strong, tough guy like me, I feel good being with you. I don't know."

"Not as good as you're going to feel. Especially after you've plucked me dry, beaten my whole fortune out of me, with your unparalleled powers of intimidation."

"Dude, give that a rest. You're whack. You remind me a little of this gorgeous babe I just met," he hesitated for a moment. "She's loaded like you are, some kinda countess or something... I gotta take a leak."

It never occurred to Curro that the "countess or something" in question might happen to be Eugenia. Much less that the dark stranger who'd awakened his basest desires, whose appeal was enough to make him demean himself, might be her kidnapper and be abusing her. Curro was in a dreamy state, entirely focused on the magnificent specimen who'd walked into his life and who so well embodied the ideal of beauty his gender and species were capable of attaining.

Harsh shouts shook him from his reverie. He looked up and underneath the blood could just make out the features of one of the most fey people he'd ever met: his mother's former hairdresser.

"Police, help, someone call the police! That beastly man just broke my nose!"

The beastly man in question was apparently none other than Alex, who exited the restaurant with the owner and three waiters hot on his heels. As Alex passed the hysterical little man, he shoved him.

"See? See?" said the hairdresser in a lilting little voice. "Someone do something, he almost killed me!"

"Shaddup, you flaming faggot, or I'll rip your head off!" came the only answer.

Manolo and his waiters were standing at a prudent distance, unsure quite what to do. It fell to Curro to approach and question the accused.

"All right, what's going on here?"

"This little faggot here followed me into the men's room and stood at the urinal next to mine so he could take a nice long look while I was pissing. If it hadn't been 'cause I'm here with you, I swear I woulda slammed his head into the crapper and made him swallow it all. He told me he'd give me a thousand euros, like I was some fucking rent boy! I'll kill you, you fucking little fudgepacker, you hear me?" Alex took a step back towards him, and Curro stepped out to block his path, while the hairdresser retreated to the sidewalk outside the restaurant.

"Police! Somebody help me! I'm bleeding to death!"

"Relax, man, it's not that serious. Come here, I'll take a look at it."

"You! Curro Morante! Libertine! I used to know your mother. *She* was a lady. You're no better than a common oaf. What would she say if she saw the company you keep? The shame!"

"Oh, get over yourself. Manolo, bring me the check. We're leaving."

"Not till the police get here!" shouted the hairdresser, shrilly. "He *broke* my *nose!*"

"Then consider yourself lucky you got off that lightly. If you'd done that to me, I would've broken your whole goddamn face. Idiot. You want the police, fine, let's call the police!" Alex elbowed Curro sharply in the ribs, none too subtly indicating an opposing viewpoint. Curro continued: "Just remember, sexual harassment can get you a pretty hefty fine—get the wrong judge and you might even do time. Then again, who knows, that might suit you just fine, you could go from urinal to urinal being the pass-around slut for the whole cell block. So go on, call the cops!"

By now the hysterical hairdresser's tablemates had joined him and they gently shepherded him away from the restaurant, thinking things were likely to go from bad to worse if he stayed much longer. Manolo, much relieved, handed Curro the check, which he paid in cash, adding a generous tip. Manolo shook hands with him, but reluctantly said a sullen good night to Alex. The snub didn't go unnoticed, and Alex shot back through gritted teeth, "Maybe next time you'll remember me, pal! You know Gagarin, the Russian bigwig? I've only been here about a zillion times with him. I'm his partner."

Curro heard this remark over his shoulder and froze for a moment, a chill running down his spine.

Gagarin? Alex's *partner*? The last bit was probably just Alex puffing himself up, it sounded like a brag he might have used before in fashionable places around town. But if he did work with Gagarin, then that babe he was talking about, the weird rich one, "some kinda countess or something" must be Eugenia. *Okay,* Curro thought, *now it's* really *time to call the cops. It's a shame, too, I was really into this guy.* While he was trying to figure out some way he could sneak off, call Carlitos in Madrid, and then make himself scarce until the cavalry arrived, Alex's cell rang. He answered it in Russian, and the short call changed his demeanor completely. He looked coldly at Curro as he finished the conversation and hung up.

"That was Gagarin, wasn't it?" Curro said, tipping his hand. "And that babe you were talking about—that's Eugenia Osorio, the model, isn't it?"

Alex considered his words for a moment before he spoke. "That's right. He knows you're here and wants to see you tomorrow at his place. He says you two have business to discuss."

"I don't have any business to discuss with that crook! He's a murdering extortionist, in case you didn't know. But of course you do know, don't you? You're one of them!"

Alex shook his head as if Curro couldn't possibly understand and then said, "I really hate to have to do this 'cause you're a cool guy and everything, but I'm gonna have to keep you with me until tomorrow, when he'll be available to receive you at home."

"Oh, he'll receive me at home, will he? That's awfully obliging of him! What he wants to do, for some reason, is to kidnap me too. Well, neither

Eugenia nor I knows anything that could possibly be of any interest to him. I'm going to the police right now. Come with me. There's time for you to break loose of Gagarin and come clean."

Alex seemed to hesitate for just a second, but when he saw Curro turn around and resolutely head back towards the restaurant, he reached out and grabbed him hard enough to stop him in his tracks.

"You try to take off and I'll break your neck right here," he said matter of factly. "Get on the motorcycle, nice and easy, and no funny moves."

***

Sleeping with the enemy. Curro thought someone should make a movie called that, and then he remembered Hollywood had already used the title. Only this wasn't a movie, and he sure as hell couldn't get to sleep. The ride from the restaurant had gone by in a blur: now he was in a secret room set up as a hideaway underneath a modest country house, far from prying eyes. A degree of claustrophobia—something else he shared with Eugenia—made it impossible for him to rest after the exhausting psychological session he'd taken part in... nd the other thing.

Once he'd been forced through a hatch hidden in the floor, a battle of wits, of lies and self-interest, had begun, in which Curro tried to talk the new villain of the piece out of membership in a mob organization with no future.

"Don't you realize Gagarin's a one-way ticket to nowhere? He's wanted on felony charges in half of Europe. Sooner or later, someone's going to lock him up and throw away the key. So then what happens to you? Are you going to hire yourself to the highest bidder as muscle, as a hitman?" Curro paused as if waiting for an answer, or perhaps to let his words sink in to Alex's head. "Gagarin is not an option for anyone able to think beyond the short term. If they don't lock you up with him, for that matter. I mean, you must be nose-deep in all the shit he's wanted for. Or aren't you?" *I should have kept that to myself,* he thought. "You've got to ditch him while there's still time to save yourself."

"Why, you got something better to offer?" asked, turning towards Curro angrily. "I mean, apart from that load of bullshit you were dropping during dinner?"

"I offer you the chance to be my companion, the man who makes me happy, a partner to travel and enjoy myself with."

"Bull*shit.*"

"The one I share my fortune with... All of it!"

"I'm not gay."

"I know that. You're the man whose portentous strength—"

"Shut the fuck up, will you? Enough of that shit! You're just trying to get laid. If you think that's gonna work with me, you've got another thing coming, pal. I'd sooner kill you."

"Alex, just a short time ago you said that you like me, you feel good around me, protected even. Can't you see that to me it could be comforting—an honor, even—to take care of, to look after, a neglected kid like you?" After blurting all this out, Curro was surprised to find himself starting to believe his own lies.

"What a crock of shit."

"Alex!" Curro, said, moving closer. "Let me go, help me set Eugenia free, and I promise I can make it worth your while. I have contacts."

"Yeah, and they're just gonna flush my whole rap sheet, right? You asked me a while ago if I'd ever killed anybody with my bare hands. Well, you know the answer to that now, don't you? Lots of times. And I didn't feel a damn thing. It's just like pissing or taking a shit."

Curro thought back to the three Russian goons he'd killed and for the first time understood a killer's reaction of this kind. "You're absolutely right. Especially if your own life is in danger."

Alex rolled his eyes. "How the hell would you know that?"

"I don't know anything, I'm just guessing."

"Well, knock it off, asshole!"

***

They were alone in semidarkness, a single naked bulb dangling from the ceiling of the secret room . Both were seated on the floor, as far away from each other as they could get in the cramped space, each pondering their own problems. Curro decided to make a move. He moved closer, uncertainly, not quite sure at first how to go about it. He put an arm around Alex's shoulder and gently gave him a kiss, which Alex didn't reject. He could feel the other man's turmoil, and his own, his heart threatening to burst out of his chest with each beat. For a moment he forgot everything, caught up in the eroticism of risk and ready to unreservedly cross the line to danger. *Here goes. What do I have to lose?*

"Relax." It was all he said.

He began by massaging Alex's temples in a way that was supposed to be rhythmic, although his nerves made that quite a challenge. After a few minutes during which he'd extended his activity to Alex's whole face, he moved lower, to Alex's sweaty, heaving chest, which rose and fell rapidly with his breath. He took his time here, savoring the moment, before the final step, spreading him out lengthwise on the rough carpet, at every step fearing the crashing blow he might receive in response. But none came. He decided to really apply himself and racked his brain for the most unusual skills he'd learned at any of a thousand different places, with a thousand different techniques. Alex gave him free rein, till his sexuality, never much below the surface, broke free, unrestrained, yielding to the pleasure of novelty. Alex too was a past master at the art of feeling pleasure, savoring it, reveling in it, and was gifted with an extraordinary ability to trigger lust in his partners, a lust always rooted in the ecstasy of surrender to a natural master, a boundlessly potent master.

Alex drifted into a natural display of authority that moved Curro; the pursuit of pleasure had taken him down paths he'd never expected to tread, and now, at last, he discovered and accepted the painful fulfillment derived from unreservedly giving oneself over to the will of a superior being.

***

Curro couldn't sleep. He was pinned down by the weight of the vigorous athlete who now slept curled over his torso. *Sure enough,* he thought, *daddy this, little tyke that, and they end up believing it.*

In fact, in his previous relationships with men like Alex, Curro had always been the one leading the orchestra, so to speak. He liked to protect and give confidence to big, burly guys who made others uneasy but who often, he'd discovered, had low self-esteem and needed support to believe in themselves.

Apart from the weight on his midriff, which he accepted without complaint, there were other reasons he couldn't drift off to sleep. Foremost among them, the thoughts racing through his mind. Had his words hit home? Had he convinced Alex that to stay with Gagarin was to back a losing horse? Or had his effort itself been a lost cause, had there really never been any chance of driving a wedge between Alex and his employer?

As he lay there he felt he couldn't be sure of anything. The position he was in—down a dark hiding hole, unable to escape, locked in a hired killer's embrace—wasn't exactly conducive to clearheadedness. Finally he made a brusque movement on purpose to wake up his beguiler.

"Alex —"

"Hmm? Lemme sleep—"

"I'm all mixed up. I think I like you, really. And I don't just mean what we just did. Being with you stimulates me, I feel more alive, more enthused." Part of Curro was speaking the truth but a larger part of him was laying a plan.

"I had a great time too. And you're totally cool, man. But lemme sleep."

"Alex," he persisted.

"Dude, gimme a break, I'm totally beat. Lemme sleep!"

Curro gave up. He didn't want to push things.

After the brief exchange, Alex flopped over, but was still unable to get back to sleep. He felt even more mixed up than Curro did. He'd never had the slightest inclination to have sex with another man. And what was even more amazing was that he'd liked it. Although, in the end, *that* wasn't really what was keeping him awake. He'd always done whatever the hell he felt like and didn't owe any explanations to anyone. He wasn't afraid to face up to new and unexpected desires. No, what he really couldn't believe was that he'd reached this level of harmony and understanding with a posh, queer, older guy he'd never set eyes on before. And his proposal—it was tempting: give up the rough life he'd led till now, tell Gagarin to shove it, trade it all for a quieter life with a guy like Curro, who promised to be anything but boring. And he was loaded. He knew that when he'd been ordered to go find him, have dinner with him and keep an eye on him. But Alex was no fool. Apart from how dangerous it would be to leave the organization he belonged to, was Curro for real, or was his proposal just a tactic for getting out of a life-threatening situation. Could he trust someone like Curro? Wasn't he just trying to put Alex off-guard so he could save Eugenia and himself?

"Alex," Curro whispered, not realizing he was making a mistake, "I don't think I even need to tell you that if you drop Gagarin and help me free Eugenia, I'll be eternally grateful. You can get away from all this, go wherever you like. We don't need to get the police involved. We could leave right now, go to my place in Guadalmina, and I'll give you everything I have there. And wire more money wherever you tell me to. Whatever you want, man."

"Yeah, right," said Alex, snapping back to reality. "So now you don't want me to be your wild little tyke after all?"

"Of course I do."

"And you don't want us to be lords of the night and masters of every whorehouse in Madrid?"

"I do, I do."

"And you don't want us to go around ripping heads off to show the world our, what did you call it, portentous and devastating power?"

"Yes, portentous and devastating, among other things."

"Shut it!"

"Alex, I want us to…to go away together. I've found things I couldn't have imagined in you, I want us to share our lives."

"Right, so that's why you want me to take your money and run."

"You can't stay here! You said so yourself. The police, your priors. We could meet up in a while, somewhere outside Spain."

"Yeah, right," he said, turning over with a dismissive laugh.

"Look, I don't think I need to tell you what I felt, you could see it for yourself."

"It was just one fuck, dammit!"

"But a damn good one, wasn't it?"

"Yeah, so? You gonna fall in love because of a single fuck?"

"Who knows, man? I like being with you, I like the whole rough thing you've got going on. You're an animal!"

"Yeah, like a circus monkey."

"No, come on, you know that's not what I mean. You enjoyed it too, unless you were faking it."

"I don't *ever* fake it. I don't have to. I'm King of the Jungle, remember?" Alex's voice changed slightly; he spoke resentfully, beginning to feel as though it had all just been a chimera.

"I just know that I like you and that we should try to fix things so they end up as good as possible for all if us. And of course I like you. Have you seen yourself in the mirror? Who *wouldn't* like you? Men, women, children. Shit, even animals turn their heads when you walk by. Yes, you are the King of the Jungle, and anyone can see that from a mile away. And that attitude you're rocking—"

"Bullshit."

Curro realized he wasn't getting anywhere. "Look, Alex, have it your way. Forget it all. Please let me go," he said precisely, slowly, in the grip of desperation. "I'll sort the mess with Eugenia out myself. All you have to do is disappear. Come back to my place and I'll give you everything I've got on me. Should be about twenty thousand euros."

"You joking? That's chump change."

"I'll wire more to you later, anywhere you say."

"You're one dumbass rich dude, you know that? Gagarin will *never* let me just take a walk. I know too much. He'd hunt me down to the ends of the earth to take me out. You don't know what a vindictive son of a bitch he is."

"Sooner or later, Gagarin's going down."

"Well, before he does, he'll take down everything he can, starting with Eugenia."

A chill went through Curro at the mention of her name. "Enough, Alex! React!"

"Get off my back! You're a fucking liar, I oughtta beat the shit outta you."

His back up against the wall, Curro decided he had to go one step further, push things to breaking point if need be. His life, among others, was on the line.

During that session of reckless abandon with his jailer, they'd sampled a variety of roles both physical and verbal. Curro was an expert—had been for years—in setting up raunchy situations to lead his partners into unexpected situations in which tone and position were reversed. He'd done the dominant master, authoritarian father on more than one occasion himself—all fiction. But seeing as nothing else he'd tried was making any progress, and with the walls closing in on him, it seemed like inaction would be the end of him. He stood up, outwardly resolute but inwardly shaky.

"Daddy says that's enough, you're a spoiled child who must be punished. Open the door, now! Obey Daddy!"

"What?" Alex wasn't sure if he was dreaming or hearing things.

"Obey Daddy!" shouted Curro, giving him a slap that echoed off the walls around them.

***

Pain! Curro's soul had been broken in pieces for quite some time. It hurt him deeply, would never heal, would be the end of him sooner or later. But his body was something else. Maybe he'd had an unusually high pain threshold; the fact of the matter was, he'd just never felt it the way it seemed to affect other people. When he'd been younger, when he'd spent his first, wildest nights on the town, he'd go back to his parents' place with bruises or scratches that he hadn't the faintest idea how he'd received. There'd even been one night, some creeps had been harassing these girls he knew and he and his group took them on; knives came out, but afterwards he'd even stopped to have one for the road at some joint on the edge of town before heading home and discovering a knife wound he hadn't even noticed. Apparently the booze and dope had worked as anesthetic.

He was sure as hell feeling the pain now, and he couldn't find a position that would relieve his howling muscles after the beating he'd taken. Because Alex had really let loose on him after he'd dared to overstep the line. Play in the midst of uncontrolled passion was one thing. Trying to assume a position that wasn't his was something else. He'd been oblivious to most of the brutal thrashing, because the second blow had knocked him unconscious, which at least saved him from seeing the fury driving the man he'd given himself to completely such a short time before.

It was an almost pleasurable pain, a pain sweetened by masochistic overtones, one he didn't entirely shun. He felt bloated, swollen, his joints refused to work; but he didn't really care, the pain he could take, and now he was back to not giving a damn about life.

Stupid, stupid. How could he have thought that a guy like Alex, straight, well-positioned in a powerful mob, a guy who'd sworn unbreakable loyalties, would drop everything—would risk his life—for the fanciful dreams murmured in a state of ecstasy by a silver-spooned guy like him. *Idiot!*

And anyway, besides his obvious appeal, the way that the "call of the jungle" turned him on, he didn't really feel anything for Alex; he could never love him. Dima's unexpected entry into his life had stimulated him, too, and Dima was a much more advisable companion. But the truth was, he could never have felt either of them to be more than a pastime. He had no love to give them. Maybe Eugenia was right, and his fear of commitment would prevent him from ever having a normal relationship, from anything except sincere friendship or flings built on play-acting. Life. Independence taken to the extreme of comfortable, consensual solitude.

CHAPTER XIX

Alex shoved him roughly, jarring him back to the present. The sun had been up for a while. The seasonal heat revived for another day.

"C'mon, move it."

Curro muttered something that Alex took as defiant.

"What? Cut the crap. Haven't you had enough yet?" Alex was looking at his watch expectantly, as if he was waiting for someone to arrive.

"More than enough, thanks for asking. I feel sorry for you, man. Wasting a chance like this..."

"Chance, what chance? A lying faggot who just wants to get laid?"

"*Got* laid, I might remind you. And you didn't exactly seem to be having a bad time..."

"Don't push me, man. I'll rip your fucking head off!"

"Jeez, you're like a broken record. Why don't you give the whole head-ripping thing a rest? It's not like you belong to one of those Amerindian tribes."

"What?" snapped Alex.

"Never mind. I'm not afraid of you, I don't give a shit about your threats. What do I have to lose? My life? Fine, go ahead, kill me! My life is meaningless. I mean, if things have gotten to the point where I'm wasting it chasing after unsatisfied, head-ripping... *ueer* thugs..."

"You're asking for it..."

"Dude, you've already given me *so* much. And it wasn't half bad. I have to admit it: you *are* the fucking master, a peerless enforcer of your own rules. And I love you for that," —*Showtime!*— "You're the greatest ripper-offer of heads who ever walked this earth! No one has ever ripped off a head the way you can... Sir!"

"Fuck, not that again. You're making me puke."

"Alex, I know you're crazy about me! Because I'm the one you couldn't intimidate, the one with more inner strength than you. Much more. Won't you be my head-ripper-offer? Let's love each other to the very edge and beyond, an endless embrace."

"You're crazy as a loon. I can't believe a word you say. You spend all day spouting horseshit."

Just then they heard a horn outside, an impatient sound. Alex cuffed Curro, blindfolded him and put a hood over his head, and then they left the hideaway. He wasn't sure where they were taking him but he guessed it couldn't be too far away, and probably near the mountain that rose up behind the town. They weren't in the car for very long, and it felt like they went uphill the whole time.

Alex pulled him out of the car, pushed him along, and didn't turn him loose again till they were already in what he guessed would be his cell. It looked like a comfortable enough suite, with a bathroom and a small living room, through the window of which he could see a swimming pool and, beyond that, the mountains. He knew at once he'd been right about their approximate location. As he took in his surroundings, Alex told him Gagarin would see him the following day. Before leaving the room he turned back to Curro with a somber expression.

"Well, Curro, I'm sorry. It's been a pleasure. I hope you get lucky with Gagarin, I really do."

"I hope you get lucky too. And as for the pleasure... vidently, it's all mine," he said with a smile.

***

Alone in his cozy little prison, locked in with no one to talk to, Curro spent the rest of the day brooding over his situation. Carlos Jiménez had warned him to watch his step around Gagarin. Well, now he'd get the chance to. He was worried, to a point; he really did feel as if he had nothing left to lose and it was only Eugenia's whereabouts and wellbeing that really troubled him. It was his chances of finding her, of rescuing her, that he kept coming back to in his mind time and again. She was the reason he'd gone to Marbella, and he wouldn't go back to Madrid without her.

Midway through the afternoon, a freckle-faced redhead came in with a tray of sandwiches and beer, which she left on a stand at one end of the room. Some goon followed her into the room and watched her movements closely. As she left, she winked at Curro and then she muttered something that flabbergasted him.

"I left you today's paper, too. There's an interview with *Real Madrid's* goalie, Casillas. He's in Bilbado and leaving for Messicos."

The door shut. *Bilbado?* he thought. *Messicos?* "Taaassis!" he shouted. *Eugenia*!

He pounced on the paper, rifling through it till he came to the sports section. On the same page as the Casillas interview he found a tiny scrap of paper, carefully taped down. He tore it off and read the terse message.

Curro, get me out of here. I can't take it anymore.
So the redhead had alerted Eugenia of his arrival.

The next day, around eleven A.M., Adrian, the second young tough, came to get Curro. Alex was nowhere to be seen as Curro was led through the mansion to Gagarin's office, where he found the Russian with some unexpected company.

"Your lordship!" said Curro mockingly, trying to figure out what Basurto's presence there meant for him. Probably nothing good, he concluded.

"Shut up, you moron," Basurto said threateningly. " And pay attention, for once."

"Why, has His Excellency the Count forgotten his manners? Aren't you going to introduce me to our host?" he asked, gesturing to Gagarin. "Let me guess: Mister Rasputin! Or is that *Count* Rasputin?"

"*Shut up*! Remember how the whole bunch of you used to talk down to me at school? You all thought you were so much better than me. Well we're not in school anymore, Curro old pal. Now I'm in charge. Around here I'm the fucking boss."

"You don't say. And here I thought I'd already met the most boss-fucking fucking boss of all the boss-fuckers that ever fucked their boss."

Basurto came closer. "Still think you're really funny, don't you? We'll see how long that lasts."

Gagarin watched the exchange, silent, smiling. Curro and Basurto spoke to each other in Spanish; Gagarin barely understood any of it, but what he did understand was enough, taken with the body language, to get some sense of the conversation and the speakers' personalities. *This Morante has guts, gotta give him that. And he's... What do those Brits say, the ones who try to avoid me when I attend events in London? 'A most peculiar fellow.'* Under other circumstances, he was certain he would have found Curro to be much more entertaining company than the preposterous 'Count'. But, he cleared his throat, and addressed Curro in lightly-accented English.

"Mr. Morante, I'm sure you are aware of the misunderstanding that has arisen between myself and your friend *Mr.* Denissov," he said sarcastically. "Am I correct?"

Curro grinned. "Would you like me to translate for His Excellency here? I'm afraid his English may not be up to our level."

"Blow me, Curro," snarled the slighted lawyer in Spanish.

"Shut *up*, Fidel," said Gagarin curtly. "Now, Mr. Morante, you'd really better cooperate. I mean, you and the lovely Miss Osorio—"

All mirth left Curro instantly. "I hope she's all right, because if she's not..."

"Calm down, Mr. Morante. She is perfectly well, and as soon as you've helped me with the Denissov matter, I'll set you both free."

"Stop, man, you're killing me. As if I'd really believe that the great crime boss is going to be nice and politely turn us loose. As for you," Curro switched to Spanish to address Basurto, "I've got a feeling things aren't going to go the way you've planned. Once the wedding's off you'll have to crawl back down to the sewer you oozed out of."

Basurto snapped and tried kicking Curro but, in his rage, lost his balance. Curro – the more agile of the two, thanks to years of sports – swung a fist; it was a feint, and in the split second Basurto was distracted, with his other fist Curro landed a punch right over Basurto's liver, to devastating effect.

"Fidel, Fidel—keep this up and I'll end up believing that we were right at school when we said you weren't the sharpest tool in the shed. I mean, really pitching in with a mobster like this, who already has Interpol breathing down his neck."

Gagarin was losing his patience. He pressed a buzzer on his desk twice, and in walked Alex, wearing his most intimidating look.

"Now *here's* the fucking boss," said Curro to Basurto, pointing at the newcomer.

"Yeah, why don't you try your shit on him," replied Basurto thorough gritted teeth.

"English! I don't understand any of this!" snapped Gagarin.

Curro was only too happy to oblige. Mimicking the halting speech of one of his British acquaintances, he launched into a panegyric on the newcomer's qualities, a pastiche of Elizabethan prose.

"How could I, indeed, try any shit on him? Imbecile! Who would dare? Do not the moon and the stars turn their gaze, the better to appreciate the cadence of he who moves like the tides? Does not the scent exuded by his epidermis bedazzle the senses? Do not the denizens of Olympus envy the harmony and looks of he who charmed the sirens? Was his virile bearing not the envy of others who, like him, boasted of the most noble blood in the universe? Could anyone resist the most perfectly proportioned ideal ever yet seen? Could anyone else ride Pegasus with more perfect horsemanship? Who among his peers is worthy even of comparison? Hercules at the completion of one of his feats? Narcissus upon catching sight of his reflection? Nay, none of them, I tell you. And what of his forcefulness, such that none dare oppose him? And what of the judiciousness with which his father Zeus honored him? Does anyone know—"

"Oh, shut *up,* you queer son of a bitch," Basurto hissed.

"I will shut up when a celestial creature so requires! I am deaf to earthly vulgarity!"

Gagarin, bored with things he couldn't understand in English, or in Spanish, and wouldn't even in Russian, gestured to Alex to cut Curro off. Alex approached Curro, who showed no signs of stopping.

"Perhaps this song of praise vexes the great usurper of the Siberian steppes? Perhaps the vastness of his ignorance induces him to believe his spurious right is worthy of being set against that of he who possesses it by divine whim?"

"Alex!" roared Gagarin.

Alex had had enough—enough of Curro's playacting, but also of Gagarin. Curro's words about Gagarin's fate had rolled over in his head all night. If he stayed with Gagarin he was doomed, and he didn't need Curro to tell him that, but if he left, if he walked away from his boss now, he'd have a small chance—a chance he was willing to take.

He had moved closer to Curro, looked right into his eyes, made a face indicative of how tiresome he found the charade, and then he turned around and made for the exit. When his hand was on the doorknob, Gagarin—his eyes bulging in disbelief—sputtered "Where do you think you're going? I told you to make this lunatic shut up! If you walk out that door now you won't live to tell the tale! I'll have you *executed*!"

"Don't you threaten me. He is out of his mind, you're right about that. But he's not gonna say a word, he doesn't give two shits about anything. Ever since the beating I gave him yesterday morning he's been spouting off like this, complete nonsense. You won't get anything else out of him. He scoffs at life, he scoffs at pain, and he scoffs at you. I'm outta here, I've had it with all this. And don't look for me, or you just might find me."

"Adrian!" Gagarin called out to the thug who stood outside the door. "Stop Alex, keep him from leaving, whatever it takes. Shoot him if you have to!"

No one would stand in Alex's way to keep him from leaving. Everyone knew their place in the pecking order and what could happen as a result of a confrontation: nothing good, especially for Adrian, who stood ostentatiously to one side to clear a path for the departing colleague who'd bested him so many times in so many ways. When he was even with Adrian, Alex said "Don't overdo it with the nutjob in there, or you'll answer to me, you hear? And leave Miss Model alone."

Gagarin called the guard hut at the end of the driveway, instructing them to prevent Alex's desertion by any means possible, and bring him back to the study. When gunshots rang out, Gagarin looked through the window towards the road. His guards lay prone on the asphalt next to the hut. Alex rode out the main gate on his motorcycle, never to return.

Curro was beaten furiously by Basurto, still stinging with embarrassment, and by Gagarin himself, who finally lost his self-control as a result of the complete lack of cooperation displayed by this absurd guest who openly mocked his threats and coercion. Adrian stood impassively watching as they worked him over.

CHAPTER XX

Curro spent a couple of days drifting in and out of consciousness. His only visitor was the redhead, who tried solicitously to interest him in some of the food she'd prepared. It was no use. He wasn't up for anything at all, such was the thrashing he'd taken from the crooks who'd thought he would be their path to Dima and the missing money. The redhead had whispered things to him a few times, things he was too wooly-headed to really process, but he gradually came to understand that she was on his side, and that she knew Eugenia, who trusted her.

On the third day he was doing a little better, enough for Ekaterina to hastily bring him up to speed and confirm that Eugenia was fit and healthy enough to make a break for it. She told him that Eugenia had been despondent after Alex had tired of using her and suddenly abandoned her; but that now she was back to her old self, and with enough grim determination to face up to the risks inherent in an attempted escape.

So the bastard used her, degraded her, he mused. Poor Eugenia, she was far from being used to such harsh treatment. Could she have been able to abandon herself to pleasure, putting issues of dignity out of her mind? Curro felt that she probably could have. She had always been a woman open to exploring new experiences, he didn't think she would slide into lasting depression over some abusive punk. Curro was convinced that Eugenia would be all right, would know how to keep her head up in adversity, with the unbowed pride that had always shown her to be worthy of her lineage.

That same night Ekaterina snuck into Curro's room. She warned him that they didn't have much time; she'd overheard a worrying conversation between Gagarin and his lawyer, heard them agree that it would probably be advisable to leave Spain and relocate their operations to Brazil. The guards' activity wasn't exactly reassuring either; not only had Gagarin brought in extra muscle after Alex's defection, but she'd seen a couple of them digging a deep hole behind the garage.

"Okay, you've convinced me," said Curro. "This is getting very ugly, very quickly. Let me out, we've got to be ready to run for it."

"No! There are more people guarding the house now than I've ever seen here, we wouldn't have a chance. Besides, I don't have the keys to Eugenia's room anymore. Adrian keeps them on him at all times, he even goes in with me whenever I go into her room."

"So what do you suggest? I mean, it sounds to me like we really should get a move on..."

"I'll keep trying to find a way to spring Eugenia tomorrow. In the meantime, keep this," she said, handing him the key to his room. "But if you do want to sneak out to get a feel for the house, be very careful. Don't do it till after midnight, when there are only two or three guards left in the house."

"Will do. Ekaterina, is it?"

"Yes."

"You're very brave. You're coming with us."

"Thanks," she said with the first smile Curro had seen from her. "That's what Eugenia said."

"And so do I."

A couple of hours after Ekaterina's departure, Curro decided to inspect the terrain beyond his cell. Noiselessly he turned the key in the lock, opened the door a crack so he could peer into the hallway, and had just taken his first steps away from the door when he heard fragments of conversation, the voices getting closer.

"... on't see why the hell it has to be us..."

"... as it coming, I'm telling you. You gotta believe me."

In a flash he was back in his room. He kept his ear to the door, hoping to pick up some further exchange, but all was quiet. He lay back down on his bed, but couldn't get to sleep the whole night.

His thoughts focused on ways they could elude the fate all signs seemed to portend. He, Eugenia and their new friend must all escape without further delay. But it wouldn't be easy—less easy, even, than before, Gagarin having now doubled the guards on the place and, apparently, getting everything ready to make them disappear before he took off. Try as he might, no clearly superior option suggested itself. He would have to simply go for broke the following morning: wait for Ekaterina, subdue Adrian, free Eugenia, and then all three together would have to try to sneak out unnoticed. A tall order, but he could see no other way.

The next morning, punctual as a clock, Ekaterina

showed up with his breakfast tray, Adrian lurking behind her like a malevolent shadow. How had she kept him from missing the key she'd stolen the night before? It didn't matter, he decided. Curro looked at her quizzically and she nodded, a signal that she'd located the key to Eugenia's room. As for the muscle, he seemed the same as every other day: serious, silent, confident.

Now. Curro distracted Adrian by asking if he could swim in the pool and when he'd be allowed into the garden. Adrian looked askance at him, then simply ignored him as the two men walked towards the door together; he seemed eager to be gone, precisely the reaction Curro had hoped his peskiness would trigger. In his eagerness to be gone he turned his back on Curro, who grabbed a table lamp near the door—the base of which had been designed to resemble a Chinese vase—and smashed it into the back of Adrian's head with all his strength. Adrian spun around as if he'd hardly felt a thing; now he was paying no attention to Ekaterina, so he didn't see her pull out of her clothes the knife she'd been hiding. She drove the blade into his chest. Stunned by the unexpected attack, Adrian stood there dumbly for a moment, which allowed Ekaterina two more quick stabs with the knife. Without a word he crumpled to the floor in a bloody heap.

Wasting no time she said, "This way!" as she rushed towards the door.

"Where's Eugenia?" asked Curro urgently.

"This way! Follow me!"

Not far away from where Curro had been held was a second door, which Ekaterina now frantically tried to open with a key that stubbornly denied her.

"Curro!" came a voice from inside, sounding both excited and exhausted. "Get me out of here!"

"Eugenia, darling! Are you all right?" He turned to Ekaterina. "What's wrong?"

"Get me out of here, for God's sake!" shrieked Eugenia.

"What's the matter?" he asked Ekaterina, his temper rising. "Are you sure this is the right key?"

"I think so, I took it off of Adrian last night."

You think *so? Great,* thought Curro.

"Get me OUT!" said Eugenia, pounding on the door.

"I'm going to search Adrian, I think you've got the wrong key," said Curro, limping back down the hallway towards his erstwhile jail.

He found Adrian struggling back to his feet; Curro had to admit, the thug lived up to the reputation Russians had for both strength and endurance. Curro grabbed a chair and hit him over the head with it, then hit him again and again, till he realized he'd lost track of what he was supposed to be doing. He threw the chair down and rummaged through Adrian's pockets: shirt, pants, front, back. Nothing. Their operation was starting to look like it had failed before even getting started. How could he free Eugenia now? Just as he was turning back towards her room, he spotted it on the floor; a keyring . Scooping it up, he went back down the hallway towards Eugenia's room, opening her door on the third try. They sprang into a warm, strong hug.

"This way!" Ekaterina interrupted them. "Follow me!"

"Where are you taking us?" puffed Curro, struggling to keep up.

"Through the servants' quarters—the garage!"

They raced towards the garage, hoping to find a car with the keys in the ignition; but before they reached their goal the stubborn sight of Adrian lurched into view. He must have guessed their destination and taken a shortcut. The girls froze; Curro took a step towards the bloody thug.

"Get lost, pal!"

"I twist each of your necks," he said, stumbling towards them unsteadily.

"Oh yeah? Show me," said Curro. Spotting an empty bottle on the floor he smashed its base against the wall. Now he sliced through the air before him, brandishing it by the neck to make his point.

Adrian was unarmed, but this didn't worry him. The Russian felt as if rage alone would suffice to finish the job. He came so close that Curro decided to charge, leaping resolutely forward. Unfortunately he'd misjudged, and in a blink Adrian had disarmed him, throwing the bottle away where it shattered.

"You die in my hands, I squeeze all air out of you." Adrian's Spanish was direct if not glib.

Curro shouted at the girls to run, to get away from there, but it was as if they were rooted to the spot. Adrian had his hands around Curro's neck, squeezing. His thoughts quickly dissipated, his mind went into the darkness.

***

"Curro, Curro, c'mon, man! Wake up! We gotta move!"

When his eyes opened he had to struggle to

comprehend anything. Next to him, shaking him, was Andy Martínez Porras. Andy! How the hell... Questions would have to wait. Andy lifted him up in his arms, as the girls watched agape, especially Ekaterina who recognized the newcomer as part of the extra muscle Gagarin had hired to beef up security after Alex's desertion.

"What happened to the Russian?" Curro asked weakly.

"Forget about him! Follow me!" ordered Andy. They went down some steps and found themselves in the garage where Tony awaited them behind the wheel of a van. He scowled, looking worried.

"Get a move on, for fuck's sake! Those guys on the gate looked at me funny when I headed in here—ah, shit, here they come."

The two guards who patrolled the outer perimeter of Gagarin's estate had been told in no uncertain terms not to allow anyone in or out; they'd been a little surprised to see both Martínez brothers going into the garage but then that was not unusual as they had dealings with their boss before. Seeing as how neither of them had come back out yet, they'd decided to take a look.

The fugitives jumped into the van, the girls in back and Andy and Curro up front next to the driver. The guards shouted for them to stop, and Tony responded by flooring the accelerator. The truck roared head-on towards the guards; they just managed to leap aside, but were on their feet in no time, the machine guns slung around their shoulders deafeningly strafing the truck's wake.

"Heads down, ladies!" Tony charged downhill

towards the main gate, a heavy wrought-iron affair, and rammed it at full speed. Impact was brutal, but the gate didn't give an inch. He backed up, bullets whizzing around them, and rammed the gate again. This time he managed to pop the gate out of the housing that moved it when someone came in. The gate skidded noisily away from them across the asphalt, and Tony opened away hard, tires squealing as they headed down the hill.

"Ekaterina!" screamed Eugenia. The three men sitting up front glanced around. It wasn't a pretty sight. Ekaterina had taken several rounds to the back and neck, her blood spreading out onto the upholstery. Her face was frozen in a blank stare: she was dead. In a thicket a safe distance away from Gagarin's mansion, they stopped and checked but there was never really any doubt: their friend had given her life to help them save their own.

Tony pulled the corpse out of Eugenia's arms and carried it away from the van, pitching it down a verdant slope into the undergrowth. No one said a word. There was nothing they could do for her. Curro still wanted to settle things his way.

Eugenia, heartbroken that she wouldn't be able to extend to the unfortunate girl the friendship she'd promised once free, cried inconsolably and clung to Curro without saying a word. Tony asked Curro where to go.

Now that's a good question, Curro thought. His Guadalmina home was out; Fidel Basurto knew exactly where it was, and besides, the narrow, winding roads in and out would be impossible if they needed to make a quick getaway. Curro decided that they should stay out of sight at a hotel, and navigated Tony towards the Marbella Splendor. The manager was an old family friend. He pulled on a cap that Andy passed him and Eugenia donned oversized sunglasses. Hoping it would be enough to prevent their being recognized, they pulled up outside the Marbella Splendor hotel. They checked into a deluxe suite under their driver's unremarkable name, Antonio Martinez.

The first thing Curro did once they were in their room was to send Eugenia off to sleep with two strong sleeping pills he'd obtained from reception. He'd been without a phone the entire time he'd been Gagarin's captive so phoning Dima was the next order of business. He called the Convent, only to be told that his friend had left the day before, apparently in excellent health. He called his own number in Madrid, but got no answer. Then he went down to the lobby to check his e-mail on one of the hotel computers, and found a message from Dima saying that as his recovery was now complete and he hadn't had any news, he was on his way down to Marbella to join Curro.

After cleaning himself up, picking at some food, and watching Eugenia sleep for a while, he called the brothers out to the suite's terrace to have a drink and talk before the three of them said goodbye. He called room service and they sent up a bottle of twelve-year-old Chivas and an ice bucket. The Martínezes had been busy in the meantime with the hotel menu and the minibar.

"Well, guys," he said, as soon as the three of them were assembled on the terrace, "the first thing, the most important thing: thanks. You saved us from certain death. Thank you," he repeated. "But what were you doing in that bastard's house in the first place? How did you get involved in our kidnappings?"

"Hey, now that was nothin' to do with us," said Andy. "As you know, Ganvino, the disco where we work in Madrid, is his. We handled management, security and, uh, retail sales..."

"You mean, dope."

"Yeah, whatever," Tony chimed in.

"So anyway," said Andy, "along comes that son of a bitch Vasili trying to elbow us outta the picture. That tip you gave us in Madrid, to get one step ahead a' him—that really paid off. We came down here and told Gagarin what Vasili was up to in Madrid. We had one hell of a face-to-face with Vasili in front of the boss and the rest of the gang. We thought we were goners. That Vasili is one convincing motherfucker, or was, I should say," he said with a smirk, "and he just about talked the whole group into believing we were the ones tryin' to take over the whole damn Madrid market."

"What group? Who was there?"

"Gagarin, his lawyer, some city councilman, and the Italians."

"What Italians?"

"Naples Camorra, not guys you wanna have walk up behind you unexpectedly, if you get my drift."

"They talked about you," Tony chipped in, "how you owe them a bunch a' cash. Well, Dima does, anyway. Hey, where is he? We thought he was with you two."

"Nope."

"But is he here in Marbella? Or in Madrid? Or did he go back to Russia? They're lookin' for him all over the place."

"Doesn't matter. He's not here and they're not going to find him."

"Fine, whatever, doesn't matter," Andy went on. "As I was sayin', it was a very tense little get-together. Thank God we did our homework, we had some of the Russians we do trust in Madrid on the phone, ready to back us up. When he heard what they had to say, he turned fifty shades of pale, the whole room could see he new his number was up. He tried to run—strong guy, he had balls, but that lawyer's place is like a bunker and the place was full of goons, armed to the teeth. He never had a chance. Gagarin had them finish him off right then and there. God, what a mess. Those guys were real animals, I better not even tell you what they did with him."

"Please don't, thanks. No need for that. I just enjoyed some excellent paté," said Curro sarcastically.

"Now with Sonia, the girlfriend—oh, that was even worse. She thought Vasili was her ticket to retiring like a queen. Well, you couldn't imagine how she ended up. See, they went out to the yacht where she was staying with Vasili, took her and—"

"No need for details, that's quite all right. You wouldn't want to spoil my digestion, would you?"

"Vasili never said a word. I gotta admit, he was a real tough guy. But Sonia? She gave a whole fuckin' concert. Turns out, Vasili was sent here from Moscow just to keep an eye on Gagarin 'cause of this whole thing with the missing cash, and to feel out Dima, see if he really knew anything. Vasili was behind all the rotten shit that happened to Dima in Madrid, which—I take it—was pretty considerable."

"Yeah, I know that. But it's Gagarin who took off

with the whole thing."

"Well, well, well, would ya look at that," he said turning to his brother, "our posh pal here knows more than we do."

"Told ya," said Andy, "this guy's sharper than he lets on."

"Told him what, if you don't mind my asking?" said Curro.

"That you know how to handle yourself around anyone, upper crust or not, and you've always been a real stand-up guy."

"Thanks, but how would you know?"

"Hah, you still don't remember me. Well, I mean, it was ten years ago, we two were just kids."

"You?"

"Yeah, you already seemed like an old dude to us," he said with a laugh.

"I'm sorry, but I don't..."

"The Carretas theater, near Puerta del Sol?"

"Ahh, good times, but sorry, I still don't remember."

"Shaddup already!" said Tony. "He'll think we're queer."

"No, man," said Curro dismissively. "It wouldn't make any difference to me anyway; but hey, if it makes you feel any better, you don't seem the least bit gay. Anyone can see that from a mile away."

"So as I was sayin'," said Andy, "we were really hard up for cash, so we went to the Carretas to see if we could turn some tricks—"

"Sounds like a magical evening. Sorry, bad joke. Go on."

"See, we've always done our own thing, my

brother and I. Just him and me. Our parents—ahh, the less said the better. Ever since we was little kids we had to take care of ourselves. Livin' on the street... Anyway, you show up, and you're really into me. I was already a little hardbody."

"This is getting interesting. Go on."

"So we sit down together in the theater, and you start checkin' me out. I told you how things were with us, and guess what, you acted like a real gent; yeah, man, right then and there. I was in bad shape—hungry, coming down with a cold, shivering—and you took off this leather jacket you was wearin' and gave it to me, and every cent you had on you. One hundred euros, which went a long way back then. Thanks to you, we were able to sleep in a room for a week instead of on the streets, and start gettin' our shit together. I never forgot that. Then the other day outside your place, when you were sayin' how fit I look and all that, that's when I realized it was you—that fairy from the Carretas theater! Ha ha! So when we heard Gagarin needed extra muscle down here; and Tarek picked up a rumor about you and Eugenia bein' kept hostage in Marbella, we volunteered.. And now... here you are, alive and kickin'."

Now Curro remembered the whole thing. In fact, he hadn't been able to get that handsome kid out of his mind for a long time, something unusual for him. He'd even thought that had been one wasted opportunity, letting a guy like that get away. But now, thanks to his snap decision all those years before in the theater, he and Eugenia were alive. He wrapped his arms around Andy in a warm, sincere hug, and even started tearing up; but now they were tears of joy, the knowledge that an act that had seemed so trifling to him had meant so much to the two young brothers. *I'm turning into an old softie,* he thought, laughing at himself.

"Andy, now I remember the whole thing, and you don't know how glad I am that my help actually meant so much to you. Believe me, you've returned the favor with interest. So, again, thank you both. But now—what are you two going to do?" He wanted to change the subject, the display of emotion made him uncomfortable. "Gagarin and his crew will know by now that it was the two of you who helped us, and they're probably not real happy with you."

"In other words, we're totally fucked. We gotta get the hell out of Spain," said Tony, rather brusquely. Truth be told, Curro had rubbed him the wrong way since the very first time they'd met.

"We was thinkin' of takin' off for a while now," said Andy. "We're blown here, and your pal Inspector Jiménez had it in for us anyway. We always wanted to give Uruguay a shot. They got five-star resorts, Spanish is the local lingo. We can make our own way, nothin' we haven't done before. And the Uruguayan babes, well, hey..."

"Then what's keeping you? I couldn't stand to see those scumbags catch up with you."

"No lettuce, bro," said Tony, rubbing his thumb and forefinger together. "We *had* ten thousand euros stashed away; problem is, it's in Madrid and the way things are I ain't stickin' my head out of the hole to go and get it."

"What about that pound of coke you were sitting on? That's gotta be worth some serious cash."

"We had to give that back to Gagarin when we had our little meeting about Vasili."

"All right, follow me. We're going down to the lobby for a minute."

At the reception desk Curro asked for the manager, the only member of staff left from the old days. He was a ramrod-straight Central European nobleman, happy to say hello to the son of some old friends. He settled them into his office, ready to hear about the important favor Curro had told him he needed to ask.

"So, Imre, we've known each other for a long time, right?"

"Of course. I mean, your parents and I were close friends."

"And you know I'm not hurting for money, right?"

"Of course not."

"Well, here's the thing. I need two hundred thousand euros. Today. I can't explain any more than that. But it's urgent, and I don't think any bank here would let me withdraw that kind of money, in cash, without a lot of questions. Besides which, just between us, I'm being watched. I assume you've heard about the whole thing with Eugenia Osorio."

"Naturally, a very sad business indeed. Is there any truth to the rumors about a kidnapping? Is that why you need the money?"

"I can't tell you anything else. Just that the life of someone very close to me is in danger, and I need that amount without delay."

"But that's quite a considerable sum."

"I need it *now*!" He raised his voice slightly. "And it has to be untraceable. That's why I thought of you."

"Curro!" he said, with mild amusement at such a request.

"For God's sake, Imre, you could raise that much with a couple of phone calls. You know every crook in town!"

"Curro, I will not be spoken to in this fashion! How dare you!"

The distinguished Hungarian Count Imre Czartoska-Pallavaccio was struggling to maintain his composure, even though he was well aware that his position as a middleman between international crime syndicates and the arms traffickers who'd recently begun calling the Costa del Sol home was common knowledge. To him, however, Spaniards had always seemed too blunt, too forthright. Was it too much to ask that things be said in a more tactful manner? He was, after all, the Count Czartoska-Pallavaccio!

"Look, Imre, if you can get me that cash in less than two hours—and I know you can, thanks to your warm relationships with some of the most distinguished families prominent locally for bribery and corruption—"

"Curro!"

"—I'll give you twenty thousand as a... commission, tip, birthday present, whatever. But it has to be within two hours. Plus, I need you to get one of those verrrry distinguished friends of yours to lend us his private jet, destination unknown, no questions asked. And it'd probably be better for you if you don't bring up my name."

"Curro, you're insane. You haven't changed."

"Make that thirty thousand for you, if you can do it this side of an hour and a half. Oh, and I need fake passports bearing the photos of these two gentlemen—you can have the hotel photographer take their snaps—in the names of Eduardo and Miguel Rodríguez Morante."

"Are they relatives of yours?" Imre asked doubtfully.

"Of course."

"I don't know, I don't know," he said, thinking the risks over. "This is an awful lot to ask for in such a brief timeframe."

"You can do it, I know you can. Well-connected guy like you," said Curro, looking him over.

"Ah, Curro, Curro. You're one-of-a-kind."

"Forty thousand and not one euro more."

"I'll see what I can do."

"One more thing, Imre old chum. Keep all this to yourself or I'll have to kill you," he deadpanned.

Two hours later the Rodríguez Morante brothers were on a private jet to London, with two hundred thousand euros cash in a briefcase. As soon as they landed, they would board a connecting flight to Montevideo. A new life awaited, and with their newly-discovered relatives—collateral lines of the Ushers—making introductions for them, they'd be very well received. And it wouldn't hurt that they were so tall, so strong, and so handsome.

***

After seeing Andy and Tony off, the first thing Curro did was leave the hotel and find a pay phone to call Marbella's police. He said he wanted to report a crime—several crimes, actually; hell, a whole crime wave—at a villa on the ridge overlooking the city. He gave the rough location of Gagarin's mansion and mentioned the missing model, Eugenia Osorio; he added that from what he'd heard it was the nerve center of a mob operation spanning several countries headed by this Russian Gagarin and his Spanish lawyer Basurto. When asked for his name, he hung up.

When he got back to the suite he found Eugenia in the bedroom they shared, awake and still utterly crushed by Ekaterina's bloody death. He brought Eugenia up to date with the latest, and she told him that while he was out she'd tried calling her parents in Madrid to let them know she was all right, but no one had picked up the phone. Could they have gone to their place in the country to get away from the media circus? Curro chided her for not having waited till he got back, and for having made the decision without asking him. He urged her not to make any more calls.

"Eugenia," he said, looking right into her eyes, "there's a job to finish here and for the time being, it's best if no one knows exactly where we are. The first thing we have to do is make contact with Dima."

"You're right. Where is he?"

Curro filled her in on what had been going on, in Madrid and Marbella, since she'd been taken. He just touched on the high points—a detailed rundown would have taken too long, so much had happened—but when he mentioned Alex, her eyes narrowed and she looked at him reproachfully.

"You liked him, didn't you?"

"What do you mean?"

"Just what I said," she answered scornfully, "you liked him, you enjoyed it, you're used to little games like that, aren't you? I'll bet you seduced him. Curro the Great Seducer, the man no one turns down, the man who gets it on with sadistic rapists!"

"Hey, now hold on, we're getting off track here..."

"You're the one who was off track here, way off track! That son of a bitch raped me, humiliated, destroyed my self-esteem, and you... you... bastard!" Now that she was free, Eugenia looked back on her captivity with clearer, embittered eyes. She felt nothing but contempt for Alex.

"Look, I didn't know anything about him. I met him purely by chance at the marina, Pam Sundheim introduced us. I had no idea he was mixed up with the mob."

"You had sex with him!"

"Eugenia, for God's sake let's not get sidetracked over this, okay? I'm telling you, Pam introduced us. How the hell was I supposed to know he was a mob enforcer? Pam herself is going to have to some explaining to do once the dust settles. You know what they say about her old man—depending on how he, or she, was tied up with Gagarin's crowd, it wouldn't surprise me if one or both of them do time."

"I don't give a damn what happens to that tramp, I never liked her. That uppity, ostentatious...*fat*..." said Eugenia.

"You're terrible," he said, chuckling. "At least you still have your sense of humor."

"My sense of humor is on life support and I feel like hell. And I'm calling Toledo, I don't care what you say. My parents are worried sick and I want to go back to Madrid now."

Eugenia made for the phone, but Curro stopped her, grabbing her arm firmly. "No!" he shouted. "I told you, we have unfinished business with those rats. We all do—surely you agree with me as far as that goes, right? Then let's wait for Dima, he's already on his way, and when he gets here we can finish what they started."

"Have you completely lost it? Are you taking the law into your own hands now? And what's this about finishing what they started?"

"We didn't tell you any of this before because we didn't want to worry you, but this whole damn mess with Gagarin started with some money stolen from the Moscow mafia, and Gagarin pinning the blame for it on Dima's father."

"What? Okay," she said, putting a hand on her tired forehead, "you've lost me."

"You haven't heard half of it. They murdered Dima's dad and mom by faking an accident in the Neva River near Saint Petersburg where they lived. Imagine how you'd feel. Dima's swore revenge and I'm planning on helping him."

"Poor Dima," said Eugenia, crestfallen. " But wouldn't it be better to go to the police?"

"They know all about this. Fact is, though, Gagarin's drawn some very influential people into his shady business ventures here in Spain, so he has protection at a very high level. My old pal Fidel is his right-hand man and I don't think there's been enough evidence of anything solid enough to ensure they were locked up. Until, maybe, now."

"Fidel? I wouldn't have thought he'd have the stomach for this kind of operation."

"Now you know. And the mafia honchos back in Moscow think Dima has the money. He wishes! We think Gagarin actually stole it himself."

"I don't get it. If Gagarin knows that Dima doesn't have the money, why go through all this? The kidnappings, the whole thing."

"Window dressing, mafia-style. The money belongs to Russia's most powerful crime family. Gagarin's actually fairly low on the totem pole. But they've told him either he recovers every last penny or they'll kill him, make an example out of him. He decided to settle his own scores with Dima's father by making it look like he took the money. Two birds, one stone, Gagarin looks diligent to his higher-ups. You and I are just pawns in a 50-million euro Russian mafia chess match. But I'll be damned if I going to let myself be taken out by a measly rook or bishop. *Now* do you understand?"

"Not really," she sighed. "But for Dima, and only because it's important to Dima, I'll wait."

"Good. I'm glad I could bring you around. Blame those scumbags for what happened to you, but don't take it out on me."

"I blame you for having gotten off on Alex, don't even try to deny it! The guy who treated me like I was worthless, the guy who stained my soul forever."

"But that—is—not—my—fault! The same guy beat the shit out of me, too! He left me feeling trampled underfoot too, made me do and say things that went against my principles too." Curro was acting, Eugenia knew him well enough to tell. "Besides, Eugenia, let's not get carried away. It was just sex. I'm sorry to have admit it but yes, he was a hell of a ride and if it weren't for the fact that he's a seriously dangerous thug he would have made me a great boyfriend." Now Curro was being frivolous, not bothering to consider the impact of his words.

"You're despicable. Weren't you head-over-heels about Dima? Madly in love with him?"

"I never said any such thing."

"Really? Well, the way you were acting in Madrid sure made it look that way. Anyway, who cares. Alex treated me like his toy, demeaned me, shredded my self-esteem, and none of that seems to bother you very much."

"Eugenia, I know you. You and I are two of a kind. You really expect me to believe that you didn't enjoy yourself, even for just a moment, with a guy like that?"

It was apparent that a huge wedge had been driven between two people who had once talked of marriage, who—more importantly—had felt themselves to be twin souls.

Eugenia shut herself in the bedroom vacated by the Martinez brothers. She'd have nothing to do with Curro the rest of the day. She spent all afternoon and evening alone, but she did keep her promise not to use the phone.

Curro, meanwhile, told his bank that his credit cards had been stolen and asked for new ones to be delivered as soon as possible. Then he visited the hotel shops and picked up a laptop computer, and a cell phone, as well as a change of clothes and some toiletries for himself and Eugenia. He had them all put on his hotel bill.

He tried calling Dima from his new phone but there was still no answer, so he sprawled out on the bed, just wanting to rest for a while. Much later he woke with a start; he wasn't sure how long he'd been asleep, but it was already dark outside. He looked at the clock: 3 AM. He took a cold shower to shake off the sultry heat lingering in the seaside air and then got to work setting up the new laptop he'd bought. When it was finally done and he checked his e-mail he was pleased to find several from his missing sidekick. The last one said he'd reached Marbella and that Angelita, despite some reluctance, had put him up in a room at Curro's Guadalmina home.

Hallelujah, thought Curro, eager for his friends support in facing the difficult decisions ahead. He knew neither he nor Dima would really have their lives back until they'd unmasked Gagarin and Basurto and seen to it that they got what they had coming. Despite the time, he phoned his Guadalmina number.

"H'lo?" murmured the sleepy voice of Angelita's husband.

"Mateo, it's me, Don Francisco. I'm sorry to get you out of bed, but it's important. I believe a friend I was expecting in from Madrid has arrived?"

"Yes, Don Francisco. He came in this morning. Well, yesterday morning, I mean. I hope I did the right thing, he kept insisting you'd invited him."

"Yes, Mateo, absolutely. I was expecting him. I'm sorry I forgot to tell you, it's just that the night I went out I ran into some friends, they invited me to a party, and..."

"Of course, Don Francisco, no need to apologize. We were starting to get a little worried, though. Just, you know, because it's been a few days and all."

"Understandable, Mateo, nothing to be concerned

about, and please tell Angelita not to worry, too. Now put me through to Mr. Denissov, please."

"Excuse me, Don Francisco?"

"The gentleman who arrived this morning. I need to speak with him at once."

"Right away."

A few minutes later he heard at last, after so many long and turbulent days, his comrade's voice.

"Curro! Where've you been hiding? I've called you, like, a thousand times, and left a bunch of messages on your voicemail."

"All will be explained. For the time being, let me just reassure you: Eugenia's with me, and she's in perfect health."

"Fantastic! Dude, you're the boss. How'd you pull it off?"

"It wasn't easy. I have a lot of news. The important thing is, we've got her back."

"Where are you? When can we meet?"

Curro was confident that in the early morning darkness, with Gagarin probably still disconcerted by the unexpected turn events had taken, it would be safe for Dima to come to them unnoticed. Once he'd reached the hotel he could lay low with them. He gave Dima the address and told him to be careful.

When Dima reached the hotel, Curro was waiting for him just inside the entrance. After a hug they went up the suite where Eugenia lay sleeping. Dima peeked at her sleeping form from her door, not wanting to wake her, just to see for himself that she was all right. Then he walked out to the terrace, where Curro was waiting to go over recent events with him.

As he sat there, not touching the Scotch on the

rocks Curro had poured for him, he learned about everything his friends had been through in the space of just a few days. Curro told him about how rough things had been for Eugenia before his arrival; about the link between Gagarin and Basurto; about the Martínez brothers' life-saving intervention just in the nick of time; and all the rest. Dima listened sedately, mostly silently, except when Curro told him about the abuse to which Eugenia had been subjected.

"I'll kill the bastard," he fumed.

"He took off. He just walked away from Gagarin, you should have seen it. Anyway, make no mistake, the people ultimately responsible for all this misery are Gagarin and Fidel Basurto. Fidel's mine," said Curro, as if they were divvying up pieces on a game board. "Enough about all this, how're you feeling?"

"Clean bill of health. Recovered and fit for whatever it takes."

"We've got to plan this down to the last detail. They're extremely dangerous—you know that only too well. First we need to get out of the hotel and find somewhere more discreet to plan the operation from. And as soon as we can be sure Eugenia's under no further threat, send her to Madrid."

"Sounds about right."

"Now we'd better both get some more rest. It's going to be a hell of a day tomorrow. C'mon, let's get to bed."

"I'll stay with Eugenia, she needs me. I've been thinking about her a lot."

"Aww, how sweet," said Curro, slightly disappointed. "See you in the morning." He gave Dima a kiss.

"Good night, Curro my friend."

Dima tiptoed into Eugenia's room, pulled off his clothes and slipped into bed next to her, wrapping a protective arm around the sleeping figure. She stirred, then tensed, startled, but relaxed at the sight of Dima's face, smiling as the snug feeling of security he radiated spread over her.

CHAPTER XXI

Curro had woken up late. He'd never been in the habit of making up for lost sleep; usually his eyes opened at nine on the dot. But that day, after his pre-dawn session with Dima, he slept eight hours in one stretch. It was past two when he finally woke up.

He lay still for a moment, remembering the night before, reviewing the all too sharp memory of Eugenia belligerently repudiating him; Dima, too, had seemed somehow less warm than at other times. Then he leapt from the bed. There was a lot to get done. He showered, phoned room service for something to eat, and was approaching the terrace—which was shared with the other bedroom—when he heard boisterous laughter. Eugenia.

The sight that greeted him brought a faint smile to his face. Gone was the stiff, distant girl of the day before; now she was joyfully chasing her beau around the terrace, while he happily played along.

"Morning, kids. How'd you sleep? Boy, I haven't slept like that for a long time."

"We slept very well, thanks soooo much for asking," said Eugenia sarcastically.

"I'm glad, beautiful."

"Oh, drop the act. Go away! Leave us alone! I can't stand you, you make me sick!"

"What's the matter?" Dima looked from one to the other, confused.

"Nothing, it's just Eugenia, she blames me for what happened to her with Alex."

"You're sssssome.... I mean, I hatessss youssss!"

"Eugenia! Stop your act, you know I don't like it," groaned Dima.

Curro gestured to him—*never mind, let it go*. No one understood poor Eugenia's occasional outbursts; no one except him, he'd been warned by Matilde once—watch out for that recessive gene that came to the fore arbitrarily every several generations. He discreetly drew Dima's attention to the sedatives and they gave her a heavy dose, mixed into her orange juice. She'd be relaxed for a few hours. Dima stayed with her, attentive, affectionate, till after a while he came back out on the terrace with Curro.

"She dozed off," he said in response to Curro's inquisitive look. "Dude, what's the matter with her? Is she sick? This thing she does, is it some posh girls' code? I don't get it, it seems to get worse each time I see her."

"Man, it's a long story. Besides, it's all just speculation... Legends, really..."

"I don't care, tell me all about it. Please. I'm all messed up. I like her more and more... I've thought a lot about the three of us these last few days, Curro. If you knew how grateful I am, how highly I esteem you.

Esteem? Curro thought. *I* hate *that word.*

"You're like a brother to me," Dima went on, "I've told you everything about my life—"

"That's not esteem, damn it! That's affection!"

"Yes, you're right. And I do love you—"

"Make sure you get your terms right! You and your Spanish granny..."

"Jeez, Curro, I'm sorry. You're making me feel like I need a dictionary to talk with you."

"Okay, okay. Now it's my turn to apologize. I just want to get all this over with. I've had it, I need a break. A loooong break," he emphasized. "So, anyway, if you want to hear the whole story, then listen up and don't interrupt. You know that Eugenia's family tree goes back right into the mists of time –"

"Right, that's why she's a duchess."

"Oh, it's more than that, much more. That has nothing to do with it."

"But she *is* a duchess, right?"

"Yes, or will be when her dad checks out. But listen! Eugenia's family descends from the ancient Visigoth kings, the barbarians who came from the North ---"

"I remember them, I've studied Spanish history."

"Good. So anyway, in the time of King Leovigildo, when the Visigoths were already much more refined than they had been, the king wanted to marry his daughter Princess Sisebuta to his younger son, Recaredo, so they would keep the kingdom in the Arian Christianity and claim the succession away from his oldest son, Hermenegildo, who had already embraced Catholicism. Now, Sisebuta wasn't too thrilled about this idea because she'd already fallen in love with a Hispano-Roman who had nothing to his name but his beauty. Sort of like you."

"Curro, man?"

"Well, it's the truth, isn't it? Anyway, don't worry, I'll leave you part of my estate when the time comes."

"I don't want anything from anybody. I'll get ahead somehow."

"Fine, we can talk about that some other time. Now, please be quiet, I keep losing my place in the story. You don't have to be a Luaces for genetics to play tricks on you, I'll tell you that. Genes can be downright mischievous. You have before you a born neurotic!"

"Curro, I think you're finally losing it."

"And I think you're the hottest thing going. Oh, that's where I was. So anyway, Princess Sisebuta fled Toledo for Merida with her beau—Isn't that sweet?—and they hid in a little cabin in the woods—see, a long long time ago there were forests around those parts. Next thing you know, she's pregnant. So, her man decides to go throw himself on the king's mercy, beg for clemency, and swear a public oath that the king's grandson would be educated in the Arian belief system. Of course, as soon as he showed his face around the royal court he was tortured, made to reveal Sisebuta's location, and then executed. She was dragged back to her family, forced to have an abortion, repudiated by the royal court, and then married off to some Asturian chieftain her father had conquered."

"What happened to Recaredo?"

"He couldn't have cared less about his sister. Anyway, that's another story—the story of Spain!"

"You have, *we* have, an amazing history."

"That we do, and yet so few people know anything about it."

"But what does all this have to do with Eugenia?"

"Sisebuta followed her new husband back to the mountains of Asturias, where her in-laws really weren't very nice to her at all. See, Leovigildo had wiped out a hefty share of the Asturian population, many of them being vassals or even relatives of Enol—that was Sisebuta's husband's name, by the way. Among others, Leovigildo had killed Enol's elderly father, and all of his male siblings. The women in the family had been raped, practically treated like slaves... So imagine Sisebuta's reception, walking into that! The Visigoths, for what it's worth, were the most Romanesque of the barbarian peoples by then, they'd adopted a lot of the Romans' customs. I mean, they were almost civilized."

"I see."

"Like you. You look like a prince. My prince!"

Curro tried to move closer; Dima's recovery was complete, he exuded such good health, such fitness that he was turning Curro on again. Dima wouldn't have it; he got up, moved to another chair, further away.

"Curro, don't be a pain. Besides, I've told you I have feelings for Eugenia. Please respect that."

"Sorry, sorry. Anyway: Sisebuta only had one ally, but she was an extraordinary one. An Asturian slave. A witch! Yes, that's what I said. A witch who'd been enslaved to satisfy Enol's esoteric interests. She helped Sisebuta escape with her, to get away through the most rugged mountains in the area till they reached the cave of Coimbre, feared far and wide for being the coven's base. It was a place notorious for its witches sabbath sessions, a place mere mortals were forbidden to go and would have been terrified to anyway. The mere mention of Coimbre triggered panic among the mountain dwellers, and none of them dared go there.

"What a yarn."

"Sisebuta was adopted by the little band of outlaws; they taught her to make potions and cast spells. While she was there she gave birth to a beautiful baby daughter; presumably, the child of one of the several relatives of Enol's who'd been abusing her. But it was all too good to last. Enol showed up leading an elite troop of soldiers. They raped, tortured and killed the witches, put all of them on a huge bonfire except the baby girl. They chopped Sisebuta into pieces, bit by bit, till they'd dismembered her. Now, here comes the extraordinary part. Before she died, Sisebuta joined in herself all the energy of her fellow sorceresses; it was sort of like she just breathed it all in, and then it possessed her. All very strange, I know, but the oral history on this was passed down from then until modern times. In fact, in an ancient manuscript in the library at the El Escorial monastery there's a drawing made hundreds of years later by a monk who studied the story, and it shows a witch being burnt at the stake while she breathes in the essence of what seem to be tortured souls. Are you familiar with Munch's painting *The Scream?*"

"No."

"Sure you are, man. It's the painting that has a close-up of this guy with a distorted face screaming in anguish, or desperation, with these unnerving red and yellow colors behind him."

"Sorry, doesn't ring a bell."

"Doesn't matter. According to the legend, that

desperation in the form of breath possessed Sisebuta, and her dismembered body exploded in a blinding flash of fire. At the same time, accusing moans started echoing off the mountains; only part of what they were saying was understood, because the moans were in a mix of witches' jargon and the Asturian language."

"What do you mean, jargon? A special way of talking?"

"More or less. I mean, the soldiers didn't understand all of what they heard, because the howls were mixed in with the mysterious language only witches understood."

"Dude, my hair's standing on end."

"They're just legends, Dima," laughed Curro. "And it was over a thousand years ago."

"Okay, so what does all this have to do with Eugenia?"

"As far as Enol's men could make out, it was a curse to the effect that none of those present would ever become chieftains of the tribe, and that leadership would pass to another branch of the family. Also that the royal bloodline would only pass through females till the end of time."

"If you mean Eugenia, she'll be a Duchess because of her father."

"Exactly. I repeat: they're just legends. Tales passed on from one generation to the next, no scientific basis. It sounds so exciting, the way some families have ghosts. Well, the Luaces' have a witch!"

"Aw, come on. Is that what all this is?"

"I can tell you that none of those gentlemen - for want of a better term—who were there at the cave that day ever became the Astur chieftain. Years later, the real Kingdom of Asturias came into being, the embryo of what one day would become the Spanish royal dynasty. Now, can you guess who those first warrior kings descended from?"

"Sisebuta?"

"Bingo!" Curro chuckled. "Part of the prophecy came true there. As for the female line taking precedence for ever and ever. I don't know, maybe they meant that the women in the family would inherit the witches' power, their mystique. I'll tell you one thing; in the Luaces family, the women are a hell of a lot more interesting than the men."

"But this whole thing Eugenia does, it doesn't seem to denote any kind of mysterious power; I mean, as far as I can see. It just looks to me like sometimes she goes a little crazy. I mean, the way she starts talking sometimes, running her esses together!"

"Hah, hah. I agree with you, I don't believe in ghosts. Besides, all that, or whatever really happened, was a long, long time ago, and anyway it doesn't match up with the real, documented record of the Luaces lineage. Much less with the genuine royal descendancy of the ancient Asturian throne. But the fact is, every so often their family produces a woman who seems to be off her rocker. Take Eugenia, the way she'll just suddenly go over the top, saying everything in this exaggerated way, stretching the S. *'You're dessssssspicable!'* I've known her for a long time, and I know some of it's an act she puts on, a sort of premeditated vulgarity; but I wouldn't be the least bit surprised if there were some ancestral genetic quirk. If you go to her family's place in Seville—place, palace, whatever—take a good look at the portrait gallery.

There are some real weird ones, I'm telling you. Not conventional ladies at all. I mean, you can tell from a mile off that there was something strange about them. Besides which, there've always been rumors that some of her great-aunts, or great-grannies, were nutty as a fruitcake." "Stop, I'm going to have nightmares about witches and ghosts."

"All right. Go back to that lovely young lady who's bewitched you," Curro grinned at his own joke, "and I'll start trying to find a safer place for the two of us. And start convincing Eugenia to head for Madrid tomorrow. I'm going to call Carlos Jiménez right now and tell him the bare essentials."

***

Dima went back into Eugenia's bedroom; the couple stayed there for the rest of the day, and the night. Curro went to the phone, several calls on his mind. The most important thing would be getting his friend the Inspector on board, convincing him to throw up a smokescreen around Eugenia's return to Madrid. Then, he needed to find a more secluded hideaway where he and Dima could prepare their next steps. He decided to start with the last chore, it was actually going to be the easier of the two.

He weighed several options before finally coming down on the side of the one that seemed safest: a discreet Sunseeker Portofino cruiser that would allow them to move up and down the coast without leaving any tracks or attracting any attention; they'd blend right into the Coast's atmosphere of imminent summer. He set the whole thing up, payment included, over the phone; the boat would be ready for them the next day at one of the coastline's quieter marinas, Port Cabopino, just a few miles away from where they were now.

When Curro finally phoned, Carlos Jiménez was royally pissed off. He'd already heard about what had gone down at Gagarin's mansion and suspected his friend might be involved, a suspicion strengthened when Curro had failed to answer or return any of his increasingly insistent calls.

"Where the hell have you been? Lemme guess: Marbella. What do you know about that whole circus over at Gagarin's place? You find Eugenia Osorio yet?"

"Do calm down, Inspector, I promise to explain everything. After all, I'm not a suspect, am I?"

"Don't get cute with me. Where are you?"

"In Marbella."

"Well, duh. Now what about Eugenia Osorio? You have no idea what kind of shitstorm's broken loose here in Madrid. Even the King's been asking if Eugenia's turned up yet."

"Eugenia's just fine. I still don't know all the details," he lied, "but she seems to be recovering nicely."

"I don't believe you. What exactly happened down there? I wanna know every last detail, you hear? Walk me through the whole thing, step by step—"

"Look, I can't tell you any more than Eugenia's told me. She was kidnapped and held against her will somewhere outside town, and no one ever told her why. But it sounds like Gagarin's group was behind the whole thing."

"What group?"

"Fidel Basurto and some other guy Eugenia didn't know—"

"We got Basurto on this too?" he asked, his mood suddenly brightened. "Excellent!"

"Sounds that way. Now here's the important part, so pay attention: it was the Martinez brothers who stormed the place and rescued her, like a couple of genuine heroes. This is strictly between you and me. Neither Eugenia nor I will ever mention their names in public. As far as you're concerned, they're dead. Forget about them. Are we clear?"

"What? Dream on. You know the justice system will have to take appropriate action—"

"Justice? Oh good, tell me another one. I've been feeling kind of blue, I could use a good laugh."

"Will you snap out of it? I'm not running a buffet line here! You can't just pick and choose what evidence and which suspects you wanna keep out of sight. Obstruction of justice, evidence tampering. Take your pick, you're gonna end up serving time!"

"Aw, c'mon, Carlitos—"

"Look, get it through your thick skull, we're not playing games here! The Director General called me into his office 'cause the Minister's been asking questions. They already know we're old friends, someone suspects you and me are up to something. I'm gonna have Internal Affairs all over my ass again in no time!"

"Carlitos, calm down. You haven't concealed anything. How could you? You didn't know anything."

"No, course not, just all about you, your Russian buddy, the Martínez brothers..."

"Dima's gone back to Russia and I haven't heard from him since."

"Yeah, *right.*"

"Seriously, man, you were right, they were after him. I had a hell of a time talking him into going back, but it's the best thing for everyone until all this is cleared up. As for the Martínez brothers, I repeat, consider them dead. Forget about them, it'll be better for all of us. I'm the only person who knows where they are, and you know me. I'm not telling a soul, much less after the way they put themselves on the line to save Eugenia's life."

Jiménez let out a sigh audible to Curro. "You're gonna end up in deep shit, my friend."

"Not if Eugenia doesn't bring them up, and she won't. Neither will I. You're the only other person who could mention them in connection with this and let's face it, that wouldn't do you any good either. Like I said, forget you ever heard of them. No one will ever be able to link them to this."

"What about Gagarin and the others?"

"Something tells me they won't be talking either."

"And how would you know that?"

"Wait, watch, and wonder—"

"You're gonna get me into even more hot water—"

"No, Carlitos, trust me. You'll be renowned as the Inspector who returned Eugenia Osorio to her family, safe and sound. You can say she contacted you herself, or you can even say I put her in touch with you, if you want, as long as you don't tell anyone I'm in Marbella. Beside, once word gets out that she's back, the media circus will blow everything else right out of the news. You know how these things with famous people are..."

"Christ, I dunno."

"Trust me. You know I'd never leave you holding the bag."

The Inspector saw no other way out of this mess. "All right, but where's Eugenia—"

"I'll tell you tomorrow morning. I'll text you the name of hotel where she's staying. But now don't be a pain and start searching hotels up and down the coast, okay? We have a deal. And promise me you'll leave the Martínez boys alone for good."

"All right, all right. Promise." Jiménez hung up the phone feeling like he'd just dug himself into a deeper hole.

CHAPTER XXII

Saying goodbye to Eugenia the next morning proved impossible. She rejected every attempt at rapprochement by the old friend with whom she'd shared so much, and with whom she'd even once been in love with. Dima's attempts to mediate were useless; deep down, Eugenia just could not get past her conviction that Curro had enjoyed himself with the man who'd humiliated her.

More heavily disguised than when she'd arrived, she walked out of the hotel's main entrance with Dima alone at her side; he sent her on her way with a profusion of passionate hugs and kisses that clearly marked a turning point in their relationship. Curro watched the whole thing from a distance, behind one of the lobby's plate glass windows. A few hours before he'd texted Carlos Jiménez, who had arrived in Marbella early that morning and was hovering nearby, hoping for the moment when he'd be heading back to Madrid amid accolades for having skillfully brought about Eugenia Osorio's liberation. By the time the Inspector reached the scene, Curro and Dima had already disappeared in the direction of the Cabopino marina.

Once they'd reached the port they quickly found their new floating home. It was a Sunseeker Portofino 48—two staterooms, bathroom, forty-eight feet long. Curro had found it through an old acquaintance, one of Trasto's former veterinarians, with whom he'd struck up a friendship at the quiet nude beach next to Cabopino's residential area. Curro's friend still looked a little worse for wear, having gotten in late from a party, but his eyes widened at the sight of Dima—in shorts, slippers and a sleeveless T-shirt, he would have been hard not to notice. He took them over to meet the boat's owner, a Brit sporting a lobster-red tan who around the same time every year fled Southern Spain's stifling heat for the more temperate charms of an English summer. As soon as the paperwork was done, Curro, a yachtsman of some experience, and Dima set sail.

That same afternoon, they watched from their floating lair as TV news carried Eugenia Osorio and Inspector Jiménez's press conference. Eugenia appeared before the flashes only briefly before excusing herself for a medical checkup. It fell to Carlos Jiménez to throw the press a bone and bear the full brunt of the cameras as Spain's news directors and editors worked to prepare coverage of the celebrity kidnapping's happy ending for their next issue or broadcast.

"Gee, you'd think he'd actually been there," Curro said with a chuckle, as he and Dima watched Jiménez's statement. "He'll be eating out on this one for a long time. He's going places."

"How do you mean?"

"Pandemonium all around him, but he's cool as a

cucumber. And his looks. He's still one hell of a handsome guy, take it from me."

"He is handsome. And strong."

"Well, well! I'm glad you admit that."

"Anyone can see that, I'd be a fool to deny it."

"Whatever. Turn it up, let's see what he's saying."

Jiménez said he was grateful for Interpol's invaluable cooperation and well as that of several other European police forces who were after the same Eastern European organized crime rackets. He regretted not being able to give more information, but he couldn't compromise ongoing operations.

"Inspector, what was the trip back from Marbella with Miss Osorio like?" asked a TV tabloid hack Curro recognized for his incisive reporting on celeb bed-hopping.

"Fine. She rested the whole time in one of the private compartments on the bullet train from Málaga, per her request."

"C'mon, give us something. Did she tell you if she'd been well treated, if she'd been assaulted, if she considered suicide?"

"I can only discuss police matters. Next question."

The inspector's attitude and earnestness were unshakeable: he wasn't going to depart from the script one iota. No gossip, no in-jokes. The ease with which he routinely handled the press did not go unnoticed by TV news directors, and he had received some very tempting offers to ditch the station house for the small screen. He turned them all down, but in time he would accept a deal to host a show on unsolved crimes, which would not only make him famous but nicely pad out his bank account.

The public never learned the whole story of what happened during the Eugenia Osorio kidnapping, nor who was ultimately behind it all. She claimed she'd blacked out and didn't remember anything. The generally held view was that some Eastern European mob had kidnapped her for ransom and that only the Inspector's intrepid operations had kept them from getting away with it.

Dima and Curro docked at Cabopino that night and joined their host, the owner of the boat, for dinner and drinks. They'd relocate down the coast to Tarifa the following morning, and lay low there while they decided their next move. Through TV and the papers they watched as the kidnapping and successful liberation of a cover girl snowballed into an international news story. On Tarifa's cosmopolitan beach, Dima discovered kitesurfing and made new acquaintances among those who'd come from far and wide to enjoy the sport in the strait's choppy, ideally windy conditions. Something in the atmosphere reminded Curro of the laid-back ambience of happier times in Ibiza. Both of them welcomed the short break, after the harrowing experiences of the last several weeks.

On the fourth day they had to face up to the fact that there was a job to be done and it couldn't be put off any longer. They hadn't heard a thing from Carlos Jiménez, and received only a couple of brief messages from Eugenia reassuring them that she was fine and urging them to come back to Madrid and not do anything foolish.

Back in Marbella, with the boat providing perfect camouflage, they boldly tied up in Puerto Banús itself, just three docks away from Gagarin's own yacht, the one where Eugenia had been held. Everyone around there knew that the huge yacht, one of the finest crafts ever to come out of the famous Santander shipyard, belonged to a wealthy, well-connected Russian who splashed out in style everywhere he went. His parties were famous, too, both for their luxury and the number of faces from glossy mags who could be seen at them (more than one of them having received choice jewelry as a sweetener for her attendance). To Curro and Dima's frustration they found Gagarin's yacht sealed off by police tape, two special forces agents standing guard. *Should've known,* Curro thought irritably. Now that the several different branches of Spanish law enforcement were finally after them, it was too much to expect for them to be out in the open like that. Now they didn't know what to do. They couldn't ask Jiménez for help because showing their hand any more would not only reveal the extent of their involvement in the previous events but also tip him off to what they were planning. Dima's contacts didn't know anything, nor did Tarek or anyone else in the Martínez brothers' former circle. Even Pam— who hung up on Curro after chewing him out for the hostility he'd shown her fiancé—sounded like she really didn't know where he was. Curro briefly wondered how much the future countess knew about Fidel's shady business dealings.

Curro and Dima spent a week casting about for some lead that would get their plan back on track. Wishing to stay out of sight, they left the boat as little as possible—generally just for provisions, and even then always somewhere away from Marbella. Cracks began to appear in their formerly firm friendship under the pressure of such open-ended confinement. Curro still had not given up all hope of intimacy, though his overtures were firmly rejected time and again, ever more firmly, till even Dima showed signs he was about to lose his cool.

"Enough already, Curro! When will you accept the fact that you can't always win? Things are not always going to go your way," he said one day when Curro made a playful pass at him. "We're friends.We're more than that," he added on second thought. "I love you, I really do, don't get me wrong, but I've come to realize that what I took for affection and protectiveness on your part was really something else. I'm in love with Eugenia, I realize that now. You can't imagine how rough it was for me, all those days with no news, not knowing if she was all right."

Curro took a couple steps back. "In other words, up mine."

"Don't be such a drag."

"Drag? Where'd you learn a phrase like that? I don't see your granny who had the Spanish Lit degree teaching you that. Tiresome, wearisome, bore... But drag, really!" Curro slumped down on a couch in the living quarters.

"What's the matter with you, Curro? Ever since we got back together you've had a short fuse and the slightest thing sets you off. Plus you can't put two words together without that sarcasm of yours."

"What's the matter is, I thought there was something between us. I'd gotten used to the idea that you'd be the muscle-bound savage I was going to polish, take with me when I travel and—"

"You're very tiresome! There, is that better? This whole savage thing of yours. I've had it, man. You don't respect me at all."

"I'm sorry, you have every right to be upset. That came out wrong. When I say savage, what I mean is that nature's endowed you with a destructive capability so great that you could wipe me out right here, right now, with just one move."

"And that turns you on that much?" Dima asked.

"Apparently so. Hey, I'm confused myself. The same thing happened to me with this Alex guy, and he's even more of a brute than you are."

"Go to hell!"

Dima withdrew to his stateroom and Curro began pondering his own attitude toward the man who'd been an unexpected hope, a new friendship. He didn't really think Dima was a savage, much less a brute. The truth was, he couldn't stand the fact that he'd been replaced in the heart of a man he liked by a girl who could be interesting and cultured, but also frivolously shallow to a degree Curro found extremely unflattering. Eugenia was intelligent, smart, she had a quick mind; but nothing that could compare to his own perceptiveness and applied Cartesian logic. Nor could the depth of her feeling compare to his; Curro's had always been more profound and enriching, even if their only recipient to date had been a worthy vagabond.

"Curro, I'm leaving." Dima stood in the doorway, a small knapsack on his back.

"Don't talk nonsense. I repeat my apologies," he

said, standing up and going over to Dima. "Sorry, sorry, sorry! Besides, I'm not letting you leave now. You'd endanger the whole operation, and both of us for that matter."

"And who's gonna stop me? Remember what you said, just one move from me."

"I'll stop you!" said Curro, as he grabbed the Viking that had been left carelessly on the sofa."

"Curro, have you lost your mind? What are you doing?"

"You're right, you're right," he said sheepishly. "I don't know what's wrong with me. I'm sorry. Do whatever you want. Here, take the gun, it's yours anyway."

"Keep it. You'll need it more than I will."

Dima was already on the gangplank down to the pier when his cell phone beeped. He read the text message, then turned around and came back inside, smiling.

"Your 'cuz' in Uruguay came through," he joked. "Here."

Curro read the message without moving a muscle: *Count and Co. at Sotogrande. Yacht: Basurto IV. Sailing for Gibraltar at dawn. Hurry up. Cousin Andy.*

"Well, good for Andy!" said Curro exuberantly as he and Dima shared a hug, their differences forgotten. "Basurto IV—that takes a lotta nerve. All right, let's get going. I'm sure these two are trying to get to Gib because they've been positioning numbered accounts and front men there that they can use to vanish for good without a trace. We've got to head for Sotogrande right now. I doubt that they have anyone actively looking for us by now, they're probably just concentrating on getting away as quickly and quietly as possible. They'll assume we've ratted them out to the cops, so they're probably scared shitless. By the way, how did you get here from Madrid?"

"By car."

"What car?"

"I drove your Jag."

"Hmm, actually, that's not so bad. It won't stand out around here. Hell, if anything we'll look poor!"

They hadn't had such a good laugh in a long time.

***

Taking just the essentials, with the Viking in hand, they left for Curro's Guadalmina home. Curro picked up some cash and asked Mateo about his dad's gun collection; he hoped at least one of them might still be in good enough shape to be operational. There were guns of every caliber, although most were for pheasant hunting, which his dad had enjoyed with a passion. Unfortunately, they hadn't been fired in so long that even the barrels were rusty, and anyway there were no cartridges in the house. Then Curro remembered his own collection of Albacete knives, added to every year by Uncle Gonzalo—a cousin of his mother's, a Spanish marine, who visited them when he was on Christmas leave from the base at Cartagena. Knives had been made at Albacete for generations, and in the eighteenth-century their blades had become famous the world over for their strength. From among them he chose one that he remembered was called the *bandolera*, a reference to the outlaws who'd used them on mountain paths throughout the south of Spain; its curving bullhorn handle was attached to a razor-sharp foot-long steel blade. For a moment he imagined himself as one of the guerrilla warriors in the regiment raised by the resistance leader 'El Empecinado', ready to slit the throats of invading Napoleonic troops.

Once they were in the car, with Curro feeling enough bravado by now to put the top down, he said goodbye to Angelita and Mateo. Their children were standing around in their bathing suits, still eying him sullenly.

"What're you kids standing there for in this heat? In the pool, now! I don't want to hear about you being out of the water at all except to eat or do what your mom tells you to do."

The kids cheered in unison and had just turned to dash towards the water when Curro called out for them to stop.

"Hey, is that any way to say goodbye to Uncle Curro? Let's have a kiss!"

As they were driving out through the front gate, Dima grinned and said, "You're really something."

"All this and—yes, he's single!"

***

Sotogrande had—some years previously—taken over Marbella's place as the summer destination of choice for Madrid's upper crust. Some very well-to-do British and Americans had acquired places there too, drawn by the area's peaceful and discreet nature; and several branches of a fabulously wealthy Filipino family who'd been the original developers and promoters of the complex also still lived there. So understated and serene were its charms that the younger set found it an extremely dull place to be, and some wag had twisted the resort's name into 'Tostongrande': the Big Bore.

The sun was low on the horizon so they decided to kill time till it was completely dark before inspecting the marina and locating the lawyer's yacht; they stopped at the nearby town of San Roque for a light supper. It was after eleven P.M. when they stole up to the port, spotting the *Basurto IV* at once: it stood out among the other craft not only because of its size but its cutting edge design.

"Boy, I can't believe how far a lawyer's income will go around here," said Curro. "He must charge one hell of an hourly fee."

"With clients like Gagarin, I'd expect nothing less," said Dima.

They moved closer to the ship, concealed among the summer evening's late crowd, and could see frantic activity on dock and deck. The ship's lights were on and its crew were busy hauling boxes and suitcases aboard.

"Christ, it looks like they're getting ready to leave right now," said Dima.

"Bingo!" said Curro, elbowing Dima to draw his attention in a different direction. A few yards down the promenade a Rolls Royce had just come to a halt, disgorging Gagarin, Fidel, and a very downcast Pamela. Gagarin charged up the gangplank then turned, gesturing from the deck to indicate—in no uncertain terms—that his attorney should get a move on with saying goodbye to his fiancee. She left the scene soon after.

"What a dimwit," said Curro under his breath. "Why the hell would she get involved with a group like this? I mean, it's not like she was hard up or anything, her dad's filthy rich."

"Ambition? Maybe she's worried about her inheritance? Daddy won't raise her allowance?"

"Ahh, love is blind," said Curro, snidely. "Dimwit. Anyway, let's get on with it before these two raise anchor. We'll have to improvise. Got your weapon?

"Right here."

Dima had his automatic at the ready; Curro ran his fingers over the *bandolera's* handle. They were as ready as they'd ever be. After the crew had finished loading and gradually spread out away from the yacht, for a break, opportunity knocked. Once the deck was deserted, they both knew they wouldn't get another chance like this. Either they went for it now, or they let them get away.

Curro took the lead, Dima right behind him. Breaking from the cover provided by the darkened shops, they slowly crept towards the boat at an unremarkable pace and, once they were sure none of the crew were within sight, shot up the gangplank and then around to the far side of the yacht, where they entered the ship through the first door they saw. They found themselves in a spacious living room, in the center of which was a spiral staircase leading up to the top deck and down, they presumed, to the guest staterooms and crew accommodations. Hearing a noise close at hand, they crept down to the lower level and, after a look around, they shut themselves into a small cabin that seemed to be unoccupied, waiting for the yacht to weigh anchor, eager to spring into action.

It didn't take long for events to depart from the plan. Though they were in one of the guest staterooms, it was near the crew area, and one of them had already had his eye on it as a way to make a long sea crossing a little more agreeable —he knew full well it wouldn't be housing any passengers. The deckhand, finding the door unexpectedly locked, swore in English and rattled the handle. Curro made a hand signal which Dima understood at once and, throwing open the door, he had an arm around the shocked young deckhand and dragged him into the stateroom before the kid knew what'd hit him. As Dima shut the door again, Curro held the knife point a couple of inches from the panic-stricken youth's face and held a finger to his lips. Once he was sure the deckhand wouldn't scream, he spoke to him in English, reassuring him that he wouldn't be hurt if he did exactly what they told him. The newcomer had just nodded when the ship began to move. They were heading out to sea.

"Just relax, nothing's going to happen to you. You don't look like one of Gagarin's hired guns."

"I'm a member of the *Basurto IV* crew. I work for the Count of Basurto."

"Do you know who Gagarin is?"

"Some Russian friend of the Count's."

"You must know more than that—what they do, what business they're in together."

"I swear I don't. The Count's a famous attorney and the Russian, well, he's one of those *rich* Russians."

"How many people in the crew?"

"The captain, me, and one other guy. The rest've been given leave and they've stayed ashore."

"And Gagarin's entourage?"

"His bodyguards, the ones he always has with him."

"But how many?"

"Three."

"Where are we headed?"

"Gibraltar."

"Okay. You a good swimmer?"

"Yes."

"Great. Now listen carefully: Basurto and his Russian pal are two mafia bosses who are both going to end up in prison. I'm afraid you are going to be out of a job. So you're going to jump overboard, now. We're still just a short swim away from land. When you get there, you can do one of two things: you can either go to the police—although in that case you may be held as a witness to all of Basurto's racketeering, which doesn't sound like a lot of fun—or just head quietly back to wherever you came from and keep all of this to yourself."

"Fine, fine. I thought something about all this smelled fishy anyway."

"What do you mean?"

"All this time we've spent sailing back and forth between Marbella and Sotogrande, and then on to Gibraltar..."

"What's so special in Gibraltar, anyway?"

"Miss Pamela's father. You want a mafia boss—real senior one—there's your man."

Curro laughed. Dima watched the conversation in silence, making sure the deckhand didn't try any funny moves.

"Now," said Curro, "you're going to go upstairs with this gentleman and indicate to him exactly where

Basurto and the Russian are, and the bodyguards, and the captain and his assistant. Then you're going to jump overboard and swim to freedom. I don't need to tell you that if you try anything funny, my friend here will have no choice but to end your life."

"I'm not taking any chances just to help those two," the deckhand said nervously.

"Fine. Now take off your clothes."

"What?"

"Surely you're not going to try to swim to shore with all that on, are you? Put on a bathing suit so you won't attract too much attention when you reach the shore. How long will you take?"

"About fifteen minutes, I reckon. Captain always hugs the coast on the way over."

"Then off you go."

The young sailor pulled on some tight swimming trunks, stuck all of his money into a plastic bag that he hid away in an interior pocket, and left with Dima. After pointing out the relevant areas of the yacht to Dima, he slipped into the water. Dima saw him swimming away with a firm, rhythmic breaststroke.

Back in the stateroom, Dima quickly sketched out a map showing where they were and where they could expect to find the rest of those on board. Gagarin and Basurto were on the main deck with Gagarin's security detail; the captain and first mate were on the bridge. Curro and Dima left the stateroom and went into the crew area, which they now knew was empty. From there they went straight up to the bridge, their presence shocking the captain and first mate, especially in view of the Viking Dima kept pointed firmly at them. Curro explained the facts of life to the stunned mariners.

"You need to get off this ship at once. Any minute now the Coast Guard will be here to arrest the gentlemen you're taking to Gibraltar. We know you're not to blame for your boss's shady business deals, so we'll give you chance to avoid drug trafficking charges if you'll kindly jump overboard and swim to shore."

"B-but," stuttered the captain.

"But nothing, Captain. It's either overboard now, or you can explain everything to the drug squad after the Coast Guard untie you when they board the ship. Your choice."

The element of surprise did the rest. After halfheartedly asking to go below decks and collect their things—Curro shook his head—both men went out to the starboard aisle and after dropping their clothes, jumped into the water and began their swim towards the shore.

"That just leaves the bodyguards. Once we're rid of them, we can give those bastards what they have coming," said Dima. "How long did you say it was from here to Gibraltar?"

"Not very long, barely an hour."

"Are you sure we're going to have enough time?"

"Now that's a good question. I'd say almost certainly not. Wait."

Curro was licensed to pilot a recreational craft and was familiar enough with the navigational equipment of larger vessels. After he'd pressed a couple of buttons, the yacht's engines sputtered to a halt.

"Now hide, quick, Gagarin's thugs'll be up here before you know it."

"Here," said Dima, passing him the automatic with its silencer on.

When the three bodyguards entered the bridge they were surprised by Curro pointing the gun steadily at them; despite that they lunged at the raiding party. Dima neatly sidestepped the first one, putting him out of action with one well-placed punch. The other two had gone for Curro, leaving him no choice but to shoot. The bullet ploughed into the larger of the two's right shoulder amid a spatter of blood. Curro swiveled the gun around, pointing it right at the third guard's chest, stopping him in his tracks just inches away. Disarmed, Gagarin's hired help were no longer a threat.

Curro began speaking to the defeated thugs in English but was interrupted by Dima, who addressed the men in their own language, in a conciliatory but firm tone. They were led away, in a straight line, hands on their heads, towards a life raft. The one Curro had shot was pretty badly wounded so swimming to shore was out of the question. Dima ordered the two uninjured guards to help their associate into one of the boats and Curro kept the gun trained on them till the waves had carried them away in the darkness.

"I'll fire up the engines again to get us out of here. I don't trust those guys one bit," said Curro.

"Don't worry, they won't be back. They know Gagarin's position and they're not interested in going down with him. They just want to make it as far as Gibraltar so they can disappear and give both Interpol and the Spanish police the slip."

"Fine, as far as I'm concerned they're welcome to run. They don't mean a thing to us."

"Same by me."

"In that case, pal, let's get to work. We're up!"

Dima felt an odd mix of excitement and sadness. His face changed, he suddenly went red with rage.

"Now I will finally avenge my parents!"

Dima and Curro burst into Basurto's stateroom, where they expected to find him and Gagarin, but that turned out to be anticlimactic; during the short time that the yacht had been stopped, both men had begun feeling jittery, worrying that their hastily prepared getaway would be scuttled by mechanical problems—they'd repaired to the yacht's lounge to relax with a drink. Both men were stunned by Dima and Curro's sudden entrance. They'd assumed all along that the two of them were back in Madrid, enjoying life again with their friend Eugenia; it had never even occurred to them that Dima and Curro would take the fight to them, risk their lives to pull off a commando raid of this kind. Neither crook was armed, both of them having been lulled into a sense of security by their guards' presence. Fidel Basurto was now utterly speechless. Gagarin, on the other hand, stayed cool, like a pro.

"Well, Dmitri," he said in Russian, "what a surprise. Glad to see you. I think it's time I explained a few things to you."

"Son of a bitch! What did my parents ever do to you? Huh? Answer me! Nothing, that's what!"

Dima passed the gun to Curro and lunged at Gagarin, knocking him over and pummeling him mercilessly with both fists.

"Wasn't I loyal to you the whole time I worked for you? Didn't I obey your orders, even put my life at risk for you? You don't deserve to go on living!"

Dima kept on pounding Gagarin, till his former

boss lay semi-comatose in a bloody heap on the floor. Basurto stared, too terrified to even blink. Now it was Curro's turn.

"You moron, Fidel, why the hell did you have to get mixed up in shit like this? Idiot. You could have just married Pam, she's loaded. You had to go and throw it all away."

"Curro, please," he said, arms raised defensively, "let me just explain to you—"

"Talk to the hand," said Curro, passing the gun to Dima before knocking Basurto off of his feet with a single open-handed blow. Then he easily landed a succession of punches on his strangely passive target. Basurto was no match for Curro, whose athletic physique and years of practicing Judo and pumping iron were now augmented by rage and disdain.

"C'mon, tough guy! Defend yourself! You were really strutting your stuff as long as you had Gagarin's muscle boys nearby. What's changed, huh?! You pussy."

With the phony Count out of action on the floor next to an inert Gagarin, the raiders felt they had the scene completely under control and, after a brief inspection of the rest of the opulent yacht, they returned to the lounge for some drinks. Curro found some single malt whisky, the lawyer's favorite, in the bar.

"Well, if there's nothing better," he said. "Shall I pour one for you, Dima?"

His friend shook his head. "Gagarin kindly left me a full glass of his vodka over here. It's extraordinary. The very best brand there is."

"Remembering the good old days, eh?"

"Nah, just a sip, you know I hardly drink."

Anchored near the coastline and feeling comfortably safe, they relaxed with their drinks. Curro switched on the stereo and reclined on a sofa, savoring his whisky. Dima, however, began feeling queasy and nauseous. He stuck a finger down his throat and vomited up part of what he'd drank, then straightened up and threw the glass across the room.

"Shit, what is this? There was something in the vodka, Curro!"

Curro moved up next to Dima and smelled his breath. Having been around horses since childhood, he recognized the smell: ket, horse tranquilizer. Things were starting to go wrong.

Unfortunately they'd been too late to discover the danger. Dima was wracked with spasms and began heaving. Curro looked around and was dismayed to find that Gagarin's crumpled form had vanished from behind an easy chair where he'd lain collapsed and apparently unconscious on the floor.

Gagarin had never really trusted his cowardly counselor, much less so after all the time the attorney had been spending lately with his future father-in-law, someone with whose style Gagarin had more than passing familiarity, having once tried to wrest control of his protection racket against the bookmakers at greyhound racecourses during his London days. This was why, since the yacht had pulled away from the dock, Gagarin had been holding onto the drink Basurto had poured for him, playing along to the lawyer's uncharacteristically boisterous insistence that they toast the new venture they were beginning in Brazil, but not actually downing the drink.

Gagarin had been down for the count, but somehow struggled to his feet while the victors had taken their rash little sightseeing excursion around the yacht. Gagarin scampered towards the Zodiacs, intending to make his getaway in one of the inflatable tenders; but his retreating bodyguards had already sailed away with one of the yacht's two Zodiacs, and Gagarin wasn't sure he could release the other one from its davit and get it going. There were two jet skis, but Gagarin didn't know how to work them either. Since he wasn't a swimmer, and actually found water slightly intimidating, he decided he'd have to retrace his steps, retrieve a gun he kept hidden in his stateroom, and try to regain control of the ship.

Gagarin opened fire as he barged into the lounge. His first target was Dima, who lay weakened on the floor, but a fraction of a second before the first shot Curro had caught sight of the attacking mobster and kicked the back of a couch which turned over forward, becoming a makeshift shield for his friend. As the couch turned over, the Viking Dima had left on it fell to the floor and spun across the ground towards Basurto. Fidel grabbed it and pointed it towards his partner; he realized that if Gagarin was smart enough to figure out why the vodka had floored Dima, then after finishing off the other two Gagarin would probably execute him next. But before Basurto could get off a shot, Gagarin pumped two rounds into him, then turned his attention to Curro. Dima, still on the ground, kicked a small ottoman that skidded across the floor into Gagarin's leg, knocking him off balance just enough for him to miss his shot at Curro, who vaulted across the room and recovered the Viking automatic from the dead lawyer. He turned to fire at Gagarin, but the Russian was already ducking back out the door onto the deck. Curro fired a barrage at the fleeing mobster and heard a muffled howl; he was sure he'd hit him. Curro sprang through the doorway, ready to finish off the crime lord, but he was gone without a trace. Curro looked over the side, into the turbid night sea. He was sure he'd hit Gagarin. He figured the wounded Russian's momentum must have carried him right over the railing, where he'd surely drown if he didn't bleed to death first.

Curro went back to Dima, who was feeling a little better. In the end, he was lucky that he wasn't much of a drinker; just a sip of the poisoned vodka had been bad enough, but really belting it back would have been far worse.

"Curro! Gagarin'll get away!" shouted Dima.

"He's not going anywhere. He went over the side."

"I'm telling you, he has more lives than a cat."

"He'll never make to the shore alive," said Curro with conviction.

Curro tossed Basurto's corpse overboard, getting rid of the gun too. After making sure they'd left no clues behind, they took one of the jet skis and headed back to the port.

The following day, once the deserted yacht had been found, the press made the most out of such a juicy story: the mysterious disappearance of the well-known lawyer Fidel Basurto in sinister circumstances; truth be told, he wasn't really missed. Only Pamela felt his absence and she was convinced that Curro and his Russian friend, who hated Fidel's business partner, had something to do with Fidel's disappearance. She wanted to stir things up with the police, but her father Mr. Sundheim told her—not for the first or last time—she'd better forget about it.

CHAPTER XXIII

Madrid, his beloved Madrid! Curro didn't know who'd coined the phrase "After Madrid comes heaven" but he felt it was right on the money. Madrid was the city where everyone wanted to live: those who studied; those who partied; those who worked; those who didn't; Spaniards; foreigners. All of them found in this city the energy they needed to take on their dreams. And for any Spaniard who wanted to triumph in any field of culture, be it in visual arts, in films, in music, or in literature, Madrid was the mecca in which one needed to get noticed. It was a cosmopolitan city, a city open to the world, where no one felt like an outsider, and where the floating population of executives employed by major multinationals had at one point seemed to never stop growing.

Despite his pleasure at being home, Curro felt as if he were drifting on his own. He'd tried everything to make up to Eugenia, but nothing seemed to work. She still refused to bury the hatchet. He wondered if there could be some tactical aspect to her obstinacy, if it was partly a gambit intended to ensure that she had Dima all to herself. For his part, Dima had packed his bags in record time, leaving Curro's to move into his new lover's place without a word. It wasn't as if he owed Curro any explanations. All this had left Curro feeling bored and lonely. Spending time with old friends was no help, they'd just beleaguer him with questions about their mutual acquaintance, not knowing that the whole adventure had put him through the wringer as well; on the other hand, staying home alone with no company except his ghosts and a glass of scotch wasn't very appealing either.

***

As he strolled pensively through the Retiro park a couple of days later, he couldn't help but remember all the good times he'd shared with Trasto. He had learned so much during that time, so much that Trasto's time in his life had left him a different person. A better person. He'd learned the meaning of thinking of others first, of leaving selfishness aside. He'd learned the discipline required to take care of another being every day, and about the responsibility this entailed. His love for his dog had changed him completely. Curro had always hated responsibility, but once he'd accepted one he never went in for betrayal or laxity. The values he'd been raised with required him to protect the wellbeing and quality of life of his companion till the end. And that's what he'd done, never feeling it as an imposition, as a duty he simply couldn't get out of, but rather with the pleasure that came from taking care of a creature you care about, a creature you'd for whom you'd gladly change your habits.

The tears came, silently. All those sunny

afternoons, and the snowy sunsets too; be it warm or cold, the two joined in an indestructible brotherhood. Why? Why had that shitty disease had to pick his dear friend? That fucking degenerative myelopathy that would destroy his neurological system and break his prey dog's pride. And it had to be a situation that would force him, Curro, to make decisions; as he had, to let him rest, to die with dignity. Shit, shit, shit. It could have been anything, a speeding car even, a sudden illness... But no, it had to be that horrible disease that had killed him a little bit at a time and forced Curro into the position of deciding Trasto needed his help to rest. He hadn't been able to say goodbye to Trasto and his inability to somehow communicate his gratitude more expressively tormented him. The day it all ended, the veterinarian's presence, his own dismay. All of it had kept him from focusing on anything except the mechanics of ensuring a peaceful departure for Trasto. He'd held his head in his hands, Trasto sniffing him trustingly; and when it was over his mind had gone blank. He'd withdrawn into sort of trance, a state of detachment in which it had been impossible to ponder anything. The guilt came later.

A sudden collision knocked his thoughts out of their obsessive loop. As he turned over and raised himself up on one elbow he saw the back of the portly man who'd knocked him over – forty-something, he guessed – and faintly heard a voice saying "Watch where you're going, man."

"You fat fuck! Watch it yourself, asshole!"

No doubt about it, his demeanor had changed, and definitely for the worse. Everything irritated him, he was much more inflexible, unwilling to give anyone a break. Nothing mattered to him. What did he have to lose? He certainly wasn't willing to take any crap off of a tubby smart aleck who'd knocked him down with such force that he had to struggle to get back on his feet. The gaggle of joggers with the other man turned around and lurched back towards him. They all looked to Curro like weekend athletes, pot-bellied losers who spent Sunday afternoons running a few halfhearted laps through the park before turning their energy to making clumsy passes at foreign tourists. They were all huffing and puffing, probably glad to have an excuse for a breather.

"Who you callin' fat?" growled the offending party, sweat dripping profusely down onto his ridiculously tight jogging shorts.

"I see lots of fat guys around here," said Curro stonily, "but I was talking to you. The fat guy with no manners."

"Man, you're getting yourself into a shitload of trouble," said the jogger threateningly.

"No, *you're* getting a lesson in how to use this park: watch where you're going, don't take up the whole pathway like you own it. Lots of people use this park – alone, with kids, with dogs. You can't charge around like rampaging hippos, knock me over like a bowling pin and then tell me to watch where I'm going. What *I'm* getting is a hunch you're a fucking hick with no manners. No wonder the country's in the shape it's in. So many guys like you on the loose."

The pot-bellied jogger, who wasn't really a mountain of blubber, but rather an overweight guy who worked out and was holding his own against middle-aged spread – except for that beer belly – stalked forward till he was standing right in front of Curro. The thought of his recent exploits excited Curro and he was more than ready to rumble. He easily avoided the jogger's first clumsy swing; the jogger tried charging Curro at speed, but that didn't work either. In fact, the charge only made his own situation worse; Curro having neatly sidestepped him, the jogger plowed through a hedge like a tank, uprooting it before flopping heavily to the ground and skidding towards Alfonso XII street, tearing up quite a bit of grass before he came to a halt.

By now a crowd had gathered, some worried, others incredulous. Amateur fisticuffs were rather unusual in the Retiro on Sunday mornings. People stood by expectantly but no one dared intervene except one distinguished old lady, a regular from the neighborhood who was out walking her little Maltese.

"What do you think you're doing, young men? Calm down, calm down."

Even after the jogger had crashed and (grass) burned, it was still a dangerous situation. His buddies weren't going to just stand by and take this kind of treatment. They all charged Curro at once, which was enough to make him recognize, at last, just what a precarious position he was in, and look for escape routes. The fastest of the group landed a kick on him which he didn't manage to evade quickly enough, and before he knew it he was on the grass near his original attacker. The first jogger pulled himself to his feet and was getting ready to pounce on Curro when a firm hand knocked him off course in mid-flight. The jogger fell again, this time on his back, and from the sound of his yelp, much more painfully. There wouldn't be any more Sundays in the park for quite a while.

"Why are you still here, assholes? Beat it!"

"Dima!" exclaimed Curro, realizing he was out of danger.

Given the firmness of the voice issuing their marching orders – and the rippling muscles on display to back them up – the battered jogger's pals looked at each other and, dejectedly, helped their fallen buddy up and then made their way slowly away down the path. The curious onlookers scattered, one or two looking back over their shoulders at the willowy young lady standing next to the peacemaker. Eugenia was unrecognizable behind the oversized shades and the cap pulled down to her eyebrows, but even so her height and naturally elegant bearing stirred interest.

"Congratulations to the happy couple!" deadpanned Curro.

"I see you're in a jam, as usual."

"Guys, c'mon," said Dima. "Enough already. The two of you make life impossible for me. Please, think about me for one moment, okay? All this is really hard for me."

"Well, who's thinking about me? It's been pretty lonesome around my neck of the woods lately. You didn't even say goodbye. Curro's B&B, that's what my home was to you."

"Curro! Don't say that. You know you're my best friend."

Curro chuckled despite himself. "Yeah, sure. That's why you made an Irish goodbye."

"An Irish what?"

"Yeah, leaving just like that, without a word."

"But I told you I was going with Eugenia, that she needed me at a time like this—"

"You didn't say any of that. You just left. Ah, never mind. See you around." Curro turned to go but Dima couldn't leave it at that.

"Curro!" he called out.

"Forget it, Dima" said Eugenia. "He's a manipulator, he always has to have his way."

"No, no. I want Curro to have lunch with us."

"Absolutely not! I can't stand the sight of him, he makes me sick. Not with him."

Curro didn't hear her last sentence. He was already several yards away, heading home.

***

He spent a whole week indoors. He left his phone off the hook, switched off his cell. He wasn't in the mood for anything at all. His best friend had rejected him, and the man who for a few weeks had raised his hopes had replaced him as easily as changing his shirt.

In the end it was Inspector Jiménez who cared enough to check up on him. He dropped by Curro's penthouse and Curro went to work in his kitchen, putting together a sumptuous lunch over which the two men reminisced about the good old days. Being the hero of the moment had made Jiménez quite the media darling, and his matinee idol looks didn't hurt.

Curro set the dining room table for two and beckoned him to have a seat.

"Man, what a jerk your Russian buddy turned out to be, after everything you did for him... Just the stuff I know about, let alone what I imagine you're not telling me... All I'm saying is, would it have killed it him to behave a little better towards you? I mean, to just go off and ditch you like that, for that uppity brat Osorio! What a total schmuck."

"Carlitos, don't be unfair. Eugenia's not a brat, she's just a preppie chick who takes life on her own terms. Deep down she's a great girl, really." Curro's words sounded forced, even to him. He wasn't sure what he really felt about her anymore.

"That doesn't excuse her behavior. I mean, hell, you were as preppie as they come, but you were always a straight up guy. My buddies back on the block I introduced you to, you impressed the hell outta them."

"Well hey, my buddies felt the same way about you!" The two men laughed. Years before, when they'd forged their friendship, Curro and Carlos had shared each other's worlds, each in time becoming a member of the other's crew.

"Besides," said Curro, "don't forget, Dima's straight."

"Yeah, sure."

"Really!" Curro answered emphatically. "He really cares about Eugenia, and it'll end up being serious, I hope, although at first that knucklehead Ignacio Osorio won't settle for anyone less than a native-born Spaniard who belongs to the same country club he does. Or a prince of international banking. But neither type turns Eugenia on. She'll end up with Dima, you wait and see!"

"Didn't you tell me he was your boyfriend, that you two were already getting it on? I remember it perfectly—"

"No, man, I didn't say any of that, you said it all yourself. I just played along. It wasn't exactly a good time to argue."

"Boy, I'll say... What with Dima beatin' the shit outta those Russians who trashed your penthouse."

Curro froze inside but didn't let on for a second. "What Russians? Carlitos, stop insisting that Dima's some kind of Russian spy who goes around Madrid mopping up the floor with other Russians. You've seen too many movies."

"Hold the phone, I never said he was a spy. But he wants revenge for his parents' deaths, you said so yourself."

"Fair enough. He hates Gagarin, who just happens also to have been behind Eugenia's kidnapping. But you know better than I do, Gagarin's gone AWOL."

"What a coincidence, you just happened to be in the neighborhood when he vanished! You sure your pal Dima wasn't with you?"

"Is there an echo in here? Seriously, if you're going to start back up again about that whole Marbella business, let's call it a day. I already told you all there is to know. Should I have my lawyer present?"

"Aw, fuck, don't go all *Law & Order* on me. Of course not, man, we're buddies. But I'm also a police inspector, and I still need to clear up the Eugenia business and the link between Gagarin and Dima."

"I told you, Dima was in Russia," Curro said, more defensively than he intended. "I was the one sweating it out in Marbella, worried sick about Eugenia. We've been over this a thousand times already."

"Right. So you want me to believe that, poof, the Martínez brothers just appeared from nowhere."

"We've talked about that too, you promised you'd forget about them. You're not going to break the deal we had, are you?"

"Course not, Curro. You know that once I've given my word, that's that."

"Precisely. That's that. Now to hell with Gagarin and all that, let's talk about something else."

"One last question—"

"Shoot."

"Name of Kasparov mean anything to you?"

"Can't say that it does," lied Curro, alarm bells going off. "Oh, wait, you mean the chess Grand Master, Gary?"

Carlos smirked, knowing he was being played. "No, the mob overlords known as the Kasparov brothers. Some Ukrainians who work for them have gone missing too."

"Gosh, I'm all broken up."

"Apparently Gagarin works for the Kasparov crime family. We hear they're lookin' for him too. Probably not to name him Employee of the Month."

"Why, Carlos, I don't think I'll be able to get to sleep at night."

"Look, this isn't a joke. This mess is driving the station nuts. Gagarin, Vasili, both of them missing, the Russians, the Ukrainians, the Kasparovs, who's behind it all?"

"Carlitos, if I hear anything, which is pretty unlikely, you'll be the first—and only—one to know. By the way, isn't your birthday coming up in a couple of weeks?"

"Yep. What a memory."

"Well, as a present let me give you a bottle of red wine, Vega Sicilia *Único*, I've still got some left from the ones the board of directors at Morante & Co. used to send me."

"Man, thanks a lot. I'm salivating already."

"Since we took the company public and I sold the stock, they don't send me anything anymore. The human condition, Carlos! Oh, and I'll send you a postcard telling you in excruciating detail what I'm up to where I'm going. I'm hoping it'll be a hell of trip and I promise you a full report."

For a while Inspector Jiménez had been having a nagging feeling, but he'd put it out of his mind. How could he ever think that — no, it was nonsense. Now, though, as he took his leave of Curro with the early birthday gift under his arm, doubt crept back in. Curro? No, no way.

***

Curro was asleep when he heard the front door open. His heart skipped a beat. He charged out of his room ready to face the intruder, but was in for a surprise.

"Dima! What're you doing here?"

"If I'm bothering you, I can leave."

"No, not at all. It's just, I haven't heard from you guys in days. And, you know, with Eugenia being the way she is…"

"She wants to make up. She's crazy about you, man, really she is. Speaking of crazy, I need your advice." Without waiting for an invitation Dima sank down onto the leather couch. "I've been calling you since that day we saw you at Retiro. Is your cell switched off?"

"Yeah, and the land line's off the hook, too. I'm just not in the mood, I have no strength for anything."

"Come on, man! I mean, a guy like you."

Curro laughed. "Like what exactly?"

"You know! So full of life."

Curro smiled inwardly at Dima's naiveté. Was he really that blind? *Full of life*? "Oh yeah? And how would you know that?

"'Cause I've seen it."

"Well, you need glasses. I've had it with everything, I'm exhausted, I just want to... rest. But anyway, since you brought up crazy— how is Eugenia?"

"Dude, how'd you know it's about Eugenia?"

"You tell me. Two plus two equals four, and Eugenia's crazy as a loon."

"First tell me what's wrong with you. Why are you cooped up indoors all day? Is it my fault, are you mad at me?"

"No! Nonsense, of course not. Why would I be? We're all grown-ups, and you need to find your own path to happiness. Eugenia's as good a way as any."

"Then I don't understand."

"Well, it's not complicated. I'd gotten my hopes up over you, that's all."

"I never gave you any reason to expect anything beyond friendship."

"Of course not," Curro said, trying his best to mask his sarcasm. "But all those nights sleeping snuggled up next to each other, they weren't half bad, were they?"

Dima's face flushed red.

"Curro, you're something else."

"Forget about it. You were a waif in need of affection, and Uncle Curro was happy to provide it. Let's drop it. What's up with Eugenia?" Curro was losing interest in a conversation that could go nowhere but downhill.

"Curro, I need you to know that I've felt for you..." Dima turned red again, "something special, something I can't put into words."

"The respect and gratefulness one feels for daddy."

"No, man!"

"So you've fallen in love with me and discovered you can't live without me?"

"Curro, you're one-of-a-kind. You know that? You treat everything like it's a joke, I never know when you're being serious. "

"Forget it. Let the whole thing be a nice memory you can share with your grandkids someday. On second thought, no, keep it to yourself. You wouldn't want the kiddies to get the wrong idea about their big, bad grandpa and this elegant gentleman he used to know."

"You're impossible, you know that? Look, Curro, to be perfectly honest, I feel really good around you, I have a great time with you. Just between the two us, better than I do with Eugenia, except when her and I are making out."

Just what I wanted to hear, Curro thought. "Of course."

"When I accepted your hugs they confused me. I kinda liked them but you weren't really there at all. I know you appreciate my body and you were enjoying it, but your mind was always somewhere else."

"What do you mean?"

"You know exactly what I mean. Even though I know you love me."

"I love you. I love you a great deal. Don't ever doubt that."

"But your heart will never belong to anyone. It already belongs to Trasto. Eugenia told me that once and you know what? She's right. I don't understand loving a dog that way, but that's the way it is. I respect that. But I can't compete with a dog, it's absurd, I can't wrap my mind around that idea."

"No one can. So let's leave Trasto alone and get back to Eugenia. Listen, she's a great girl, and I know her better than anyone does so I know what I'm talking about. And I know you two were made for each other and you're going to end up together."

"You really think so? I hope you're right!"

"I'm positive. And as for her quirks, yes, she's just a little neurotic. But honestly, who isn't? I think what Eugenia really needs is love, lots of love. There's nothing love can't do. Eugenia never really had a father figure. I don't know if you've heard this already but her father, before and after he got married, couldn't keep it in his pants. He bedhopped like a crazy man. Sonsoles would never have gotten her hooks into him if it hadn't been for money, but the swinging never really stopped. Eugenia was raised by nannies and maids and never felt the authority of a father's presence. That's why she was so hung up on me, and she confused that feeling with love. She was never in love with me, and I was never in love with her. She just saw me sort of as the grown-up who'd chew her out when she really needed it. Something no one had ever done, definitely not that dimwit Ignacio. In you she sees a self-confident, strong, supportive man she can lean on and trust. You have to love her, and tell her enough is enough when she gets out of line."

"So how do I handle her dad, anyway? I mean, Ignacio can't stand me, he thinks his daughter's way too good for me. We've all spent a lot of time together the last few days and the slights and putdowns I've had to take. If it weren't for Eugenia I would've bashed his face in."

"Why not rip off his head?" said Curro in a faraway voice, his thoughts elsewhere.

"What?"

"Nothing. Never mind. Anyway, forget about Eugenia's father, he's out of the picture. Eugenia's mom is the one who wears the pants in that family, and she and I get along really well. And don't forget to schmooze *Auuntiieeee,*" Curro couldn't help it, "and Pepe. They call the shots, too."

"What do you mean?"

"I mean, Eugenia's parents pay attention when they talk. They owe a lot to Pepe, he did a lot to get the Luaces' finances back on track. He's managed Sonsoles' assets for years, and managed them very well, too. Pepe will be in your corner, I'll take care of that."

"Her father will never accept me, Curro. I'm a nobody and Eugenia's a duchess who's loaded."

Curro now came over and sat next to Dima on the couch. "Look, Eugenia's father is a twit who hasn't read a book in his life. He's nothing but a nice façade propped up entirely by his wife's money. Eugenia, with her peerless elegance and class, is the first swan to come paddling out of that gene pool after generation upon generation of ugly ducklings. Yep, in Eugenia the recessive swan gene seems to have come to the forefront—along with a drop or two of Sisebuta," he joked.

"They think I'm a gold-digger, that I'm only after Eugenia for her money," said Dima gloomily.

"As soon as you two are engaged, I'll settle a dowry on you. I have no direct heirs and since Trasto, my natural heir, is no longer with us," Curro said, very seriously, "I don't feel any obligation to anyone. Trust me, Ignacio won't stand in your way. Besides, he must be crazy—I mean, just think of the beautiful kids you two will contribute to the Luaces dynasty."

"I can't take money from you."

"We'll see about that. And now, on another topic, my friend the Inspector was here. He's a little miffed, but that won't be a problem. I told you, he gave me his word not to stir up things surrounding Eugenia's kidnapping and to forget about the Martínez boys. He didn't even mention Fidel Basurto and he's seriously off-track as far as Gagarin goes. He did happen to mention that a hit squad sent by the Kasparov family have gone missing—oh, congratulations, you were right about their accents, those three stiffs were Ukrainians after all. Anyway, the important thing now is that this whole murky mess with Gagarin, the Russians, the money... All the pieces are falling into place."

"You think so?"

"No doubt about it. The Kasparovs ordered Gagarin to find the money. But they didn't trust him, so they sent their own team, the Ukrainians, to find you and do whatever it took to learn where the money was stashed. As for Vasili, he was sent out from Moscow to keep an eye on things and report back, but I think he decided to go rogue and try to find the money and keep it for himself. At least he got what he had coming to him.

"So, what do you think will happen now that Gagarin's gone and Vasili's not filing status reports? How will the Kasparovs react?"

"They'll probably blame Gagarin. Since he's disappeared, it wouldn't surprise me if they decide he was behind the whole thing to begin with. If that's the case then you'll be in the clear. Still, we'd better watch our backs. An organization that big will have informants everywhere."

"Tell me about it."

"But as soon as you marry Eugenia, that'll be the end of the mess. Eugenia's kidnapping ended up being international news; they won't want that kind of attention focused on them. Remember, Eugenia hasn't named names to anyone; I'm the only one who brought up Fidel and Gagarin. Eugenia's fame will put them off of trying anything. I mean, even the King's interested in her wellbeing. Like I said, you should just forget about the Kasparovs."

Before taking his leave, Dima urged Curro to drop by Eugenia's sometime over the next couple of days. She wanted to smooth things over, apologize, and rebuild their relationship.

"I'll call you," said Curro.

"I hope so," said Dima. "I don't know how to thank you for everything you've done for me. I'd be lying if I said I didn't start to feel something beyond just conventional friendship; but the very idea overwhelmed me, I couldn't understand or accept it, because..."

"Let it go. Don't forget, though, I want to be godparent to the first kid you guys have, and it has to be named after me."

"Ah, Curro. How our friendship's confused me. I dunno, I dunno."

"Give it a rest, man! Enough already."

"Besides, your memory of Trasto was always there, and no one will ever be able to compete with that."

"Yes, Dima, Trasto is always present."

After Dima left, Curro felt better and he realized that staying cooped up in his penthouse wasn't doing him any good. He decided to make an effort, get out for a while, go for a walk. Now he loved walking. *Thanks, Trasto!*

With his mind obstinately focused on his dog, his thought turned to the only two men who, however briefly, had distracted him from his pathological feelings of guilt. The extraordinary coincidence of Dima and Alex having both crossed his path, one so soon after the other... Were they really so similar, or was it just a superficial resemblance? Both were classically beautiful, both came from turbulent backgrounds that had shaped them for life, made them fighters. They were both survivors of hostile environments that had stamped them out as natural leaders. Both, despite their appearance and their recent past, had middle-class roots: one, with a family made up of KGB officers and exiled Spanish intellectuals, the other with the owners of a circus. And each in his own way had manners, a code, and the word respect was part of their vocabularies. These few traits, then, made up their resemblance; that, and a certain kindheartedness.

Dima had made a profound impression on Curro; his handsomeness, his disposition, his ability to take on new interests, his eagerness to learn. All together they'd singularly endowed him with what it took to spur him, Curro, to once again feel a certain degree of hope. He would definitely have been the most suitable option, if things had somehow worked out differently, or so he told himself..

Alex—what a whirlwind of emotions he'd kicked up. His magnetism, the stubborn brutality he exuded, as opposed to the timid, overgrown kid he carried deep inside. All of that made him a challenge difficult to resist, an impossibly intriguing one.

Words, words, words... When all was said and done he was just daydreaming. Neither of the two would really distract him or entertain him, save for a short time; Curro was too given over to self-imposed solitude. It was something that couldn't be shared; it required intimate communion with oneself.

As soon as he got back home, he got to work. There were things that needed doing.

He sent his friend the Inspector that postcard he'd promised, in the form of a sealed letter absolving Dmitri Denissov from any responsibility in certain events that had taken place over the past several weeks. He described in great detail for Jiménez his experiences with the Russian mafia and the role he'd taken on. He described how sportingly he felt he'd risen to the challenge fate had sent his way, and that he didn't feel in any way guilty; circumstances had forced his hand, and he'd had nothing to lose. As he accepted responsibility for the collateral damage, Curro couldn't help smiling at the thought of Carlitos' jaw dropping as he discovered Curro's toughest side—better yet, his most violent, lethal side. He was sure his old drinking buddy, who'd stuck up for him so many times, could never have imagined that a posh snob like Curro Morante had anywhere in him the grim resolve—and the skill—to do away with another human being. Warming to his subject, Curro threw in the thug Dima had killed in the men's room at the Royal Theater, and Basurto and Gagarin too. The more the merrier.

He went down to the building super's workroom and gave the letter to Feliciano, with strict instructions to send it in two days. Not before, not after.

"Traveling again, Don Francisco?"

"That's right, Feliciano. Tomorrow or the next day."

"Will you be gone long?"

"I'm afraid so. It's going to be a very long trip."

He spent the rest of the afternoon listlessly reading the sports pages and surfing the net. His e-mail accounts were overflowing, even the one he used the least, the address only those closest to him had; there were several unread messages and he went through them all till the very last one, the oldest one, really threw him for a loop. It was a confession he'd been forwarded, unexpected enough to make him shout out loud with surprise.

CHAPTER XXIV

The next day he knew it was time to pay a call on Eugenia; it couldn't be put off for any longer. He was eager to make peace with her and to try to make her see that he couldn't have avoided the unavoidable, and to tell her to fight for her relationship with Dima, to make him a part of her life. Curro had a very strong feeling that an engagement would soon be announced that would scandalize the more conservative sector of Madrid's upper class. If Ignacio Osorio was going to be too much of a pain, Curro would put him in his place—he knew just the way to do it. It wouldn't take him very long to lay out a few irrefutable truths if the outmoded duke's opposition became a problem.

He walked over to Eugenia's from his place, doing a little window-shopping on Serrano. Curro didn't really enjoy shopping, unless it was absolutely necessary, but he'd planned this route because it took him by a frame shop where he had them mount a photo of him with Trasto, which he was going to give to the couple. He had a few other surprise presents for them that he was sure they'd like, especially Eugenia.

When he got to Eugenia's condo, José, the

building super, was standing outside the main door having a smoke.

"Don Francisco! How nice to see you, it's been a while."

"Not really that long, José, but you know, it feels like a century."

"You're right. Are you here to see Miss Eugenia?"

"Yes, we're having lunch."

"Don Dmitri, that friend of yours who was here when Miss Eugenia disappeared—he's upstairs."

"I know. I hope you'll be as nice to him as you've always been to me."

"But Don Francisco, you're practically family."

"Before long Don Dmitri will be too."

"You don't say!"

"Keep it under your hat, José, but I'm counting on it. Why, does he rub you the wrong way?"

"Not at all, he's a very polite young man. It's just that… What will His Grace the Duke say?"

"His Grace will be delighted, I'm sure. He couldn't ask for a better husband for Eugenia."

"I like him, and Miss Eugenia seems more focused, if you don't mind my saying so."

"Of course not! Who better to say so, you see her every day. And I agree, I think Eugenia's found the mate she needed. Anyway, I'd better go on up. Say hello to your family for me."

"Will do, Don Francisco."

Having been tipped off by the super, Eugenia was waiting for Curro by her front door, and the two of them squeezed together in a warm hug as Dima watched contentedly. Once inside they sat down in her living room and chatted over some cold beers, potato chips, and olives. Eugenia had also put out one of Curro favorite snacks, *boquerones en vinagre,* filets of small whitefish marinated in vinegar and spices. He loved the dish.

"I brought you guys a picture of me with Trasto, I hope you'll give it pride of place."

"Of course," said Eugenia. "But hey, slow down. We need to convince Daddy first."

"Don't tell me you're actually going to pay attention to your father for the first time ever, and over something important. Where's that rebellious spirit I know so well?"

"You know what daddy's like," she said apprehensively.

"I don't want to hear it. You two need to set a date, and the sooner you pick one the better, or I'm not going to have time to slim down enough to fit into my morning coat. By the way, here's my wedding gift. I hope you use these at the ceremony."

Curro took out a little box he placed on the table next to their snacks. It was Eugenia who picked it up and opened it, letting out a little gasp.

"You must be kidding! We could never take these!"

The box contained jewel-encrusted art deco cufflinks Curro had inherited from his father and which he almost never wore; and a bracelet, also bejeweled and in the same style, that had been an engagement gift to Curro's mother. Having no children and no nieces or nephews to leave them to, Curro had decided to offer them to his friends as a token of friendship. He'd never been attached to material things, much less now that he'd settled his scores and apathy had again taken over his demeanor.

"You tell me, who better than you two to enjoy these, and after you, your children and grandchildren? Otherwise they'll eventually be inherited by some cousins of mine to whom they won't mean a thing. They're yours to keep."

"You've lost it," said Eugenia. After admiring the present for a while, Eugenia asked Dima to put the little box in with her other safe-keepings in the bedroom, and while he was out of the room Curro leaned over and lowered his voice. He had a confession to make.

"Don't tell Dima, but I opened a checking account in his name at my Swiss bank and transferred a tidy sum to it. He'll easily be able to maintain you in the style to which you're accustomed."

"He won't take it, you know that. He won't take money from anyone."

"Well, it's practically his money anyway. So, start putting everything together. You're getting married."

"What about my dad?"

"He'll be delighted, with the money especially, just you wait and see. Besides, that hangup about Dima being a commoner, it's very passé. I mean, your mother herself, if you don't mind my saying so—"

She laughed. "You mean the Pérez-Benzo de Torres dynasty? Sometimes if we're arguing I pick on her and call her a peasant."

"Hah! Your dad's more of a peasant than she is, despite his pedigree."

"Curro, Curro. Same rapier wit as ever."

It felt wonderful to Curro to be laughing with

Eugenia again. Reuniting with her was one last piece of important business he had on hand.

Dima returned, ignorant of his coming good fortune; he was already a millionaire without even knowing it. They went through to the dining room. Eugenia had borrowed her mother's cook to make oxtail for the three of them, knowing it was a dish Curro was particularly fond of, and she served it with a bottle of magnificent red Alión. They stretched the meal out with coffee and Port, and Eugenia told the cook she was free to go, her maid would tidy up the following day.

Later on, just when Curro was getting ready to reveal Dima's new status to him, the doorphone buzzed. José, the doorman, told Eugenia that two foreign-looking gentlemen he'd never seen before were on their way up, having insisted they'd been invited to join her and her guests for coffee.

Eugenia returned, ashen-faced. The voices in the background that she thought she'd recognized made her skin crawl.

"You're never going to believe this," Eugenia began. She hurriedly relayed what José had said, then added, "But I'd have sworn I heard Gagarin's voice."

Curro raised an eyebrow at Dima. "So, this isn't over yet," he mumbled. The prospect made him nervous. Or maybe not.

An apartment door was not going to stand in the way of Gagarin and one of his toughs. They had to prepare, and fast. Curro told Dima to grab anything that could be handy for self-defense. Since they'd dumped the Viking automatic into the sea when they'd left Basurto's yacht, they had to fall back on kitchen knives. They never even considered calling the cops, much less Inspector Jiménez; Curro knew that after so many lies, with more than one dead body in the equation, a sudden bout of honesty wouldn't reflect too well on them now. The two of them would have to finish the job themselves. They sent Eugenia out the service entrance to take refuge with her downstairs neighbors. Curro told her not to move unless she heard strange sounds; in that case, she was to call the Inspector, whose number was in the cell phone he handed her.

Curro nodded approvingly as Dima hid one of the butcher knives under an oversized cushion on the couch. When the unexpected guests walked in, Curro and Dima were waiting for them near the entrance like perfect hosts. There was no escape; besides every story has its ending and there was nothing to be gained by delaying this one's.

Alex was first through the door, followed by Gagarin, brandishing a revolver. "We meet again, Mr. Morante," said the crimelord in English. Curro's eyes met Alex's but his expression was impossible to read. What was he doing back with the mob? Gagarin stepped further into the room. "Dmitri! I hope you're finally going to tell me everything you know."

"Mr. Gagarin!" said Curro unimpressed. "And here I thought you'd been flirting with the mermaids all this time." He turned his attention on Alex, who was still indecipherable. " Alex!"

"What?" he asked dully.

"Nothing. But come in, come in," said Curro, wanting to keep control of the situation before Dima tried anything. "Let's talk business. Right this way, make yourselves comfortable. Would you like some coffee, Gagarin?" said Curro sarcastically. "How about you, Alex, can I get you anything?"

Both men shook their heads. They were taken aback by their apparently cordial reception and looked from left to right wondering if there was something they'd missed. The Russian sat down, while his outrider stood at his back. Curro sat down facing Gagarin, Dima standing behind him.

"Do you mind if I have a Scotch? Surprises like this do rather strain one's nerves."

Gagarin eyed him suspiciously. "Help yourself. Alex, go with him."

"Relax, man, don't you see we're unarmed? Dima, shall I bring you anything?"

Dima said nothing. Curro went to the kitchen followed by Alex, where he poured himself a Scotch on the rocks. Alex's closeness made his pulse speed up.

"How'd you hook back up with that scumbag? We thought he was sleeping with the fishes. Literally."

"Yeah, well, you're a lousy shot. You missed."

"I heard him shout in pain."

"I dunno. There he is, don't ask me how. Yesterday morning he showed up at my mom's place threatening to kill her if she didn't tell him where to find me. He wanted my help to find you guys. It wasn't exactly rocket science, everybody knows who Eugenia is."

"He lied to you. He knows damn well where she lives, and where I live for that matter. As if he's never had us followed!"

Alex slammed his fist on the counter. "I don't

care. All I care about is my mom, he left two second-rate tough guys guarding her, so I had to get back with this son of a bitch—but it won't be for long. First chance I get, I'm gonna fix him good. Shitbag thinks he's gonna get away with threatening my mother?"

"Won't be for long, you're right. Just as long as it takes you to murder us." Curro took a sip of his Scotch.

"Look, he's got my mother!"

"Then you're here to help me put an end to my tedious existence," he said turning. "That's really considerate of you. But I'd appreciate it if you'd give Dima a break. Like you, he's a great guy who just needed someone to take care of him. And his only crime is trying to survive, like you, and crossing paths with that undesirable thug. You and Dima are two sides of the same coin."

"Knock it off with the cheap talk, don't try to bring me around. I don't know why I'm even listening to you. You're a rat, you're no better than him. All I care about is my mom. They won't release her until I come back with Gagarin safe and sound."

"After he's finished us off, he'll kill your mother too. And then he'll kill you."

"I gotta try it."

"Your call. Aren't you ever going to trust me?"

"No. I don't trust anyone," Alex said, firmly.

"Alex!" Gagarin was getting impatient.

Curro and Alex went back into the living room. "Here we come, don't be nervous," said Curro. "I was just trying to talk him into killing you, but unfortunately I didn't get very far. That is one loyal henchman you've got there."

Gagarin laughed. "You're crazy, Mr. Morante. Now, let's talk money. Oh, and where is Miss Osorio?" he asked, looking around. "If she's gone to ask for help she'll not see either of you alive again." His tone intensified. "Where is she?!"

"Not here, as you can well imagine. She's in a safe place. And don't worry about the police. You see my hands? They look clean, don't they? But they're stained with blood, just like yours. Forget the police! Money talks, horseshit walks."

"Don't start another one of your monologues!"

"You must know very well that neither Mr. Denissov nor anyone in his family had anything to do with the disappearance of that money—50 million euros, wasn't it? Don't lie to me, Gagarin, where are you hiding it? All this is just play-acting to look good for the Kasparovs, isn't it?"

"My patience has reached its limit!" shouted Gagarin. "Where is the money?" Gagarin looked at Dima. "Your lives aren't worth one miserable ruble to me. Let's start with Mr. Morante, who doesn't seem to care whether he lives or dies. Alex?"

"I don't think my relationship with my inner self is any of your business," said Curro sarcastically. "You're just a lousy scoundrel fate's put in our path, nothing else."

"Alex, shut him up."

"Fifty *million* euros? You son of a bitch, you were only gonna give me chicken feed!" Even though Gagarin was armed, the speed of Alex's unexpected attack left him unable to react in time; the two shots the criminal warlord got off did nothing more than shatter Eugenia's huge picture window. Alex wrested the gun from him and stepped back, now in control of the situation. Dima, meanwhile, grabbed the hidden knife. He sat down, wielding the knife, staring intently at Gagarin, while Curro stood between the two of them and Alex.

"Alex!" Curro said. "Stop for a moment, think about what you're doing. Put the gun down, we have no beef with you. You know full well what Gagarin's like, he was going to leave you high and dry—if you were even that lucky. I swear to you I'll find a way to rescue your mother, you know I can do it. Trust someone for once in your life, dammit! Forget about him, let Dima and him settle their differences on their own. You must know that son of a bitch killed Dima's parents."

Alex stood for a moment, keeping the gun pointed at them, and took a long, hard look at the man he'd served loyally and who'd repaid that loyalty by holding his mother hostage. Nervously, he lowered the gun and took a step back, resigning any interest in the fate of his former boss. Gagarin erupted, swearing to Alex that he didn't have the money and offered him a share of the profits from the last job he'd pulled. Alex didn't bother to answer.

Revenge, finally, was Dima's for the taking. Dima stood up, slowly, and put the knife down on a shelf. He started walking around his onetime mentor who, when he tried to speak, got a kick in the face that split his lip in two. He sat down and stared at Curro, who took the hint and gently nudged Alex off towards the far end of the room. Dima stood again and moved closer to Gagarin, shouting at him in Russian. For a moment it seemed as though Dima wanted to annihilate him just with the strength of his voice. But he wasn't finished; in fact, he was just getting started. Dima picked Gagarin up, grabbed him by the lapels and began throwing him around the room, bouncing him off the walls. Gagarin, silent after the first impact, flew through the air like a broken puppet.

"We should really finish this up," said Curro. "I know Eugenia. I'm sure she's called the police."

"I'm not through yet," said Dima icily.

Curro fell silent and began wondering if he'd convinced Alex that they were on his side. He hadn't put the gun down, hadn't really taken a clear stand, for that matter standing off to the side, it was as if his mind were somewhere else.

Dima, meanwhile, was squatting down on top of Gagarin, beating frenziedly. Curro thought he was dead. Probably had been for a few minutes, in fact.

"Enough, man," said Curro. "The clock's ticking."

Dima was still engrossed in his broken puppet. He grabbed Gagarin's neck and throttled him till a snap echoed through the room. He'd broken the mobster's windpipe. It was all over too soon. Dima would have preferred it last longer.

The sound of sirens outside broke the mood. Curro went to the window and saw patrol cars skidding to a halt on the pavement, the first officers jumping out, led by Carlos Jiménez. The model, hearing her plate-glass window shatter from her neighbors' apartment below, had assumed the worst and dialed the Inspector's phone number. She didn't really tell him anything, but he ordered her to stay put till he got there himself.

"Traitor!" said Alex, raising the gun again.

"No, man, it was Eugenia, she's downstairs listening and the noise scared her. I assure you we want nothing to do with the police either. You already know about Sotogrande, Gagarin told you that. But it was also us who made the Kasparov clan's Ukrainians disappear. Have you heard about that?"

"Yes."

"Alex, listen to me. There's no time. I'm going with you." He turned to Dima, whose eyes widened. "Both of you, help me! We've got to hide the body!"

Dima and Alex picked up the body, one at each end, and followed Curro towards the service quarters, where they locked the corpse into a closet in the laundry room. Curro handed his friend the key.

"Dima, I'm going with Alex."

"What?" said Dima, stunned. "Why?" He sounded disappointed.

"If they find him here they'll start asking all kinds of questions and we'll all be under suspicion. You know that once Carlitos gets an idea into his head... Besides, Alex left us alone and now he's on our side."

Dima scowled. "Whaddya mean, on *our* side? Have you forgotten Eugenia? Outta my way, I'll kill him!" he shouted, shoving Curro to one side.

"Aw, don't make me laugh," said Alex with his usual bravado. "All right, try it! Let's see what you got."

Dima lunged at him and both of them rolled around on the floor, Curro now master of the abandoned gun. The two antagonists rained punches on each other, and when Curro tried to separate them an accidental blow knocked him away from the scuffle.

"You idiots," yelled Curro. "Carlos is gonna be through that door any minute now and we'll be completely fucked! I've never seen two guys as stupid as you two!"

Ignoring him completely, the two boxers kept up their assault on one another, each landing so many crushing blows that any normal opponent would have bit the dust long before. Curro, fed up, fired a shot in the air, realizing instantly it had been a mistake and that time was running out. But the unexpected report at least stopped the fight, and Dima grabbed the gun from Curro.

"I oughtta kill you right now, you rapist piece of shit," Dima growled, looking Alex right in the eye. Alex met his gaze, held it.

"Go ahead, I'm right here!"

"Will you two knock it off?" shouted Curro. "Carlitos will be here any second!"

"Who the hell is Carlitos?"

"Friend of mine. Police inspector. Dima, give me that gun, it'd be better for all of us if no one sees it around here. And say goodbye to Eugenia from me. Tell her she was a great friend and I'll never forget her."

"You sound like you're never gonna see her again."

"Who knows?"

"You're gonna run right into all the cops!"

"Don't worry, I know my way around the building. We'll sneak out through the garage."

"Curro—"

"We have to run. Remember, stay away from my apartment and get rid of Gagarin's body. Explain the situation to Eugenia, she'll know how to get it out—after dark, through the garage. And you tell Carlos Jiménez this whole mess today was my fault. You hear? All of it! Knock yourself out."

Dima didn't know what to do. His closest friend, his only remaining family, really, was abandoning him and leaving, possibly forever, with that despicable gypsy. Curro moved closer and hugged him tightly. He also took away the gun.

"By the way, I finally managed to open that e-mail attachment you forwarded to me from the convent, that one you couldn't open. It's very revealing. Watch your inbox, I'll forward it back to you. When you read it, you'll understand."

"Curro, man, where're you going?"

"Dima, I love you. I'll always carry you with me. Good luck, my friend! I know you'll have it," said Curro, his heart in a lump, not daring to look his friend in the face.

"Gimme back my gun!" said Alex as they quickly exited.

"Here," he said handing him back the gun. They were much more likely than Dima to need it.

They took the service staircase down to the garage, which was shared with the adjacent building; they walked calmly up the ramp and left. Dima felt himself even more orphaned than after his parents' death.

Once the police had arrived and taken up positions, their presence gave Eugenia the courage to take a chance on returning to her penthouse. She went in, hesitantly, finding the apartment empty and the living room a complete wreck. She proceeded gingerly down the hall, looking into every room as she went; in the kitchen she found Dima looking as if he was about to come unglued. She ran to him, hugging him passionately.

"What happened? Where's Curro?"

"He just left. He's fine."

"And the others?"

The sound of approaching voices startled them. It was Carlos Jiménez, striding resolutely towards them, after leaving two officers posted at the front door, which Eugenia had forgotten to shut.

"All hell broke loose, I'll explain later!" hissed Dima into Eugenia's ear. "Just follow my lead."

The inspector stood before them, visibly irritated.

"Miss Osorio, I clearly instructed you to sit tight till I got here. Is this what you call paying attention?"

"It's just that—"

"It was my fault," said Dima, cutting her off. "I went and got her, I didn't want her to worry."

"Why is it I seem to find you everywhere I go? I thought you were in Russia."

"I just got back yesterday."

"Sure you did. Mind telling me what went on here? Where's Curro?"

"He left a while ago, Inspector."

Eugenia put a hand on the inspector's arm, leading him back towards the living room and—unbeknownst to her—away from the evidence. "Call me Eugenia... Carlos. After all, you are Curro's friend. And you did save my life," she said, in a tone not lacking irony, which Jiménez noticed.

"Fine. Call me whatever you want. But now explain to me, what is all this, and where's Curro?

What's with these foreign guys the super mentioned to me?"

"I was a witness, I'll explain everything, Inspector," said Dima.

"Carlos," said Eugenia firmly, "Can I get you anything?"

"No thanks," he replied. Then, looking at Dima, he said, "What the hell happened to your face?"

Dima realized how he must look after trading blows with Alex. He took a few deep breaths to relax. Then he sat down. How would Curro handle this? With a certain distance... ith irony... nd, above all, with bald-faced lies. *Here goes...*

"What , this? Oh, two guys tried to snatch Eugenia's purse this morning. I stopped them, no big deal. They landed a few blows, but you should see how *they* look. Say, Eugenia, would you pour me a Scotch? Now, Inspector," he just couldn't bring himself to address the cop informally, "today at about two P.M. Curro came over for lunch; Eugenia had invited him. Everything was going just fine till he found out we're getting married. Then the shit hit the fan. Curro got all jealous—"

"Hold it. Who's getting married? You and Miss Osorio?"

"Eugenia, call me Eugenia."

"Or you and Curro?" asked Jiménez pointedly.

"What? What're you saying?" Dima sprang to his feet.

"It's just that it surprises me that—"

"I don't care what surprises you. I'm not queer and I'm not having any snide remarks."

Dima had, at a stroke, thrown off the leeriness,

fear even, that many Russians seemed to exhibit before any member of State security services. Even he, a former soldier who was all grown up, tended to feel uncomfortable when faced with a member of the police. But this had just changed. Somehow, he'd taken on some of Curro's personality and from that moment on he'd behave more confidently. Carlos backed down, aware of the mistake he'd made.

"I'm sorry, excuse me. That was outta line."

"Eugenia, bring the Inspector a Scotch."

"I don't drink," said Jiménez.

"Neither do I. But sometimes..." Both men smiled.

"So, as I was saying, Inspector, Curro went nuts. I don't know who he was jealous of, Eugenia or me, but it was definitely a jealous rage. He started insulting us, then he trashed the place. I mean, just look around."

Not bothering to look at the room as invited, the inspector continued. "Tell me about these foreigners. They were Russians, weren't they?"

"Yes they were. I'd never seen them before; they were friends of Curro's, he'd asked them to stop by here for coffee after lunch. He said he was interested in setting up a gym specializing in martial arts, a venture I'd be managing. But we didn't really get any time to talk about that. Curro was drunk... Before I knew it the whole jealousy thing started up again, Curro grabbed my gun and ... I have a firearms license, I was in the Russian Army. Okay, the license isn't valid here, but I haven't used the gun, anyway."

"Of course, of course." Jiménez didn't believe a word, but what to do? There was no evidence, yet. "Tell me, where did you keep the gun?"

"In the bedroom."

"Loaded? In plain sight?"

"In a drawer in the nightstand. We're still worried about Gagarin; Eugenia can't get to sleep at night..."

"Right, right."

"Curro went to the bathroom and when he came back he was pointing the gun at us."

"He'd completely lost it," chimed in Eugenia. "When he came back from the bathroom it was like he was a different person."

"He pointed it directly at me," said Dima, "I was sure he was going to shoot me. Then, just before he pulled the trigger, he aimed the other way and took out the window."

"Right, right."

"Carlos, you can't imagine. It was horrible," said Eugenia. "Look, I'm still shaking like a leaf."

"What about the third shot?"

"Same time," said Dima, "he pointed the gun up and fired a shot in the air. The bullet's lodged in the roof, see? Over there."

"Oh yeah, there it is. Kids, Curro would be proud of you. But he's better at dissembling. If you want to lie convincingly you have to do it with more poise, like he does."

"Carlos!" Eugenia acted offended.

Jiménez stood up in annoyance. "Oh, come off it. Do I really look that stupid? We got several witnesses say there was at least fifteen minutes between the first shot and the last one."

"They must be mistaken."

"That's enough. I see you two are quick learners but, all the same..."

The couple fell silent. They had nothing else to say. They'd been confident that the Inspector would put his friendship with Curro and the promise he'd made above strict adherence to the law. That he wouldn't squeeze them too hard.

"Where's Curro? Where'd he run off to? What happened to the Russians?"

"Inspector…Carlos," said Dima, "We really don't know. After the shots I sent Eugenia to run and hide at the downstairs neighbor's, that's where she called you from. Then, when they heard the sirens, the Russians got jumpy and Curro led them out down the back stairs."

"I'll bet they went out through the garage this building shares with the one next door," Eugenia added. "Curro knows every nook and cranny of this building."

"Right. And you have no idea where he might be?"

"No idea," said Dima. "He took off with no explanations."

"All right. I'm done here. When Curro resurfaces we'll talk again."

***

Carlos Jiménez Moreno left firmly convinced that some funny business had been going on in the penthouse just before his arrival. But lacking any evidence that a crime had actually been committed, he decided it best to let things stand as they were. Eugenia Osorio's kidnapping had already had enough media repercussions without putting her back in the headlines. Besides, the case had officially been solved, he himself taking the praise for that; better not to do anything until he had more information, he didn't want to step on his own dick.Eugenia and Dima breathed more easily once he was gone. After Dima picked up the bullet shells, they settled into the living room and talked about Curro's strange behavior in leaving with Alex.

"He's always been like that, does whatever he wants, whenever he wants. That creep's got Curro wrapped around his little finger."

"You think so?"

"No doubt. I've known him my whole life. Seedy guys like that, they amuse him. I hope he doesn't get Curro into trouble, I don't trust that bastard any further than I could throw him. Ah, let's talk about something else."

"Surely Curro doesn't like that guy *that* much. I mean, he's just a lowbrow street punk with no manners," Dima said, sounding almost jealous.

"Well, Curro does like guys like that, dear, they turn him on. What do you care, anyway? It's not like Curro's your *boyfriend*!" Eugenia was getting hot under the collar.

"He's my *friend* and I love him as a *friend*, that's all. If it hadn't been for him I would have killed that son of a bitch. We got in a fight. Now I'm glad Curro stopped me. I just want to start a new life with you and leave the old life behind me."

"I'm glad too," said Eugenia, without much conviction.

CHAPTER XXV

Curro and Alex had no trouble avoiding the cops. They'd walked up the ramp of the shared garage onto the street around the corner from Eugenia's building. They turned left towards Paseo de la Castellana and then walked towards Plaza Cibeles, a stone's throw from Curro's penthouse. They walked in silence, each with his own ghosts. Only when they were at the door to the building did Alex speak up.

"Where you taking me?"

"My place. I live here," he said, putting a key in the door.

Alex stopped. "I'm outta here. Have I been speakin' Chinese or something? My mom's being held hostage!"

"Calm down, Alex—"

"Like hell I will!"

"Look, I need to sit back for a moment and have a drink. I think it'd do you some good too. If we settle down and focus, we'll be better able to work out how to rescue her."

"I'm gone, man," Alex said with his hands in the air. "I don't need you. I'll take care of this myself."

Curro took hold of his arm. "Alex! Slow down for just one minute. Don't you think it'd be best to organize ourselves, come up with some kind of plan? Look, I think I've done pretty well so far. Trust me."

The young hunk shrugged and reluctantly nodded his agreement. He hadn't thought things through, he would have just gone to the circus yard and went in swinging. Curro was right. They needed to make a plan before rushing into action.

"Fine, but let's not waste any time, all right?" he said, following Curro into the foyer.

Once they were inside Curro's penthouse, Alex gave himself a quick tour, then said approvingly, "Nice shack!"

"You like it? Thanks. It's not too bad."

"Not bad, he says. You could fit about ten apartments the size of my place in Marbella into this one."

"Make yourself at home, Alex. I'm going to pour myself a Scotch. You want anything?"

"I'll have one too."

They sat facing each other on the terrace, the late spring sun still shining warmly.

"Alex, before we do anything, bring me up to speed on your family so I can get some idea of what we're up against. Don't hold back. When you said your mom's being held hostage at her place, you meant the circus, right?"

"And how would you know that?"

"Ekaterina. She told Eugenia."

"Oh. Yeah, my mom still lives there, even though it's closed down now. People don't go for traditional circus stuff the way they used to: you know, clowns, lion tamers, tightrope walkers. Now it's all about lights, sound, theatrics. That ain't a real circus!"

"Where is it?"

"Outskirts of town. City Hall let her have a vacant lot next to the pool at Lago, in Casa de Campo Park."

"Man, that's not the outskirts! That's five minutes away from downtown."

"Whatever. You know where it is?"

"The pool at Lago? Of course! I've never been swimming there, but I've been by it dozens of times. Casa de Campo's practically my second home. I used to go there with my dog all the time. And eat there, at Currito's. Anyway, getting back to the subject—so who's left at the circus, then?"

"My mom, my aunt Tula, and a few of the performers who've spent their whole lives with us and got no place else to go. Everyone lives in their own wagon."

"Your dad?"

"Son of a bitch might as well be dead, for all I care."

"What happened, he abandoned you and your mom?"

"The fuck do you care?" Alex said sullenly.

"Same old story, handsome playboy, place to place, woman in every port. Don't tell me if you don't want to, it's none of my business."

"Yeah, well, you nailed it, man. Son of a bitch. I dunno how many brothers and sisters I've got running around. The bastard dumped my mom when she was pregnant with me."

Curro nodded and said, "The usual story."

"Naw, man, see, he kept coming back, every time he was hard up. Till about ten years ago, he disappeared for good. I heard him slappin' my mom around and I gave him such a whipping he lost interest in ever coming back. If my mom hadn't stepped in I woulda killed him. You know, I don't even know why I'm tellin' you this shit."

"I inspire trust in you," said Curro, who couldn't help the warm feelings Alex stirred in him. "Who actually owns the circus?"

"My mom. Her family have always been in the circus biz. You ever hear of Bonin and Bonet?"

"Of course! The legendary circus clowns."

"Well, Bonin was my great-grandfather. He founded the circus, and it's been in our family ever since."

"So then, your circus is the Bonin Brothers Circus."

"Yeah, that's the one," Alex said proudly. "Now it's officially the Peres Circus."

"So your mother must be Rosita Peres, the tightrope walker!"

Alex looked impressed. "Dude, you know your stuff."

"She was the most famous tightrope walker in the world! Didn't I hear about her having a bad fall a few years back? She was the only one who didn't use a safety net, right?"

"Yeah, she broke her back, never the same after that. She's not doing too bad now, though."

"I didn't even know she was still alive, I thought she was a lot older than that... And you're her son!" Curro said.

"Yeah, I came along late. She was over forty when she had me."

"Imagine that. I never knew she had a kid."

"Here I am, the one and only."

"Man, you are full of surprises, you know that? Very interesting. But now, getting back to our problem. How many people are at the circus right now?"

"When I left, no more than three or four, including my mom. Aunt Tula lives with her but she wasn't there yesterday."

"Those guys holding your mother hostage—you know them? Are they dangerous?"

"Never saw the fuckers before. Definitely not part of the Russian mob. The Russians think Gagarin's dead. Bastard! He was gonna give me peanuts outta that fifty mil."

"So then, the hired guns—"

"Dude, I dunno, some lowlifes he picked up somewhere. They're definitely not any of the kids Gagarin had working as bouncers at his discos—they all know me and they wouldn't have dared. I got a good look at 'em, they didn't look like all that much to me."

"How about if we go take a look?"

"Now you're talking!" said Alex, jumping out of his chair.

"Hang on just one moment," said Curro, going into his study. He sat at his computer, opened the drafts folder and sent Dima two messages; the one whose contents had so surprised him, and one he'd written himself. His eyes welled up.

They set out for Casa de Campo, Curro guiding the car up Gran Via, its early twentieth-century Modernist buildings gleaming majestically in the afternoon sun. The famous street's sidewalks heaved with a mass of people speaking in accents of every imaginable origin, in numbers enough for all of them to feel, in the capital, a bit of the home they'd left behind. At Plaza de España they turned towards the Estación del Norte, a onetime railway station now converted into a gargantuan shopping mall, and then went into the long tunnels that stretched beneath the Manzanares River, just a weak shadow of the abundant waterway it had once been. When they emerged on the other side it seemed cooler; temperatures were in fact a few degrees lower on that side of the river, thanks to the lush foliage that made up the park that locals sometimes referred to as the Lung of Madrid.

The lot where the circus had come to rest was in a clearing adjoining the lake. As they approached the big tent on foot, they were surprised by the eerie calm enveloping the place. Alex looked around and saw no one in the ring, or in any of the walkways around it; he led Curro back to the area where the wagons were parked. As they closed in they heard raised voices:

"Rosita, listen to me, we have to call the cops!"

"My boy said to wait till he gets back. I'm afraid I'll get him in trouble."

"Him? Rosita! I'll bet that Russian's already bought the farm."

"But Alex's hands are tied! He thinks I'm still being held hostage!"

Alex picked up his pace and hurried around the side of one of the wagons. "Mom!"

A delighted Rosita turned towards her son. "Alex, my darling!"

The explosion of love that followed surprised

Curro. He wasn't used to such open displays of affection. Mother and son locked together in an extended embrace punctuated by loud kisses and nuzzling. Rosita held her boy's face in her hands, alternately kissing him and just holding him to look at him, while the battle-hardened veteran of a thousand dirty fights sobbed happily.

"You're free!" said Alex jubilantly.

"And so are you!"

Curro stood back, watching from a distance, comparing the scene to his own memories. His relationship with his father had been cold, almost non-existent; not so the link he'd had with his mother. He'd adored her. They'd always understood each other perfectly, linked in unspoken complicity. Concha Solloso knew all, and said nothing. She would have preferred a son who took a more active role in the family business; above all, a son who would have given her grandchildren to spoil rotten; but she soon realized that would never happen. In spite of that she was always supportive of him. But physical contact, touching—there had never been any of that, and it was something Curro had needed. For that reason, this extravagant display of affection made a profound impression on him.

Brushing aside these thoughts, Curro turned to analyzing the members of this little circus gathering. Rosita must have been about seventy, but she was prettier and, apparently, more agile than he would have expected for someone who'd been through such a serious accident. Slightly built, her wrinkles didn't completely obscure the beauty for which she'd been justly admired as she performed around the world. On the other hand, the gigantic woman standing next to her brought back confusing memories for Curro. This was Alex's Aunt Tula. Taller even than Alex himself, about six and a half feet, Curro guessed, and she must have weighed close to 300 pounds. She seemed to share nothing at all with her elder sister save the bright blue eyes.

Rounding out the group were a couple of dwarves, a man and a woman, who—judging from their wizened appearance—looked to Curro as if they'd hung up their costumes a long time ago.

"And who is this gentleman?" asked Rosita, once she'd settled down enough to notice Curro's presence.

"This is Curro, Mom," he said proudly, "he's a friend who helped me lose the Russian. Curro, this is my mom, Rosita; my aunt, Tula; and 'The Pepitos'."

"Delighted, ma'am," said Curro, approaching the *artiste* with an outstretched hand, which she ignored, pulling her towards him for a kiss. Aunt Tula, more reserved, shook his hand; she looked at him penetratingly, as if the newcomer stirred up some memories. "The Pepitos" simply waved at him.

"My boy's friends are always welcome here," said the mother, looking him over with the eye of someone who's traveled the globe and developed keen psychological insight to show for it.

"So, Mom, what happened? Where are the guys who were holding you hostage?"

"Two words: Aunt Tula. C'mon, have a seat. What're you having, sir?"

"Scotch, if you have it, thanks. And please, call me Curro."

"Only if you call me Rosita."

"Deal!"

***

The tale of the famous tightrope walker's captivity and release would have been worthy of the attention by a master of Italian neorealism.

Gagarin had showed up outside Rosita's wagon in the early hours, backed up by two young thugs on the make who were delighted to get such a simple job. The crooks had already reconnoitered the twenty or so wagons parked in perfect formation and not seen a soul. Aunt Tula, as it happened, had left early on circus business; the family wanted to keep their operating license valid and it was time to apply for renewal with the city. And "The Pepitos"—he was Pepito, she was Pepita—had hidden as soon as they'd spotted the foreigner and his hired guns skulking around outside. They weren't sure whether or not to step in; they were brave enough, but armed with nothing more than their tiny bodies, they'd felt it best to wait and see if an opportunity for them to make a difference presented itself.

Alex's arrival had dampened the two young hoods' bluster. The two greenhorns knew him by sight, and once they saw him, they started to remember some of what they'd heard about him: he wasn't the kind of guy anyone wanted to make an enemy out of. The look he'd given them said all that needed saying: if he survived whatever the Russian was up to, they'd be sorry they were ever born. Gagarin left with Alex, leaving Rosita nominally in the power of the two nervous punks. "The Pepitos", meanwhile, were on the lookout for Tula, whose circus tagline had been "The Strongest Woman on the Planet".

When she got back the dwarves were waiting by the entrance to tip her off. She didn't hesitate for a moment; they'd soon put a stop to this. They worked out a plan whereby the dwarves would distract the apprentice scumbag who was guarding the door to Rosita's wagon. They'd say the police wanted to talk to her about an illegal connection the circus had made to the city electrical grid. Even if she was "indisposed," the lookout would have to go through the motions of asking her what to tell the cop who was waiting outside the gate.

"Who're you?" asked Pepito.

"I'm a pal of Alex's. He should be here any minute, we were supposed to meet up here. You?"

"We work for his mom. There's a policeman outside who wants to see her, something about us having a line to a power grid that shouldn't be there."

"She's busy right now."

"Fine, then you come talk to the cop. Talking with police is not my strong suit."

Gagarin's lookout went with the dwarf after checking with his buddy, who got even more nervous at the thought of a cop on the premises. As the young tough walked around the last of the wagons toward the gate he ran straight into Tula, who slammed him to the ground with a single push. Before he had time to react she was sitting on him, her full weight pinning him to the ground, preventing him from moving, almost preventing him from breathing. His chum heard the suffocating thug's initial shocked shouts and ran out of the wagon, gun in hand, leaving Rosita behind. Like his pal, he was still a novice at nefariousness and faced with the sight of the circus giant crushing his buddy, with law enforcement supposedly at hand, self-preservation trumped the chimeric paycheck Gagarin had promised him. He ran like hell. Then Tula got up, grabbed her erstwhile cushion by his clothes and dragged him to his feet, shouting, "Get lost, you punk! And don't you dare come back!"

***

Curro had enjoyed the tale, laughing along with the rest of those present. But he felt himself being watched—studied, even—by the others, especially Aunt Tula, who made no attempt to conceal her distrust of the newcomer. "The Pepitos" said goodbye and went back to their wagon. Discreet, quiet onlookers since childhood, they were acutely sensitive to moments at which their presence became superfluous.

Tula stood towering over him, arms crossed, a sight striking enough to warrant a feature report in *National Geographic*, like the freak of nature that she was. "So who's fancy pants here?"

"I told you, Aunt Tula, he's a friend of mine."

"Spouting lies as usual. This guy? Friend of *yours?* Your friends are all a bunch of lowlifes. They can go to hell."

"Aunt Tula, I deserve a little respect."

"You'll get it all right—*very* little, same as you show us. I mean, to bring a gang like that down on our heads! At least anyone can tell your new pal here is a real gentleman," she said mockingly.

Curro laughed heartily. "Don't get the wrong idea, ma'am, I assure you that's only a façade. By the way, now I can see where Alex gets his guts from. Clearly runs in the family."

"Stuff the flattery, that don't work on me."

"Shut your filthy mouth!" shouted Alex, bewildered at his aunt's animosity.

Tula had been one of the few people in Alex's inner circle who didn't fear him. Even back when his thirteen-year-old self had already been terrorizing the other members of the troupe, his aunt had stood up to him. And given him a slap more than once. Gradually things changed. Alex could have whipped his aunt without breaking a sweat, despite the extraordinary strength she could still muster to amaze circus audiences. They loathed each other. Alex always accused her of badmouthing him behind his back; Tula accused him of using the circus as a front for illegal activities.

As for Rosita, she wanted to know more. Her son had long since joined a world she'd never approve of, she wasn't about to pass up a chance like this to demand some explanations from him. Before hostilities between Tula and Alex had a chance to escalate, she stepped in.

"Enough already!" She looked at Curro. "Could you just give me a moment with my son? He has some explaining to do."

"Of course. I should be going—"

"No, no, please stay. Tula, behave yourself."

Once he was alone with Tula, Curro helped himself to some more Scotch and stood up; the folding chair was torturing his backside, and he couldn't help but smile at the thought of Tula attempting to use one of them. She was seated on a sturdy-looking stool, the same kind the circus had used for some of its elephant acts. Despite the stool's robust construction, the abuse it had endured had left it looking like an accordion.

"So, friend of Alex's, huh?" she asked belligerently. "I know you from somewhere. I can't remember where, but I know you."

"I'm sorry, but I just don't. Anyway, I assure you, I'd remember if we'd met."

"What do you mean?"

"Well, Tula, you don't exactly blend into the scenery, with a physique like that."

"You making fun of me? I'm warning you, I have a very short fuse."

"No, Aunt Tula," he said provocatively, "would I dare make fun of a phenomenon like you?"

"I am not your aunt. And you're not fooling me, you and Alex are up to something. What else would a real smoothie like you be doing hangin' around my nephew?"

"Life's full of surprises, Auntie." Her tone was starting to really get under his collar.

"I am not your Auntie! You tryin' to put one over on me?" She approached, menacingly.

"Look, Tula. Alex is my friend, and I'd like to help him turn his life around. Deep down he's a good kid, in spite of all the trouble he's gotten into. Okay, you're right, he and I come from different worlds; but I feel a strong urge to reach out to kids like him. I can't help it! He's just a boy who needs some protection—"

She snapped her fingers. "Now I remember! It's you, the Protective Faggot!"

Curro closed his eyes for a moment, focusing on a

flurry of images that suddenly came flooding back. Now he remembered too. That enormous woman had been the wife of the Norwegian ambassador's chauffeur, back when the ambassador had lived in the same building as his parents. That rough little guy from some small town, who Curro had hooked up with. It had been a huge scandal. One day in the garage, Curro had gone up behind him, gripping the yearned-for firmness, finding a man who didn't react badly– no, who went along with it. He'd been a family man, and Curro had promised him the moon, for him, for his kids; even though, at the time, he had no money of his own yet. Eventually Abilino—that had been his name, an object of Curro's early desire—had asked for his help (to enroll his kids in a bilingual school, no less); Curro couldn't pay up, and then all hell broke loose.

Abilino had showed up with a furious woman—Tula!—who demanded damages, and interest. Curro had nothing of his own, just the trifling allowance his dad gave him every Saturday, and could do nothing but shrug when threatened with being disgraced throughout the neighborhood, having the truth revealed to his own family. Tula would have beaten him up right then and there if three of the other chauffeurs hadn't happened by; even so, the three of them combined could barely hold her back. The ambassador and his wife found out about the scandal but said nothing; they'd grown friendly with the Morantes and their only daughter displayed evident interest in Curro, an interest they'd hoped would in time be reciprocated... A delusion. Curro's interests lay elsewhere.

In the end, Abilino was fired, but given a glowing letter of recommendation for a job in the government motor pool; but Tula, who'd looked the other way for as long as she'd held on to the hope the promise of compensation would be honored, never forgot how humiliated she'd felt as a woman by her husband's behavior.

"Now I remember you, Tula. God, what a sorry business," he said theatrically. "How's the family? Abilino, the kids... I heard that in the end you got them into that school you liked, and that Abilino—ah, Abilino, what memories—he settled into his government job well, served longer than several of the Cabinet Secretaries, is that right?"

"How dare you! You shameless rat! It was your fault everything changed. After you Abilino was never the same again, he wouldn't touch me. I even heard him whisper your name when he was dreaming. I oughtta kill you!"

"Tula, I'm sorry, I really am. I was just a kid, it was a whim, I couldn't help it. Abilino was so, so, solid-looking. I couldn't resist, I've always been a slave to my appetites. It's pathological. I lack any capacity for forbearance."

"Is that all you have to say? You ruined my life! Nothing was ever the same after that!" she shouted, and then burst into tears.

The sight of the imposing figure reduced to tears made Curro extremely uncomfortable. But what could he do? It had all happened a long time ago, and he hadn't forced anyone to do anything; it was true that he'd made a promise he couldn't keep. But Abilino had enjoyed himself. Boy, had he enjoyed himself. He'd even called Curro from his new job, been kind of a pain as a matter of fact; Curro had a hard time getting rid of him after that. He wasn't going to bring any of that up now, he didn't want to enrage Tula's inner beast any more.

"Tula, I'm truly very sorry. My behavior was inexcusable. Why don't you sit down and relax a little? We've all been through an extremely stressful situation. C'mon, sit down and I'll make you a drink."

"Extremely stressful situation," she mimicked. "Pretentious twerp. Fairy."

"Relax," Curro insisted. "We're celebrating. Everything turned out all right."

"Easy for you to say, you're just one of those guys who gets turned on by my nephew and wants to score with him."

"And if I were? So much the worse for me, Alex isn't gay."

"I know that, but I also know my nephew: he likes money more than a wino likes a twist-cap. And you're made of money."

"Tula, let's be serious. I'm Alex's friend and I came here to help him sort out the hostage thing with his mom. I'm not looking for trouble, least of all with his aunt."

"Well, you're gonna find it, whether you're looking for it or not. I know what guys like you are like. Why else would you be hangin' around Alex? Don't think you're the first guy to go weak-kneed at the sight of him."

Curro had just about had it. He was tired of trying to reason with a woman who'd formed an unshakeable opinion of him and his character, an opinion from which nothing would ever make her budge. His serene veneer was starting to crack.

"Let's drop it. Tula. I'm starting to get a headache. Let's just enjoy the night sky till Rosita and Alex come back out."

"You make me sick! Look at you, sittin' there without a care in the world. Faggot!"

"All right, that's enough, you disgusting moose!" hissed Curro, his patience finally overwhelmed. "You think just being an old hippo gives you the right to insult people? I haven't done anything to you! It's not my fault you can't get laid! I doubt anyone after Abilino ever had the slightest inclination to go spelunking under your skirt!"

"What did you say?" Tula roared.

"I said you oughtta ask your nephew to do you a favor and give your rotten beaver a workout! I'll pass, thank you very much!"

Tula completely lost it. She grabbed Curro by the neck, lifting him like a feather, then crushed him between her body and the side of one of the wagons. The more he moved, the more violently she manhandled him. He tried to break free from her by kicking her legs, he even tried to bite her. It was no use. Tula's size made such maneuvers impossible. When he was out of strength, in desperation he tried headbutting her sternum, and the she-giant lost her balance and fell backwards onto the ground. She was already getting back to her feet to give battle, when Alex and Rosita came running up, having heard the sounds of the scuffle.

"What's all this?" Rosita asked, alarmed.

"I'm sorry, but your sister's crazy," said Curro.

"Tula, are you all right?" she asked, helping her little sister get up.

"Curro here is the Morantes' little boy, the ones who lived where Albi used to work. He's the one who put those ideas into his head."

"Ha ha ha!" Alex rolled with laughter. "The one who talked him into batting for the other team!"

"Alex, please, don't pick on your aunt, she had a really hard time of it. Tula, try to calm down, go lie down for a while."

Tula, who hadn't been young for a very long time, walked off to her wagon slowly, hurt, defeated again. Once they were alone the three of them looked at each other in silence. Rosita and Curro were saddened, embarrassed by their glimpse at such long-held suffering. Alex was attempting to stifle a grin.

"Mr. Morante," said Rosita, "can we take a walk? I'd like to talk with you."

"As you wish, Rosita."

Alex's face went serious. "Mom, don't talk him into a coma, okay? I can't imagine why you wanna bend his ear anyway."

In one hand Rosita held the cane she'd used since the accident, and put her other arm through Curro's. As they began walking, he was afraid she'd begin reproaching him for his past misdeeds. They walked along for a while in silence, till Rosita said accusingly, "I hope you're not going to steal my son from me."

"Rosita! For God's sake, what are you talking about?"

"You heard me. You stole my sister's husband from her."

"Juvenile hijinks. I assure you I'm truly sorry. More so now that I've learned she's Alex's aunt."

"You love him, don't you? And you're going to

take him with you. Until you get bored with him and trade him in for someone else."

"No, Rosita, that's where you're wrong. I don't love him. And believe me, I regret that. If I did love him, not even my respect for you would keep me away from him."

"I don't understand."

"Let me explain. I'd love it if I could love him, and rest assured that I could make him happy. But it can't be. My heart's already spoken for, for all eternity. Besides, Alex isn't gay. He's a man's man, from head to toe. I can't envision him holding another man's hand and looking tenderly into his eyes. He's not the slightest bit homosexual."

"You're telling me? I'm his mother! I know he likes women, but I can also tell, from the conversation I just had with him, that you've made an impression on him. He's changed. I noticed it as soon as he came back from Marbella, when he told me he'd had it with sleazy cons and he wanted to make a fresh start, free from bad influences. What happened between you two in Marbella?"

"Nothing special, we were each doing our own thing. Let me tell you something," he said, stopping as he met Rosita's gaze. "The only reason I was in Marbella was to act as a mediator in the Eugenia Osorio kidnapping. You'll have seen something about that in the news, right?"

"Yes, I saw it on TV. What does my Alex have to do with all that?"

"Nothing. A friend introduced him to me, Alex was working as his bodyguard."

Her face broke into a frown. "You expect me to

believe he's not involved in anything shady?"

"Ok, so he's spent part of his life on the edge of the law, if not actually on the wrong side of it. And he's spent time in places, and with people, that haven't done him any good. But believe me when I say he was just dragged along by the tide. I know him well enough to say that that's all over now. He's woken up. He doesn't want that kind of life anymore."

"That's what he told me. What did he have to do with that Russian who showed up here?"

"They had some unfinished business. He keeps his cards close to his vest, he wouldn't tell me anything else about it."

"He wouldn't tell me either."

"Trust your son. He's made up his mind. I'd bet he won't be giving you those headaches any more."

"May the good Lord hear you!"

They walked on in silence. Curro thought it was time for him to step off the circus stage, as it were, and focus on the decision he'd made to get the rest he deserved. He wanted to get out of there without further delay. He hoped Alex wouldn't take it too hard.

Near the exit of the circus grounds, Rosita grabbed hold of him and said, her voice quivering, "To tell you the truth, now that I know you a little better I'm sorry there's no place in your life for Alex. I'd feel better if I knew he was with you."

"Rosita, don't be silly! You just asked me not to take Alex away from you."

"Let me ask you something. Do you like Alex?"

"Of course I do. Anyone with any taste at all would. He's great, he's hot to trot."

"Then I don't get it. If you say you like Alex and

you say he's changed and you trust him and that he's gotten away from all those bad influences, why are you rejecting him? I don't get this eternal commitment you mentioned, either. Are you already in a relationship? Alex just told me you're not, that you and Miss Osorio have called it quits."

"That's right, we have. The other thing would be hard to explain, it'd take me another eternity. I like Alex, I already told you; but apart from the fact that he's not gay, I'm very tired. I gave myself completely to that other relationship I told you about and I lack the strength or willpower to take on a new whirlwind of emotions from scratch. No, Rosita, love's over for me. Now I need a rest. A very long rest."

"Are you still in love with Eugenia Osorio?"

Curro laughed. "No, not at all."

"Then?"

"You wouldn't understand, Rosita. Let's drop it. The party involved is no longer with us."

"Say no more. Poor Alex! Competing with a memory..."

"That's it exactly. One more thing: like I said, I'm going away for a good long while and I'd like to be sure that Alex has the means to make a fresh start. Talking practically, do you have... Will Alex have enough money to start over with?"

"Everything I have is tied up here. I don't expect you know much about circus props and technical equipment, but mine's one of the most advanced in the world in that respect. I have a very appealing offer from the Rotling Brothers Circus... I'll sell my big top to ensure Alex has a better future, I've made up my mind."

Curro placed his hand on hers as they continued to walk. "Doesn't that tear you up? The circus has been in the family for generations."

"It does sadden me, but for Alex I'll do it with pleasure. Just between us, I'm tired too. The years weigh heavily on me, and..." She held the sentence for a moment before adding, "I have terminal cancer."

"Oh, I'm sorry to hear that. It'll be hard on Alex. He adores you."

"Keep it to yourself. As you can see, I'll be departing this world before you do, in spite of how tired you feel."

"Let's not make any bets, Rosita."

"What do you mean?"

"Nothing... Just some nonsense of mine. I'm happy to hear that Alex's future is assured. I'd happily have given him some of what I have... Or all of it."

"That's very kind, but it really isn't necessary. Alex was right, you are just a bit crazy. I'd feel better if, when I leave this world, I knew he was still your friend."

"I promise Alex will be my friend till the end of my days."

When they got back, Alex was waiting for them at the entrance to the circus. He was smiling, but wasn't quite able to conceal the look of concern, of worry, that had come over his face. He was eager to say goodbye to his mother and take off towards a new horizon, which he guessed, and hoped, would be more comfortable. What could they be talking about, he wondered. He knew his mother and knew she'd be trying to squeeze something about the last few days out of Curro. But he trusted in Curro's ability to mince words and only mention the nicer side of their shared adventure. Even so, the time spent waiting for his mother and his new friend felt like an eternity and his fears and doubts bloomed.

Alex told them that Aunt Tula had gone off to her caravan, not before she'd sworn to take revenge on the thief of affections. Alex reiterated to his mother his firm resolve to face a new destiny alongside the unexpected ally fate had sent his way. Rosita abided his wishes, though she knew he was chasing after the impossible. She made Alex promise that he'd keep her up to date with his new life, and made Curro promise to look after Alex. Only then did she let them go. The odd couple faded from her view the same way they'd appeared, in silence.

***

"Where we goin'?" asked Alex, surprised by the route they were taking. They'd not driven through this area before and it wasn't on the way to Curro's home.

"We need to talk."

"About what?"

"About us, Alex. About you and me."

Alex made a face, an expression loaded with meaning if one knew how to read it. Deep down he'd never been able to shake the feeling he was chasing a chimera. He clammed up and let Curro take the lead.

Curro parked where he had so many times before. Along the perimeter of the Casa de Campo, near the entrance to the amusement park. They got out of the car, and walked along deserted paths, away from the noise of the attractions, in silence. On a mound from which they could see the spires and domes of the city's churches against the night sky, they sat down, still in silence. It was Alex who spoke up, after a few minutes:

"I had a hunch..."

"I used to spend whole afternoons here with Trasto..." Curro began as if lost in thought.

"Everything always goes tits-up for me. The one time I trust someone, look what happens."

"... ill what had to happen, happened, and I had no other choice."

"You're not even listening to me. It's like you're on the moon."

"Sorry. I was listening. You were having a hunch..."

"I mean, you're blowing me off, right?" he asked incredulously. "I'm a fool."

"Alex, let's be serious. Tell me, what idea of our future did you have? You just walked back into my life this afternoon, because Gagarin forced you to. Where were you, what were you thinking of doing? I hadn't heard a word from you and I didn't expect to."

"I see. What does it matter where I was? Near Madrid, chillin' at this babe's house, lettin' time take its course. I wasn't too clear on what to do."

"Now on the other hand you seem to be very clear. You want—and your mother's given me some hints in this regard—us to run away together. Where? For what?"

Alex took a small branch in his hand and examined it, as if trying to blot out where the conversation was headed. "I dunno! Don't make me any crazier than I already am. This's already been eatin' my brain enough for the last few days. I thought you were into me..."

"I like you a great deal, Alex. In a way I've never liked anyone."

"You got a funny way of showin' it!"

Curro looked at him more closely. "You want me to believe that you've suddenly fallen in love with me, as if by magic, and want to spend the rest of your life with me? Alex..."

Alex tossed the branch aside impatiently. "Curro, whaddya want me to say? I just know that I feel good when I'm with you. And I got nothing else going."

"Aww, that's sweet. So the gentleman here is lonely. Or, rather, since he can't stand anyone else and is tired of everyone else being afraid of him, well, here's Curro, a comfortable daddy to cling onto."

"I mean I've been adrift for a long, long time and then you hit my life like an earthquake. I never thought I'd do it with a queer. Much less, that I'd like it. Besides, I like *you*, you're a totally cool guy."

"Gee, what a precise and sincere explanation. I never thought one fuck and a gang-banger of your caliber—Grade A, I mean," he said with a smile, "would make me reevaluate my life either. I've been confused too, although I haven't really pondered our relationship very much. I thought you'd disappeared forever, that the time we'd spent together was just a mirage. And now, here you are…"

"Eager to change. And to build a future."

"By Uncle Curro's side. Alex, I don't know if that's possible. I haven't gotten over Trasto's death."

"Trasto?"

"My dog. I told you about him at home."

"Yeah, I remember, but I don't get it. Whaddya mean?"

"I can't forget him, it's terrible. He's always present, day and night. I had to have him put to sleep and I feel guilty about it. All the time. People tell me to just get over it but how can I make them understand? I've given up, in every sense of the word."

"I understand you. I've been around animals my whole life. Whenever we had to have one put down, it really sucked. When Cain got leishmaniosis and we had to put him to sleep, it really hit me hard. He was a great pooch."

Curro recoiled from Alex as if he'd just been delivered a physical blow. "A great pooch. I loved my dog, damn it!"

"I loved Cain too."

"You just don't get it, man. I loved my dog! He taught me a lot of things about companionship and loyalty, he was always by my side. I've never had a serious relationship, just flings; Trasto became my emotional compass in a way no one else could. That's the way it is, why delude myself?"

"Relax, dude. Okay, you loved your dog. Got it. Does that mean you and I can't be friends?"

"We can be; but I don't know if I'll be able to give you what you deserve. I'm not up for anything. I've had a few terrible months, there's no place for me in this world anymore. I'm all out of enthusiasm."

"I can give it back to you, no doubt about it."

"I wish!" Curro said with a bittersweet smile. "I'm not so sure. I don't think anyone can."

"You don't know me! You'd flip with me. We'd have the best times together."

"Sure! Like Eugenia Osorio."

"Okay, that was a low blow," snapped Alex.

"You're right, that was a low blow. I'm sorry." He changed his tone, made a mock bow from the waist. "My apologies to the gentleman."

"Don't start, Curro. Man, you really know how to make me lose my cool. You tryin' to piss me off?"

"No, God no. Who would ever want to see the divine wrath of the god of dirty war."

Alex stood up and slapped him in the face. A second later he was hugging him remorsefully.

"Sorry, dude. Dickhead!"

"I'll only forgive you if you give me a kiss on the lips. But no tongue, you hear? Rome wasn't built in a day."

"Yuck! Not a problem. No tongue."

"Besides, if your tongue's like the rest of you I'd probably suffocate. Is *any* part of your body average-sized?"

Now Alex smiled. "'Fraid not, sorry," he said with a laugh.

Unexpectedly, Alex leaned towards him, gripping Curro, and gently planted a loving kiss on his lips, a kiss which left him dumbfounded. Curro reacted by passionately pulling Alex closer. They held each other that way for a few seconds.

"Who would have thought? What a kiss! I had no idea you could do that."

"Now you know, dude. Want another?"

"Pleeaaaase..."

Alex laughed again. "Have you always been this way? You're always egging everyone around you on."

"To tell you the truth, yes, I can't help it. If

anything I'm more so than I used to be. I guess it's the fatigue life makes me feel. By being provocative, I feel more alive. I don't know, I feel less bored that way. It keeps me going. But you're right, I've always been that way. It's the house specialty."

"You, bored with life? Aw, come *on.* You never slow down, you live life the fullest. Almost more than I do."

"Well, I'm bored, fed up. I'm not in the mood for anything. And there's nothing to be done about it."

"That'll change soon enough, just you wait and see. We make a good team, you and I. Now, you come here," he said, pulling Curro into an affectionate hug.

"You crazy? Who's your daddy, the fucking master who can do it all?"

"Youuu..."

"Then snuggle up in daddy's big, strong arms."

"Ha ha ha. You're nuts, you know that?"

They spent a long time like that, Curro with his arms wrapped around Alex, Alex yielding to the comfortable feeling of being protected.

***

Both minds flew far away to remote places. Alex silently begged fate to let him enjoy that glimmer of happiness on the horizon. Would he at last be able to shake the evil cloud that seemed to have lurked over most of his existence? Would he be able to give himself to another man? He wasn't gay; but he didn't really care. Curro wouldn't love him, either. But he was sure he'd be able to love Curro like the best of friends, and he'd enjoy Curro's experience as a man of the world. Curro had much to teach him, he was certain of that.

Curro, on the other hand, was going through an intense emotional debate. Did he love Alex? Would he find in Alex's company the lost serenity he so badly needed? Could he think positive if the reward were worth it? Would he be able to free himself from the deadweight that his guilt over failing Trasto meant for him? A multitude of questions, and only one answer: No. He didn't love Alex, although he liked him, was amused by him. And he was attracted to him. A lot. But that wouldn't be enough to face down his pain. Nor to make him change his habits and take renewed pleasure in the new ones. No, for him all that was over. He would never find a way to shake off tedium and apathy. And guilt, which had taken root in his spirit.

He began sobbing. They were inwardly-oriented tears, almost devoid of external tremors. He wished he could love Alex, the image of him had often been in his mind in those first days after he'd come back from Marbella. He was so handsome! So daring! So self-confident! Someone he could treat as an equal—after a bit of polishing, to be sure. But the raw material was there. He would be an apt pupil, unselfconscious, asking question after question, ready to learn more and more.

After the intense distraction that Dima had represented, Alex's brash appearance onstage had challenged his vision of his own future, allowing him to fool himself for a few days into thinking he'd escape the fate that he'd marked out for himself. Deep down he'd known all along that this fantasy was doomed to failure, but—always fond of folk sayings—had chosen to tell himself that *hope springs eternal.* Hope, however, had turned its back on him, returning him to the harsh reality of a heart that had nothing to offer. The tenderness that Trasto, his Trasto, had triggered in him would never be repeated, replaced, nor even shared, with anyone ever again. He knew that, he'd known it always; but he was at least grateful for the tenacious certainty at such an important moment. Another wave of tears came, but tears of joy this time, elicited by his certainty of what lay very close at hand. Finally.

The strength of the emotion sweeping through him confused Curro. He'd always laughed at people who let sentimentalism rule them. He'd bragged of the rationalism that set him apart from more primitive reactions; he'd scorned those who let reason be swayed by passion. But now, right now, he found that he was unable to follow his own precepts.

His heart's pounding, his growing agitation, finally stirred Alex, who'd been resting in his arms oblivious to the turn his future had just taken.

"What's the matter?" he asked, seeing Curro's grimace.

"Nothing, Alex, it's just... It's through."

"What do you mean?" Alex asked, confused.

"I'm leaving, Alex. You've got to understand me."

"But I don't understand you," Alex responded, alarm growing on his features. "Tell me."

"I can't take it any more. I've explained it to you. I'm fed up with everything... nd I don't know how to face it without my dog. I'm sorry, I really am, but I have to leave you. Forever."

"Curro, you're freaking me out. What do you mean? Where are you going? You're just going to have to get used to living without your dog. Everyone does it."

"That's exactly what I can't do." Curro now fought back tears harder than ever. "I'm not going to explain it again. Everything, nothing in my life matters anymore. Besides, I don't want to. I don't want to live without him."

"Well, you're gonna have to, dumbass. What other choice do you have, suicide?"

"Congratulations, man, you've finally got it."

Alex looked wearily at Curro, fed up at the thought of another provocation.

"I'm outta here. I've been an idiot. What future could I possibly have with a nutjob like you?"

"Alex, please—"

"What?!" he said as he got roughly to his feet.

"I'm dying," he said with conviction. "Now's the time, I know it. I'm going to die. All I ask is that you stay with me, please. Don't leave me alone. Help me, man... My love."

Alex turned, saw Curro's contorted features, and understood that his extravagant friend was serious, and needed him as the lead actor to make sure the curtain went down. In spite of Curro's determination, he resisted the absurd request. He stammered, "Let's go back to your place. We can talk tomorrow. C'mon, dude."

"Tomorrow is today, and today's already the past."

"Curro, I can make you happy. I can!"

"But I can't make you happy, my love. Come on,

hold my neck tightly and squeeze it gently. First give me a kiss."

"What are you asking of me?"

"One kiss, my love. And just squeeze softly, I'm dying by myself."

EPILOGUE

After Inspector Jimenez's departure, Eugenia and Dima had fallen into a pensive mood. They spent the rest of the afternoon snuggling together on the couch, neither feeling especially talkative. Curro's having gone off with Alex lent an almost surreal air to a day already full of surprises. Only when dusk settled did Dima snap out of the dreamlike state. Gagarin's body had to be disposed of.

That same night Dima got rid of the corpse. He talked himself hoarse insisting Eugenia let him do it alone, but it was no use. Eugenia, who'd already been through so much in recent weeks, insisted on sharing the risk with her lover. Besides, she knew the perfect place to dump the body. Dima wrapped the corpse in a blanket, slung the huge bundle over his shoulder, and they went down to the garage, piling into the Range Rover Eugenia used for trips to the countryside. They pulled out into the rush of Madrid's evening traffic. The model guided her vehicle onto the highway towards Andalusia, which she left near Aranjuez, turning towards Chinchón. Halfway there she left the main road for a bumpy dirt track.

"Where are we?" asked Dima.

"This estate belongs to some cousins of mine, the Perezes."

"I think I met them at your aunt and uncle's place when I was there with Curro."

"Could be. They all look like my mom: good-looking, green eyes, dark."

"That's them. You wanna stop here, or..."

"No, further in. It's fine, there's no one here."

"How do you know?"

"They never come."

"What about the groundskeeper?"

"His place is all the way at the other end of the property. This isn't the main entrance, this is just the one they use for tractors and heavy machinery."

"And it's just open like that, no gates, anyone could drive right in?"

"Spain's like that. You know how we are."

"I don't get it. Whoa, stop here, this is perfect."

Eugenia did as she was told. They were in a hollow, hidden from view, surrounded by rocky scrubland. Dima pulled Gagarin's corpse out of the vehicle and carried it a few yards to a clearing where nothing grew. He threw it on the ground and went back to the Range Rover for a jerry can full of gasoline, which he poured all over the body. Then he realized he'd overlooked the obvious: no matches. He went back to the Range Rover looking worried; neither of them were smokers. But Eugenia, grinning broadly, handed him a dirty lighter through the window. He walked back to the body and on the third try lit a rag that he threw back onto the dead mobster. The clothes burned quickly, and as the body went up in flames the acrid smell of singed flesh wafted through the air.

Dima stood watch until he was sure the body could never be identified, then went back to the vehicle.

***

They spent the next day trying to track down Curro. No one had any idea where he might be. Dima found some acquaintances of Alex, but had no luck locating him. They went to the Peres Circus, but a wall of silence met any inquiries about the owner's son. He and Curro seemed to have vanished into thin air.

That day Eugenia also had a tense meeting with her parents to inform them of her decision: she was marrying Dmitri Denissov, whether they accepted him or not. Ignacio Osorio, no less blunt, warned her that there would be consequences. He couldn't prevent her from inheriting the title in due course; but the family fortune was a different matter, and if she refused to see reason she'd never touch a penny of it. Unfortunately Curro had been mistaken in his prediction regarding the Aguirres' reaction. They, too, made it clear to their niece that they found such an eccentric match intolerably unacceptable. Dmitri Denissov! Was she out of her mind?

Years later, they'd remember that night as the turning point, the moment everything changed. The evening news reported that the body of businessman and society playboy Francisco Morante had been found at a remote spot in Madrid's Casa de Campo park. He seemed to have died in the early hours of the morning, in circumstances yet to be explained. Eyewitnesses who'd found the body said there were marks around his neck but no other signs of violence; in fact, they said, the deceased's face looked tranquil, at peace. The news anchor cut to footage of impromptu remarks made by Inspector Jiménez saying investigations were ongoing, a full statement would be released later, and that at that point the police weren't ruling anything in or out. As he walked away from the cameras the microphone just picked up his words to the young cop with him: "What a shame, ending up like that."

Eugenia had burst into tears at the news while Dima, staring intently at the TV, began sobbing slowly himself. Their greatest friend had left them. She lost the confidant, the accomplice, of so many years' worth of adventures; he'd lost the man who'd made him feel protected, and respected. Curro's spirit, the memory of his charismatic personality, would stay with them for the rest of their lives.

Dima suddenly remembered one of the last things he'd ever heard his friend say: "By the way, I finally managed to open that e-mail attachment you forwarded to me from Segovia. It's very revealing. Watch your inbox, I'll forward it back to you. When you read it, you'll understand." The nebulous remark had intrigued him but everything had happened so fast after that he'd had neither the time nor the inclination to check his e-mail. He'd forgotten the remark until the news report suddenly cast everything in a different light. He raced to the computer, logged in; sure enough, he saw two unread messages from Curro, sent the day before.

"Eugenia!" he shouted hysterically.

"What is it?" she answered, concerned.

"C'mere, look at this! I don't believe it!"

As Eugenia stood by his shoulder, he began reading out to her, tears in his eyes, the first of the two messages. In it, his father had written the following:

Dear Son: I hope you're all right. If you're reading this it means something bad has happened to your mother and I. As you'll know, Gagarin's cast the blame for a missing fifty million euros at my feet. He's telling the truth this time; it was me. I was tired of seeing your poor mother struggle so hard to make ends meet and I couldn't stand seeing you risking your life fighting and doing shady jobs for those people. Now the money will be yours. It's in a safe deposit box in your name at Crédit Suisse in Zurich. When you go there ask to see Mr. Müller, he's in charge of the private accounts section. You'll have to open one to legally assume ownership of that much money. He'll ask you some questions, but trust him. With this I send you my love and that of your mother. Good luck, son."

Dima was overcome with emotion and couldn't talk. He got up and gestured to Eugenia to read on, to open the second message, the one written by Curro. It said:

Dear Dima: Congratulations! You're a millionaire. Your dad—what an ace! Bit of a rascal, too, I'm sure he and I would have gotten along really well, ha ha. You'll just have to get used to your new life as a rich man, with Eugenia by your side. As you can see, I'm telling you all this in writing, because I'm no longer with you. Try to be happy for me. I need to rest, and soon I will be resting, and well. Have no doubt that I'll be fine where I'm going. I've given this a lot of thought. Anyway, back to the important stuff. When you go to Zurich, go to the bank's main office and ask for Krauss Hauer, he's the director and I discussed your case with him. You won't have any problems. I went ahead and opened up a private account in your name, so there won't be any uncomfortable questions. Man, when it comes to money the Swiss are something else.

I say goodbye to you full of love and with the joy of knowing that a better life awaits you. Spend your money wisely. Set up down south, or even outside Spain—somewhere the Osorios can't make your life miserable. They are such a tiresome bunch—a total drag, ha ha. Please reiterate to Eugenia my affection for her and ask her to forgive me for not writing to her directly. I have so much stuff to do.

Eugenia was shaken, but more in control of herself than her despairing companion. Curro's prediction that she'd end up in a stable relationship with Dima would come true. She thought about the time she'd spent with the man she'd once thought would be her companion on life's journey, the father of her children. In the end, sadly, they'd failed each other. They were both looking in different directions; each putting themselves first. Life had brought them together for so many years, and ended up driving them apart; it couldn't be helped. Both had known that neither would ever be willing to sacrifice their utopian idea of happiness. Curro had been the first to go in search of it, perhaps he'd finally found it; as for her, she was now getting ready to embark upon a different kind of journey, one entailing a loving, more fulfilling future. She looked at Dima, whose face showed that his thoughts were far away, in distant worlds, and she went up to him, put her arms around him and hugged him tenderly. It was her way of giving him her condolences. For his parents. And for Curro.

Look for these titles from Riverdale Avenue Books:

The Passionate Attention of an Interesting Man
by Ethan Mordden
http://riverdaleavebooks.com/books/21/the-passionate-attention-of-an-interesting-man

Sacred Monsters
by Simon Sheppard
http://riverdaleavebooks.com/books/5124/sacred-monsters

The Two Krishnas
By Ghalib Shiraz Dhalla
http://riverdaleavebooks.com/books/5122/the-two-krishnas

Chulito
by Charles Rice-González
http://riverdaleavebooks.com/books/5126/chulito

The Best Kept Boy in the World:
The Short, Scandalous Life of Denny Fouts
by Arthur Vanderbilt
http://riverdaleavebooks.com/books/5142/the-best-kept-boy-in-the-world-the-short-scandalous-life-of-denny-fouts

Fifty Shades of Gay
by Jeffery Self
http://riverdaleavebooks.com/books/27/50-shades-of-gay

Monarch Season
by Mario Lopez-Cordero
http://riverdaleavebooks.com/books/1045/monarch-season

Made in the USA
Middletown, DE
29 September 2015